The London Wife

Susana Cory-Wright

COPYRIGHT

Published by KDP

ISBN: 9781520413341

All characters and events in this publication, other than those clearly in the public domain, are fictitious and any resemblance to real persons, living or dead, is purely coincidental.

Copyright © Susana Cory-Wright 2017

All rights reserved. No part of this publication may be reproduced, stored in a retrieval system, or transmitted, in any form or by any means, without the prior permission in writing of the publisher.

Kindle Direct Publishing

In memory of my father, Alfonso Torrents dels Prats
1925-2014

and

for my children Emma, James and Maximilian and as always for Jonathan

Gus is the Cat at the Theatre Door.
Her name, as I ought to have told you before,
Is really Asparagus. That's such a fuss
To pronounce, that we usually call her just Gus.
Her coat's very shabby, she's thin as a rake,
And she suffers from palsy that makes her paw shake.
Yet she was, in her youth, quite the smartest of Cats —
But no longer a terror to mice or to rats.
For she isn't the Cat that she was in her prime;
Though her name was quite famous, she says, in her time.
And whenever she joins her friends at their club
(which takes place at the back of the neighbouring pub)
She loves to regale them, if someone else pays,
With anecdotes drawn from her palmiest days.
For she once was a Star of the highest degree —
She has acted with Irving, she's acted with Tree.
And she likes to relate her success on the Halls,
Where the Gallery once gave her seven cat-calls.
But her grandest creation, as she loves to tell,
Was Firefrorefiddle, the Fiend of the Fell.

Old Possum's Book of Practical Cats

T.S. Eliot

One

There is always something absurd about the past.

Max Beerbohm

London 1917

On a cold day in February 1917, the recently widowed Lady Tree was catapulted unsteadily through the revolving doors of His Majesty's Theatre. Of course, it was *his* theatre no longer. The shock of the meeting that had just taken place behind the walls of a building that up until now had been the hub of her professional life, made her gasp as cold air hit her lungs. The document outlining Maud's future – or what was left of it to be more precise - burned a hole in her pocket - well the hole was there already; it was a wonder the paper hadn't slipped through the lining into the hem of her threadbare coat. Above, as if mocking her now, enormous billboards announced the war-time hit *Chu Chin Chow* - its garish design a far cry from the Shakespearean productions more generally associated with Tree. She remembered how horrified her husband had been when his manager first suggested they stage a musical. A musical! Why, the closest Tree ever got to music being performed in his beautiful theatre was in 1910, when their dear friend Sir Thomas Beecham hired His Majesty's for an opera season! Actually the great conductor was not *quite* so dear now that he had left his lover of twenty years, (their *other* dear friend) Lady Emerald Cunard, for a younger woman. And married her! But that truly was another story…

Maud leant against the pillar of the theatre, trying to steady her breathing as panic rose in her throat. Around the base of the plaster and above the sandbags that have been tied to the

Corinthian pillars, there are more posters advertising the show. The fact that neither she nor Herbert wished to be involved with the production will haunt her always. With a gloved hand, she traced one of the Chinese figures with its embroidered gown and exaggerated, slanting eyes. Risqué with more than a touch of panto, it is not unsurprisingly tremendously popular with soldiers on leave. Not so the Lord Chamberlain, whose cheeks inflated rapidly at the sight of scantily clad young ladies flitting about the stage. While sympathizing with his demand that 'this naughtiness be stopped,' Maud couldn't help but marvel at the vision of the camel, donkey and snakes that made up Charles Street's latest menagerie. Tree merely commented from the pit, that the whole production was 'more navel than millinery.' That, of course, was so typical, so utterly Tree, demonstrating exactly the kind of wit that she had once found... She frowned. Found what? Oh the wretched man! The girls were the least of it! Still, the show was proving staggeringly successful. Audiences loved the big dance routines and dramatic sets with their touch of the orient. It appeared to pander to the current fascination for all things Asian, and there was no denying that was bringing in a bob or two tho' for how much longer was anybody's guess.

It was the 'guess' that formed the substance of the meeting with the theatre's trustees. Maud was still reeling from the discovery that in reality this theatre was as much Tree's as the next man's - that the complex loans and debentures procured at the time of its 'purchase' meant that for all these years they had done nothing more than lease it, and furthermore that less than half is to come to her – the other half is to be given to... Maud grimaced. How many times had she written to Danes asking that the accounts be shown her? How many times had Danes oh so faithfully replied that without Tree's consent, this was impossible. Danes seemed incapable of turning a blind eye; as incapable of lending her 5 shillings as he was of advancing her tickets to her own husband's matinees! It infuriated Maud that Danes, whom she had known when he was little more than a scrawny boy should be so protective, especially when he of all people knew what it was to be without. *Well now they are both dead* – she thinks bitterly – *both actor-manager and actor's manager and all that is left behind is a paper trail labyrinth of debt...*

It had begun to snow again during one of the coldest winters in recent memory, but already the pretty white blanket was turning to ice and in the half-light everything appeared eerie and grey. Maud sniffed and snuggled into the oversized fox-eating-its-tail wrap, taking care not to touch the dead animal's face for in truth the thing made her shudder, but it was the warmest bit of clothing she possessed – everything else had gone to garner funds for the war effort or to clothe her own daughters. She stroked it absent-mindedly, for bits of it were indeed very soft. Any other day the thought of how she must appear with this limp, dead animal hanging from her neck and her Regency style shoes, fashionable in the '80s, would have greatly amused her. Large, tarnished buckles that were once *le dernier cri* protrude above sagging stockings. Or maybe they'd never been a 'cri' at all but simply cast-offs from that funny little Sheridan play she'd starred in –*The Critic* – in which she and most of the cast had found themselves completely floundering. It was harder still to believe that this laddered material enclosing her legs was once even silk. However, in comparison to what their boys at the front had to endure, her cares seemed pretty unimportant. Men at arms were struggling with far harsher conditions, as she kept reminding her daughters. And yet... and yet at times like this, it was hard not to feel a twinge of irritation at the drabness of it all and yes, a visceral yearning for the splendour of the many houses she has known. And of course for one house in particular...

Belfield.... whispered a small, imagined voice. No, she mustn't think of Belfield – not now, not ever! Especially not when she was about to lose the theatre! One loss to replace another... was that the knack of survival? And yet... and yet... with her thoughts reeling, how could she *not* bear to think of it? His Majesty's, Belfield, *Tree*... The things and people she holds most dear, all gone. What better moment to think of Belfield and remember and be calm...? She closed her eyes. Shutting out the lawyers' laborious comments, the monotonous reading of a will that amounted to nothing more than one long catalogue of loss, (hers mostly) she sees herself once again at Belfield. The thought of that other place, that sometime home, at this very moment when she is drowning in despair, feels like an emotional life-raft and she pricks out its memory with desperate fingers. *Yes it truly is a physical yearning,* she thinks as the clammy coldness of shock subsides in the wake of bitter-sweet recollection.

She willed her breathing to steady itself just as the see-sawing of the two places that have exerted such influence over her – His Majesty's and Belfield – heaved to and fro... Belfield was always heaven, always a haven. Still is. Even though she should think to the future, she indulged this internal dialogue. Ferociously she clutched at the truant voices in her head, for even these were comforting. And she was tolerant of their candour.

Didn't she play a Mrs. Candour from *The School for Scandal?* She giggled at the memory. *No, no, no! No digressing! Back to Belfield if you really must. Be truthful!* says another voice. *The house was damn cold and not always so comfortable, now was it?* No, she concedes, not always. In the early days when there were no hot pipes or stoves, the arctic blast along cold, long passages was enough to send guests scurrying back to the rooms (and fires) for warmth. But even minor discomforts were forgotten while the past was bathed in a benign light. Maud remembers only the colour to be found in the house's pictures and furniture, and the delicious scent that always seemed to permeate lovely rooms. Above all, although they could not know it then, weaving through those days was the luxury of time and a way of life that was slowly disappearing. *But*, says that pesky little voice, *the house alone would never have been enough. After all it never was for its true owners. You enjoyed it because you had the other. You had the theatre – you still do. There will be other theatres, other plays and roles.*

Yes, thought Maud, *of course there will and I will get through this. There have been difficult times before and I have survived. Barely, but I am still here. But oh, I never expected to do without His Majesty's.* This wonderful building in the French Renaissance style with its Corinthian colonnade and great dome was more than an old friend, it was quite simply the one constant – the backdrop to both her and Herbert's greatest professional successes but also their most acute domestic dramas. The glamour of their beautiful theatre, modelled on other grander rooms, an extension of places they had grown to love, was the foundation upon which Maud has constructed her life, from which she continued to find solace and meaning. And yes, at this moment she would have given almost anything to wing herself back to a time when her entire being was consumed with procuring the roles guaranteed to provoke Tree's jealousy.

But now *his* was the greater revenge. Unbidden tears welled in her eyes. The one consolation from the bitter grief of Tree's death was the knowledge that the theatre was hers – hers and their daughters' to continue their work. While she would always yearn for Belfield, not just for its flag flying grandeur but its romantic woodlands, formal gardens and fountains, she knew it could never be hers. And no matter how much she worshipped its every crevice and shaded grove, she will always be a visitor and an increasingly infrequent one at that. His Majesty's on the other hand was her spiritual and actual home. She had been involved with every step of its construction, refurbishment and decoration. And it was because of her flair for extensive networking that she was able to secure financial backing from the great Anglo-German bankers Lord Rothschild and Ernest Cassel. Tree had been on tour in America at the time, leaving Maud to effectively run the show. And run it she had. She was tireless in approaching playwrights and actors, persuading, cajoling, *entreating* them to direct their talent in her direction. And they had, oh how they had! When the theatre first opened its doors on that sweet balmy September evening it was to an audience that included ambassadors and princes, Anna Pavlova, the Bancrofts, the great Ellen Terry, and the Prince of Wales. But Tree was its undisputed new Sovereign and Maud his unrivalled Queen. Their success knew no bounds and when Tree was knighted and Maud led him onto the stage (rushing it had to be said from her own performance at a neighbouring theatre) and Tree began his speech... "Some achieve greatness..." the audience erupted and Maud's happiness was complete.

She has never however, in all the years of their mutual antagonism and jealousy, ever anticipated this. Never in her wildest fears, or most secret negotiations with *her* has she anticipated having to share... and to link... their... children! Maud felt uncontrollable rage rapidly replace any vestiges of grief or nostalgia. But much worse, was an overwhelming and hideous impotency at not being able to retaliate. *With one smooth blow, Herbert my love, you have killed off any residual anything!* How hollow now, all those final entreaties to carry out your wishes! How meaningless those letters from America wanting to 'settle' things, wanting to make things right! And all that hard won harmony and the sacrifice on her part, of the only chance of happiness she might have had with another, in the end, amounted to nothing at all. *Why did you even write to me? Why tell me that you longed for us, for home! Because you didn't... You didn't long for us, did you?* What then? *I would kill you*, thought Maud, *if you weren't already dead.*

"You alright love?" Maud blinked. Her thoughts were so dark she assumed it was dark outside too, but now registered the fact that it was still light outside with a great deal of noise and bustle. Taxis and buses streamed past, pushing against slushy, snow-covered pavements while people gathered at street corners to grab the latest news headlines. She looked behind her. Had someone spoken?

"'ere, 'aven't I seen you before?"

A child with a woman's leer was trying to sell her a flower - not a nurse in training then, which was Maud's initial thought. The girl had been leaning in towards her but now straightened to examine Maud more closely.

Maud sucked in her cheeks - a Pavlovan response. She'd be ready for her cue in her sleep! She had once famously said she never acted a part she couldn't learn in an evening. She raised an eyebrow over what she knows was still, an arresting blue eye.

"I knew you was famous!"

"Well..." began Maud deprecatingly, modestly, and had she been younger and the speaker of the opposite sex, she might just have allowed herself a blush.

"I '*ave*, I '*ave* seen ya...!"

The child/woman was older than she appeared at first glance. In the right light, she might have passed for twelve years of age, but now Maud noticed small breasts straining against the cheap material of her waistcoat, and a slim ankle above boots that are far too big. The bare skin exposed at the shins is paper-white smeared with coal smudges, but the eyes that peer down are hazel coloured and clear and beautiful.

Of course you've seen me you silly goose! Maud wanted to say - *I'm on the steps of my husband's theatre aren't I? This is -was – our theatre until... until it became their bloody love nest. But I was its leading lady – she never came out. Not in public anyway.*

"I 'ave seen you! I 'ave!!" the girl said again twirling in delight and revealing patched petticoats dyed an interesting buff colour– in fact almost the same interesting colour as Maud's own.

"Oh! 'ave got it! You was in *Cinderella* wasn't cha?" The girl was triumphant. "You was! I know you was!"

Maud was taken aback.

"Uh... no," she said firmly, except those same wilful voices reminded her that indeed she had been. Only Maud wasn't sure she would call it a play – it was pure panto – and one of Barrie's.

He had taken an age to persuade her. By the end of a long lunch during which copious amounts of alcohol were consumed, he had finally got to the point. "It's not just *a-a-any* C-Cinderella," he stammered, his entire face convulsing.

"N-no?" Despite her best efforts, Maud found herself stammering in return.

He made a huge effort. "No. It will be a *n-new* one with a n-new title. I've called it *C-Cinderella & the G-g-g-glass S-s-slipper or P-r-ride P-p-unished.*"

What, a kind of Austen revisited? Maud had felt uneasy even then and should have stayed longer to better inform herself, but they were both so exhausted by the exchange that Maud accepted with alacrity. She would have agreed to be the pumpkin itself had it meant a quick exit.

The child's tone sharpened accusingly.

"You was the witch, you was."

Maud's mouth opened ready to deny everything, only no sound came. Slowly however, the flower girl's face began to recede to be replaced by scene after scene of that appalling production. It might have been all right – even the likes of Ellen Terry were being forced to stoop to roles they'd never have considered in their youth – but Barrie's show was something else entirely. Or it might have been had she not been so exhausted travelling up to Salford. Maud realized too late that she was in fact too old to be staying in digs, and certainly beyond performing one play at a matinee and an altogether different one in the evening. She had become so confused and given off so many different cues, changing her wig once too often, that even the audience had felt compelled to join in, crying with one voice, "Which witch is which?" Maud shuddered involuntarily.

"Nah!" the girl snapped her fingers and in the same movement managed to insert a dying carnation – Maud didn't like to think from where it had come – into the fox's mouth.

"Ugh!" Maud took an instinctive step back so that her back was pressed against the pillar.

"I've got it!! You was in the circus!" Thrilled with her deduction, the girl began to jig in a motion that made Maud faintly nauseous. She braced herself to touch the fox's head and remove the flower. She drew herself up to her full height.

"I was never, ever in the circus," she said emphatically in her sternest Comtesse de la Brière – another Barrie creation – albeit a more successful one.

Sensing that she might have misjudged the older woman's mood, the girl resorted to straightforward haggling.

"Buy me flower, lady – 'elp a poor girl do!"

And suddenly Maud was jolted into kinder territory. She plunged her hands deep into never ending pockets, digging further still into the lining itself, to fish out a coin amid the boxes of Woodbines she keeps for her soldiers and the dried out carmine dye papers for emergencies.

"Ah... bless ya, lady..." said the girl with such utter relief that Maud once again felt her heart sink at the futility of it all.

"Go and warm yourself up my girl – get yourself a nice cup of tea," she said doing her best to sound cheerful. *Think of doing some war work instead,* she wanted to say, but "Go on with ye -" is what she actually said, her voice subconsciously reverting to one she has not heard since she was a child – one she has tried the best part of her working life to erase. Maud stopped herself appalled but the girl merely shrugged and with a knowing smile muttered something that sounded like, "Not so grand after all, eh my lady?" and sloped off into the shadows as soundlessly as she'd appeared.

No, my girl, that is something you've got right. Not so grand at all. And now what? The memory of where she has come from never fails to strike terror in her heart. She hasn't risen so high only to come crashing down! But what was she to do? There was plenty of war work – she was inundated with requests for recitations and was on the Entertainments Committee for countless hospitals, but it was all unpaid work of course. What will happen now? In the next weeks, if not months? Without His Majesty's... without a steady income? Maud clenched her fists. She shouldn't be in this mess. *And I wouldn't be if you'd kept to your own bed dear Herbert, or even hers.* And then from nowhere she remembered those letters. *All the distance in the world cannot divide our hearts – can it?* Had she really ever written that? To *Herbert*? How she had loved him! And hated him – how angry she was now that he was dead! And the children...? No wonder there weren't enough funds to keep the theatre going, let alone ... more tears squeezed from her eyes only these were hot and rebellious.

She blew her nose, thumped her own chest. She mustn't cry – it was too disgusting to see an old, badly dressed woman sniffing... She was an actress – *so you keep saying* – said that same sly voice – *oh yes and a professional! Well act like one! You've experienced worse situations than this!* It was true, there had been so many moments in her life when she had thought all lost only to pull through. She was an *actress*.... Tree had always said that an actor was limited to his personality – he played upon himself. Well whom could she play now? What character could possibly convey all that was in her heart? Ironically, endless parts of the 'other woman' came to mind, Mabel Vane or Mary Archerson both quintessentially the wronged lover, women with hearts of gold– the kind of woman Maud knew only too well. But where, pray was the part for the wronged wife?

Snow fell more heavily now, tiny ice particles stinging her cheeks. Was it snowing, she wondered, as far as Belfield? She closed her eyes, imagining the castle covered in a dusting of snow, its upper turrets clipping the clouds amid protective, ancient hills. Was Violet even in the country? *Dear Comfort, my only comfort.* Was there really a time when she had considered her thus? Maud was overcome by a sudden longing for her friend. Why, she would go to Belfield, to Violet, this very moment! What was she waiting for? How silly not to have thought of it before. Waves of relief washed over her. Violet would know what to do and even if she didn't, Maud would be able to sleep at Belfield, recover her strength. She was so very tired... In her relief at having an immediate plan of action, she moved too quickly, the oversized buckle of one shoe catching on a baggy stocking. Lurching sideways she tripped on the icy bottom step only to fall unceremoniously, legs akimbo.

"I thought I'd find you here my lady."

Maud stared first in disgust at the culpable shoe and then slowly upwards, squinting in the half-light. What a busy time of day this was proving to be... already two conversations and she still hadn't left the theatre! This time she recognized the voice...

"I'm sure you didn't think it would be quite like this."

"Well, no."

The accent was unmistakably Scottish, unchanged in the twenty years that she has known J.G. Littlechild, Private Investigator. She adjusted her vision to take in the vulpine features of the man who looked down at her but did not proffer a helping hand. They studied each other warily. At last he stretched out a gloved hand and Maud, thinking it was to assist her, held out hers. Instead, he dropped a thin white envelope onto her open palm as if loath for any physical contact.

Maud stared at it uncomprehending.

"Tell me no," she said weakly.

"'fraid so, my lady."

"What ...*posthumously*? Is it even possible?"

The man had the grace to look uncomfortable. "Wouldn't know about that. All I know is that it's New York this time."

Maud didn't take her eyes off his face, outstaring him until he looked away first.

"So not Putney."

"No, not Putney." In other circumstances Maud might have been amused that even Littlechild used the name Maud had given Herbert's mistress some thirty years ago, but at this very moment humour eludes her completely.

"Does she know?"

"Not yet."

"I see."

Littlechild straightened but still did nothing to help Maud to her feet. *To think I'm even paying you!* Instead he fingered the rim of a very smart bowler. His spats looked new too and were spotless despite the snow and grit from the salted pavements.

"It means my fee goes up." He looked down at his boots. "Too old for the war in case you're wondering."

"I wasn't," said Maud. She wanted to say, "Please, talk to Danes," but realized with a pang that of course this isn't possible. "You'll have to come… back in a few days time. Today has been… well… I've had a … shock."

She could not bear to touch the envelope. "It's in here is it?"

"As always." Littlechild bowed obsequiously. "I'll come back then, my lady," he said flashing none too white teeth. "And mind I find you here."

"Oh you'll find me here," said Maud tightly, summoning every nerve and sinew in her body not to hit him but to rise to her feet. She towered above him sucking in her cheeks in a Mrs. Allonby stance. With one final attempt at grace she flung the fox wrap over her shoulder.

"Tomorrow at 6?"

Maud considered this little man, never mind little child. Her eyes narrowed but she stayed silent. She nodded. *Interpret that, my good man, as you may.*

Two

*Sometimes these cogitations still amaze
The troubled midnight and the noon's repose*

T.S. Eliot

May 1887

Herbert Beerbohm Draper hovered in the wings on the set of *The First Night* or *Le Père du Debutante* as it was originally called, and which like a good number of the English plays being performed at the time, was lifted – if not downright plagiarized - from the French. In spite of himself, Herbert was mesmerized by Mr. Alfred Wigan whose artistry had transformed the role of Achille Talma Dufard (what a name!) into one of hilarity. Like Herbert, he was also a wizard with make-up. Herbert peered more closely as Wigan came to stand a hair's breadth away. He could certainly smell sweat mingled with mascaró but was the wool hair bonded directly to his skin or to a stretch cap? Hebert could have found the answer to this question himself had he wanted to – Wigan was so close now Herbert could almost separate the strands of hair with his fingertips. He would do it! God's nightgown he would! His heart heavy – thudding now – Herbert held out a shaking hand when in the same instant, Wigan pirouetted away. Herbert frowned. 'Pirouette' could not adequately describe the alacrity with which the actor leapt across the stage, nor the man's supreme confidence in being able to execute such a move. If Cobbler's wax had been applied as adhesive, such vigorous exercise, as Tree well knew, would be impossible. Under the footlights, his face would reveal the evidence - unavoidable streak marks of melting lard - as the wig gradually slid down his head. What had the man used? And *Gott in Himmel,* was that lead oxide on his face? That wonderful translucency was almost impossible to reproduce with coloured fat even when mixed with Dutch rouge, but the terrible side effects were well known. Surely an English actor of Wigan's stature knew this? Or maybe he did and didn't care. Perhaps it was even over-use of the stuff that caused Wigan's characteristic tic – Herbert would go as far as to say partial paralysis – and not good acting at all? With a delicious schadenfreude, he contemplated a future without his rival and one in which Herbert's own skill with the newly invented Leichner greasepaint – a German creation no less – and yet to reach England - was allowed a free hand.

    And now in his physical one, Herbert fingered the letter his boy/dresser had just pressed upon him. But Herbert was torn between wanting to hear the rest of the piece - silently Herbert mimed the lines anyway - and a desire to rip open the delft blue envelope. Addressed to Mr. Beerbohm Esq., it had the thin, spidery script Herbert generally associated with maiden aunts in his native Germany – the ones responsible for stuffing him so full of specht and liverworst sausage that he spent much of his school life feeling just like one. Once in England and away from their kitchen, Herbert rapidly lost weight. Until that was, his mother died and his father married one of the aunts. Herbert's father had had to marry his former sister-in-law in Switzerland, the only country at the time not to consider this union anything less than incestuous – but had now found employment for himself and his only son at London's Corn Exchange. Herbert was not to remain 'an only' for very long however. The frailness that had all too soon overcome Herbert's mother, was not evident in her sister – she presented her new husband (her former brother-in-law) with six children in quick succession. Max, the youngest, was by far the most precocious.

 Corn and its exchange interested Herbert not in the slightest, nor did any aspect of working in the city for that matter. There was something however, that did. Something so powerful and all-consuming that Herbert sometimes wondered how he had survived at all in Thuringia. Herbert hardly thought back to those early days but when he did, it was not to remember that Thuringia was indeed beautiful with its vast expanses of green forests – forests that became a magical icicle wonderland in winter. No, it was that there in Thuringia Herbert had first read, not Goethe or Schiller who both haled from that same green hinterland, but Shakespeare. And although Herbert still pronounced Shakespeare's blank verse with what Shaw was later to call a peculiar and guttural lisp, it was the beginning of a life-long obsession. Everything about the great man excited Herbert. Herbert poured over prompt books, analyzing every stage direction, every costume change and at night, alone in his cold, mice-infested attic room his passion alone kept him warm. At night he wrestled with the one question that would dominate his career. How best to represent the greatest of playwrights? Was it to appeal to the spectator mainly through the eye? For in his he imagined lavish sets each more spectacular, more dazzling than the last. Or was Shakespeare to be left alone, a mere literary legacy? That was truly the question. Yet surely it was possible to do both? Surely by deeply impressing an audience visually, its heart might throb more fiercely to the beat of the poet's wand?

What Herbert was absolutely clear about was that he was not made for the city and he and it must part company. He would leave the city, he would leave his father's house and he would kiss goodbye to goose-fat dumplings. Now that he was being neither fed nor clothed, Herbert was going to have to find employment if he was going to realize his dream. But his brain, teaming with so many thoughts of Shakespeare was unbounded by his own personality nor was it limited by his own mental horizon. On the contrary, an arrogance and utter belief in his duty to interpret Shakespeare as best he might, caused it to soar and now an idea that was only half formed began to take shape and fly. When Herbert thought about the theatre in general and who best to interpret the full meaning of the poet's works, the answer lay always with the actor. After all, Herbert concluded, it is the actor who captivates his audience with a compelling voice. It is the actor who is the intermediary between the writer and his work, the audience's imagination and inappropriate accessories. So Herbert's first step would be to learn to act. And he was learning. And he was happy in the pursuit of his goal. One day he would have a theatre of his own devoted to producing Shakespeare's plays – and the greatest tribute to the bard's genius would be that his work would belong no less to his, Herbert's time, than to Shakespeare's own.

If Herbert ate little and seldom paid for the extra coal to stoke the fire of his simple lodging, there was notwithstanding, one area that he was not prepared to sacrifice (although he certainly suffered) for his art and that was in the question of women. Glorious womanhood in all its shapes and subtleties was irresistible to him and to his delight he in turn was irresistible to her. The comeliness, freckles and Teutonic colouring that was commonplace in the land of his birth was matched by striking deep-set azure eyes, all the more noticeable now that he had lost some of the roundness so encouraged in Schnepfeuthal and so little prized in London. The surprising lisp that somehow formed when he spoke English was not evident when he spoke German although it was with an accent that even his father was at a loss to explain. And as much as Herbert revered Shakespeare, for words of love Herbert turned to his native tongue. In German, his voice was perfect. It was the scent of a woman that always proved his undoing...

Herbert shook the hair out of his eyes in a disarming, coltish gesture that did not go unnoticed by the female members of the cast. Hovering in the wings opposite, the young Henrietta Hudson, understudy for the part of Arabella Fotherinjoy, caught her breath. Catching Herbert's eye she was so flustered, her stays so tight she thought she might faint. Instead she averted a sudden urge to gag by coughing once again. Unfortunately the second cough distracted Wigan into thinking he had missed his cue – or at any rate skipped one. His face registered a panoply of expressions – *at least it still can* thought Herbert sourly while the audience, unaware of the damage about to be inflicted on the performance, found Wigan's initial surprise amusing. However, as bewilderment grew among the cast and they began bumping into each other in confusion, gentle titters gave way to mocking guffaws. Wigan's white face, made all the more stark by carbon hydroxide chalk, was soon streaked with emil noir as dye trickled down his cheeks in distracting rivulets. Having inadvertently skipped three pages, he could only watch helplessly as the ensuing chaos unfolded and he and his fellow actors hurtled towards a climax in a play that depended on each scene being painstakingly played out. It was Herbert's turn to smile. The colour seeped from Miss Hudson's face and then spread in a wonderful stain (carmin red perhaps?) along her bosom – a bosom that was now pumping up and down so vigorously that surely a nipple would soon be exposed? It was more than he could have hoped for at this time in the evening. Herbert drew himself to his full height. He gave one final toss of his head and turned to give Henrietta Hudson the full impact of his blue, penetrating stare. He noted her smooth unlined throat, and her tiny, unnaturally so – waist. No wonder so many women were prone to fainting! Her lips were full and red and eager. He took a step forward, the letter fluttering from his fingers.

"Sir?" Herbert looked down at the thin hand stopping him in his tracks. The boy – his dresser cum general dog'sbody and no more than twelve years old – was surprisingly strong when he wanted to be. Herbert's hand was already on the boy's shoulder ready to steer him out of his way when he was momentarily distracted by the scent wafting from the heavy mauve paper. The scent... heady and intoxicating reminded him of another place - a place not remotely connected to maiden aunts. No, this was the perfume of a rich young heiress, recently married, *unhappily* married, nicht, *widowed* who- Tom waved the letter under his nose.

"You ain't never had a letter like this!" he said proudly.

"Haven't," Herbert instinctively corrected taking the letter off him."You've not opened it?" he added suspiciously.

"Sir!" Tom objected. "There's a seal, Sir."

Herbert smiled, "So there is."

"But no coat of arms," added Tom with some contempt. "So can't be anyone grand like."

"You never can tell, my boy, you never can." He sniffed the paper. "You read it to me Tom, but let's not dilly dally. I have a ... meeting." He glanced across the stage. *Good, that young Miss Hudson was still there*. He glanced again. In fact she looked turned to stone. *Be stone no more!* He was momentarily distracted by images of Hermione in *The Winter's Tale. And who would play her? Now that would be a play to produce!*

"But Sir... you know..."

"Good for you to practice..." Herbert blew out his cheeks impatiently. "But come along, my boy." Herbert handed the letter back to Tom.

Tom hesitated before reverently breaking the wax seal and sliding his nail under the rim. Still he hesitated.

"Yes, Yes, go ahead," said Herbert. "We have anything?"

Tom glanced at the page, panic strangling his gut and then breathed out in relief. It couldn't have been shorter with simple vocabulary and no alarming new words.

'Dear Mr. Herbert,

Should I go on to the stage?

Yours truly,

Helen Maud Holt (Miss)'

"Hummf." Herbert took the letter and with a final sniff, scrunched it into a ball allowing it to fall at his feet. Tom obediently scooped it up.

"Oh Sir!" said Tom making swiping moves in an attempt to smooth out the creases.

But mild protest became a yelp as he was suddenly thrown against Herbert and together they were both hurled centre stage. Blinded in the footlights, they froze before vast red velvet curtains swooped shut, swishing along the floor like the hem of a hooped ball gown. Wardrobe mistresses, understudies and general theatre staff whirled into action backstage but it was too late to stop the second curtain, the safety curtain from crashing down on top of them. Landing on his back, one of the last things Herbert remembered thinking was that it was a surprising relief to be able to close his eyes in sleep without having to make love first.

*   *   *

A few hours later, sprawled in an armchair towards the back of the stage, and still holding a cold cloth to his head, Tom Danes was suffering less from pain or even shock than downright hunger. What had the evening been about then? A play gone wrong from the start and then the calamity with the broken whatsit – some word beginning with p that Tom was never going to remember – enough anyway to send plaster and ceiling crashing onto the stage. It was a wonder no one was killed was what the company was saying. All Tom knew was that he could murder a pasty, a sausage, a steak and ale. But food seemed to be the last thing on his master's mind before the performance and it certainly doesn't seem likely that was on it now, seeing how he's vanished and all. It was never on his mind. Even lying there unconscious when Tom had thought he might be dead, Herbert had calmly got up, asked for a drink of water and fled if not into the night, then certainly somewhere into the bowels of the theatre. It was Tom who was left dazed. He still was. But that was due to hunger. Not something that ever seemed to affect his master... That was the difference between them. Tom was always hungry. Herbert never. In fact Tom Danes had become so sensitive to his master's mood swings that he could tell from the simple inflection of an eyebrow if it was going to be an eating day or not. This trick was not born of a great need to understand Herbert or any man for that matter. Tom gauged his entire week, his day – he'd go so far as to say – his every hour to the ebb and flow of hunger that raged over the troughs, ravines and pot holes of his stomach.

      And then Tom had a brainwave. So much so that he sat up ignoring his throbbing temple. How could his master *know* that Tom was hungry? He too has suffered a blow to the head and has probably forgotten to eat. It was Tom's job – nay his *obligation* – to make sure his master was fed. But where exactly was his master? Tom threw down the cloth, noting with mild interest that it was somewhat bloody. Some kind person had left a candle and matches at his feet. He lit one and for a moment watched fascinated as shadows flickered, his own with them, along the empty seats. He will go to his master's dressing-room and wait until he returns. He has done it before. In fact Herbert has been known to vanish mid conversation without so much as a by-your-leave.   Yes, Tom knew very well just how capable Tree was of disappearing. It was never for very long though, and soon after Tom would be summoned to Brighton or Stalybridge or whatever godforsaken music hall Tree will have washed up at and whatever time of day or night. And then it was arms about Tom's neck as he was greeted as a life long friend, a strong pint in a pub with a log fire to warm him and fresh horses to carry them both to the station in the morning. Then it was long stories – not all were boring. The ones in which Tree recounted tales of his childhood summers spent in Marienbad where he, Tom, must (*must absolutely*) visit if only to breathe in the pungent pine-cone air – air that pricked the lungs with invisible holes so that oxygen rushes to the head forever clearing it – these were the ones Tom liked best.

"I will get to the top you know," said Herbert during one of his vanishing acts to Leicester while glancing up to the tips of imaginary conifers.

But Tom was tired of hearing about dreams and mythical feasts. He was hungry and wanted his bed. He understood neither the Grantham ale nor accents. "Of the tree?"

Herbert, flushed from beer and the log fire and the excitement that any stage appearance always gave him, looked at Tom at first with impatience and then delight. "Of my profession… dear boy – of my profession."

The following morning when they returned to Hampstead Heath where he, but not Tom lodged with the other fled-from-the-city-would-be actor George Alexander, Herbert placed his hands in an affectionate gesture on Tom's shoulders announcing to the disinterested landlady, "From this moment on, I wish to be known as Tree… Henceforth," he added grandly, exposing a frayed shirt cuff, "I will be Herbert Beerbohm Tree."

Herbert was a good man – but there was a lot of hanging around for not much consumable reward. Sometimes Tom felt a warm rush of feeling – he wouldn't have gone as far as to say pleasure – when he heard his employer called by his new name, but he would have felt just as great a thrill were his innards groaning from too much sausage stuffing. Once up close, he would like to see a fat to bursting roast hog, its jaw jacked open with a juicy green apple or an entire lamb trussed upside down on sticks. And quite frankly given half a choice, he'd have had just one of the delectable German sweets Herbert has told him about, than be credited with a name change. In an agony of craving, Tom conjured up visions of sugar covered cinnamon biscuits and piping hot cherry strudels. And sweet, milk white dumplings with strawberry jam and apricot brandies – eau de vie - or the kind of schnapps that snapped off your head without warning.

Somehow though, they always seemed to end up with the driest piece of cold mutton and tea so pale and tasteless Tom had once confused it with the water Tree soaked his paper sticks in – tortillons he'd called them – Tom couldn't get used to pronouncing such a foreign word. Had they had anything to do with the turtle soup Tree sometimes described, Tom might have paid attention. But these Turtle whats-its, were what Tree used to blend lard (once Tom had very nearly been tempted to spread this on a hunk of bread long rejected by their resident mice) and the coloured powder he put on his face.

It wasn't that he was mean – Herbert always shared whatever food he had, if and when he remembered to eat, but that was not often. Tom was also beginning to understand that Herbert could talk passionately enough about anything long enough, to forget about everything that was not theatre. Tree was so often distracted and vague his face only really came to life when he was near a stage. *Do you see that?* Tree would ask him, *do you see the way the voice drops and lifts, drops and lifts?* And he would shake his head in wonder. Tom Danes could see no voice but what he could see absolutely brilliantly was the pile of half penny pieces that sure as blazes were not coming his way - at least not quite yet. And if Tom stayed, in spite of his constant state of near famine, it was because he had to believe Tree would come good, that he would in fact climb to the highest branch...

And if Tom was sceptical that his master's success would happen before Tom reached manhood, he had only to remind himself of one of Tree's more recent performances. Tom had never seen an audience as enthralled by Tree as it was when Tree played Milky White – Tree assured him this was in itself a pun – or as the aged, half-blind Colonel Chalice blundering and stuttering as if already relying on his other sense of hearing when that of his precious sight was failing. The applause was thunderous all right but Tom knew that Tree's ability in this instance was not entirely due to talent, that Tree had only exaggerated the part because he'd not had time to learn his lines. Theatre critics wrote of 'the charming way' he strained his head as if genuinely deaf when Tom knew very well it was simply because Tree was desperately trying to listen out for the prompt box. Had they had a proper meal, Tom couldn't help thinking, perhaps *all* their concentration would improve.

So there was always the prospect of success – he knew this. Still Tom put up with his master in ways he knew were beyond what was expected of him. But tonight after their little shock Tom felt empowered to ask only that they share a bottle of ale together, even a pie... the thought alone made his entrails growl all over again. The candle began to hiss and splutter as Tom made his away through corridors of scenery and props. Most theatres at night gave Tom the creeps with their eerie riggings and the odd creeks and groans that sounded so much like a ship's moorings. He had yet to become accustomed to the smell and hiss of gas in the damp, dim corners. When an open window set leaves scuttling across the stage floor or a door slammed somewhere in the gods, Tom used every ounce in his being to suppress a desire to run. Tree's temporary dressing room was an upstairs storeroom and as far away from the stage as it was possible to be. The silence of a theatre out of hours was thundering and if Tom virtually slept on his master's doorstep it wasn't out of loyalty, but fear.

The candle was not bright enough to light much distance and Tom used his hands and memory to feel his way up the stairs to the top floor passage. And lo there was light! At the end of a sepia coloured tunnel, a thin beam was as welcoming as a lighthouse is to a ship caught in a storm. Tom scrambled towards it just as a draught blew out his candle. But something made him hesitate before knocking at Tree's door. Were those voices within? Or perhaps he had merely imagined them. Perhaps the sounds were coming from his stomach! He took a deep breath before knocking. What would he say now that he was there? That he was hungry? His master would think him insane. But he *was* hungry. A final gut-wrenching rumble decided him. Tom knocked as loudly as he dared. There was no reply. What could have happened to the man? Was he alive? He knocked again and again there was no reply. After the sound of his knocking had died away it was deafeningly quiet and very cold and late. Without his candle Tom felt less brave about retracing his steps. Instead, he crouched on the floor by the door preparing to stay there all night if needs be. Besides, the light, feeble as it was, was strangely comforting. Soon he had slid into a half-sitting, half lying position and soon after that, he was asleep. It was not for long however, or so it seemed. Suddenly the door was flung open and Tom slumped forward with it.

"Tom!" Herbert thundered, positioning himself against the darkness as if he were casting his voice to the back of the Bijou Comedy in Folkestone. Tom looking up saw only Herbert's lips, which enlarged in the half-light and coloured Mongolian brown formed a perfect 'O'. Instantly they re-shaped and through them his voice dropped to a sudden whisper.

"Ah... there you are."

Tom had heard him speak in just such a way only the week before when Herbert played the village priest. Tom also knew there had been no one more captivated by that performance than Herbert himself. As Tree took a step backwards, Tom fell onto

Tree's bare feet and into a pit of gas-light. Tree shook him off gently as though he were a pup while Tom stood sleepily before him combing his hair with his fingers. Herbert steadied him while in the same deft movement turned him so that his large velvet clad body in a robe borrowed from *King John*, blocked his view of the room.

"I need you to do anything for me."

"Something." Tom automatically corrected under his breath.

"*Bitte?*" Tree frowned.

You keep making the same mistake! How many times must I tell you?

For a moment they looked at each other as if they could read each other's mind. Herbert's eyes narrowed, Tom's belly began to rumble. If he could only sleep a full night the hunger didn't bother him so much but if something or someone woke him... Tom glared at his master. *To be woken in the night is to awaken the ravenous beasts that claw at his stomach...*

Tree smiled. "You have something?"

"...'Oy 'erbie..."

Tree's smile became a grin. "I think even she has heard this."

"Actually I think the entire theatre can hear it!"

There was another sound coming from the room and in a bold move Tom ducked under Herbert's arm to get a closer look. He could just make out the delectable top half of a beautiful girl, naked breasts bravely bobbing above the pulled up bed sheets.

"It's Miss Hudson to you love, or 'im –" the girl smiled winsomely showing even white teeth and dimples that danced over pink, smooth cheeks. She twisted all the better to see Tom. "You're just a boy!" She said surprised but then added "Mind you don't go jawing with the rest of the company, about you know, this."

Tom stared. *She* didn't seem undernourished.

Herbert cleared his throat. "Hen– Miss Hudson would like–"

"Ooohh!" said Miss Hudson breathlessly. "That don't 'alf sound posh…" She wet her lips allowing the sheet which in reality was just the underskirt to another costume, to slip from her breasts. "If tha's how it is…you should say Miss Hudson *desires*…" Tom's own lips and mouth and tongue were suddenly bone dry. "Miss Hudson *desires*… 'erbie…"

"*Liebling gottschieninging*…"

"Ya what?" said Miss Hudson dropping the sheet.

And whatever Miss Hudson desired was never revealed to Tom because suddenly the door shut in Tom's face. And then opened just as suddenly.

"I'll pay you more," Herbert said now. He was always saying this actually. "I'll pay you more but you must negotiate. I'm not doing something for you." Tom wasn't sure what 'negotiate' meant but he did know that the pay was always the same, in that he never got any.

"Tell… whatshername– "

'The letter I gave you earlier…?'

"Yes, that one. Reply. Go in person. I'll pay you more but tell… her I have no idea. I mean if she should go on the stage. I have no idea. Oh… and Danes?"

"Yes?"

"Tell her she must call herself Maud."

Three

! Pay! Pay!

November 1899

Mrs. Beerbohm Tree, dressed in a mink-trimmed gown was standing at the very edge of the stage of the Palace Music Hall ready to deliver Kipling's final lines. Her dress was crimson to echo the red of the British troops and swathes of its velvet train spread like a pool of blood around her. Her waist was reduced to the size of a child's by ingenious corsetry (and nerves) and secured by a white fringed sash. She extended her arms, reaching out to the audience. Beyond the footlights, female spectators who before this evening would rarely have set foot in a music hall were bedecked in so many jewels that light glinted and shimmered off the walls. Erect feather headresses bobbed amid a sea of catskin top hats. Anyone who was anyone in the beau monde of 1899 was there to support the delectable actress with her flaxen hair and almond-shaped green eyes. While many acknowledged her husband's genius and obsession – his theatre was now given over entirely to a Shakespeare Festival – he had his own share of critics. Maud's generosity, her vast network of friends cast over every echelon of society and her ability (commended most heartily by the men) to overlook Tree's flagrant infidelity, endeared her to aristocrats and actors alike.

Maud could feel nerves tingling to the very tips of her fingers and her bosom heaved. She was proud and excited by what she had done. The audience gathered like subjects before a sovereign. It was there for her and her alone. Not for Tree but for her. Briefly, she closed her eyes thinking it all a dream that when she opened them everything would vanish. But it didn't. The music hall buzzing with chatter and approval was still there as were all the lovely, beautiful creatures in their coloured silks, the men ramrod straight in white tie. This audience was here for *her*. It was delicious and empowering. But the evening had not come about without effort. Maud had not only learned Kipling's poem in an afternoon but had secured an advance, the unpublished text and a six-week solo run at the Palace. It was a coup she wanted to share with Tree. Foolishly she thought he would share in her delight.

"A music hall?" He was incredulous. "Did I hear correctly?" Except that he could never pronounce his 'r's and the word came out as "cohwecally."

In a heart sinking moment, Maud wondered why on earth she had ever thought Herbert might be happy for her. She shifted her weight awkwardly from one foot to the other, wishing she could make herself invisible. On receiving Kipling's script, delivered by the author himself to their home at 77 Sloane Street, she could hardly wait for the great man to leave before grabbing her bicycle – and peddling furiously, to tell Herbert in person. Impulsively she had made her way directly to the Dome of Her Majesty's theatre – that enormous fifty-foot hall at the top of his theatre where Tree now based himself. *Tree at (D)ome* was what it amused her to tell people.

She was somewhat surprised to find him home at all and even more surprised when the door sprang open almost as she knocked. Despite the vastness of the space behind him, Tree held the door ajar and Maud was forced to wait on the threshold like the aspiring actresses she knew he entertained there. He was wearing a multi-coloured dressing gown – the one he was to wear for *Joseph and the Brethren* – although it was early in the afternoon even for Herbert. She had pushed her bike through St. James's park, then up a crowded Haymarket with its crush of omnibuses and horse-drawn cabs. Catching sight of her reflection, she thought she looked rather fetching in her new hour-glass biking dress and little straw boater. And independent. She had a contract in her pocket and rode a bicycle in divided skirts – it didn't get more emancipated than that! But now beads of perspiration slid along her spine and spread to dampen her muslin leg o'mutton sleeves. Smooth and glossy on leaving the house, her hair had reverted to a frizzy, curling mass. Any confidence she might have had was devoured by his stare.

"It's for the war effort – I've pledged half my earnings."

He stood firm, all unmoving velvet, arms crossed across his chest. *Protecting his heart.*

"Why stop at half?"

Maud's heart was pounding painfully but she lifted her chin defiantly. *Was he being sarcastic?* "All right then, I'll give it all."

Tree slowly uncrossed his arms and when he spoke his accent was particularly marked.

"You really do go out of your way to make a fool of yourself," he said. Then with an injured sniff added, "und me."

The lapse into German made her want to giggle and her mouth twitched.

"Oh I'm not, really I'm not," said Maud. "I'm just trying to do my bit."

Tree snorted. "By appearing in a place where there is smoking and drinking and women dressed in their undergarments?"

Oh, as in the Dome, as you are now?

She held his gaze, noticing as if for the first time the way his tongue darted round his teeth, the way his eyebrows rushed to meet each other, the way his pupils vibrated like marbles spinning round a glass bowl. And as always the antagonism that was never far away flared up between them.

"Does it matter where it is? As long as we donate the proceeds? Everyone is trying to shoot Krueger in whatever way they can," said Maud.

Was it always so airless up here? Colour spread under his fair freckled skin. He wasn't certain, she could tell, if she was challenging him.

"*We* are filming the first ever Shakespeare," he said carefully as though explaining to a backward child. "I've added a tableau – the signing of Magna Carta. *King John* will be patriotic, glorious – a reminder of the values we hold dear. We should remind the populace *why* we are fighting."

"True of course," conceded Maud smiling sweetly. "But isn't it enough that we are?"

Herbert shook his head. "Oh Maud, Oh Maud."

She thought he would dismiss her then, but tightening the cord on his robe, chest expanding, he launched into a detailed description of his latest project.

"It's like this," he said. "For my play, as for any of my plays, I will borrow everything that the arts and sciences have to lend. My *King John* will be as worthy and munificent a production as I can afford. Obviously, I expect a great turn-out, hundreds if not thousands..."

"Obviously," murmured Maud.

But he hadn't finished. He would prove yet again, he told her, that Shakespeare should be treated not as a dead author but as a living force speaking with the voice of a living humanity. *Especially pertinent now and then* – He took a deep breath and for a moment Maud feared he might begin a new speech but instead he paused, reaching a climax.

"And then?" Maud leant forward, curious in spite of herself.

"And then?"

Tree looked at her as if she had failed to follow anything he'd been saying.

Maud looked blank.

"I do a magnificent death scene."

"You are ... King John are you not?"

"Funny. Ha. Ha." Tree scowled. "And still you would parade yourself... like some common... common..."

Maud made her almond eyes widen innocently. Tree had always said he loved her eyes.

"Yes?"

"You insist on –"

"Y-yes?" Maud feigned confusion but in that moment of looking up at him, she felt an unbidden stab of desire. To deflect from this, she moved quickly to look over his shoulder. Tree took a step towards her blocking her view.

"You really (weally) would do this? You would appear in a place where there is no interest whatsoever in the play or art in question, but every interest in consuming as much refreshment as possible."

Maud clapped her hands as she had done in her role as Jenny Northcott in *Sweethearts*.

"Yes, exactly right! Oh thank goodness we understand each other."

Tree made a choking sound. "You know as well as I do that any attempt to turn a public house into a theatre would only end in turning the theatre into a public house. We cannot do something."

"Something? We're not trying to do *anything* other than raise money for the Boers and their families! What is being performed hardly matters. As long as the recital isn't overlong that is…" Here Maud made clear reference to the length of the Shakespeare plays Herbert produced. Again he made a dismissive gesture but she continued. "And if it means people dig into their pockets then all the better. Do you see the daily newsreels? Do you read the eyewitness accounts? It's heart-rending. Rudyard has told me about it himself. He knows how it is. He was there."

Tree's expression darkened. "Rudyard? You are friends?"

Maud made a dismissive gesture. "You know we are. We met him together, remember? Not here but in America. On tour – that time in Washington after our performance at the White House. He was seated beside me at Mary Leiter's."

Maud mentioned the woman who would later become Vicereine of India. How could he not remember their exhilarating tour of '95 when they had been alone together for the entire sea journey to New York – where Duchess had leant Maud her most prized jewels and these were still insignificant in comparison to the wonders that American women possessed? She had been his leading lady then and the press had gone wild for her, calling her 'erudite' and 'beautiful' and Tree had been wild for her too – as she had been for him.

"Yes we are friends. You know how it is."

And suddenly Tree smiled and so did she. They did know how it was. They knew how it had been between them, how it would always be.

"Your letters and gifts?" he said, referring to her system of sending (sometimes complete strangers) a note, a gift, free tickets to Tree's productions (never it seemed to him to her own) and in this way creating a vast network of acquaintances and friends. As a consequence of this candid approach she was to become friends with politicians, bankers, aristocrats and the greatest artists and writers of the day.

"It works."

"Ah... yes." Tree did a *Beloved Vagabond* expression – a Germanic, eccentric one of pained understanding.

Maud knew the part and was not taken in. She had no wish to turn the conversation to her. "This war is already becoming the most expensive and longest running," she said brusquely.

"Precisely, little mouse. That is why it must be Shakespeare."

Maud, thrown by the sudden tenderness tried a different tack. "Have you *heard* Kipling's poem?" And instantly realized she had made a mistake.

His shoulders flexed in annoyance but it was she who began to feel desire ebb, to be replaced by irritation. And as for the accent she used to find so amusing, so alluring...

"How could I?" he said loftily. "No one has yet. Besides *King John* achieves just the same … patriotic rabble scrabble if not more. You know Falconbridge's speech is one of the most rousing you will ever hear. Kipling is… *jingoistic.*" He said disdainfully. "Look, put very simply, your so-called performance detracts from mine – from what I am trying to do here at Her Majesty's – to pay homage to the greatest writer to–"

But Maud was becoming tired of all this Shakespeare talk.

"Why? Why does it detract from yours?" she said impatiently. "It has nothing to do with you. You don't *like* that I have chosen to perform in a music hall?" Her voice rose shrilly as it would in a few years time, as Agrippina. From great tragic depths it was transformed from feline intensity to a gentle caress – the tigress defending her young. "Ah Herbert… *meine*… long lost husband… do not confuse the actor with the part."

"I don't."

"Alright then, if this production of yours is so… so innovative…" Maud could hardly believe herself. "Then include me," she heard herself say. "Let *me* play Elinor."

Tree was utterly still. *Would he actually? Probably not…*

"All right, it's a concession I admit," she said quickly. "Constance then, I'm practically the same age as she was anyway."

"You know I can't do that," he said at last.

She looked at this man to whom she'd been married for a decade, with whom she had a child, whom she had loved and hated and might one day love again. Perhaps.

"Why not?"

Tree also made his eyes widen as he had as Svengali to look at her levelly, the man who had seduced her, made her love him and then discarded her.

"Because my dear Maudie," he said evenly, "both parts demand extraordinary *sympathy.*"

And with those words, Maud went from relative calm to rage. In an instant. Her breath was ragged as she lunged at him with both hands – nails drawn to rake his face.

"Then we shall repent each drop of blood," she panted tearing at his robe, quoting Constance and the part she would never play. *"That hot rash haste so…"* She pulled at his hair…*"Indirectly shed."*

As she lurched towards him, Tree leaning lightly on the open door stumbled backwards into the brightly lit room. For a moment she thought they would tumble together but he gripped her arms, then her waist. Her breathing was jagged as she emitted a feral shriek – exaggerated certainly, slightly hysterical but oh so pleasurable! Feeling remarkably liberated, she recovered herself quickly and bursting with curiosity, pushed past him. She blinked. The place was much bigger than she had imagined. It was a vast Persian carpeted banqueting hall with wide, twinkling chandeliers, enormous dining table and overstuffed sofas. She couldn't wait to tell Violet that she had seen the place at last! The walls were crowded with tableaux from Tree's Shakespeare productions. Maud raked over them now for those in which she and Herbert had appeared together. There should have been dozens. Her eyes darted from one gorgeous portrait to the other, and all the more conspicuous by her absence from them. And then she spotted the 1892 Haymarket production of *Hamlet* in which Tree had been the prince of Denmark and she Ophelia. Surely there would be a picture of her? The oil was after all a magnificent one. H. M Payne had depicted Hamlet sporting a goatee and moustache. She remembered how its bristles had tickled her skin, as had the thick velvet of his emerald green tunic. And she saw herself – a tiny Ophelia whose hair falls in curls down the back of her exquisite silver gown. But while Tree was represented in all his forty-year-old manhood, with every gem of his jewel-encrusted belt exquisitely represented, Ophelia was seen only from the back. She might have been anyone.

Maud suppressed a nick of pain, her attention diverted by the crackling fire at the far end of the immense room. And on the rug in front of that delicious fire a blonde woman sat nursing a child. Beside her on the rug, a fat bonny boy of about eighteen months played with his toys. There was a stunned silence before the mother, who had turned at the commotion, exclaimed, "'erbie!" In turning, her nipple had become dislodged from the baby's mouth and now he began to howl. Maud looked from the baby to that pink, taut and now that she thought about it, exceptionally pert nipple and to Herbert, turned even whiter than he had appeared as Boris Ipanov in *Fedora* – before that is, Mrs. Campbell's own make-up managed to wipe off all of his Leichner greasepaint, leaving him with ridiculous zebra-type stripes.

"*'erbie?'* " echoed Maud, more in shock that this woman should use *her* term of endearment for him than from the scene that presented itself. And when she tried to say more, the words stuck in her throat and no sound came.

"They are –" In Herbert's nervousness the words came out as 'zey' –"Zey are ...understudies."

Maud, willing herself to be someone else, let alone be somewhere else, heard voices in her head – deafening voices crowding in on each other – Mabel Vane, Mary Archerson, Marie Wilton, Hermione and Titania and all the betrayed, betraying women as yet unknown...

"Understudies?" questioned the woman.

"*Understudies?*" repeated Maud when the din behind her eyes had lessened. "And for what play, pray might that be?"

*   *   *

And now, several weeks later, Maud was a success. She was inundated with requests to recite and her costume of the evening was recreated in the Fashion pages of women's magazines. *The Lady* went as far to state that furriers were fast running out of trim with which to edge velvet dresses. The *Globe* that very morning had written a glowing review with specific reference to the war. '...the theatrical profession,' it said, 'always prominent in deeds of charity, are coming forward nobly on behalf of the soldiers, wives and families. The noblest of all is that of Mrs. Tree.' Her spirits soared on reading that one. She had carefully cut out articles from half a dozen dailies pasting them into the large cloth-bound books she kept for cuttings. She cast her eye to the first floor balconies smiling for his grace the duke (Sunny) Sunderland and to the box that held dukes Portland and Manchester – complete philistines but whose archaic and intractable perception of actresses was something Maud encouraged – anything if it would support her cause. She couldn't help but wonder at these people who were now her friends and the far cry their Belgravia drawing rooms and country estates were from the pub in Marylebone where she was born. In the first row sat dear W.S Gilbert (yet to be partnered to Sullivan) together with the nearly stone-deaf Burne-Jones. She was a particular idol to elderly Lotharios, with a seemingly endless capacity to listen, and marvel at the days in which their exploits (and their physiques) were famous. Of course the present day Lotharios pestered her for advice and occasionally, if they thought they could get away with it, a quick fumble before a show. With the rumour that the Queen was due to attend, the hall had attracted record attendance – the upper classes were here as much out of curiosity as a desire to do their bit for the war effort. Not that it could be avoided. *The Daily Mail* had Boer War coverage at fever pitch with Kipling's poem printed on silk mementoes, commemoration programmes and pamphlets.

Maud scanned the darker corners looking for *her* (and *him*) and only when she was as sure as she could be that *she* wasn't there, did she place a hand on her hip, throw back her head and reach high above her with the other as though reaching for an apple on a high branch. *Of a tree?* Ha. She modulated her voice in the way she'd been trained to – in the way that Herbert, with his strange intonations and sometimes guttural rasp – was incapable of doing. She could almost feel the frisson among the crowd – the men leaning forward in anticipation, the women sensing this excitement in their men, shifting as well – at one with their partners, diamond necklaces sinking deep within rose-powdered bosoms. Maud smiled, exhilarated by the power she commanded – at this moment holding the entire room in her thrall, queen – if not of Her Majesty's of every single man and woman in this place. And when she spoke there was a collective hush.

"When you've shouted Rule Britannia –" she could hear the rustle of silk. *"When you've sung God save the Queen."* Her voice rose and sank. *"When you've finished killing Kruger with your mouth."*

The men began a low approving murmur almost a battle hymn in itself.

"Will you kindly drop a shilling in my little tambourine
For a gentleman in khaki ordered South?
He's an absent-minded beggar-"

The murmur became louder and when she reached the last line:

"Pass the hat for your credit's sake, and pay – pay – pay!"

The house erupted with top hats, coins, even jewellery being thrown onto the stage. Diamond broaches, sapphire rings and bracelets landed on Maud's train to lie there sparkling as if displayed on velvet trays. There was a roar as the audience leapt to its feet cheering. Maud shielded her face as more and more coins were hurled in her direction. Her heart hammered in her chest, her ribs heaved against her tight stays as if doing everything in their power to break the ties that bound them.

"Bravo!" shouted the men. There were cries of "Hear, hear!" and then Harry Cust, MP for Bermondsey, journalist and lover of women leapt effortlessly onto the stage as he would from one polo pony to the other, and sliding on one knee, grasped her hands. A lock of his hair fell forward and he tossed his head to look up at her.

"You are, dear lady," he said in a voice thick with emotion, his moustache tickling her skin as his lips skimmed her hand, "a very part of England."

It was more than she could have hoped. The Palace manager came on to the stage to conclude the evening but was booed off as Maud took bow after bow. Only Cust refused to leave, standing steadfast beside her as increasingly heavier objects were thrown in their direction. She felt fragile, empowered, beautiful and beloved. And yet the only person whose approval she wanted, the only person for whom she wished to shine, was with another.

"It's no good," Cust said at last, ducking as an enormous stone broach whizzed past his head, "You'll be harmed if you stay."

Maud acquiesced, carefully shaking her train so that the bounty that had collected there scattered on to the floor. Reluctantly, she followed him into the wings. Cust took Maud by the hand as if she were a child and led her through the warren of narrow stairs and back stage storerooms to the area set aside as a dressing room.

"There's someone to see you Maudie," he said. "She wanted it to be a surprise."

Maud's smile was broad. There was only one person who dared not appear in public just at this time but who would not fail to support her when she needed her most. Violet Lindsay was Maud's closest friend and they had known each other since childhood, when Maud's older sister had been employed as a governess to the Lindsay children. The only child of a shy vicar's daughter and a hero of the Crimean war, Violet was beautiful, bohemian and fascinated by the theatre. Initially theirs had been an unlikely friendship, the heiress and the coal miner's daughter, but from the moment Violet set eyes on her new playmate she recognized a rebellious spirit to equal her own.

Later they would both know the heartache inflicted by adulterous spouses and over the years provide each other with even greater comfort and solace. Maud benefitted from Violet's patronage at a time when actresses were still marginalized by society and in turn Maud introduced Violet to some of the greatest writers, painters and musicians of the age. Violet cared not a fig for what society thought of *her* and she came and went from the grand Belfield Castle as she pleased, gaining a reputation for being raffish and whimsical in the process. Maud however, was all too well aware that Violet was an aristocrat and the same rules did not apply. Violet had married Lord Henry Manners in the same year Maud married Herbert Tree and although her husband would not become a Duke for a few years yet, Violet was commonly known as "Duchess." She was also an original member of a group of intellectual aesthetes devoted to artistic pursuits, known as the Souls. Entry to this elitist club was granted if the candidate possessed 'a soul above the ordinary.' Under the guise of taking tea with Maud, Violet was also in the process of conducting a secret love affair with another Soul member, Harry Cust.

Duchess was waiting for them, Harry's evening cloak draped over her shoulders. Her lovely auburn hair was gathered into a loose chignon held in place with diamond clips, and in her ears the Belfield sapphires reflected the mauve/blue of her enormous slanted eyes. Violet, like Maud had been in love with her husband when she married, but early joy had quickly turned to disappointment and anguish. 'He says he wants children,' Violet wrote to Maud in the first year of marriage, 'but he doesn't try one bit.' She all too often spent the week alone at Belfield while her husband was in London staying at his club. The reality was that he did 'try', just not with her. Tonight she wore the ubiquitous violets pinned to a burgeoning bosom and had got her wish. She was clearly with child but the child was not her husband's.

"My darling," she said in that low, modulated calming voice Maud loved. "You were wonderful – so wonderful you should see what the *The Era* is saying about you! Nothing but praise and more praise! Heaps of it! It talks of your charitable works - why even the Reverend Waugh says actresses are the kindest people. Well that's certainly been my experience..."

Duchess splayed her arms either side of her in a gesture that would have seemed affected on anyone else. Cust stood behind her chair toying with her hair and Duchess snuggled blissfully into him. In profile, Cust bore an uncanny resemblance to Violet's husband. Both possessed the same high forehead, the same straight nose and neat moustache that barely disguised full sensuous lips. But there any similarity ended. While Henry Manners might be Marquis of Granby and the purveyor of exquisite manners (as befitting his name) he was considered a philistine by the Souls who he in turn found dull, eschewing everything they epitomized. His interest in the theatre was limited to the beautiful actresses with whom he flirted and fathered love-children. Cust by contrast, was considered to be the most brilliant man of his generation, the one most likely to become Prime Minister. And while both men and women were drawn to Cust's magnetic personality the same could not be said of Henry Manners. Cust not only recognized Violet's artistic temperament but also her vulnerability. Would that Tree recognized *hers*, thought Maud - or her success.

Maud poured herself a glass of water. There were flowers on her dressing table and her heart skipped a beat. Violet followed her gaze.

"They're from us ducky," she said reading her mind. "There's been nothing whatsoever from *him*. Sorry."

Maud leant against the wall, hands behind her back. Violet may have found solace elsewhere but Maud still yearned for Tree with all her heart. She considered Violet so happy in her new love and tried her utmost to suppress the slingshots of envy.

"It was never meant to be a competition," she said at length. She reached to pluck a rose from a vase and breathed in its scent. *Winchester Cathedral*. She fingered its thick, creamy petals.

"Wasn't it?" she said thoughtfully. "Herbert once said he couldn't bear it if I became more famous than him."

Duchess pulled away from Cust. "Tosh," she said forcibly, even for her. And then she smiled with the smile that turned a man's resolve to lust. "It was just that he wanted you at home, waiting."

"Fawning, you mean."

Duchess shrugged. "You shouldn't have cared so much."

"As you never did?"

Violet's eyes misted.

"I'm sorry," said Maud hastily. "I didn't mean that."

"No, you did." Violet sat up straight, imperious. "Of course I cared but about different things. I cared – I *care* about my drawing. All I've ever wanted was to draw and Henry continues to do everything in his power to prevent me. You have to learn to get what you want but not show you mind. You love the stage. I know you do."

"Sometimes."

Violet made a face. "Not tonight?"

"Of course tonight."

"The whole of London is hers tonight," said Cust kindly. It was not for nothing he was considered London's most glamorous womanizer.

"Tonight is different. It's not always like this," said Maud. "It's such hard work just to – well just to keep one's head above water."

Violet stifled a yawn.

"Life is hard," she said nonchalantly. "Everything is ... That's not the point."

"Then what is?"

Maud noticed how Violet's long lashes fanned a full, smooth cheek. Chance or providence, Maud reminded herself, had thrust someone like Violet before someone like Maud. It was a friendship Maud treasured above all others. Nonetheless, her dressing room seemed suddenly too small to hold them all. The gilt table, which had looked so elegant earlier in the early evening light, now seemed insignificant and altogether too spindly to cope with the vases of roses that cluttered its surface. Violet brushed against the little table causing it to shake precariously. She looked as if she were ready to drop her child at any moment. Maud hugged the wall shrinking against it, suddenly depleted. Sometimes Violet could have just this effect – just by being Violet she was somehow so much *more*. She was so beautiful, it was difficult to tear her eyes away from such perfection – even her clothes, bohemian as they were, made Maud feel hers were over fussy in comparison. As though she had tried too hard – which of course she had.

"Don't compete," said Violet with that uncanny ability she had of being able to read Maud's mind. "That's the point." Her hair had loosened from her chignon and perfectly coiled curls hung to her chin just skimming a twirling earring. Not a single lock had managed to escape Maud's.

Maud raised an eyebrow. "No?"

Duchess shook her head, "At least not with Tree."

Maud had to resist a sudden urge to ... cry.

"No, darling. Do more. Do..." and she reached up for Cust to kiss him fully on the lips. "Do... Ibsen!"

Four

Youth will come here and beat on my door, and force its way in.

Ibsen

November 1899

"I don't want you to!" The child in her starched flannel nightdress stared stubbornly out of the window, her face pressed against the glass. Her little fists pounded the frame. Her cheeks were hot from so much crying. "I don't want you going out."

Maud snuggled into her fur cloak as much for support as warmth. For two pins she would have stayed. The brightly lit front room with its roaring fire, bowls of flowers and freshly painted walls was feminine and pretty and utterly inviting. "I have to. You know I do darling. Although I'd so much rather stay home with you."

"Then why don't you?" Viola glared at her mother. "And I don't like your clothes. Boring dress, boring shoes."

"Oh…" said Maud examining her narrow ankle. "I thought they were rather good."

"I don't want nanny." Viola glowered menacingly. She was tall for her age, grave with dark hair tied up in ribbons to help it curl, and Maud's bright blue eyes. Luckily, thought Maud, she didn't have Herbert's red hair. "I won't have her."

There was an uncomfortable silence as Maud heard nanny approach and so rather too loudly said, "But we love nanny. Come along Vi – come and give her a kiss."

Nanny looked as though a kiss from Viola was the last thing she wanted.

Viola glared. "If you love Nanny, then you kiss her."

"Now darling."

Maud filled her reticule with a shilling note, handkerchief and rouge.

"You can wait up for a bit but you need your sleep – you want to be a bright forward child of nine don't you, rather than a slow backward one of six?"

Viola stared. Sometimes her mother could be incomprehensible. Despite the fierce expression on her face she was breathtakingly beautiful. At least to Maud she was. Her baby cheeks were smooth, the skin clear. Her small hands were perfectly shaped.

"I want Daddy."

"Oh…" It came out more as a groan. It was the last thing Maud expected her to say.

"I want Daddy. I want Daddy now!"

Maud hesitated. "Aren't you happy Vi – here with us?" she shot Nanny an uncertain look. But Viola with this new thought gave in to renewed sobs, banging the pane with renewed vigour.

"Darling, you'll break the window."

"I've been waiting for him all evening," sobbed Viola. "You said he'd come. You said!"

Maud sighed. "I said he *might* come, sweet pea. But you know how busy he is. I'm sure he wants to-"

"If he *wants* to then why isn't he here?" She began to hiccup uncontrollably.

Maud put on her gloves, smoothing the soft pink kid in the crevices between her fingers. In five minutes she'd be late for curtain call. As it was she'd had no time to eat and was feeling giddy, as if her inner core were sinking into itself. She sat beside her daughter on the window seat pulling the resistant little body on to her lap. The gas lamps had already been lit along Sloane Street and outside a cab awaited to take Maud to the Royal Strand Theatre. She buried her face in Viola's clean soft hair, her chubby feverish cheek against hers. She longed, just this once to be at home and to curl up with Vi for the evening. She closed her eyes, breathing slowly in an attempt to quell the irritation that was beginning to tingle. She really did have to go.

In truth she didn't know why she was doing this latest play except that Duchess had suggested it and William Archer (who had translated it) and Elizabeth Robins (who produced and played in it), were so enthusiastic.

"Don't you *see*?" Duchess had said. "Your play will be in such contrast to everything *he*'s doing! You want to be noticed? Then this is the way to do it! Ibsen is so terribly… *avant garde*." Her voice was raspy. "Everything about him is…" Duchess shivered, imagining, Maud shouldn't wonder Ibsen's very own fingers slithering down her back. "… well so *earthy*…" The way Duchess pronounced the word made Maud's own back shiver. "It's the theatre of the continent, darling, bared to the minimum, *stripped*…."

Well it certainly was that. Robins' production involved very few props, in fact only two– a wooden table and brown velvet curtain – *confounded brown curtain* even – or so Oscar Wilde had called it, appalled by the drabness of the production and the number of equally drab women in the audience. Constance had written hastily after her husband's acid review on account of a darling little broach Maud had sent her, to reassure her that her husband was too much the aesthete to completely understand.

"Then it's a success!" a delighted Duchess declared. "That's the whole raison d'être of European theatre! A simple stage setting and even fewer props is a background for *ideas.* It's so… so pure after all the garishness… of Tree's *excess*."

It was clear Duchess was converted. Maud was still in two minds. She quite enjoyed sumptuous costumes and yet Archer had written to her only that morning to tell her how much he had enjoyed the production (and her diction!) Surely that had to count for something?

"I tell you what my darling," said Maud now, her mind sharply hauled to the present by the hot tears on her hand and the well-aimed kicks to her shin.

"What?"

Maud pursed her lips at her daughter's impertinence but she continued evenly.

"After tonight's performance, I shall hop into a handsom – and go along to see how Falstaff – I mean Daddy – is doing and I shall tell him that he simply must come home. I shall invite him here to supper tomorrow."

"Why not now?" Viola continued to hiccup.

"Now Viola my love, you know why not. Tonight isn't possible. Both Mummy and Daddy are in the theatre and then it will be too late. But tomorrow-"

"You're just saying that."

"No I'm not." Maud unlaced Viola's fingers firmly from her own. "I promise he'll come tomorrow."

"Promise? Promise? Promise?"

Maud kissed the top of her daughter's head, crossed her heart and hoped to die.

"I must go but I promise, I promise to at least go and see Daddy." Under her breath she added. *But I can't promise he will come.*

*   *   *

Maud was exhausted by the time she left the theatre after her performance. The theatre of 'ideas' was proving to be somewhat leaden and particularly unyielding given that much of the action took place behind the confounded curtain. The audience was lacklustre, struggling to follow the plot and none of the actors had gelled with each other but Maud did find Mrs. Wilton's: 'I don't give up happiness merely because it comes so late…' intensely poignant. Maud too was weary of little, cold theatres and even colder dressing rooms and late nights and a lonely bed when she got home. Her Majesty's in her mind seemed the complete antithesis – bright and opulent and lush and full of noise and allure. And yet as loath as she was to seek Tree there, she was even more loath to return to Viola a promise unfulfilled. Her heart leapt at the thought of seeing Herbert just as it was fearful she would not find him alone. She had not stopped loving Herbert but she had not been able to hold him. Flattery from others was the attention he craved. The chase was everything but once he got what he desired he no longer wanted it. She had known this about him from the very start but like so many women before her had hoped she would be different, that she would be the one though. Slowly she had come to realize that there would never be only one for Herbert. He had a great capacity for love, he once told her. It was only now, however, that she was beginning to understand what that really meant. There were footsteps behind her and Maud turned to let the person walk on. The footsteps gathered momentum. Maud stopped short with a woman all but bumping into her.

"I'm sorry," said Maud strident and then her voice softened to an "Oh Elizabeth!" as she recognized her co-star.

"I saw you leave the theatre but you walk so quickly! It went well don't you think?" Elizabeth Robins, the American born actress whose husband, fully clad in a suit of armour had so famously thrown himself in the Boston river in protest at her refusal to give up her profession for him, and died there, grinned at her in an alarmingly friendly way. Her hair like Maud's was piled in a knot on the top of her head and like Maud she was wrapped in a floor-length fur trimmed cloak. Beneath a seemingly untroubled brow her deep-set blue eyes were determined, unflinching. Formerly, Elizabeth had been aloof towards Maud but falling in love with William Archer, the dramatist and well-known Ibsen translator and like herself a

Norwegian speaker, had softened her. She was positively friendly now, thought Maud.

"William believes the part might have been written for you," continued Elizabeth. "It is exceedingly subtle yet effective."

Maud pulled up the hood on her cloak as the other actress fell into step beside her. "I've tried to play it that way."

"And succeeded." Elizabeth was a little breathless trying to keep up. "It's the most modern play Ibsen has written to date."

"So I believe."

"There is one thing... I should say-"

"Y-yes?" Maud wondered how, if at all, the Ibsen might be improved.

"Do you think you ought to speak the line, 'and I don't give up happiness merely because it comes so late' with a different feeling, almost tears? I have thought of it as spoken with defiant pride, not pathos. Don't you think she rather abases herself before her natural enemy, Mrs. Borkman, in admitting that touch of feeling? As I say I am not bigoted on the point..."

"Not at all," replied Maud stiffly, never one to take criticism kindly. "I'm glad you ... have spoken plainly."

Maud burrowed deeper into her cloak. She was certain this was not all Elizabeth wanted from her. Elizabeth was a determined, aspiring playwright, already known for her outspoken, New Woman beliefs. Her unwillingness however, to allow her work to be swallowed up by actor managers such as Tree had not made her popular. Not that she appeared to care. Maud was used to fellow actors trying to gain favour with her so as to get closer to her husband, but Elizabeth did not appear to need Maud's influence or anyone else's for that matter. Elizabeth placed a small, strong hand on Maud's arm forcing her to slow her pace.

"I'm always so afraid to read the notices," she said disarmingly, eager to appear as critical of herself as of her fellow actor. "Bad ones or even just and kindly critical ones harass me if

I hear them in the midst of my work. They lower my confidence so I go to my work the next day with scrap ends of praise and blame flashing through my mind." She smiled guiltily. Maud felt herself warming to the younger woman's openness.

"I don't think you have to worry."

"I tend to overdo the good things and the bad are probably worse. I try to wait a week or so and then I read what's said."

"That sounds very sensible. We're all at the whim of the critics." Maud began a much slower amble in the direction of the Haymarket.

"You don't take a cab?"

"I prefer the air."

"Then I'll accompany you, if you'll allow it."

Maud inclined her head although she would have preferred to walk alone. She wanted a few moments to compose herself before seeing Tree, prepare what she might say. But Robins was buoyant. "I never thanked you –"

"Thanked me?" Maud echoed uncertainly, mild panic setting in as her mind raced. She wrote so many letters and sent so many gifts it was hard to keep track sometimes of what she'd sent and to whom. It was only ever W.S. Gilbert who addressed her as NKL (Nice Kind Lady) she remembered clearly. Of course Robins' 'notoriety' since her husband's suicide leant her a certain cachet, but she proved to be a serious actress with her sights set on writing and producing her own plays. There was never any suggestion that she intended to capitalize on personal tragedy.

"The book of verse?"

Elizabeth Robins nodded eagerly.

"Swinburne?" Maud ventured hopefully - a stab in the dark.

"Tennyson."

"Ah yes…"

"I –" she hesitated –"William and I will be doing *Little Eyolf* next. He has almost completed the translation. Mrs. Campbell is to play Rat Wife."

"Oh… good." Maud's tone was so ebullient that Elizabeth shot her a suspicious look. But Maud was being sincere. Did allocating the main role to Mrs. C mean Maud *wouldn't* be asked for the play? She certainly hoped this was the case. Maud fancied something a little lighter next time and a play that required more props. They moved forward together towards the Haymarket.

"I hear your novel has been a success." Maud began generously enough but then recalled too late that Robins' latest publication had been compared to Ibsen's *Rosmersholm* and was a gloomy (if not downright spooky) tale set in a rambling house in which an old retainer warns a young woman that the house is no place for the young.

"I have long been interested in the occult," said Elizabeth, "we know so little do we not, about the soul of things?"

Maud managed to get to church most Sundays but that was the extent of her thoughts on the soul of things or anything else for that matter. She was too busy learning her lines and chasing after Viola for one thing. Elizabeth appeared to be waiting for an answer. Her intense blue eyes were bright with curiosity.

"You grew up in America?" ventured Maud eager now to get to Her Majesty's. Tree's banter, though infuriating was somehow less taxing. Elizabeth, however, was merely warming to her subject.

"I did – Staten Island as a matter of fact. I attended many a séance there. It was foretold that I would be an actress."

In spite of herself Maud shivered. Elizabeth nodded knowingly.

"And after Charles died – my husband – I tried to contact him."

"Contact him?"

"Yes, through a medium. There are many who believe that the spirit exists independently of matter."

"And did you? Manage to contact him I mean."

Elizabeth paused. "No," she said. "But you should come with me to the Society for Psychical Research – I have recently joined. They seek to submit spiritual phenomena to the scientific test."

"Goodness…" said Maud weakly. "And how do they do that?"

"Come and find out. Do you never wonder…?" But the rest of her words were lost in the shrieking of horns and clattering of hooves along the cobblestones of the Haymarket. The streets were awash with cabs and carriages waiting to collect evening-clad spectators from theatreland and ferry them to the supper rooms and clubs of Piccadilly. *Henry IV* would have ended by now. Maud felt her heart pound in her chest. Tree would be taking his last curtain call. The vast velvet curtains would be swishing into place. He would be turning to Danes for a glass of water… *We have done anything.* He would be saying to Danes as he said to him every night after a performance – Danes who waited for him every night, always so patient. *Yes, you've done something.* Tree would pat the lad on the back and they would head up to the Dome. There was a time when Tree would take the stairs two at a time to *her* dressing room and the Dome was the attic it should have remained.

"Do you ever wonder where we are going?"

Maud stopped abruptly as they rounded the corner and Her Majesty's loomed before them, grandiose, imposing, *home.* "Why we're here already. It's just here," she added hastily to reassure her friend. *Not difficult to miss…*

Elizabeth shook her head. "No, not the theatre itself. I meant… afterwards?" Her voice had dropped to above a whisper and she had that far-away look Shaw described in her of being able 'to send thought across the footlights.'

"Afterwards?" repeated Maud and all at once she realized that Elizabeth must be worried for her safety and how she was going to get home. And what on earth must she think of her walking alone through the Haymarket? By day the theatre district was safe enough but after dark it was another place, mysterious, dangerous and potentially compromising in all kinds of ways. Even if a society woman met her own brother in the company of an actress she would not acknowledge him, nor he her. There were unwritten rules and if a lady wanted to be considered as such she did not appear alone with a gentleman even of her own class. And actresses walking as they were doing now unchaperoned, in the Haymarket were too often mistaken for the kind of women they were not. Elizabeth's eyes bored into hers but Maud was only surprised Elizabeth minded. She was, as far as Maud knew, completely uninhibited by convention. And given the bent of their conversation, protected by ethereal spirits.

"I hadn't thought that far to be honest – " said Maud and then stopped mid sentence. "God's nightgown! They can't be here for Tree!"

The side entrance to Her Majesty's was almost entirely blocked by groups of giggling young women – some of them only just out of the nursery. They were without exception lavishly dressed in satin evening dress and velvet cloaks, their hair spiked with feathers and jewels. They pushed excitedly against each other, jostling for position.

Elizabeth smiled, steering Maud away from the throng.

"No, for Hotspur." Robins nodded to the large rosettes the girls wore with the initials K.O.W. emblazoned on them in gold capitals.

"And what does that mean?"

"'Keen on Waller.' Falstaff, your husband, is jolly good by all accounts, but it's Waller the girls queue to see."

Pleasant relief turned to amazement. "What, *Lewis* Waller?" Maud wondered if recently she'd had reason to write to him or send him any accompanying gift. She didn't think so. She did recall though that a few years before, they had both acted in *Julius Caesar*. Maud had been a daring, barefoot Lucius. He had a buttery voice, languid and rich. She remembered how he irritated Tree on account of it and Shaw was always comparing them – or rather *unfavourably* comparing Tree to Lewis. Maud frowned. Yes, now that she came to think of it, he *was* rather good looking, with those boyish looks that some women clearly found attractive. Clearly.

"*The Graphic* calls him an 'idol.' And I don't know if you've seen him in britches?"

"No, but I've seen him in a toga," murmured Maud.

"Well then you'll know what I mean."

"I don't remember being bowled over … no."

Elizabeth smiled kindly, "But that's because you were – *are*," she corrected herself, "in love with your husband."

Maud felt herself flush. "Don't be silly."

"I'm not," said Elizabeth. "If you weren't why else would you be here?"

Maud stared at her. She was right of course. Why else would she be here and at this late hour? But if it was clear to Elizabeth Robins…

"Oh dear," said Elizabeth. "I know what it is you feel," she said warmly. "I too have had come to terms with loneliness."

"You, Miss Robins?"

Elizabeth winced at the formal use of her name.

"Yes, Maud. I'm sure you have heard it but William Archer is married." She said it proudly, defiantly, but was also the first to look away. "I have known loneliness," she continued again less harshly "but I have come to terms with … my past and I will not sacrifice my ambition. You mustn't either…" She gestured to the chattering girls. "If you ever get the matinee hours approved," she said quickly, "you'll have to do something about these women! I've passed this way most evenings and it's always the same thing. But surely you know this?" Robins' tone implied she knew the reverse was true. "You'll have to get Danes to let you in," she added, "it's no good trying from this door."

"I'll manage, thank you Miss Robins." Maud's tone was chillier than she intended as she disengaged her arm.

Robins studied Maud thoughtfully, struggling with all she wanted to say but settled for something less, a gentle smile forming on her lips.

"You never answered my question."

And which one would that be? Maud wanted to ask wearily, but before she had a chance to reply Elizabeth pressed on.

"I meant," she said "when I asked you about afterwards, I meant do you never wonder about the subliminal self?"

Five

So shaken as we are, so wan with care.

Henry IV, Part I

Thankful to be alone at last, Maud slipped into the theatre. The lights were low and the black and white marble floor of the vestibule gleamed like a giant chessboard. Dominating the vast space was an enormous portrait of Tree as King John. Given that the play had only just finished, the paint could hardly have dried thought Maud ruefully. The audience had almost completely dispersed from the foyer, and firemen attached to their hoses were just exiting. Maud was proud to see that Her Majesty's was still one of the earliest theatres to employ firemen at every performance – an essential precaution given the recent Exeter Theatre tragedy in which 180 people died. Maud shuddered. A piece of scenery ignited by a gas burner had fallen on to the stage and within minutes the entire theatre was engulfed in flames. Over 100 children were orphaned that night. Maud thought of Viola with a renewed pang and the reason she was there at all.

Maud took the crimson velvet stairs two at a time, her heart in her mouth. She was doing this, she reminded herself, for Viola. As she climbed higher, her feet sinking into plush carpet – no luxury had been spared in its refurbishment – she could almost hear the theatre encores calling for "Tree! Tree! Tree!" Memories bounced off the walls. How many nights had Maud returned home alone to Sloane Street while her husband, generally acclaimed as the greatest actor since Irving, joined his cabbie in the Cabman's Shelter or Junior Turf Club as it was grandly known, preferring to stay there until six in the morning drinking coffee and playing backgammon. She thought of all the estrangements… letters, thoughts, searing rejections. Good heavens they had more than skillfully written their own script in the melodrama of their life! In fact Tree had written not so long ago on tour from Belfast:

I know that my manner is harsh with you but I have not been able to control myself... I think it best for us both that we should not be together too much for some time. Do not imagine I do not blame myself – I do always but do not imagine either that my attitude towards you has been due to my relations with another...

Not be together too much for some time! The words crucified her. *Why*? More importantly *how* had it come to this when she loved him so? When had their estrangement begun? It wasn't enough that she loved him with every breath in her body, with every fiber of her soul. That everything she did was for him, to attract his attention. The truth was that their estrangement began the day they married.

And now all Tree could do was encourage her – oh so infuriatingly - to be happy. Was he a fool? Didn't he understand that her happiness depended on him? On being wanted by him? He had always said that he wanted her to have as much joy as life could procure. But he had also said he didn't think she had always had the wisdom to distinguish pleasure from happiness. She was beginning to think he was right but not in the way he imagined. After all, what wisdom was there to be had in living alone, in loving a man who no longer loved her? Besides which any pleasure he had given was accompanied by untold pain. And yet... and yet... how she wished she didn't need to beg him – how she wished he were coming down these very stairs in his frockcoat and catskin to greet her, to accompany her home! There was stillness now in the building; all props had been carefully stored, furniture returned to its rightful place and the steel safety curtain hoisted into position. (That was another direct result of the dreadful Exeter Theatre fire). And darkness, not the eerie black that she knew so unnerved Danes, but the enveloping warmth and relief that comes after the show. She gathered her cloak, less to keep warm than to disguise her shabby costume – Marie Wilton's final scene had not merited grand clothes nor had the New Century Theatre of the Strand.

Maud felt her way, by memory, down the little winding passage to the huge nail-studded door of the banqueting hall and then through the heavy curtains that screened off Tree's inner sanctum. But the usual gregarious supper party generally associated with 'Tree at Dome' was missing. Tree loved to be surrounded by an excited, chattering crowd after a performance, with Danes dispatched to procure food from the neighbouring

Carlton restaurant. But not a whisper emanated from within the room.

"Is that you?"

Maud could only wonder exactly who 'you' was. She took a deep breath as though to recite Merivale. Everything was as she had last seen it – the green floors and armchair and the roll-top desk bearing his father's picture. Below, the rooftops of London glimpsed through the high set-up windows, seemed worlds apart.

"No, Herbie," she said gently.

"Maudie?" His tone too was unexpectedly gentle and for a moment they appraised each other quietly without any of their usual animosity. Tree, still dressed as Falstaff, was slumped in his chair by the fire, one leg outstretched, his prosthetic stomach lurching unnaturally.

In spite of herself, Maud couldn't help smiling.

"Anything is funny?" he asked growling.

Maud unfastened her hood and sank close to her husband, although it was hard to think of him as such, on a stool by the fire. His cheeks were cherry red from the heat of the flames. With his soft white-haired wig and whiskers he looked as he might in old age. A narrow leather belt was almost entirely lost in the vastness of his stomach. He wore over the knee ochre coloured boots and a grey felt cloak edged in plum velvet was thrown over his shoulders. A sword balanced against the stone hearth. But his eyes darkly made up beneath bushy eyebrows were troubled.

"You are."

Herbert's eyes swept over her to linger on the cheap fabric of her dress. "So are you. More of the baize curtain type drama, I see."

Maud drew a deep breath ready with a witty riposte and then grinned sheepishly. She touched her skirt.

"Sordid suburbanism at its best."

Tree looked surprised. "*I* said that."

Maud nodded. "About Scandinavia. You also said it was a place congenial only to mushroom growers."

Tree smiled broadly. "Did I really?" Tree stared thoughtfully into the fire. "There *is* a kind of conspiracy between the actor and the audience," he said at length. "I mean of course the actor must be adroit at adapting his personality to the character he is portraying. If the actor imagines himself to be a fat man he will be a fat man to the audience. But–" Tree patted his belly, "it is not the outer covering which causes this impression; it is the inner man – who talks fat, walks fat, and thinks fat."

"So Ibsen is not entirely off track?"

"Not entirely, but equally an audience will not be offended by appropriate accessories," he replied gravely.

Maud recalled how once to illustrate this very point Tree had said it would be better to have no scene at all if depicting ancient Athens, than a view of the Marylebone Road. Maud had been born in a pub in Marylebone but after the Ibsen experience, she was beginning to see what he meant.

"It pains me to say this but even I miss the excesses of His Majesty's."

Tree acquiesced graciously. "Unlike Shakespeare I have never implored the spectator to supply by his imagination, the deficiencies of the stage..."

"No, and I applaud you in your effort."

"Thank you." He inclined his head once more. "I have always felt it better to strive for the higher even if we miss it, than to clutch at the lower, even if it be within easy reach." He looked at her sharply. "Is something wrong? You are too... *nice*."

"And you... too ... quiet."

Herbert sighed. "I don't feel it."

Maud touched his sleeve. "But it went well didn't it?"

"Well? Well?" said Tree impatiently. "What is well?"

"The audience –"

"Some, not all–" Tree's 'all' was particularly German with extra emphasis on the 'lls.' "Shaw of course didn't like me."

"But he didn't like me either! Not this time… " Her voice trailed. "He does say Falstaff is an unrivalled part for the right sort of comedian," she added cheerfully.

"He said that about Irving," said Tree testily.

"Oh … did he?" *Not the right moment to bring up Waller then…* For a moment Tree glowered.

"Yours is a new kind of acting, Herbie," said Maud gently. "It's not going to please every critic all of the time. You know that. The same applies to me. Put it behind you – think to your next production. What next?"

"I am uninspired."

Maud let out a strangled guffaw. "You? *Uninspired*? I don't believe it! Your homage to Shakespeare is… inexhaustible. Why not do… I don't know…something not performed often – something stimulating."

"*Henry VIII*? Irving played Wolsey in the Lyceum production, Ellen Terry was Queen Kath-"

"You think that… cheerful?"

"You said something stimulating."

"Yes," agreed Maud, "but you've just done *King John*. There's been so much talk of war. It's all so drab and dreary. Why not put on something completely different to distract from the gloom? After all isn't that our business? To entertain?"

Herbert sat up crossing one leg over the other. He examined his ankle.

"What say we do *Hamlet* again? A revival, only this time we could do the uncut version–"

"What all five hours?"

"No, you're right. Dinner is so necessary nowadays."

Maud said nothing.

"I do look good in black hose, you must admit I was a magnificent prince."

If overtly romantic ... Maud refrained from mentioning Irving once more. Clement Scott had devoted pages to unpicking the problem with Tree's Hamlet and how much more he had enjoyed Irving's.

"And your Ophelia..."

Ah... now Scott had loved *her* Ophelia. Maud had ordered fresh flowers for every performance so that she could rip them up on stage. Scott wrote in his review how this had given Maud's acting the desired edge... He claimed hers was the most persuasive, the most graceful interpretation in years and that her performance had left a most delightful and lingering impression...

For a moment they sat in companionable silence remembering so very differently, the same production.

"I have it!" Herbert's eyes were ablaze. "*Corialanus!*"

"Herbert!"

"All right... " his carmine painted lips pursed and then he stroked his beard. "What about...what about... *A Midsummer Night's Dream?* What about that?"

In his excitement he leant forward as she did, towards him.

"Perfect!"

He was so close she could feel his breath on her cheek.

"Although I refuse to do a Poel," he said softly. "Mit out scenery und placards: 'This is a Lion. This is a Wall.(*vwoa*l)' Too much like your Ibsen."

"He's not 'my' Ibsen," said Maud and although she wanted to contradict him but she couldn't. "You don't have to do anything. You've always said that illusion is the whole business of theatre – so do something… do something spectacular! "

"You mean I don't always?" His eyes narrowed but she could tell he was pleased.

"You know what I mean, make this as gorgeous as it is possible –"

Tree slapped his thigh as Falstaff might have but the words that he spoke were his own. "We'll do it for the New Year – it's the end of a century – the end of an era. 1900 Maudie, think of that."

"1900!" Maud echoed. It was too big a thought. "Oh yes!"

Maud was taken up with his enthusiasm. It was like the old days, the first days of their marriage when they planned their theatre engagements, productions, future.

"We need cheering up – the defeats in the Transvaal have been too many this week. Take us back, Herbie, to what is beautiful and civilized and great. Do it as beautifully as you know how – transport us to the Fairie world. Take us to the limits of the conceivable!"

"Rabbits."

"I meant figuratively."

"And I mean literally. I want real rabbits nibbling real foliage." He leant forward, his huge stomach bulging in odd places.

"Und birds und nature und brook."

"Und?"

"Wasser! There must be wasser!"

Maud smiled. "Water, yes absolutely –" her eyes twinkled with a delicious thought. "In which Bottom might check his reflection!" Maud knew this would appeal to Tree's vanity. She felt as if she were already in someone else's play with no inkling of its ending. "Your reflection. You could play Bottom."

Tree raised his eyebrows. "How would you know?"

"My memory hasn't completely… faded."

Tree sat back in his chair, very still.

"I would have thought you would like me as Oberon."

Maud wanted to say she'd have liked him in any guise. Her eyes were level with his. "No, that demands … " *What had he said to her once of a role? That it demanded sympathy*…? "A voice… it demands a voice. I mean… a stellar actor… to complement you of course," she added quickly.

Tree pursed his lips – put his hands together as if in prayer then flexed them as if cradling an orange.

She took a deep breath. "What about Waller?"

Tree looked at her thoughtfully. "Yes, always better to choose someone who has gained his spurs in the wider field of our arduous calling than an unknown– I was about to suggest him myself."

Tree reached for her hand and Maud had a sudden longing to squeeze his back. The sense of familiarity between them was both comforting and seductive but she would not respond. She was determined on that. Her hand lay passive in his. He examined her fingers one by one.

> "*And touching hers, make blessed my rude hand*," he quoted softly.

Maud caught her breath. *Forgive them for they know not what they do*…She placed her other hand on his but so it was flat, barely touching.

"Good pilgrim, you do wrong your hand too much."

He tightened his grip. "Oh Maudie, I know I do."

Maud tried to pull away but again he gripped her hard. She could smell his sweat mingled with greasepaint.

"You know how you upset me," she said, wanting him to acknowledge at least some of the anguish he caused her yet confused by the pulse beating at her temple and the desire that had not abated to have everything right between them. He let go of her hands and slumped back in his chair, his feet planted firmly on the carpet. Forgetting he was wearing a wig, he attempted to run a hand through his hair. The result was more deranged than comical and Maud suppressed a giggle that was half way to becoming a sob.

"And you upset *me*! I am in a perpetual fever when you are on tour with me! I cannot do something! And then I cannot work which is necessary for us all– this you do not seem to realize…"

"Your women…"

He was dismissive. "Ach… falling in love is just… a … a…hebit."

"Then correct it! Fall in love with me!" Maud regretted the words almost as soon as she'd said them but by then Herbert's eyes had lit with that passion she had enjoyed herself once and was jealous of when it was re-directed at others.

"With you? With you, little mouse?" He frowned as if a thought had just occurred to him. "And if I played Bottom would you then be Titania?" He smiled roguishly. "Und then you would have to fall in love with me!"

Maud took a deep breath. "Maybe." *What was she saying? Had she gone mad? Violet would never forgive her! She wondered if she would forgive herself.* She tilted her face up to his beguilingly; her eyes she knew looked catlike in the firelight. "Well maybe I might fall in love, but only for a short time. I believe all love affairs should be short, don't you? Shall we say we will stay in love but only for the duration of the play?"

He looked at her in astonishment as though she were a completely different person. She certainly felt like one tonight. She felt as if she had lost her reason. She was *supposed* to be asking Herbert to dinner – *surely that would come…* ! She was supposed to be talking about their daughter Viola not Shakespeare and love! Herbert got to his feet and loosened the tie at his waist. Maud gulped in alarm and then a gargled laugh stuck in her throat. His false stomach slithered to the floor between them. Gallantly Tree kicked it away and reached down to pull Maud to her to feet. He tugged off his wig.

"Just for the duration of the play?" he whispered his whiskers tickling her ear. These too he peeled off, throwing them into the fire.

Maud nodded for she could not speak.

Tree touched her face, tracing the contours. "Would that more actresses were like you!" His lips found hers. "You amaze me little mouse, you enchant and bewitch me. You do see that you do anything to me, yes, you do see?"

Six

Castles in the air – they're so easy to take refuge in. So easy to build, too.

Ibsen

Maud lay sprawled on an oversized day bed in the Queen's Dressing room at Belfield. With its turrets and towers flying its flag from the top of a hill, Belfield was every bit the quintessential fairytale castle Maud had read about in books. Countless visits never failed to impress upon Maud a sense of awe or history – William the Conqueror had awarded the estate to the first Lord Belfield after the Battle of Hastings – nor disbelief that she should be there at all let alone as a valued guest. Moreover the suite of rooms she had been allocated was one of the grandest in the house. The bedroom walls were lined in Chinese silk purchased by Duchess on special trips to Paris, with yards of matching billowing drapes hanging from the half tester bed. A palmette motif embossed the cornice of the small sitting room, while heads of mercury were carved on the secretaire and bookcases. Draughty floorboards were smothered in thick Persian carpets. But Duchess had insisted Maud have the most important guest rooms in the house for no other reason than she was immensely proud of the newly installed plumbing. A mahogany wardrobe opened onto a long and narrow corridor where a hollowed-out wall had been created to allow space for the ever-expanding girth of Belfield's other most frequent guest, the Prince of Wales.

Maud smoothed the yellow damask beneath her fingers, delighting in the way the silk strands gleamed in the soft light. She rested her head against plump cushions, twisting her long plait dreamily. It was twelfth night and she was expected to perform or recite something for the evening's festivities. The house was at its grandest for the celebrations. Fires crackled in the numerous fireplaces and the delicious scent of pines wafted on the air from the twin Christmas trees ablaze with real candles. There were garlands of rosemary and ivy with bunches of mistletoe and holly tucked into every spare nook. The huge chandeliers were hung with Victorian Kissing rings stuffed thick with moss and sprigs of yew. Watchmen, gong-men, lamp-and-candle men cased the house and grounds, vigilant to the guests' every need. Six housemaids had polished the floor in the Regent's Gallery and silver and plate shone from every available surface. For the occasion, a track had been inserted along the floor in the Servants' Hall for beer to be trolleyed along and the footmen were dressed in white tie. The following day there was to be a 'reindeer sleigh' and housemaids would sport antlers tied to their bonnets to pull couples in sledges along the frozen lake.

Maud was content. She had half her Titania part off pat and she hoped to have learned the whole by the time she returned to London in a few days time. In any event she had to have learned it by then as they opened at the end of the month. Fittings for costumes were also taking place and Maud had taken extra care over the shimmering gold cloth she had chosen for the flying fairies, imps, sea-urchins and wood-elves. She was as excited as Tree by the beauty of the production. For the fairy invasion Oberon would tap each of the nine pillars in Theseus's palace with his wand and they would glow from within, fading only when the fairies crept away, darkness fell and the curtain came down. Her good friend Julia Neilson, delightful as the fairy King, wore an electrically lighted breast-plate and a spikey crown reminiscent of the image of Britannia. Surely both Trees were doing everything in their power to brighten these troubled times when there was so much sorrow in the land?

And Bottom? Tree as Bottom was nothing short of hilarious with his bibulous visage, flesh-coloured tights and voice thickened with indulgence that was well suited to the intonation of his spoken English. Maud smiled to herself; Bottom had been loving and attentive during rehearsals and afterwards there had been cosy little suppers at 77 Sloane Street followed by even cosier nights when happy Viola finally went to bed. Maud hugged herself, warm in the delicious memory of those nights… She still scanned the theatre during rehearsals for signs of *her* but so far there was nothing to suggest that Tree was wandering. In fact it had been remarkably easy to resume their life together. 77 Sloane Street seemed to burst at the seams once more with his gusto for life and the endless stream of people needing to be fed before the theatre, or at least happy to watch *them* eat. She wasn't enchanted with all his friends – Godwin, a celebrated architect and member of the Costume Society– had reappeared in their lives almost as quickly as Tree had and was still too inclined to whisking Herbert off till the early hours of the morning. Maud approved of neither his black hat and long cloak nor his much-publicized love affairs. On the other hand, his sometime companion and mother of his children, Ellen Terry, had become a close friend.

"If you please Ma'am," said a maid poking her head round the door. Maud, jolted from her daydreams, looked up confused.

"Yes?"

But the girl had ducked behind the door holding her foot against the door-jam. She was flushed as she heaved a baby's cradle into the room, placing it in the corner by the window.

"Good Heavens!" Maud exclaimed propping herself up on cushions.

The maid bobbed a curtsey. "If you please, ma'am," she said, "Her Ladyship says she wants to come and chat while she feeds my Lord Haddon."

"No, that bit is fine," said Maud. "I've just never seen such a – a contraption like it."

"Not many have," said the girl.

For a moment the two women contemplated the extraordinary ebony cradle in wonder. The 'cradle' was designed to represent a swan. It had an oval basket body woven in silver mesh while its long neck was gold leaf. From the swan's 'head' gauze curtains were pinned back with wide satin ribbons. Its bed was freshly made up with exquisite monogrammed linen sheets.

"I think I'd quite like to be a baby again," murmured Maud.

"It was a present from The Prince Regent, the Prince Regent that was, that is," said the girl. She smoothed down her apron and attempted to push unruly hair into its cap. "To another Duchess of Belfield. Lord Belfield says all little Lord Haddons are to lie in it."

"As indeed they must," said Maud still stupefied. She believed her first cradle had been a bottom drawer. And she didn't like to think where the maid had slept.

"Darling," drawled Duchess coming into the room carrying her baby. The maid flushed, bobbed another curtsey and scampered. Duchess ignored the splendid baby's bed and sank onto the window seat beside Maud, positioning her child on her breast. Maud could hardly tear her eyes from her. Violet's hair too, was loosely plaited, and in a violet velvet peignoir that matched the purple irises of her eyes she had never been more beautiful. "A penny for them," smiled Duchess.

Maud picked up the book – *Enoch Arden* – her party piece – but how could she possibly tell Duchess how she felt?
Receiving no response, Duchess persisted, "You haven't explained the change."

"Change?"

Violet's lashes briefly fanned her cheek. "Yes, change. You must know that you are different... calm... beautiful even?" She said the last almost ruefully. It was not an adjective usually applied to Maud.

Duchess's soft voice was soporific and Maud found her thoughts drifting once again. It was twilight, the sun slowly sinking behind the line of silent, snow- covered hills. Inside everything was warm and luxurious with the delicious anticipation of a wonderful evening to come. Duchess rocked the baby's cradle with one foot though the baby was firmly rooted to her breast. The rocking motion made Maud drowsy and she stretched languidly, imagining herself sung to sleep by forty-seven fairies with battery-operated wings and Bottom... She rotated her ankles so as to better examine her pretty slippers, wondering what colour she should dye them. What colour would Tree like? And was it time to change for tea? As always it was a stretch to bring enough clothes to Belfield, expected as they were to change up to as much as six times a day – more in the hunting season. Maud was not mistress of the army of ladies' maids who arrived with trunks full of dresses, which then had to be laboriously ironed and got ready for the mere hour or two in which they were worn. Nor did she possess the magnificent jewels that were required not only to adorn sloping bodices but buckles, shoes and heads. When she was older, Viola would accompany her mother, but in the early days, Maud borrowed Duchess's 'tweeny' or in-between maid who was clumsy with furniture, let alone hair. But this time she had enjoyed the preparations and been especially creative with paint. These shoes would be a different hue entirely by the evening and one dress would be re-cut and sewn and presented, she hoped, in such a novel fashion on the last evening so as to be unrecognizable from the first. Not that Violet minded, known as she was for her original dress sense herself – original that was even for the Souls. But Maud was not a Marchioness and she sensed that she must never dress as it was presumed an actress might, and that she must be more elegant and recherché than even Margot Asquith herself.

"So?"

"I'm sorry," said Maud. "What were you saying?"

Duchess raised knowing eyebrows. "I was saying that you have beauty, my beauty? I want to know why."

"Well I've never had it before." Maud took a breath. This was the moment. She could tell Violet and not tell her. She met her gaze levelly. "Even you – favourite of of the gods that you are – must know that a woman is beautiful when she is loved."

Violet's eyebrows knitted together. "Yes, that is true…" she said touching her sleeping child's head, a smile once again hovering on her beautiful mouth. "And as you can see, I am in a constant state of beauty."

"And he doesn't mind?" said Maud hastily, anything to deflect the conversation away from her.

Duchess met her look unflinchingly. "You mean Belfield?"

"I mean Cust."

"I'm sure they both do – one because he is not the father, the other because he is. But there is no greater revenge." Violet's eyes were inky pools. "My husband will never know if the child is his."

"And that's a comfort?"

"Oh Darling!" Violet rounded fiercely. "Darling!" she repeated more softly this time. "My love was killed off years ago, in one blow as I pray yours is for Herbert."

"He has children by her," said Maud bitterly, the happiness at the start of the day beginning to see-saw.

"As does Belle Field." The slur was deliberate.

The women looked at each other, reaching into each other's soul for the peace that eluded them.

"There is another way…" said Violet, threading her slender fingers through those of her baby's. "It may not help you but it does me. Keep your true feelings and your own true self hidden."

Maud thought of the part of Mabel Vane. "Masks and Faces then?"

"That sort of thing yes, but more than that. Don't let your precious health be hurt by this – *they* aren't worth it. And you can dissimulate enough for Herbert to never discover the truth about how you feel."

"I think it's too late for that," said Maud under her breath and bowing her head so that Violet wouldn't see her smile. She could still feel Tree's lips on her neck, the insistence of his hand on her shoulder.

"Is it?" asked Violet, misinterpreting. "I don't think Belfield has noticed anything different – he hasn't seen that the loveliness is missing from the ordinary wifely care one can bestow from a sense of duty or kindness."

"I'm not sure that I could do that. I feel it so much."

"But so do I!" declared Duchess passionately. "I have just learned to hide it and to distract myself."

Maud studied the exquisite detail of the Chinese silk wallpaper. A pair of herons hovered precariously above a slender peony branch. Cherry blossom was seemingly sprinkled across a duck egg blue background while the palest yellow butterflies floated by a burnished kumkwat. Delicate gold birdcages hung from golden chains were drawn separately on the doors of the rosewood and lacquer wardrobe. Maud had no wish to dwell on their husbands' infidelity, not when her present happiness was so ethereal. And such lovely interiors made it easier to forget...

"Then who is the real actress?"

Violet shifted the child in her arms and leant over the ornate cradle to place him between the starched baby sheets.

When she hadn't replied, Maud said, "I've never asked, but do you love Cust?"

"Sometimes," replied Duchess truthfully. She sat back on the window seat, flushed and very lovely. "Sometimes not at all. Belfield broke my heart and now I believe I break his. Cust cares for me. He knows my moods, my joys, my sorrows. He is devoted, attentive and a wonderful lover – except when there's a child."

Maud looked away, an unhappy memory spiking her optimism.

"I know how it is."

Violet's baby began to stir, raising his head like a kitten, his eyes tightly, blindly closed, his fists resisting their swaddling. He had a shock of black hair and Violet's pale skin. His mouth began to purse and Maud wondered how long it would be before the little lord began to howl.

"If you had a little boy... Maudie..." Maud winced so that Violet rushed on, "Enough of this – we're becoming far too gloomy! I shall come to town too – we can stay together. I shall open Arlington Street. Oh darling, what fun we can have! I want to have fun. I've been cooped up so long!"

"Cooped up? You mean all of two weeks! And it *was* because you were having a baby!"

"Yes well... it feels like a lifetime. Tonight will be a party at any rate. You know that I've asked Squiffie and Margot– she's breeding again – although between you and me I don't know how they've managed it – he's away so much up and down the country with all his Liberal politicking." Maud raised an eyebrow but

Violet steamrolled ahead. "They arrive tomorrow with Henry James – I know you know him and Nielsen – such a novelty to have a woman play Oberon! A stroke of genius on your husband's part I must say. Oh, and J.M. Barrie who my dear, has just published the most shocking little play about a woman who pushes her husband out of their carriage!"

"Is that shocking?" Maud smiled playfully but Violet responded in a different vein.

"Not as shocking as my friendship with you darling," said Violet nonchalantly. "Not that I'd change it for the world," she added quickly, "but you do realize ducks that the Souls view my association with an actress as almost too much, even for the most raffish among them."

"I see," said Maud now very miffed. "So they don't mind any of the other... transgressions." She had wanted to say they don't mind Belfield's but couldn't bring herself to use him or the baby's innocence as a tool in her defence.

"Oh darling, you know how we *love* the theatre! In fact I insist on walk-on parts for all my gels in the Spring. Even Terry says she has begged parts for her daughter and your husband has been most obliging, as he has with mine. I know you get endless requests."

"It's different with friends."

"Possibly, but Henry doesn't ... love the theatre as you know, I have to do everything I can to – "

"But he loves actresses –" The words rushed out unbidden and sank into the concrete silence that followed. Maud could have kicked herself. "I'll talk to Herbert, of course," she added quickly, reminding herself that she was after all a guest in this house, "about the girls."

"Oh would you darling?" Violet's tone was smooth yet toneless. "Now who else is coming?" she asked briskly looking to her bejewelled hands as if they could speak. "And ducks, I do hope they get a move on. We want great festivities tonight don't we? With simply *everyone* contributing." She rattled off a guest list that included local landowners and friends. "Then there's that dreadfully boring ex -King of Portugal with the terrible moustaches – and Dukes, Portland and Manchester (yawn) although I know *you* like him and Lady Mount-Temple – so ancient now I wouldn't be at all surprised if she died on us, but she was such a good friend to dear Constance Wilde."

"What a sad business," said Maud lifelessly. "Constance died so young yet *he* is still alive."

"Only just, I gather and not at all well."

"Still in Paris?"

"Yes." Violet examined a particularly fine diamond and emerald ring, trying it on one finger and then the other. She breathed on it, wiping it against her bosom. "And Waller," she mumbled into her chest.

Maud's head jerked up. "What do you mean 'and Waller?' Is he living in Paris or not well?"

Violet feigned a yawn.

"Neither – well his wife Florence is. I mean in Paris. So I invited him."

Maud recoiled. "But why?"

"Well, Florence, he says, is so busy buying up plays – you know what these Americans are like at the grand gesture – that she's had no time for him this holiday – no time I think for him for longer than that, reading between the lions as the gels used to say. Anyway the point is that she's away and I thought… well darling his voice *is* divine and my gels are mad for him. I thought you might be too. Just a bit."

"Well I'm not. You're wrong Vi, it's not him. I wish you hadn't."

"Oh darling… I am aren't I? I was so sure it was him!"

"It's not."

"Oh well… we'll have fun whatever happens. And you can rehearse *Dream* or at the very least *Pyramus and Thisbe*."

"Yes and 'Wall' and 'Lion.' I'm not sure we have so many scenes together."

"It doesn't matter – he can stand in for … Bottom."

"Very funny. And a recurring joke I might add."

They began to giggle.

"You're not cross then, darling? I couldn't bear it. It would make my milk go all funny."

"Would it matter? You're not feeding much anyway."

"No… you're right. Oh good, we can go to London even sooner! Which reminds me. I've got a present for you." Violet reached under the pillow to produce a small box.

"Go on Maudie – I can hardly wait! Open it!"

Maud smiled, pleased beyond expression. What could it be? A little bit of jewellery would be more than she could hope for, but then Violet had so much…and she was always saying how she didn't care a fig for any of it and Maud might borrow if any time. Maud undid the ribbon with shaking fingers. She held her breath, ready for an effusive and sincere thank you. But the oh! of delight came out flatly as a K.O.W badge fell onto her lap.

"You're incorrigible," she said briskly, hoping her disappointment didn't sound.

"Oh God darling, I do hope so. Glad you're pleased."

Maud made a thing of noisily wrapping up the badge in the tissue paper, retying the gift with its ribbon, shaking out her rug, looking for her book of verse, and in the meanwhile keeping her face well hidden. By the time the baby began to stir she had regained her composure and when Violet said, "do ring for nanny darling and shall we have a drink?" was able to sink back into the enveloping soothing ease and effortless extravagance that was Belfield.

Seven

It's a sort of bloom on a woman. If you have it, you don't need to have anything else; and if you don't have it, it doesn't much matter what else you have.

J.M. Barrie *What Every Woman Knows*

Maud's maid (or at any rate the girl on loan to Maud for the duration of her visit) was doing her best to ensure that every step in preparation for the afternoon was as laborious as possible. Or so Maud thought. The girl's fingers fumbled with the many tiny buttons of Maud's chemise and she had piled her hair so high and so tight that Maud felt like one of the extras for Tree's 1888 *Pompadour,* rather than the emancipated young woman she felt herself in her heart to be. Used too, as she was to her mistress's minute waist, the maid had laced Maud's unnaturally small, so that she could hardly breathe sitting down and could only speak properly if standing ramrod straight. And Maud had neither jewellery nor out of season blooms – more costly than pearls at this time of year – to soften the effect. The reflection in the oval mirror that stared back at her was one of tetchiness and discomfort. There had been no sign either of Herbert since breakfast, so Maud dismissed her maid and set off down twisting turrets and long galleries to look for him.

It had begun to snow again and by the walkways and terraces of the gardens below, a thick blanket was beginning to cover the balustrades and statuary. The gardens were Violet's creation and from a casement window, Maud could just make out the Corinthian column she and Violet had purchased together in Italy. Maud sped down the cantilevered staircase to the Guardroom with its vaulted ceiling and collection of weapons and armour. Her feet hardly touched the cold, black and ivory patterned stone that fanned out beneath her to frame the single canon that welcomed the visitor to the castle. This part of the house was silent, as if oblivious to the festivities soon to begin in the ballroom. And although log fires blazed at either end of the room and boughs of holly and trailing ivy adorned the mantelpiece, it was hard to believe there was anyone at home. Maud retreated up the stairs and through the Grand Corridor to the second floor library. And there, leaning towards the window for light and consulting the Grantham train timetable, was Herbert. A dusty travelling cloak was draped over his shoulders but rather than appear dashing, his appearance was as dishevelled as usual, and had Maud not been so shocked by his obvious impending departure, she would have found his lack of 'toilette' amusing. She could always tell when Danes doubled as his 'man' as his shirt was collar-less. Both servant and master were equally bewildered by the accoutrements involved in dressing a gentleman. But while Maud never ceased to wonder at the contrast between the lives they had known and the glamour of the ones to which they were exposed to now, Tree viewed each rich interior and its accompanying exigencies of dress as mere costume to be worn against the backdrop of theatre.

"You are... leaving?"

Maud's heart was hammering so hard against her corset she thought it would actually pierce skin. Tree turned with the humbug expression she had seen him adopt when playing Beethoven. She knew – but why, oh why had she not heeded her instinct? – it had been premature to feel happiness with him again.

"Oh little maus," he said, and she hoped it was embarrassment and not just the heat from the fire that made his freckled skin turn pink. "You know how empty the country always seems!" He made an expansive gesture and Maud followed his gaze to the clock on the flag tower through the window. And she marvelled that 28,000 acres of rolling white hills after a fresh snowfall could spell romance for her while to Tree it was indescribable desolation. "There are no people!" he added.

"Just a house party of 25 with double that in servants."

He made a dismissive gesture. "There is so much to be done still with *Dream* –"

"That can't be done here?" Maud's voice was sharper and shriller than she intended.

"Ach…" he replied impatiently, his mouth pursing at her retort. "It's not the theatre! It's not *my* theatre."

She yearned for him to pull her into his arms almost as much as she yearned to undo her corset, but she was rooted to the spot with a sudden exhaustion and a pride that stopped her from throwing herself at him as she had done when she played Olivia in *Twelfth Night. As she had planned to tonight… After all it really was Twelfth Night!*

"No, it's not." And yet if she wasn't gentle he would go and who knew for how long? She swallowed, forcing her voice to be calm. It took all her willpower not to slap him. How could he disrupt their lovely time here? "Oh Herbert, isn't it just a little bit like Marienbad?"

But reminding Tree of his beloved Germany, of his most favourite place in all the world and the one to which he returned yearly to work and rest did not produce the desired effect at all. He used his foot to spring his body forward, away from the window and frowned impatiently. His tongue began to dart around his mouth as if trying to taste any last vestiges of alcohol. It was a maddening habit.

"You want me to feel something I simply can't," he said quietly.

"No, I'm not even asking that," said Maud, holding his gaze until he was the first to look away.

"I can't," he repeated.

"Or won't?" Maud could have bitten her tongue but it was too late, the words were out.

"Can't," repeated Tree stonily.

She paled.

"Ah maus…" he said, more gently this time. "It's like writing on oily paper – it's just not possible – it's, it's… a feeling of mental impotency!" He looked pleased with himself for coming up with the analogy.

She had no idea what he was talking about. She felt only an engulfing wave of disappointment. Why did she mind so much? What was it that Violet was always saying to her? *The heart has its reasons that reason cannot know?* Yes, that was it. Her foolish heart had a life of its own. And for no sane reason it wanted Tree. She would try one last time. She must drive the bitterness from her heart if there was any hope of keeping him. She could do this if she could only find a part – a role she could emulate and one she did not have to feel or over-think. There must be a hundred parts that required such a change in tempo, mustn't there? She fluttered her eyelashes.

"I'm not asking you to love the place, only to stay one day longer. It's the last night of Christmas, Herbert. We're to act our scene together. You–" she moistened her lips. "And I."

He grimaced as if in pain. "Are we by Jove?" he said. " Then act it we will!"

Maud's heart began to slow its furious pace. Thank God, she thought, thank God! *This is where he must throw off his cloak and pull her against him as he had done at dome. This is where* – She closed her eyes. *His lips should be close... his breath on hers...*

"Then you'll stay?" she murmured. Even to her mind her voice sounded like a caress... it was the softest she could make it.

"No, I must go."

Her eyes flew open. He looked at her piercingly then, his eyes slits of tepid-coloured glass. "Ah Maud."

"Yes?" she croaked. She couldn't help the tears in her eyes. The tears were everywhere now, coursing down her cheeks, her neck. She brushed them violently away.

"*Yes?*"

He was unmoved. If anything her emotion irritated him.

"You must know," he said gruffly. "You were tantalizing to me."

"Oh Herbert I – "

"Once."

Maud gulped in shock. *Once?* And then he was gone and she stood shaking, her knees knocking out the petticoat of her gown. Her heart roared in her head, blood pounded through her ears. She could neither see nor hear. Instinctively she felt for the library table in front for support, but then as her fingers closed over the soft leather binding of a doubtless priceless tome, she grabbed it fiercely and hurled it blindly with all the strength she could muster. As its fine, parchment pages ripped from its spine and were strewn over the rug, she gasped in horror.

"Oh God, Oh *God*!" she exclaimed aloud.

"Don't be a goose. Go after him!"

"What? *No*!"

Maud froze as Henry Cust revealed himself by waving a hand from where he'd gone undetected at the far end of the library. Soon after a foot saluted from behind the globe and metamorphic chair that converted, as required, into library steps.

"You!" Maud added unnecessarily but doubly dismayed.

"Go after him," repeated Cust.

"What's the point?" She moved towards the door. She wanted to crawl away from this mortifying scene. And in front of Cust! Of all people!

"Wait a moment," said Cust from his cosy alcove corner. He reclined in the low chair Duchess settled her subjects when she was drawing them. Indeed Violet's sketchbook and pencils lay beside him on a small table as though she had only just left the room. The half finished sketch showed a man in profile, his beautiful head thrown back, his shirt open at the neck. A book was propped open on his thigh held in place by a slender, manicured hand, flashing with precious gems. The other arm trailed over the arm of the chair, touching the rug by his side.

"I- I didn't see you."

"No, well I could hardly interrupt that little scene. I had no idea which way it would play."

"Ugh...!" groaned Maud as she felt a corset string give way. She bent down on all fours to gather the pages from the scattered book.

"He'll never change," volunteered Cust. He leaned his head on his elbow managing to convey a notion of movement without actually moving. Maud had finished gathering up the torn book by the time he'd uncrossed his legs. "I don't suppose you ever guessed these weren't real?" Cust's eyebrows twitched in the direction of the books on the shelves above him. "These sham ones make up part of the jib door that leads –" he grinned. "Well, you know where it leads."

Yes, thought Maud, I do know. She fixed her gaze on Pope's *Essays* alongside Walton's *The Complete Angler* for future reference.

"Look, if you want one hardened Lothario's advice – you can't change him so don't try – you'll only break your heart in the process."

"It's already broken if you must know, but thanks."

"Not at all."

Maud's stays cut into her rib cage and as she straightened she felt the world spin. Sweat trickled down the back of her neck.

"Steady old girl," said Cust, whose voice emanated energy and concern while his limbs remained absolutely inert.

"Oh get up man and help her!" came the unmistakable melodious voice of Lewis Waller.

Maud sat back down heavily as Waller swam before her eyes.

"Et tu Brutus?" she said lamely.

"Lucius? I thought it was you. I *hoped* it was you."

Waller smiled, recognizing his former co-star. Now he helped her into a reclining position, keeping his hand on her shoulder as if to keep her pinned to the spot. And as the warmth from his fingers filtered along the iron tight bands of her corset, she suddenly remembered a strange little note he had written her at the time.

Shall I be very selfish if I hope that 'Brutus' may be just a little bit missed?

Maud couldn't recall the circumstances. Had he been absent from the play? Why did he imagine she would mind? Had she? She was certainly aware of him now and the intensity of his concerned look.

"Just how many more people are going to pop up in this room?" she said faintly.

"Well if he couldn't interrupt *you*," said Waller pointing at Cust, "I couldn't interrupt *him*!"

"It could have become very complicated."

"A farce."

"Bedroom farce even."

"We need Duchess for that."

"Yes, well."

"He's an idiot!" said Waller passionately.

"He's my husband," said Maud rather prissily – not exactly what she intended.

Waller took her hand and bending over it said, "I wish he wasn't."

Cust looked at them both with one of his more energetic expressions, a raised eyebrow curbing the tic that passed for a smile when he wasn't exerting himself overmuch.

"I rather think I'll change for dinner," he said uncrossing a long elegant leg. But between saying and doing there was still a wide Sargasso sea. He remained rooted to his chair, which retained the imprint of his beautiful form long after he had gone.

"I really don't feel too good," said Maud. One scene was quite enough for one afternoon. She felt neither witty nor beautiful, both elements necessary to enter into any repartee with Waller. She closed her eyes as once again she felt her skin prickle and nausea sweep over her.

"I'll help you to your room," said Waller soothingly – his warm, rich voice rolled over her jagged heart like a temporary balm. Before she had a chance to protest Waller lifted her to her feet, placing one solid arm around her waist. He was much stockier than Tree, shorter and altogether stronger and she leaned into him in relief. Cust had still not moved a toe in their direction. As she stood, her legs went weak and without hesitating Waller swooped to lift her in his arms. She could feel his fingers between the whalebones of her corset and the thin cotton muslin of her undergarments.

"I say Waller, dear boy…."

Maud could feel Waller's breath on her cheek.

"Yes?"

"I think I might be taking tips from you…"

* * *

The dining room, with its newly fashioned alcoves and fireplace built from two Venetian lion heads Duchess had discovered once again on her travels with Maud, was lit with dozens of candles. Large gilt baskets of azaleas covered most of the surfaces and the air was intoxicating with their scent. Against freshly painted walls, in a shade of green Maud had never seen before, were portraits of long forgotten dukes and duchesses. The low hum of chatter and the tinkle of wine being poured into crystal greeted Maud as she slipped into her chair. She was unfashionably, unforgivably late. There was a momentary pause in the otherwise smooth flow of conversation. Belfield frowned, muttering something along the lines, "We thought you might have got lost!" which was met with low guffaws from the male dinner guests. He wore a richly scented gardenia in the lapel of his white evening coat and his freshly trimmed whiskers made him appear debonair and playful. Seated on his right was Margot Asquith, wife of the future Prime Minister, exquisitely dressed in a ruby red velvet gown by Worth. Triple rows of pearls cascaded down her flat bosom and more pearls were liberally wrapped round her wrists. An egg-sized aquamarine set in a band of diamonds sparkled from her finger. A pristine white fox wrap hung on the back of her chair. Her shrill voice cut above the others, cheerfully gossiping about everyone, calling the Royal Family 'kindly louts' and the Prince and Princess of Wales 'Beauty and the Beast' until no one was left with a shred of reputation.

Violet in contrast, was simply dressed in a pale muslin gown, her improbably tiny waist even after the birth of her child, accentuated by an enormous sash held in place by fresh violets. Under the table, Maud could see she was holding hands with Cust. The Duke shot her a look from time to time but otherwise his attention was held entirely by the King of Portugal and Dukes Portland and Manchester, regaling them with tales of his latest amorous conquests. Their duchesses sat with glacial expressions on their faces – due less, Maud was certain, to aristocratic froideur, than to the fact that their enormous tiaras while sparkling and exquisite, were nonetheless so heavy they could only turn their heads by moving their entire upper body. Maud thought they looked like rather exotic owls cooing and tweeting in unison. At Maud's end, Henry James, already a dear friend, was also a deathly dinner companion having difficulty in keeping up and always a couple of topics behind in conversation. James was not helped by Asquith, who having turned down leadership of his party was returned to the bar. He was neither as witty nor as catty as his wife and as a result a good deal less fun. Nor would anyone mention the Queensberry affair, as Madeline Wyndham, seated between Herbert Asquith and Henry James, was a distant cousin of Lord Alfred Douglas.

It fell upon the delectable Ettie Grenfell, the most celebrated hostess of her time and one of the most beautiful, to resurrect the floundering conversation. Ettie, wife of the first Baron Desborough, enthralled everyone who met her, exciting the old and young alike. Famous for dazzling house parties at Taplow (where the view was said to stretch the soul), her guests vied with each other to be the wittiest and the most memorable. Friends with politicians and members of the royal family she was as popular a guest as hostess. She avoided musicians but lionized writers and actor managers, especially Tree. She was also a devoted mother, as besotted with her young sons as they were with her. She now turned her beautiful face with its flawless complexion and enormous doe-like eyes to H.G. Wells and in her husky, strange intonation demanded an outline of the scandalous new book, *Ann Veronica* she knew he was writing. The female guests were agog with curiosity, fascinated by the relationship he depicted – part mentor, part lover – of an older gentleman with a younger woman.

"A sort of modern Svengali," volunteered Maud.

"Indeed," said Ettie eking out the word so that it appeared to spread over an entire sentence. "I-i-i-n-n-n-deed." She touched Wells's arm in a pretty little gesture, her hands appearing perfectly white against the black cloth of his coat. "But why did you ever make a *man* the mentor?"

"What do you mean milady?" asked Wells.

"W-ell..." said Ettie slowly through half closed lids. Her head, listing towards the light on a neck that appeared unnaturally elongated by an enormous double necklace of rubies, cast oblong shadows across the table. "Why not have an older *woman* embark on a relationship with a younger *man*."

There was a small silence.

James Barrie took a sip of wine.

"Did she say *Peter Pan*?"

"No," said the actress Julia Neilson who was to play Oberon to Maud's Titania in Tree's forthcoming production.

"Ah, so you've read my play?" inquired Barrie. "*Her* husband turned it down." He nodded in Maud's direction.

"I was thinking of a beautiful…" Ettie's eyes were dreamy.

"B-boy?" volunteered Barrie.

"Exactly…"

"I think…" said Maud.

"Better not!" whispered Waller loudly, his eyes crying with amusement.

"Protestations of ecstasy and devotion…" pronounced Ettie breathlessly.

"To his m-mother!" said Barrie.

"Oh yes!" Ettie clapped her hands. Her own mother had died in childbirth and as a consequence she considered all mothers with a Madonna-like reverence. "Devotion from him…"

"Ardent joy from *her*!"

"He must be malleable but not prickly."

"And she must exude confidence, maturity but *deliciousness* all the same," said Waller for the sake of it.

"You enjoyed saying that," hissed Maud.

"There might be other… children…" Ettie's cheeks were flushed. She adored intensity. "But this boy is a *rival*…"

"An in- in-f-fatuation…"

"And absolutely no physical consummation."

"Good God man!" interjected Asquith."

"He wakes!" cried Margot.

"No that's not at all what it's about." Wells scratched his head perplexed. "It's really much more subtle than that... more of an observation on the New Woman."

"New woman, new woman! Who's offering me a new woman, eh?" Belfield guffawed loudly poking the King, Carlos I, unceremoniously. His Queen nodded uncertainly. "Si, *mulheres*," she agreed with her lady-in-waiting who scrabbled in her reticule for her dictionary.

"Here we go..." breathed Duchess.

"But listen here Maudie," said Cust attempting a rescue of sorts. "You've acted in one of those so-called feminist plays, yourself."

Maud put down her fork as a footman in a white waistcoat whisked away her untouched quails in aspic while other arms elbowed the air passing plates between them. A gilded peacock was brought in next on a silver platter, its tail cascading down the maid's back like an exotic scarf. "Ibsen."

"Ibsen," intoned Belfield gloomily.

"They say," said Maud, "or at least my brother-in-law Max says, that the New Woman was born intact from Ibsen's brain."

"And would you say you were one?"

"*Me?*"

"Would rather be a b-beautiful m-mother," persisted Barrie.

"Not exactly-"

Cust raised an eyebrow. "As in the kind of mothers in Faust of whom Mephistopheles speaks in awe."

"What is... he... saying?" asked Queen Amalia.

"He speaks of Goethe, your Majesty," replied Cust smoothly, allowing a glimpse of the brilliance that once earmarked him for the premiership – a brilliance that was soon dissipated by women and drink.

"Is that C-Cust speaking?" ventured Barrie. "Th-that man got m- me quite intoxicated l-last night," he said in a loud whisper "b-but it was worth it."

Cust bowed over his glass. "Flattered dear man," he said gallantly, "though 'tis a sentiment I'm more used to hearing from women."

There was laughter while Queen Amalia flicked through her dictionary.

"Goethe? You say," said the Portuguese King. "The German?"

"The German," agreed Cust firmly. "You see for Goethe, mothers are the creative force that plant the notion of Ideas, Forms and Archetypes in the human psyche."

"Is that why Peter rejects his?" said Maud tartly. Barrie had begun to twitch and his little moustache was getting in the way of his glass as he tried to drink.

"Oh no!" said Ettie. "He ... *longs* for his... for *her!*" Ettie had withdrawn her hand from Wells's arm but had stayed close, her bosom pressed against his forearm. "He's just an innocent." Ettie formed the 'o' beautifully so that the entire table concentrated on her luscious mouth.

"Ah..." said Cust leaning back in his chair. "But is he? Does he? What is so innocent about persuading children to leave their mothers? Who has noticed that this boy has no love in him, changes side quite blithely in a fight and kills without conscience?"

"Wendy does..." suggested Duchess. She picked a violet from her waist, tearing it into little shreds alongside her plate. "She doesn't like his conceit..." She looked at Cust pointedly. "Nor his *greed*..." her eyes ran over his face lingering on his mouth. "Or cock-i-ness..."

"So in the... absence of a mother...?" Maud said hastily as the dinner guests all swivelled to look at their beautiful hostess who was so clearly in love with another. Maud had not intended to speak aloud. A nagging memory was pulling at her. A slice of the

Twelfth Night cake was placed before her, confusing her even further. Images were scooting around her mind. She looked up to catch Belfield's unusually thoughtful expression.

"Childhood can always be recaptured and can b-be just as touching, just as captivating - anything is p-possible when you escape from being a human b-b-eing... away from the adult world." The diminutive Barrie seemed to have shrunk in his high-backed chair. He gripped his cutlery with force and his eyes, which had never seemed so before to Maud, now appeared sly and sinister. "My p-play will open the day after B-b-oxing day. I know your h-husband will regret it." He glared at Maud.

"I'm certain he will regret all manner of things," she said smoothly.

"But not his Manners," Waller bowed gallantly in Violet's direction and everyone laughed.

Maud closed her eyes, as much to shut out images from the past as those hovering round the table. She felt rather than saw, Waller's gaze upon her.

"Just tired," she mouthed faintly. But he did not return it and when he spoke his tone was almost fierce.

"I know what it is."

The conversation splintered once more into snippets, heads bobbed above glass, earrings glimmered against cheeks, the sounds becoming as fractured as the light. In the many mirrors, the powdered, liveried servants appeared as if from a by-gone age. She sensed Waller speaking, perhaps his words were even directed to her but she couldn't make out their meaning. That famous liquid voice was sonorous, hypnotic – merging and blending, rising with the cadences of the other sounds in the room. She smiled feebly, her eyes fixed on the Duke's face. It at least remained steady, unaltered. And yet... and yet as their eyes met and hers locked into his, a grimmer memory struggled to make itself known – make itself known and then declare itself. She was the first to look away. *Oh no!* Had the words been hers? Had she even uttered them? And yet gauging by the stunned reaction, by the silence cutting through tiara and diamonds and flickering candlelight, someone had spoken, screamed even. She rose unsteadily, gripping the tablecloth in one trembling hand, while the other pulled at an imagined choker. With the dawn of recognition came panic as for the second time that day Maud felt the room tilt unnaturally. Somewhere, somehow... it came to her at last... that voice...

* * *

"Cheer up, man... " He was firm, commanding, not without empathy, she could see that now. "It won't be long before you find yourself another woman..."

But who had said it? She pressed her eyes tightly shut – a gentleman's voice – a voice not unlike... she remembered it's jauntiness – its carelessness – the carelessness of privilege. And she standing in the shadows in the stairwell shifting her weight from one foot to the other lest he notice the coal on her boots – tho' why he would see her at all was a wonder. Somehow she thought if she hid one foot, both would be less noticeable. And then the crack of bone against bone as someone else... no ... not someone else but her father, her own father hitting the gentleman square on the jaw, except that blood poured from the man's nose on to the snowy silk evening scarf around his white tie, spattering it in one go. But her father had made no apology – had sobbed – even.

"I don't want a new woman – you bastard –I've never wanted another woman!" he has said raising his fist.

Maud had cried out, "Don't Father!" and both men had frozen having forgotten all about her, and his man had come running ready to pull her father from him and fell him to the ground. And then surprisingly the gentleman had held up his hand – the long slender hand with the unusual jewelled signet ring placing it at first in front of his long, no longer straight, yet still beautiful nose.

"No, Hargreaves, let him be. He's quite right of course. Why would anyone want anyone else but her?"

And then the gentleman had touched Maud's head – her dirty, lice-infested hair gently – as if she were a lady and not a coalman's daughter. Maud had shrunk even further against the wall, suddenly cold and hungry and alone and wanting more than anything to be part of his world and not her own – wishing it with such an intensity tears pricked her eyes.

"The girl needs a mother..."

No! Maud had wanted to protest – that's not it – not why I'm crying.

"She has me." Her father was fierce. He bent his head, beating back his sobs. "This should never have happened!" he spoke loudly so that she jumped.

But the gentleman was bored now and his man placed a thick black cape that buttoned down the front around his shoulders.

"You'll pay for this!" her father had hissed. "No one does this and gets away."

The gentleman's back was towards her now and for a moment she thought it sloped forward.

"Everyone pays... in the end..." he said.

And when the gentleman had gone her father had spun round to her and with the drink rising in him and that wildness pressing against his temples he had knocked her to the ground.

And all at once Maud understood how it was and who he was. Her chair fell backwards, a rung snapping in two onto the fine Persian rug. Waller leapt to his feet too late, as grabbing uselessly for support she went tumbling, tumbling into the welcome and blessed darkness.

Eight

Question your desires; Know of your youth, examine well your blood.

A Midsummer Night's Dream

January 1900

Outside the dressing room entrance of Her Majesty's Theatre, on the corner of Charles II Street, Tom Danes stuffed the last of the wayward rabbits into its cage, cursing as he felt damp excrement slide through his fingers. He slid a cabbage leaf through the bars, wondering if he shouldn't in fact be saving it for himself for later. His pockets always bulged with ends of salt sticks or muffins, and now that Christmas had been and gone he had great wedges of fruitcake and slices of suckling pig and roast turkey hidden away for good measure. He straightened up wondering if he had time to nip to The Swan Inn for a pint, but it was only an hour before the little buggers had to be on stage and given the fact that most of them did not nibble at the real foliage or bran or indeed frolic in any meaningful way at all, he doubted he'd have time to even snack on the delectable slab of apple boudin he'd found drying away in the Dome. He blew on his hands to warm them – he hadn't had time to feel cold and under the awnings that wrapped round the building, both he and the rabbits had been protected from the odd snow flurry.

He pushed the cages flush against the wall and let himself into the stalls entrance. He could hear laughter from the audience like a dull sea roar – the kind you hear from a trumpet shell. And a grand audience it was too – he had seen the women arrive in their rainbow array of silk gowns holding their trains in one hand, fans in another and gentlemen in white tie and tails, top hats so shiny they mirrored the overhead chandeliers. Tom was curious for the first time in his life about one of Tree's productions.

"It will be anything else," his master had said gleefully after the first successful rehearsal. "You will see Tommy my boy, illusion is the thing! The entire aim of all art is Illusion – to gain this end all means are fair. Everything is anything else!" He had pressed Tom's shoulder with one hand as impatiently he pushed back his fringe with the other. "The country needs this – anything comforting – romantic. Something is so... gloomy."

Once Tom had substituted Tree's 'anythings' for 'something' and the 'something' for 'everything', Tom was able to make some sort of sense of what Tree meant.

"And..." Tree wagged a long finger in front of Tom's nose. "Do not forget this: all that aids illusion is good, all that destroys illusion is bed."

Bed? Surely... Tom looked at his master. Did he really mean what he thought he meant? In his case, he probably did. Anything of course was possible.

"I mean who wants (it came out vants) a green (gween) baige (bwaige)curtain eh? Bed... absolutely bed..."

Bad. He must mean bad. "Er... no one Sir..."

"No... the baige curtain..." Tree frowned demonically, "is the beginning of everything that is boring (bohwing)." Tree's voice shrank to a whisper. "Everything in short that smacks of... sordid suburbanism..."

Tom blinked, the flicker of understanding he had experienced earlier, extinguished completely.

"In that compound of all (his mouth formed a perfect 'o' and his tongue circled each 'l') the arts which is of course the theatre," continued Tree whose pale eyes were now like sharp flints of stone and his cheeks feverish, "the sweet grace of restraint is of course necessary...But!" he steered Tom to the edge of the stage where they stood looking up. "But," he said holding Tom's head steady, "the scenic embellishments should not overwhelm the dramatic interest or the balance is upset – the illusion is gone!"

Tree dropped Tom's head and swept his arms wide, the breadth of the stage. "Is illusion destroyed by getting as near as we can to a picture of the real thing? That is the question."

All Tom knew is that for the moment, food was easily come by. There were plenty of pubs near by and the Carlton (if you mentioned Mrs. Tree) was happy to provide meals at any time of the day or night, on credit. And if he timed the rabbits right he'd be able to see the whole of the first act uninterrupted. He took a last bite of cake although he wasn't really hungry, but you never knew with Tree whether 'a short interval' became two days or didn't happen at 'oll'. He wiped his hands one last time on his knickerbockers and stuffed his flat cap into his pocket. He let himself into the auditorium closing the door silently behind him. There were no empty seats by Tree's famous new flat stage, so he crouched in a corner by a fire hose. He glanced around quickly – somehow by night the gold statuary around the three tiers of gold boxes shone more brightly and the glittering jewellery in the audience perfectly enhanced the dazzling effect of the production. The stage was unrecognizable from the chalk markings and sheets doubling as pillars Tom had seen only the day before. Now above Theseus's palace a huge shield spelled Athens in Greek with recreated Corinthian columns and a mosaic-painted floor with intricate Grecian borders running the width of each ceiling border. Tom along with half the audience, gasped at the splendor of it all. Some of the fairies switched on battery-operated glow lamps at key moments, such as Puck's incantation over the sleeping lovers, while mechanical birds sounded in English beeches. A lawn of thyme and wildflowers provided Titania and her fairies with a natural carpet and huge garlands of evergreen hung amid branches of real trees. Mendelssohn provided the background music.

But while visually, *Dream* really was the stuff that dreams were made of, leading Tom to surmise that there might be more to his master than he had previously thought, even Tom was aware of certain well… blunders. To begin with, Waller lost his famous voice completely and his general ability was said to be somewhat weakened due to what *The Stage* later called in its review, 'a sorry rheum.' Tree's Bottom was 'distended till it spread over the whole play' leaving Bernard Shaw to quip that the Shakespearean forest couldn't be seen for the 'Beerbohm Trees.' That was not all. Quince stuttered his prologue; Lion roared himself into a coughing fit and when Thisbe knelt over Tree (as Bottom) to ask, "Dead, dead, my dove?" Tree reacted with a violent coughing fit, proving to be very much alive. There was more. 'Moon' dropped his lantern because it was too hot. With only Thisbe's mantle to hand, 'Moon' grabbed the mantel, leaving Pyramus without the aforesaid mantle with which to apostrophize. Thisbe and Pyramus took so long to settle into death that Quince in exasperation finally threw a blanket over them both and sat on them. Only Max Beerbohm, loyal to his brother, declared the illusion of fairies admirably achieved by the troupe of many children that peopled the production.

The best was yet to come. Tom, in forgetting himself quite completely in the magic of the play also forgot the rabbits and was forced to enlist the help of the duty firemen. There was a panicked scramble to get the cages backstage in time for the second act, by which time the animals were so shaken about they came out squealing. The rabbits burst out of their confined spaces running hell for leather onto the stage, ignoring the bran (to Tom's partial relief) instead making a bee line for the artfully strewn roses along Titania's bower. The fairy 'children' shrieked and the battery-operated lights came on in super quick time. Only Mrs. Tree, in her costume of spun gold, in yards and yards of chiffon, sporting diaphanous wings and a crown of crystal blossom, seemed oblivious of the commotion around her. But something was wrong. She seemed to sleep-walk through her part, looking undeniably beautiful but somehow absent, her smile fixed. Her usual flair and ability to command her audience was neutralized in flat tones and such a genteel air that Tom had to agree with the critic in the audience who hissed, "We're not out of the 19th century yet Titania!"

Tom sat forward on his haunches, his hands gripping his knees. Oberon (played by a woman, which Tom thought just downright wrong), entered with her /his train of fairies from one side of the stage whilst Titania processed regally with all 42 children trailing behind her scattering rabbits and bran in their wake. Tree in the wings, now assuming his director's hat, hissed loudly "Skip! For Godsake you're fairies, *skip*!" and Titania, moving at a snail's pace leant heavily on a wand as if for her support. In the recreated moonlight, her face was translucent and her entire figure shimmered against the painted woodland.

"It's a fairy from South Kensington!" someone whispered loudly. "Mrs. Tree looks as though she's stepped into a drawing room."

Oberon halted in her presence, holding out a hand to stop his own fairies from careering into Titania's.

"Ill met by moonlight, proud Titania," he/she said.

Maud gazed at Oberon with a beatific smile on her smooth features but didn't speak. There was a long silence. Too long a silence. The audience itself began to mouth her response.

"What, jealous Oberon! Fairies, skip hence: I have forsworn his bed and company." Under her breath she whispered, "As he has mine," continuing to smile benignly while the lights round her head rotated in an on/off motion and the rabbits turned their attention to the real daisies sewn on the hem of her gown. Maud seemed unaware, not even attempting to kick them away.

"Tarry, rash wanton: am I not thy Lord?" Julia Neilson (Oberon) spoke in a deep voice, but her spikey crown rendered her more like Britannia than King of the fairies. Her breastplate too was electrically lit and now pinged so brightly that Maud blinked involuntarily. She turned her head owl-like as if it were weighed down by the crown jewels.

"Rash wanton?" her voice was extremely clear as if in an elocution class. "Rash certainly, but not so much wanton as pregnant!" She placed a hand lightly on her belly lest there be any misinterpretation.

There was a collective titter from the audience and a roar from Tree, "Well so is May!" that was mercifully drowned by the whoosh of the colossal velvet curtain swinging into place.

But so did the safety curtain swing into place and because Tree had rushed centre stage, for the second time in his career it crashed down neatly on to the crown of his head.

* * *

Tom was very glad he had kept the turkey stuffing wrapped in newspaper because, as it turned out he didn't get another opportunity to eat sitting at a table for the next 48 hours. He patted the package from time to time just to make sure it was still there. Its mere presence was of comfort for he knew that he would not go to sleep with those terrible gnawing pangs he had so often known when he first started out in Tree's employment. Not that there was going to be much chance to sleep, he was sure of it, be it keeping sentinel outside the Dome, or in his own bed in Shoreditch. There had been times when Tree slipped out of his theatre to visit 'his other wife' and their 'other home' on Putney Hill but Tom never asked and Tree never said and there was an unspoken bond of secrecy and silence. If Tom felt the odd twinge of discomfort as custodian of this information, he never let on, his narrow, sometimes half closed eyes appearing simply not to see. Other than that he was quite content to look after Tree and his theatre. However, he had never been quite so ping-ponged before his master and his wife as now. Tom alone had always dealt with Tree's business and domestic arrangements, but tonight for some reason Mrs. Tree seemed to think that he (and the entire company) was at her disposal, that because she was the aggrieved party as she saw it, they should all rally round *her*. Whereas Tom was quite sure Tree was feeling that he was the one wronged.

He now knew why it said in the bible that one slave couldn't serve two masters. Having the two of them at each other's throats was making his work nigh on impossible. It wasn't as if Maud had left in a huff once the stage debacle had settled down. If only she had! No! She had hung around half the night as she'd done during rehearsals of *Dream* till 3 and 4 in the morning as if *guarding* Tree until the entire cast was grumpy and unsettled. And work to be done there was. Tree demanded a doctor so the beautiful Constance Collier, Tree's sometime leading lady, appearing as if from nowhere, offered Tree hers which immediately made Mrs. Tree suspicious. Wasn't *she* the one who had usurped her? She hissed at Tom. Wasn't *she* the one who played the Goddess Pallas Athene in Tree's *Ulysses* which she, Maud, had set her heart on playing? Hadn't she, Maud that is and surely Tom knew this, planned her entire costume to be gold so that her hair and slim figure would be shrouded in a gold veil, backlit in gold so that she would appear more than mortal? And wasn't Constance the trollop (nothing divine about that) who couldn't for the life of her pronounce all those Greek words that positively tripped off Maud's tongue so easily, given her background in the Classics? Tom could hardly keep up with the number of questions she threw at him but didn't seem to care whether he answered or not. Something about rhetoric someone else said. By the time Tom opened his mouth to say something, Maud was well into her stride, asking Constance bluntly now if she too were having an affair with her husband. Mrs. Tree kept changing colour, going red and white faster than Puck's electric lighting. At last she seemed satisfied with the answer while Tree continued to cover his face with his hands moaning, "Do anything, please. Do anything!" But Tom was sure it was more to hide away from these women, than because he was in any kind of pain. Maud then dragged Tom into his 'office' – well Tree called it that. To be honest Tom was hardly, in it, he spent so much of his day running errands for his master.

"You must book me a passage on the ferry and vagon lit," Maud commanded. "I am leaving for France! And someone must fetch my Baedeker! I never travel abroad without it."

The 'someone' Tom might have known would be himself. But when Tom enquired when she intended leaving, she said she had to leave that very night – she also listed travelling essentials apart from the Baedeker, clothes from Sloane Street and a book of Racine, misplaced but without which she could not leave. Care had to be arranged for Viola. Exile in Paris was no place for a child, did you know. Tom didn't and hardly knew where to begin with Maud's demands while Tree's though more varied, were just as extreme. His head needed stitching but he was more concerned with the cracked proscenium arch (this was not a word Tom often used in his current vocabulary, but one that he learned rapidly over the next week or two) caused by the excessive weight of the steel safety curtain. So not like last time, then? What last time? Oh that… no nothing like. The fact that it had been abruptly pulled was just a coincidence. Notwithstanding the repairs would be costly, another theatre must be hired in the interim and the actors paid retaining fees. At eleven o'clock at night, while still waiting for a doctor deemed suitable by Mrs. Tree, Tree hit upon the idea of the Waldorf and then spent the rest of the night (blood spilling down his face) tearing between the two theatres effecting an immediate move.

"Oh and Tom," Mrs. Tree appeared from behind a lobby pillar still sporting her electric crown and gossamer robes studded with glow lamps, "There's something else you must do for me."

Tom dropped the piles of clothes and books Tree had ordered from the Dome – he too was abandoning the theatre but in his instance for the Garrick Club and Tom was going with him.

Maud didn't wait for an answer but thrust a piece of paper in his hand.

"Find this man," she said. "And send him to me in France." She threw back her shoulders. "Tell him I will pay his expenses but he must come as soon as possible."

"Very good, Madam," he said, putting the paper straight in his pocket without looking at it.

"Oh and Tom?"

"Yes?"

"Tell no one."

"No, Madam. And where is 'he' to go?"

Maud looked down at him as if she were indeed Queen of the Fairies.

"Oh the Ritz, Tom. The Ritz." And with that she turned on her heel, flicking her toga style robe over her shoulder with éclat before disappearing once again into his study.

And then of course there were the rabbits. Tom never wanted to see another small furry jumping creature again in 'oll' his life. He was sure some must have come a cropper – he'd lost count quite literally of the cages he'd left outside the building, never mind backstage. By the early hours however, Tom had accounted for most of them and hustled them once more into the cramped spaces from where they came. He sat on top of the last cage exhausted. He had seen Mrs. Tree off in a hansom cab, a portmanteau brimming with an odd assortment of clothes from wardrobe and a travelling cloak that Pegotty wore in *David Copperfield*. She had taken one of the rabbits for company and left Tom with a pile of letters to be hand delivered – you know it's faster – even Violet Belfield's was to be delivered to Arlington Street in the event that Lord Granby was not to be found at his club.

"You could just as well send it round to Violet Vanbrugh's dressing room," she said bitterly. "That way Henry would get it a darn sight sooner."

Tom held her gaze. Vanbrugh was another of Tree's one time leading ladies but Belfield's current paramour.

"I'll take it to Arlington Street," he replied firmly.

Yes, it had been a long night and now that the dawn was breaking over the Haymarket gaslights flickering in the weak wintry morning were finally being extinguished. Street sweepers were out brushing away the last of the night's debris. At least he wasn't having to clear up the mess left by the rabbits and the copious amounts of foliage and woodland hauled in from Richmond Hill no longer needed on the stage – or *this* stage at rate. Tom couldn't begin to think about the logistics of transferring everything to the Waldorf. But there was time for all that in the morning. He unwrapped his packet of turkey stuffing and the end of a bread roll. He chewed on it carefully as if it were the most delectable food in the world, which of course it was to him. He tasted the salt gravy as though it was piping hot, as though it was splashing down his chin and he licked his lips with gusto. He leaned his head back on elaborate lead piping. It was cold but he didn't feel it he was that relieved to be out of the theatre and for a few hours at least away from the Trees and yes even his master. The pants and sighs and 'Woe is me!' were too much – enough to grate on Tom's nerves of steel. He would close his eyes for just a moment or so. No use in going home at this stage. He'd only have to turn round in an hour or two to make the long journey back into town.

Tom's mother had died in the years he had been with Tree and half the time there seemed little point in returning home when he was so needed at Her Majesty's. Now that he didn't have to, he still hoarded food and could live on virtually nothing. He spent 2 shillings a year on a pair of new boots, but if he needed a shirt he helped himself to one from wardrobe. Mrs. Tree was a great one for mending too and if she was sewing her husband's clothes she often gathered up Tom's as well. His one indulgence was a pint from the nearest pub in whatever town they happened to find themselves in, and the odd flutter on the dogs. He would have a short kip and then go in search of eggs for Tree's breakfast. Some actors ordered in chops or buns and milk but it was always the same for Tree. Tom stretched his legs all the better to dig into his knickerbocker pocket for the remnants of a humbug he remembered having put there some time ago. He found the sweet and the piece of torn paper Maud had thrust into his hand. He sucked loudly, luxuriously.

'L.G. Littlechild. Private Investigator,' he read. "All manner of personal work undertaken. Putney 3256."

And his heart sank.

Nine

The lunatic, the lover, and the poet, Are of imagination all compact: One sees more devils than vast hell can hold, That is, the madman; the lover, all as frantic

A Midsummer Night's Dream

The heavy damask curtains were closed tight – not even a single neat line of light seeped from under the thick silk lining. In this way it was impossible to tell whether it was night or day. Maud had lost all sense of time, all sensation of hunger but was overcome now, and in complete contrast to the raging energy that had gripped her on the night of *Dream*, with an overwhelming desire to sleep. She slept but woke most nights from a nightmare in which she was drenched in perspiration. Even the sheets under her were sopping, the back of her neck was wet and if she felt the skin above her breasts, rivulets of water ran between them as though she were squeezing a sponge from her bath between them. And every night it was the same dream, the same sensations, the same asphyxiating fear. She saw herself, she saw a woman, a mother dying in childbirth drenched in sweat and blood. She saw dirty sheets and a dirty pillow, and on that pillow thinning tangled strands of what had once been a thick glorious mass of blond tresses. She saw two children sobbing and a man with dirty hands and boots. She felt her own head jerked back.

"Say goodbye," he said gruffly. "Say it."

"No!" the little girl shrieked something defiant, bigger than him or the small wailing voice within her. "No! I won't."

"By God you will!" The man slammed her face down against the wet eiderdown, against the motionless thigh, the staring eyes and before he could strike her again they were both startled by the thin

cry of the newborn babe from somewhere among the mysterious and terrifying folds of the bed, that cried and died as if the effort of opening its mouth was too great. And he too froze – she could feel the muscles in his back against hers, his forearm a bar of iron against her cheek as he pulled back. An older woman entered there, dirtier than him if that were possible, with the same sweet smell of drink.

"5 shillings it is," she said "alive or dead."

The man jack-knifed to his feet and crossed the room in a leap and with one swift movement had the woman against the wall, his hand at her throat. The smallest boy began to cry but the girl stared fascinated by the woman's feet dangling above the floor.

"Enter this house again and I'll kill you," he snarled. The woman spluttered, her face growing from under his fingers, spreading and inflating like butter under a knife. He gave her a final twist and dropped her so that she fell coughing and spluttering, clutching her throat.

"And take this!" he said gathering a mass of bloody rags from the horrible mass on the bed. "Take the brat – don't bother with a burial!"

The little boy shrank against the wall beginning to snivel. The girl hissed at him to shut up. And then in a grown up voice, one that wasn't hers at all, one that she could imitate, she said, "That's not a brat." Her voice was ice on the pond, ice in the larder bucket, ice inside the broken window. "That's our brother."

*   *   *

There was a scraping sound like a steam train braking suddenly, the tearing of silk as the curtains were ripped apart.

"Madame, *venez voir!* It's royalty."

Maud winced in the alarming glare of light that burst into her room onto the silk sheets, the velvet bed coverings and the exquisite fresh linen pillows. There were bouquets of sweet scented flowers in front of mirrors and on highly polished surfaces. Walnut furniture and pale upholstery were in perfect harmony in a room that was feminine and light, warm and spotlessly clean and luxurious. She felt her belly for the imperceptible swell that was still there, that refused to budge. She reached for a bowl into which to be sick. The maid paid no attention, her eyes drawn to the place Vendome in front.

"It's so exciting!" she said. "You must get up."

"What kind of... royalty?" Maud wiped her mouth on a linen towel watching in fascination as her fingers trembled. She caught sight of her reflection and winced. Sleep beckoned her back, beckoned her under...

"You must get up, now! Come and see. It is the English."

Maud's eyes struggled to focus and then closed, so much easier to –

"You don't say."

"I do say. So many ... children and servants and dogs."

"Children?" Maud's eyes fluttered.

"And ... *equipage*."

"Luggage?"

"Yes... no... I mean equipment. Art tools, easels, très Bohème."

Maud pushed herself onto her elbow, then onto her knees, clinging to the four-poster for support as the floor and the ceiling rushed towards her. She felt as weak as a kitten. If she knelt straight she could see out the window. Four horse-drawn carriages had pulled up directly beneath them. Footmen ran to help a nanny carrying a baby alight, followed by three little girls identically dressed. A woman wearing a purple travelling coat came next. As her small foot touched the carriage step, she lifted the veil from her enormous hat. Maud shrank back. It was Violet, Violet outside her hotel window, here in Paris and wasting no time now in directing the various trunks that tumbled onto the pavement.

"*Debout!* Please! They must be kept upright!" Clear modulated tones rose in the clear air.

"Good Heavens! Lord Haddon!"

"The English prince?" the maid had opened the window and was leaning over the balcony.

"No, not a prince," said Maud. "But an English Lord...Oh *Lord*... I mean...I know who it is! Quick! Help me back to bed."

The girl turned from the window. "You should get up Madame," she said not unkindly. "It's not good for you... you should eat something too. You leave the tray... always it is untouched."

Maud sank onto her haunches still holding onto the bedstead as though it was a sinking ship and she was clinging to the wreckage. Her fingers clawed at the rich bedcoverings as if they were life-rafts. Once more ensconced in the enveloping down she sank, a tremendous relief overcoming her.

"I'm not hungry. And please..." Maud turned her face to the pillow. "If anyone asks for me, please say I am not to be disturbed."

The maid replied in French and from her tone it was clear that Maud was being scolded. The girl bustled round the room but gradually the small disturbances quieted and Maud realized she was alone once again. She pressed her face into the sweet smelling pillow, comforted by the fact that though her dreams might be nightmares her physical surroundings were real. But with her eyes shut, she was haunted by the same sequences: the squalor of that other room, the smell of blood and dirt and death. She remembered or rather saw, the cobwebs in the corners, the peeling paint, the rims of brown rust round the basin and the mud that caked on the bottom of the eiderdown and along the newspapers laid on the floor to hold the blood. This time she woke up with a start, drenched once again in sweat and a pain stabbing her breast.

"Do you actually *want* to lose the baby?"

Maud blinked at the vision standing in front of the window, looking for all the world like an angel in copious amounts of pleated linen, the trademark violets at her waist.

"Are you real?"

"As much as anything."

"Or something."

"Come again?"

Maud shook her head into the pillow, thinking of Tree.

"You never travel with the children."

"And you never take to your bed." Violet glanced round the room, opulent even by the Ritz's standards. "Who's paying for this?" Maud noticed she hadn't once addressed her with her customary 'darling.'

Maud shrugged. "I hadn't really thought."

Violet approached the bed. "Well you better had and quickly. Or you'll end up a pauper!" She might just as well have added 'again' but didn't. She re-opened the curtains only this time the light was muted. It was almost dusk, the breeze from the open balcony doors sweet and refreshing and for a moment Maud had a great desire to thrust her head out and inhale the fresh air. Violet's stern look persuaded her to stay put.

"It's time for action," she said calmly. "I admit to not being a great advocator but in this instance it is necessary."

"I'm afraid I disagree." Maud shut her eyes firmly.

There was a frigid silence and then a sharp click as Violet flicked open her fan.

"I have come with two questions – very important ones and everything I say from now on depends very much on the answers."

Maud yawned.

"Can't they wait till morning? I'm awfully tired."

Violet snapped her fan shut as she rang for the maid. The determined expression on her face made Maud's heart sink. Violet pulled an elegant Louis XIV chair closer to the bed, arranging herself prettily – prettily and patiently. Maud knew that demeanour better than her own. Violet said nothing and nodded graciously when the maid who arrived shortly afterwards curtsied, stuttered a 'Your Grace,' and placed a tray on the bed beside Maud. There was clear orange blossom tea, a poached egg and bread. Maud wrinkled her nose against the needles of nausea that began to prick her stomach.

"Eat," commanded Violet. She poured them both a cup of tea as Maud elbowed herself into a sitting position. The egg was perfectly done and it broke over the white bread – the kind of bread her mother used to give her before-

Violet set down her cup, placing the silver spoon carefully on the edge of her saucer, examining the beautiful porcelain with a practised eye.

"If the baby is a boy will it make a difference?"

"What do you mean?"

"Eat!"

Maud tried to swallow just as her throat closed to repulse the food.

"I mean if the baby that you are so determined to abort is a boy, will you forgive him?"

Maud took a sip of tea, the fragrant blossom the lightest of tastes along her tongue. In spite of herself she smiled.

"The baby? Or Herbert?"

"You're being difficult. I meant Herbert."

"What does it matter? No matter what, the world will forgive him," said Maud quoting from a short Barrie play she had acted in only recently.

Violet did not return the smile. "But it always does, we know that. It's whether you can. It's whether your boy like my Haddon, can be enough."

"Boy? Girl? Why should that make a difference?"

Maud took another sip of tea the hot, hot liquid invigorating her. Violet looked at her closely.

"In that case you cannot leave him. It simply must not be allowed to happen."

"You can't be serious!"

Violet's eyes were purple pools, her cheeks flushed in a manner Maud had seldom seen.

"Deadly."

Maud sat up, pushing herself into the bedhead for support. "But you! You of all people know what it's like."

"And it's because I know, that I can advise you." Violet removed the flowers from her waist, smelling the petals one by one. "You cannot divorce. It would mean the end of your career, the end of Tree's, the end," she finished darkly, "of Viola's chances. Do you want that?"

"No of course not, but this sudden conformity comes from where? Are you sure you are the best person to advise me? You who have had three, no four children by three different men."

Violet was not offended. "I do not deny it. But I did because I could, *can*. I am a Marchioness, one day I shall be a Duchess. You darling," and here she smiled, "are an actress. A very loveable one!" she added hastily, "but still an actress. And you are wrong. Like you I cannot divorce but it doesn't matter. In theory of course divorce is open to us but the reality is very different. I would lose my children for one thing. Society would snub me,

Cust would..." Violet tossed her head. "I have all the privilege that wealth can afford me and more importantly, the freedom."

Maud put a trembling hand to her hair.

"Then what am I to do? I can't go back. I won't go back."

"Oh but you can."

"It would be too painful."

"Of course it will be. Do you think I don't shrink at *his* touch now? Do you not wonder how I sit sometimes night after night biting my tongue raging inside, wanting to lash out? Wanting to hit him? Wanting to wound him for destroying my dreams, for stealing those precious years when I was so in love with him when I thought we were strong, that nothing could come between us, that we would lie always in one another's arms? That I should never seek another's?" Violet's voice rose passionately and then she checked herself. She got to her feet to stand by the window. The sun setting over the Vendôme column turned it pink and gold beneath an inky skyline.

"There is another way. A better way," she said at last turning, only slightly but her look was still far away, her beautiful figure outlined against the Corinthian pilasters.

"I want him, I want my husband." Maud suppressed a sob. "I want the man I married."

"And a child cries for the moon."

For a moment the room sounded only with Maud's low sobs.

"It's not that he doesn't love you," Violet said at last more gently.

"Oh I'm certain he cares," said Maud bitterly, "but along with a dozen others."

"You have to accept that a man like Herbert, like Henry... well they are not ...exclusive... they will never be."

"But God forbid that we should behave like *them*!"

Violet shrugged. "It was ever thus. The world will forgive *him* but condemns *us*."

"But it's intolerable!" Maud punched the pillow. "How can I bare it? How have *you*? I can't go on... I don't want to."

Violet fingered the curtain damask, rubbing her slender figures over the embossed silk.

"First of all you must get strong." Violet's tone was firm though not enthusiastic. "Then we gather information-"

"Oh no!" Maud sat up, the sudden action making her dizzy.

"What is it? Are you in pain?" Violet was by her side in an instant.

Maud shook her head. "I'm all right. It's not that. I've hired a man. All expenses paid. He may very well be on his way now."

"What do you mean hired a man? To do what?"

"He's a detective." Maud looked away. "I'm ashamed to say. I was so consumed with rage – so jealous–"

But to her astonishment Violet smiled. "No, that's good, that's very good," she said. "That's exactly what I meant by gathering information. This way you'll *know*."

Maud grimaced. "But do I want to?"

"Yes, my darling I'm afraid you do. As I said, it's a time for action." She drew a chair beside the bed. "There's so much to do. SO much you can do and I will help you. But you must tell me what is it that you want besides the obvious."

"I want Herbert," Maud said stubbornly.

Violet made a face. "*Besides* Herbert."

Maud closed her eyes. What was there to say? Her whole life had revolved around him for such a long time. And before that?

She had simply survived. The image of the tiny room with the blood-stained newspapers slid before her eyes and she groaned.

"I want to act... I can't not... act...but in a different theatre from Herbert's –in the new theatre – the theatre of ideas, the theatre of the continent."

Violet clapped her hands then gestured to the square beyond the window. "Et voilà! I was so hoping you would say that. Now then, this man?"

"Littlechild."

"Yes. We must stop him coming. For one thing we need him *there* not here. These creatures are costly enough without incurring unnecessary expenditure. And another thing, once you're well we need to find you an apartment. This is heaven of course but we'll both be bankrupt if we stay here much longer."

Violet's eyes narrowed. "This Bohemian look..." Her eyes swept over Maud's unwashed hair and still damp night-gown. "It's mine sometimes but never yours. You can't afford to look like this. You must always, always be elegant, coiffée. I am a sculptress – I can get away with it. But I'm being harsh..." Suddenly Violet stood up. "And I've tired you I can see. Look, we'll start with small things... and in the morning you will give your first interview."

"My *what*?"

"Oh... darling this..." she waved her hand vaguely, "all requires precision. It's a campaign; if it were a military one it would be no less exacting."

Maud downed the last of her tea, comforted in spite of herself. "And how long is this... campaign going to last?" she asked mildly.

Violet pursed her beautiful lips and tilted her chin in a most coquettish fashion.

"Oh... I should say about... nine months."

Ten

And, as imagination bodies forth The forms of things unknown, the poet's pen Turns them into shapes, and gives to airy nothing A local habitation and a name.

A Midsummer Night's Dream

Maud sat at her desk in an area of Paris that wouldn't be fashionable for another twenty years, but it was every bit as Bohemian as Violet had promised. Her apartment was in a former 'domain' in Notre Dame des Champs, a small cul-de-sac off the Boulevard St. Michel and a stone's throw from the Luxembourg gardens. It was small but there was an extra bedroom for the baby and nurse. The shared stone staircase was reminiscent of a more romantic, precious age and tall wrought iron gates dipped in gold hinted at the formidable ghosts of a forgotten city. A fountain in the secluded courtyard with its rhythmic trickling of water was soothing to the ear, and with spring in the air Maud's spirits lifted further. Maud worked assiduously, following a plan Violet insisted would succeed. A pile of newspapers and magazines lay at her feet from which she snipped articles for the scrapbooks she had begun collecting. She hadn't progressed further than reviews of *Dream*, none of them particularly flattering. 'Nothing whatsoever is left to the imagination, not even the wire suspending Puck... nor the cord which makes Oberon inseparable from his electrically lit sceptre,' said *Sporting Life*. She looked for reference to herself and found one. 'The Titania of Mrs. Tree was graceful, though it was scarcely worthwhile taking her away from the Palace and her praiseworthy task of earning £100 a week for the War Fund for what many others could have done just as well...' There were more comments along that vein stating that hers was a Fairy Queen from South Kensington whose revels were limited to Queen's Gate.

A little harsh, thought Maud though not entirely unhappy. Given the circumstances she was damned if this production went down in the annals as being a success. Besides which she was generally too busy to worry about theatre critics at Her Majesty's when she had more than her fair share to contend with in Paris. Most mornings she gave interviews or was photographed, gratified to see that her style was said to emulate that of Violet's in their matching muslin gowns and picture hats. The *Lady* called Maud a 'vision of sunshine and indescribably beautiful – a dream of white chiffon.' Elsewhere she was portrayed as wearing the 'most charming gowns in her own particularly graceful clinging style.' The *Sunday Times* said she 'dressed with her usual elegance of taste.' Society pages featured Maud surrounded by celebrities such as Nelly Melba, Lillie Langtry, Lewis Waller and Irving – the latter (even more than the former) designed to irritate Tree as his relationship, notoriously difficult with the other actor manager, was well documented. Maud was photographed drinking tea at the Ritz with the great Paderewski. Photographs of Maud's London home mimicked the articles appearing in the French capital with columns requesting advice on how to balance both career and home life. And in America, a series penned by a New Woman, doggedly attempted to understand Maud's position. She was called a lady scholar and 'a versatile mathematician.'

Maud began to enjoy herself to the extent that when a precocious young journalist unabashedly inquired about the ten-year gap between the births of her children, Maud was not offended. She appraised the young man with such an intense stare that he coloured violently. "Well by then, monsieur," she said coyly "I had learned to wait in queue." On another occasion she had sighed in a way designed to elicit support. "Yes, life can be very disappointing. Nothing comes off (she pronounced it 'orf') except buttons." And now Maud set about doing what, apart from acting, she had always done best – networking by way of extensive letter-writing. And she had new targets. Invigorated by Violet's belief in her, she was full of plans. Strindberg was on her list because he was unpopular in America, and Maud had a soft spot for tetchy Scandinavian writers most guaranteed to attract Tree's attention. *'Do you mean to put an end to the actor manager?'* Tree wrote to her in fury. *'Do you mean to do away with my theatre?'* *'Mais non,'* she replied sweetly, *'but tu vois, I am interested in a theatre of ideas.'* At Violet's instigation, she had sent Winston Churchill three volumes of Shakespeare and a charmingly worded note. "But he's a boy!" Maud protested. "A boy no longer, Maudie. He's back from the Boer war and more importantly he's now a *politician*," said Violet and was vindicated when they received a joint letter of thanks. Maud wrote to Ellen Terry to be friendly, to Violet Vanbrugh (mother of Belfield's love-child) *keep your friends close and your enemies closer*, and to Barrie and Maugham so as not to be forgotten when they got round to casting their next plays. She approached French and English playwrights and became friends with Proust's lover, Reynaldo Hahn who asked her to write the prologue to his biography of Sarah Bernhardt.

She had less success with her banker friends. '*Yes, I did receive the note and it has worried me ever since,*' Carl Meyer replied after a decent interval. '*I know of no way of turning £50 into a lot of money except by burglary or murder and neither requires any capital.*' Anyone and everyone who was of interest socially, culturally or politically became the recipient of Maud's little notes and small tokens of remembrance.

"And then there's Florence West," said Violet coming into the apartment after a visit to Rodin, with whom she was collaborating on sculpting a bronze statue of St. Catherine of Egypt. She was re-visiting Maud after a few months spent settling the children, including Viola, back in England at Belfield with a governess. Violet removed her cloak – one of her own creations, and draped it over the back of a chair. Her matching dress was no less extraordinary. It had enormous epaulettes and was made of canary yellow velvet. A matching yellow bow that at a glance might have been mistaken for the bird itself, perched amidst a nest of fine straw on the top of her head. She, or rather the hat, nodded in the direction of Maud's baby's room, empty at present as she was out for a walk with the nanny.

"By the bye, have you thought of a name?"

"I was thinking of calling her Felicity."

Violet smiled, peeling off yellow kid gloves and pulling up a chair to sit beside her friend. "How... optimistic."

"I think so." Maud returned to her scrapbook. "Why Miss West?"

Violet leaned across the desk for a more recent copy of the *Illustrated London News,* scanning the society pages. Violet's thumb rubbed against the paper and she appeared suddenly to be deeply absorbed by whatever it was she was reading.

"You do mean Waller's wife?" said Maud in a bored tone.

Violet was silent and Maud knew she wouldn't divulge a thing more unless she showed more interest. But two could play this game. Maud went on cutting out bits of theatre-related articles. Presently Maud's curiosity got the better of her.

"You do mean Lewis Waller's wife," she repeated.

Violet threw down her paper. "I do, I do!" she said excitedly. "You need to befriend her. She's actually rather nice."

"Mmm... not sure I do." Maud snipped out a large photograph of Tree and then considered cutting off, if not his head, then other bits of his anatomy.

Violet studied her hands, and noting a bit of clay between her fingers from her morning's sculpting began to wipe them with her handkerchief.

"Mrs. Wa- Florence is an actress. She's rich. She buys up interesting plays and she's Clement Scott's sister-in-law." Violet mentioned one of the most influential theatre critics of the age. "Oh, and she's in Paris at the moment looking at plays of the *Grand Guignol*."

Maud looked up, scissors poised. "You mean horror plays?"

"I mean the Théâtre Antoine."

Maud shuddered. "Yes I've read about him, it. He says if he doesn't make enough women faint of an evening he hasn't succeeded."

Violet clapped her now clean hands. "I know. How thrilling!"

"I'm not sure I'd call it that. But yes, and?"

"*And* you goose she's coming to tea. Well not here. The Ritz again I'm afraid."

"But they're French–"

"*All* plays are French."

"But horror? I'm more of a Barrie girl – with a sprinkling of Ibsen."

"If you want to break away from Her Majesty's then this is the way to do it. Besides I'm not necessarily talking about acting…" Violet tossed her newspaper onto the pile on the floor. She reached into her reticule to pull out an enormous key.

Maud raised her eyebrows.

"I don't understand."

"Do you remember that first day at the Ritz when I came to find you? When you had just left Tr–?"

"I remember," Maud cut in quickly.

"Well, I said then that I had two questions."

Maud frowned, struggling to recall anything much about that time other than her attempts at forgetting its very existence.

Violet touched Maud's arm. "I asked you about boy children," she said gently, "but there was something else."

Violet's deep, velvety purple eyes were misty with emotion.

"Y-yes?" said Maud almost coldly. She wanted to get on with her activity. She picked up her scissors. She'd had an age to reflect on her life and it only made her feel sad to look back… But Violet took the scissors from her and put a key in her hand in its place.

"What would you do with this?" she said, closing Maud's fist around the key and then covering it with her own. "With your own theatre?"

Maud's heart began to thump. She pulled away.

"I don't understand." Except she did. "Vi?"

"Oh darling... I couldn't resist! Charles Wyndham was happy to lease it for a couple of months in the autumn."

"Lease it?" she echoed.

"Oh Maudie, are you being deliberately obtuse or is it post baby? Why *Wyndhams* of course! As in Charles Wyndham – darling he's a cousin. He's always said he'd do anything for me, well now he has! Such an angel! Oh there's so much to think about and plan now that you're well."

Maud sat back in her chair. "I'm not sure I'm all that recovered," she murmured but Violet had leapt to her feet and was now pacing the room excitedly.

"Florence will explain everything later on,' she said. "When you meet her. She has her sights set on two plays – one, *Au Téléphone* – about a grisly murder – a man is on the telephone when he actually *hears* his wife and child being killed. Can you fathom it?"

"No, I can't. How terrible!"

Violet stopped her pacing momentarily. "Yes, but a tremendous theatrical opportunity!" She clapped her hands. "It will be all thunder storms and grey lighting!"

"Maybe *you* should do the play," said Maud under her breath, but she went unheard. Violet was warming to her subject.

"And can you *imagine* the man's horror of being helpless to go to their rescue?" she said, her eyes wide and becoming wider by the moment. Her hands were clasped to her bosom, puffed out in its fine linen blouse. Tiny tucks and buttons fluttered under her chin and her skirts twirled as she spun on her heel. "You do see how in this instance the telephone is an instrument of *torture,* not communication? Do you see how rather than overcoming space and time the telephone paralyses the listener within the very space he is trying to evade?"

"I don't yet but I'm sure I-"

"I think it too *weird* –" Violet said then added in delight, "a genuine play from the Continent!"

Maud's expression owed less to pleasure than to wonder at the sight of an impassioned Violet. She placed the key carefully on the desk and turned the page on her scrapbook.

"And considered by all accounts perfectly unwholesome to normal appetite."

"Tch!" Violet made and exasperated sound. "Look, you either break from Tree's style of theatre or you don't. You can't have it both ways. Antoine's is certainly... *raw* but... inexpensive to produce – apart from the lighting – you'll need green footlights for the effect perhaps, and has a small cast. It's perfect."

There was a small silence. Violet was actually panting.

Maud sighed. "All right Vi, all right, and the other?"

"Ah... the other..."

"Well?" Again Maud was compelled to feign more interest than she actually felt.

"The other is more... complex. First of all the French title is *LÉnigme*."

"And the English?"

"*Which?*"

"*Which?*"

Violet nodded.

"Doesn't sound quite as ... to use your word, 'weird' as the other."

"It explains the plot."

Maud leant towards her. "Which is?"

Violet's hat bobbed vigorously. "'*Which* of them in the darkness and solitude of the night, creeps down to admit you? Which would be the moth to the treacherous light?'" The yellow bow on her head dipped. "Oh! It makes my backbone unhinge!" she cried.

Maud grimaced. "You're the actress, my comfort," she said lightly. "I really don't know what you're talking about."

"Oh Maudie, at one point Lenore – you could play her - says, 'We don't want to be edified, we want to be shocked!'"

"The *Grand Guignol* at its best, then."

"Yes. No." Violet made a sweeping gesture. "*Au téléphone* is that certainly. This is different. The play is about betrayal." Violet paused. "And adultery."

There was a moment's silence as both women looked deep into the other's eyes.

"How much adultery?"

Violet looked shifty. "Quite a lot – enough to attract attention – that of the critics, that is. But we want that."

"We do?"

"And reputation. It's all about a woman's reputation."

"And that's where the horror comes in?"

Violet made a face. "There are two couples and an extra – the lover."

"You're right," said Maud with feeling. "This is a grand gugnol kind of play."

"Just wait," said Violet. "Just listen. It's an interesting play, it is. Essentially it poses the double enigma, whether a man who has caught his wife's lover is bound to kill him, and then there is the question of which woman the man is in love with and therefore which husband is deceived."

"I see. It sounds... confusing."

"You don't like it?"

Maud smoothed the pages of her book. "It's not that but the play seems to be focused on the faithless wife. There is no faithless husband?"

"No."

"But centres on the husband's right to do himself justice? With the underpinning sentiment that the lying wife whose soul is all deceitfulness is not worthy of the name wife?"

"Yes. Exactly-"

"Killing is too good for her."

"Maudie!"

"A man has no right to play the lover to his wife when he has just proclaimed his readiness to kill her like a beast."

"You've read the play?" Violet at last stopped moving round the room and sat down on a small chair by the window. She pushed it open even further and a delicious scent of lilacs and freshly mowed grass wafted in.

Maud sighed. "I don't have to. We've lived it, haven't we?"

"Not to this degree! Infidelity does not balance murder."

"Of course not, but I don't think we need take this to heart."

The women looked at each other. Maud could see disappointment etched on Violet's face.

"All right Vi-" she said at length. "Maybe I'm interested. There. But we'll call it *Caesar's Wife* – who must be above suspicion. No 'Enigma or Which.'"

Violet sprang towards her friend.

"Oh Maudie! I can't tell you how pleased I am! But you must, must buy the rights immediately! Before anyone else does, including Frank Harris! Although I've spoken to him and he's happy to help with translation – oh darling I know your French–"

"...Is deplorable. We might get Max too, I mean for translation." Maud giggled. "That would annoy Herbie."

"Anything you want darling."

Maud tilted her head thoughtfully. "Of course the play's plot is not completely irrelevant. How on earth are we going to treat a subject that can't be referred to on the English stage except at the gaiety between a wink and a laugh?"

Violet moved to tidy herself in the small mirror above the mantelpiece and collected her cloak. "That is as they say, your problem. I'm only here to facilitate."

"And there are actors to hire," Maud said thinking aloud.

Violet half turned. "You could of course act in the plays as well."

"What? And all by the autumn?" Maud's voice was faint.

"Er... there's actually a third play." Violet tied the cloak's enormous yellow velvet ribbon under her chin. "But it's nothing – an Irish farce – something called *Irish Assurance.* A bit of comedy probably wouldn't go amiss sandwiched between murder and adultery! No rights or translation involved. I was thinking in terms of a triple bill."

"So... *three* plays by the autumn!" Maud looked doubtful.

"You've got some catching up to do."

"I've just had a baby."

Violet pulled a face. "Not 'just' and that's an excuse. Besides you miss the theatre, don't you?"

Maud inhaled the sweet spring air. "More than you can know. It's the smell of greasepaint mostly. I never thought I would."

"Well then." She put on he gloves. "That's settled. I'll expect you for tea today at four. Don't be late. Like most Americans in Paris, Miss West is a stickler for punctuality."

* * *

Maud checked her reticule and hat – a vast circular sphere of straw piled with roses, ribbons and a bird not unlike Vi's yellow bow. She felt faintly ridiculous but Violet assured her it was exactly the kind of get-up Florence West would expect of Herbert Tree's actress wife. She unfurled the delicate mauve veil so that it cupped her face, tickling her eyelashes. She wore a blue glacé silk gown with a heliotrope bodice embroidered with a feathery leaf motif. Buttons of iridescent beads in a glittering combination of diamonds and burnished steel completed the coat. Beneath this she wore a blouse that boasted what the fashion pages were calling the 'new sleeve.' It was rather more daring than anything Maud had previously owned, being made of shirred chiffon and completely transparent. A tiny mauve belt with diamond clips encircled her waist, and she wore the palest green kid gloves (a whole size too small) with the intention of making her hands appear enchantingly slender. She might just have gone a little too far this time in her willingness to please Violet, however, for she was having trouble grasping her parasol. The baby Felicity was out again with her nanny and Maud was late. Unable to properly flex her hand, Maud pushed the door with her foot and almost bumped into someone standing on the landing. The woman seemed unperturbed, as if she'd been waiting for her.

Maud let out a surprised, "Oh!"

"Mrs. Tree?" The speaker was a tall woman – the tallest woman Maud had ever seen – heavily veiled and dressed in mourning.

"Yes?" Maud's reply was hesitant, impatient and panicked at the thought of further delay. Besides which she had to strain her neck to look up.

"May I come in? It's a matter of some urgency."

"I- I was just going out." Maud didn't mean to sound ungracious.

"I must speak with you." The woman's voice was husky, seductive almost. Maud hesitated, trying to make out the woman's face through her own veil. She'd never met such a tall woman before and it was disconcerting. Maud, who was so used to being in command, felt at a disadvantage. She was also plumper than Maud but with thick blonde hair piled under a tiny black hat. Maud could see nothing whatsoever of her face.

"It's very important." The speaker's tone was insistent, urgent. "To me."

Maud wiggled her fingers. The tips actually felt numb.

"Oh very well," she said at last. "But I can't stop very long, I have an appointment. Your name Miss..?"

"Mrs." The woman gave the title emphasis. "Reed."

Maud stood back to let the woman pass. "Very well Mrs. Reed, do come in."

She stood for a moment as if blind, her arms held out so that instinctively Maud took her arm to lead her to the window seat but the woman shied away from the light.

"Hurts my eyes," she said, her whole body turning away.

"Is there something the matter with them?"

The woman hovered, watchful, stealthy.

"I am losing them, is all," she said and then suddenly a memory stirred, a troubling memory, but it sank just as quickly as it had surfaced, without trace between them.

"I'm so sorry." Maud guided her to a chair.

"You don't know me, do you?"

"No, I don't think so."

"It's the lead oxide what does it," said the woman. "I was told not to over- use it, so I guess it's me own fault but it did work a treat at first. I used to leave it in overnight coz the effect drove 'im wild. But it's eating away bit by bit – first me skin and then the eyes."

"Lead oxide?" A cold, fearful shiver made Maud tremble. "You were … an actress?" She could hardly say the word.

"And a promising one… when I met your husband." The woman loosened her veil to reveal the most damaged side of her face. The skin under one eye was mottled. Blisters along her lip and chin seeped with pus. A cancer of sorts had begun to eat away at the nostril. Maud forced herself to keep her gaze steady.

"Ain't pleasant is it?"

"I've seen worse," said Maud truthfully. The woman let the material fall into place and Maud was relieved. She didn't want to show or feel pity or censor what she needed to ask.

"You know Herbert?" Maud's tone was harsh to disguise her curiosity.

"You could say that," the woman smirked behind her veil. "'erbie and I–"

"What did you say your name was?" Maud's heart began to thump and she suddenly felt light-headed. She unloosed her lace cravat and the fetching silk jacket, wanting to rip them from her flesh. If only the gloves had allowed it!

"Reed."

Maud frowned, her mind racing. "Reed." She repeated the name carefully as though it were foreign, distasteful. "But it wasn't always, was it?"

There was a silence. "No it wasn't'. I was born Pinney. My first name is May."

The room began to spin. Maud tried to straighten her fingers and the discomfort was sobering. She tried once more and her fingertips went numb – not pins and needles numb but painful blocks of hard matter too heavy to be carried. Slowly her heart stopped its erratic beating, the room came to a giddy stop and sticky perspiration dried at the back of her neck. Where a moment before she had been panicked out of her skin, she now felt icily calm.

"Why have you changed your name then? You're not... married?" *There thought Maud – I dare you! That is something you will never have, no matter how many brats you bear! You will never marry!*

The woman squirmed. "All but in name, love. I'm Mrs. Reed, that's all that matters."

She peered at the woman. *This was her, wasn't it? The woman at dome? The woman – girl back then who had been sitting on the rug by the fire nursing a child while the other–*

Maud sat down on the window seat abruptly, but instead of sinking onto the soft cushion the tight corsets kept her upper body ramrod straight – just like her fingers were too, sticking as knitting needles out of a ball of twine. This poise though was an advantage. "Why Reed?" she said imperiously. *If there was ever a time to pull rank...* "You didn't think you'd be a reed to his tree did you?" *No!!! She didn't say really say, that aloud did she?*

But May Pinney seemed to think this pleasing. "Something like that," she said placing her hand on a still plump belly.

"And you've... just had a child?" She asked incredulously. *Another child!*

"Yes, a boy."

"A boy? Ah..." The pain ripping through Maud was jagged and uncontainable. If it weren't for whale-bone holding in her stomach, she'd have slumped forward.

"And another on the way."

No! So Herbert doesn't mind a freak, thought Maud but didn't say it.

"What do you want…?" said Maud at last faintly. "Is it money? Now that you can't work?"

"Oh it's not money!" May was scornful. "You really don't know anything do you? No dear, I don't need or want money. I, *we* have a perfectly fine house in Putney, on Putney Hill if you must know. It's called Daisyfield – in fact a Miss Potter, Beatrix I believe she's called, paid us a visit only the other day. The house you see used to belong to an associate of hers at the Academy. A Mr. Brett, I believe."

Maud's vision went momentarily black but she saw all right. *I, we have a …fine house.* It wasn't possible. *How* was it possible? Her ears roared with sounds that faded in and out. She looked at the veiled figure bobbing to the cadences of her own speech. She caught something about the Byam Shaws being frequent visitors, even Ellen Terry. *Her* Ellen Terry? Would this never end? This May creature seemed to have days of chat in her. Did she and Herbert not talk?

"I'm not wanting anything," said May.

"Then why are you here?" said Maud tartly. "I have to go out."

May dropped her veil into place. "I'm not wanting anything," repeated May once again, "except for you to stop talking about Herbert's affairs."

"That *I* should stop talking!" Maud was incredulous.

May nodded, or rather the veil moved. "That's right. And to people who really have no sympathy for you but merely relate the stories." May began smoothing the creases in gloves that Maud now realized were expensive and fine. In fact now that she took a closer look at the woman there was a great deal about her that looked expensive. There really was nothing pathetic about the former actress at all. She had turned her affliction into an empowering tool, she was clearly being looked after and she seemed despite her illness, dare Maud think it, happy? Pregnant and happy…

"You see, I in turn have heard that Mr. Waller gossips to members of Her Majesty's company, which can only place yourself in an even more ridiculous position. I mean," she lifted her head proud and high so that Maud's own extravagant hat suddenly seemed the one out of place, "I cannot imagine in what way you think your position improved by this indiscreet behaviour."

"*My* position?" croaked Maud. "Why you–" Maud stood to take a swipe at her but May caught her by the wrist.

"Oh and Herbert has a message. He says he really does want you to always be your own sweet self."

*   *   *

"You didn't come!" Violet was furious. "I practically *give* you a theatre, a play, an *angel* and you don't show!"

"Go away!" Maud huddled under the bed clothes squinting as Violet ripped open the curtains. "You're making a habit of this!"

"Yes and for a reason!"

"I can't do it."

"Yes you can."

"Did you know she calls herself Mrs. Reed?"

Violet paused. "What, a reed to his tree?"

"That's what I said." Maud looked surprised. "It's no good. I'm going to go away."

"You *are* away."

"I mean leave the stage. I can't go on. My heart is broken. This time well and truly. And she's in foal again. "

"Naturally."

"And they have sons. Lots of them." Maud raised a tear-stained face to motion to the pages and copies of birth certificates spread over the bedspread.

"Littlechild?"

Maud nodded.

"'I beg to report,'" read Violet aloud, 'that I went to Mr. Minton, the Registrar of Births and Deaths for the West Hill Wandsworth District and obtained certificates of birth of Juliet Reed born 14 May. Father Herbert Reed. 'Good God."

"Does it say that?"

"No."

"And Claude." Violet shuffled the papers.

"And Paul. And Robin."

"God's Nightgown!"

"And Peter."

"I see."

"And she's so... disfigured!"

"What fat from so many children?"

"No from lead oxide. She was an actress too. Which means he must really love her. I mean to be so ugly and still…"

"Herbert loves himself first and foremost. No one comes second to that except perhaps Shakespeare. *She* must tell him how wonderful he is a million times a day. That's all that is."

"Do you think I should have tried harder, should I have been more like *her*?"

Violet shrugged "What you have to do is get out of bed and see Florence. But *beg* forgiveness first."

"I can't, Vi – not this time. It's over."

"It's never over! But enough! Really, did you never have a decent nanny? So much wallowing! Look, we've done our preparation. You've built a wonderful reputation – you're in all the society mags and papers. The theatre world, the *bon ton* loves you but now my darling, it's time for revenge. You must think to the future if nothing else, to Viola and Felicity. You can't let that woman *win!*"

"She already has."

"No, she hasn't, she's not his wife. She can never be that."

"Well she's as good as. She said so herself and she's right. She's the one he goes home to. She's the one in his bed! Look Vi, I haven't the heart for this. I'm tired of always having to pretend, of putting on a brave face, of going on stage to be funny when my heart is in pieces. I'm done with cold rooms after long hours travelling and still to be looked upon as little better than a –" her voice broke warming to her subject, "I'm sick to death of being someone else. I'm just so tired."

"That I understand."

"So let me go back to sleep."

"No!"

"Look, what's the use? It's clear Herbert wants, *is* with someone else." She turned her face into the pillow. Violet came to lean over her, throwing back the bedclothes and gripping her shoulders.

"Yes, but there's something that you love better than him even if it's hard to admit it now. Something that is bigger and bolder – something he loves better too than all the women put together."

"Oh not the bloody theatre?" Maud sniffed. Vi raised an eyebrow.

"Yes, the bloody theatre. So go out and do what you love – the rest will take care of itself. Oh and by the bye…" Violet gave her a final pat and moved about the room tidying her clothes. "I've heard that Max is engaged to Constance Collier."

Maud's eyes shot open and her heart leapt with delight. "Really? Gosh that *will* make Herbert mad!"

"So that makes one less from the opposition."

"Perhaps, but I can't always rely on Herbert's brother marrying his leading ladies!"

"No, but you have to learn not to mind."

Violet paused, her arms full of satin under slips and the beautiful shirred chiffon blouse.

"Darling, you will get through this. You really will but the trick is to do it, survive I mean, without bitterness."

*   *   *

'Dear Miss Pinney,' wrote Maud, eyes intent on a page that was illuminated by the lamp on her desk and the moon rising high behind the open curtain.

'I feel you should know that I learnt some time ago about your relationship with my husband. I learnt that one of the members of his company had met you at a party at your home and that you had been seen driving with Herbert. If grief and bitterness wrung no betrayal of this secret from me, the years have been kind to me in teaching me to forget.

In conclusion, my 'position' is accordingly an absolutely satisfactory one and you must not, please, give yourself the trouble of trying to analyze in what way I hope to 'improve it.'

Maud sprinkled the page with sand and scrawled her signature through the grains so that the ink would not smudge. She felt astonishingly better for it. Violet was right. She would not give up. She would not give in. She would visit Miss West the very next day and take her a chamois-bound edition of Hall Caine's latest play *Catherine* that she herself had a mind to produce. And then she would go home. But not quite yet. Paris life suited her. It was more relaxed than in London, but then she was less well known here. Or at least as being someone's wife rather than appreciated for herself. The French loved women and they loved actresses most of all. Maud was flattered in a way she wasn't in London. The fact that Herbert had a mistress amused them no end. It was perfectly acceptable – more than that, positively encouraged. They simply could not understand why Maud should be put out.

She sat by the fire, not that one was strictly necessary at this time of year but these stone buildings with their high ceilings could still be cold at night. It was an indulgence she knew. She felt the warmth heat her cheeks. She wore nothing but her pretty loose peignoir free of uncomfortable stays, her feet encased in delicate honey-coloured slippers edged in mink. Momentarily distracted by how exquisite her feet appeared in them she failed to notice a letter being pushed under the door. Instead, after a while she reached for her own writing case – a finely stitched little Florentine leather box George du Maurier had given her after the success of *Trilby*. Ah... thought Maud fondly. *Trilby.* The play had been their professional turning point. Proceeds from the show, written by du Maurier, produced by Tree and acted in by Maud, had led to the building of Her Majesty's. The trouble was, thought Maud, that every thing, every memory lead directly or indirectly back to Herbert. But how deep had been this last wound! How painful it was to remember him in the early days of their courtship! She heard footsteps retreating down the outside stone stairs, and twisting in her chair she saw the letter in the shaft of light from the corridor. She had only a few steps to take to retrieve it and resume her delicious, supine position. She stretched and crossed the room quickly, unimpeded by the usual hobble skirts or train and bent down to pick it up. Once again ensconced among plump damask cushions, she let the envelope rest in her lap. She recognized the writing at once.

I want you –
> I want you dreadfully
> I want you now
> I want you always
> And I can't have you at all!

And for the first time in a long time, Maud hugged herself and smiled.

Eleven

Thou shalt not die; die for adultery! No: The wren goes to't, and the small gilded fly Does lecher in my sight. Let copulation thrive.

King Lear

London 1906

"You cannot produce (it came out pwoduce) a play about adultery!" Tree, still dressed as Fagin for his latest production of *Oliver Twist* looked less malevolent than deranged. His eyes were wild, the pupils darting as if desperately trying to make out an invisible script. His ragged overcoat was stained – Maud wasn't sure if this was from over-indulgence in the part or out of it. Either way the pull of attraction she normally felt towards him was curiously absent. He descended the stage steps, crossing the distance between them in easy strides despite the floppy buckled shoes he had assigned his character. The result thought Maud, was definitely more Shylock than Fagin.

"But why ever not?"

"Can you not see the boards which must surely come? 'Mrs. Tree plays the guilty wife!'"

Maud's eyes narrowed and she steadied her breathing. "You don't know whom I am playing," she said very carefully. "The whole point of the play, if you care to read it, is that no one knows beforehand the answer to 'which?' – hence the title. Besides, it's being talked about and according to dear Oscar it's better-"

"Yeah, yeah – we (ve) oll know what Oscar said."

"Und I suppose *he* is in it?"

Maud gave him an arched look, "who's 'e' 'erbie dear?"

Tree's eyes blazed beneath bushy eyebrows. Some of his teeth were blackened and he had a balding spot on the top of his head. Maud could only hope this was a wig.

"You know who I mean!" He stroked his very ginger beard.

"I only hire the best," Maud replied sweetly. She patted her hair, wetting her lips in a coquettish manner.

Tree appraised her menacingly. "You obviously want to burn! And you will burn yourself with this... *experimental* thing! It was bad enough in *Fwench* but in English...! And don't think it's because it's so ... unsuitable or that, as you might suppose, I feel at all (ol-l) threatened. On the contrary it is *you* who should be. No, it's simply impossible to feel any interest in either the men or the women. Your play is full of *barbarians*!" Again the 'r' came out over-rolled with a distinct German accent. The accent was becoming more pronounced – Maud liked to think in her absence and in Putney's company.

Maud feigned surprise.

"And your play is full of noble characters is it?"

"Ach!" Tree exploded. "Some – you know Nancy–"

"I know Bill Sykes. Look," said Maud calmly, "I admit the Théâtre Antoine is in stark contrast to the... *lavishness* of His Majesty's but if you look at Strindberg and Bell and Achurch, they are all going that way. I really do believe it's the future. It is a very exciting step forward, Herbert, not something to be ... feared. "

"I'm not afraid!"

"Then what?" She was genuinely curious. His hands, puffy and white were splayed before him. They shook like jelly fish.

"It's just so ugly! Brutal und... *realistic.*"

"The nooks and crannies of human existence, Herbert. You should... try and adapt."

As he loomed over her alarmingly now more Sykes than Fagan, Maud suddenly had a vision of someone else, someone else's passionate eyes yearning for her in love not conflict. She had a vision too of his wrists holding her hands steady, wrapping his arms around her waist, his breath on her neck... *I love you and you only in all the world... know that you are the only real love of all my life...*

"What is it?" Tree said gruffly. "You have anything?"

And then Maud began to laugh a low rumble that began in her belly and rose and kept rising till it gurgled in her throat. The relief of being free of Tree was immense, for that was what it felt like at last and after all these years... Oh the blessed relief!

"Yes, yes!" she gasped "I do! I *do* have something! I've just been too stubborn to see it." She began to hiccup she was laughing so hard. "I must go!"

"*Go*? But you've only just got here. Ah I see ... you go to withdraw it? You will stop making such a fool of yourself? With all this Independent Theatre stuff and me as a consequence?"

Maud tilted her head in its new and rather fetching bonnet. For the first time ever she was unmoved by his earnest expression, his thinning hair, the intensity of eyes, which when she came to think of it, were somewhat demonic.

"No, Herbert. Of course I'm not going to withdraw it, whatever gave you that idea?"

* * *

"It's a success!" exclaimed Waller, reaching for a dish of devilled kidneys. Little spirit lamps warmed rows of silver dishes brimming with porridge, eggs and all manner of roast meats. The breakfast table groaned with toast, marmalade and pots of Indian and China tea. Even when there were only two of them, Waller insisted on eating well. Maud, smiling at his enthusiasm helped herself to a slice of melon. There were nectarines from Taplow that Ettie Desborough had sent earlier in the week. The fruit had arrived in large crates packed in wood shavings for freshness.

In between mouthfuls, Waller continued, "Winston Churchill begs a corner in Viola's box – or indeed anywhere he says! And an Arthur Edward suggests his services for further staging and then there's someone who addresses you as N.K.L? What is that?"

"Don't be jealous," she said, noticing his tone dip. "Nice Kind Lady. And I call him Nice Kind Gentleman. That must be Gilbert. Such a dear but very married."

"As are we."

"Just not to each other," said Maud dryly.

"More's the pity."

Maud ignored him. He sulked, took another helping of kidney and bit into toast oozing with melted butter.

"And what now?" he said pushing his plate away and wiping his mouth with a large stiffly starched napkin. "Now that you have all London at your feet and the papers call you a brilliant and fascinating actress, embarking on what the Americans call a 'stellar' career, will you make a bid for fame on your own account?"

"That has to have been your brother in law, Clement Scott?"

"No, but Clement does dedicate paragraphs in *The Drama of Today* to stating what a genius you are – he says everyone should go and see this 'really clever show.'"

"And so they should!"

Maud settled back in her pretty negligee contentedly. "And the King?"

"Loved it. It's not every day you get a standing ovation. The *Whitehall Review* says you deserved it and I quote, "for you have striven to climb the heights on the upward slope of Art where sits ambition."

"How ... poetic."

"That's the *Review* for you. And now?" He was growing more insistent, more impatient.

"I shall return the key to Charles Wyndham. But not immediately."

"Oh?" There was no disguising his relief. "Oh..." he smiled, understanding her at once.

Maud allowed the shoulder of her gown to slip from one shoulder. She undid the plait of her hair, entwining the ribbon around Waller's fingers so that they were joined briefly together.

"Right now," she said very softly, "at this very moment, I would very much like you to make love to me."

*   *   *

"The largest, grandest most extravagant thing you can find!"

"Like this, Duchess?" Viola's clear young voice rang with excitement.

"Yes my poppet that's perfect!" she said as Viola donned a circular frilly pink silk hat that looked rather like an elaborate strawberry ice. She wore her best coat and a serge skirt of grey cloth with a white blouse and looked only slightly out of place as she rushed about Duchess's bedroom in Arlington Street trying on hats.

"But push it to the back of the head."

"I'm not sure I approve, Duchess, of dragging her into this," hissed Maud, appalled at her own picture-hat of black velvet with half-a-dozen ostrich feathers grouped round the spiralling, upturned brim. She wore a white skirt edged with five rows of mink and a coat-bodice with triple shoulder-capes also edged in fur. A deep black velvet waistband was held in place by a gold buckle and a jabot of plisse tulle and lace cascaded in descending rows from her chin to her waist.

"Nonsense! All fair in love and war as they say. Besides we're off to the theatre!"

"Mmmn..."

"And there's not much time. That bow darling should be higher – higher! Much! You know sweetie what we're after. And talking of sweeties I've got two simply *huge* boxes of chocolates." Duchess swooped down on to a low table, hardly able to bend her stays were so tight. Her gown was the loveliest shade of terracotta with a satin skirt. The velvet bodice had a pouched front arranged over a yoke and tiny vest of white satin. Her vast hat had a white satin brim and a white and black tulle veil. From the left side of the black velvet crown, a black and white Paradise osprey rose erect from a chou of white satin, while an enormous diamond hat-pin in the shape of a violet held the whole together.

"Some afternoons the Palace smells like a confectionary shop so many gels are chomping their way through piles of the stuff!" she winked at Viola and turning to Maud said under her breath, "Last part of the campaign. I'd say we've done frightfully well!"

Maud smiled weakly. "I'm just not sure about *sabotage*."

"Oh don't be a goose! Think of Putney, *Daisyfield* if you must."

"That's the problem, " muttered Maud, "I'm not sure that I want to ... anymore."

Violet blinked. "Then think of your ratings. This can only help. Come on girls! Look lively!" And she swept out of the room, her head forced into an unnaturally high position by the moving bird perched on top of her head.

Duchess, her daughters, Viola and even Felicity with her nurse, folded themselves with some difficulty because of their hats, into various hansoms and carriages and were soon trip-trapping along Jermyn Street. Maud's heart thumped with trepidation at the subterfuge of it. Huge boards above the newly christened His Majesty's Theatre, now that Edward had succeeded Victoria, announced Tree as Prince Tosan and Maud's own friend Lena Ashwell as Princess Yo-San, in his Oriental drama, *The Darling of the Gods*. Oriental or not, it was certainly dramatic as its author David Belasco had been accused of plagiarism by Winifred Eaton. Not to be deterred, Belasco in a swift counter move, in turn accused Winifred of libel and had the woman arrested at the play's New York première. Duchess cared little for this somewhat histrionic background to the play, intent only on getting as many of her female friends as possible and the largest hats, to the matinée.

Duchess, who by now really was a duchess, greeted her peers and ladies and members of the Souls, ordering them in turn to raise their chins ever 'higher, higher!' She had reserved some thirty seats in the front rows and other strategically chosen places throughout the theatre and now the chattering women, their skirts rustling, catching, tearing as they cluttered the aisles were intent only on creating as much disturbance as possible. Armed with colossal boxes of bonbons the women arranged themselves on the edges of their plush velvet chairs, their hats all but entirely blocking the view of the audience behind them. Directly in front of her sat the formidable actress, Madge Kendal herself, wearing a hat the likes of which Maud had never seen before. Boasting every conceivable decoration including a tiny but distinct birdcage, it was a miniature stage in itself. As though only recently flown the coop, overly stuffed birds jostled in position with small toys, and fruits including waxed peaches. The entire hat was then wrapped round in a spotted veil as though it were spun sugar. At the back beneath a tidy organza bow, peeped a tiny pair of binoculars that seemed to be staring back at Maud to follow her every move. An even smaller inscription neatly printed beneath said: 'Drop 6 shillings in the slot and I will keep my head still.'

Maud let out a loud "Ah!" and the curtain rose in a gigantic flourish, the newly repaired safety curtain just grazing the rooftop pagodas of old Japan. Cherry blossom and a crescent moon framed a scene of breathtaking beauty. Cascading waterfalls and little bridges crisscrossed a turquoise lake while exotic birds flew across the stage. Lovely women in brightly patterned kimonos took tiny steps along flower-strewn paths. But while Maud could only gaze in silent wonder, Duchess encouraged her friends to voice their opinions loudly against much sucking of sweets and unwrapping of noisy paper. There was a collective and somewhat confusing odour of chocolate. The modern woman it seemed could not endure afternoon drama without it. The hats did indeed bob with increasingly regularity, inciting anguished cries from the gentlemen with a plea to keep quiet or better still to remove the hats altogether.

"Not possible!" Duchess stage-whispered loudly, "'aven't me maid to undo all the pins!"

"What!"

"Sh!"

"What did she say?"

"Hasn't her maid."

"This is ridiculous! I shall get the manager!"

"Oh you can't do that – we're getting to the good bit."

"Yes but I can't *see* it!"

"But you can *hear* it! Just think of yourself at the opera – this is only a version of *Madama Butterfly*. Surely you know the ending to that?"

"Oh for goodness sake!"

"Sh!"

"She's not... ?"

Maud steeled herself. "Oh yes," she said blithely, "Herbert's affairs begin with a compliment and end with a confinement."

Only this time there were no tears to blink away.

* * *

In the absence of her maid, she allowed him to remove her hat. His fingers were gentle, more patient than she would have been in her desire to free her bound hair. He placed the many hairpins carefully on her dressing table but continued to stand behind her.

"They finally arrested one woman from a box!"

"Whatever for?" His tones were drawn out. Their conversation a prelude and utterly irrelevant for what was to come.

"Well it does seem silly now. For obstructing the view, for causing a disturbance."

"And did it?"

"Oh certainly. But then I don't entirely trust Violet. There's no doubt it was a fiasco."

"And justified?"

"No, I was enjoying the play."

He spread her hair as though it were a delicate shawl about her shoulders, his face close to hers. She could smell the clean linen smell of him so close just behind her.

"I should have been there."

"You're here now."

His eyes met hers in the glass. "But are you?" He turned her to face him. "Are *you*?"

*   *   *

It was the same again, the sweat-drenched sheets, the blood-soaked floor. Only this time just as Maud struggled to wake, knowing she was dreaming, the dream altered, dragging her with it to that other place, the theatre and that cold wet night when they waited in the shadows to meet the man in the cloak. *What were they doing here?* She asked her father and got a slap for her trouble. There were slaps for everything it seemed. Slaps for speaking and slaps for keeping quiet. The clever thing was to know just how important it was to speak at all. Her cheeks still smarted as they made their way along the dingy corridors, the rabbit warren of corridors in the basement below the stage where gigantic cobwebs hung from the rafters. And then they emerged to a kind of light and the tall man in his beautiful evening clothes came out of the shadows to greet them. A woman stood slightly behind him, she remembered that now. She wore a pale pink satin gown with enormous puffed sleeves, elaborate bows tied at the elbow that were part of her full-length evening gloves. Ropes of pearls hung round her neck and there were even tiny pearls sewn onto the bodice of her dress. Taking a step forward he impeded her advance by holding out his arm and Maud saw the flash of that unusual ruby ring. But then in her dream even that turned to blood as it began to saturate the woman's dress.

Maud woke panting, her hair plastered to her scalp. In her dream her mother's face had become hers.

"It's all right, you are safe now," he said.

"I never feel safe," sobbed Maud.

"Then don't think of never – know that there is only this moment." His fingers caressed her throat, her shoulders, moving to her back. Their warmth spread itself under her skin. She moved into the shelter of his arms as she clung to him. "Know... that in this moment you are safe – that there is nothing else. That you are loved."

Twelve

What's past is prologue.

The Tempest

"Can't this wait? I'd thought we'd sup together?"

Maud was still in her costume as Agrippina and to her mind she looked gorgeous – formidable yet deeply alluring. A burgundy velvet toga edged in a Greek Key pattern flowed over one shoulder, contrasting with the purple shot silk sheath encasing her slim figure. On her head was a gold crown that wonderfully accentuated the golden strands of her hair. The press had been more than enthusiastic. She was described as passionate, ferocious and tiger-like 'with an energy which is feline in its ferocity.' She liked that very much. She was certain that last bit could be attributed to Arthur Symons. She would write to him tomorrow, send him something special, a cigarette case maybe. One critic had gone as far as to say that Maud had thrilled her audience with an instinct closer to that of a tiger than a human being. But the feather in her cap was the letter from Henry Irving, Tree's greatest rival and first actor to be awarded a knighthood, praising her magnificent performance. *'...Certainly my name and my heart are both at your disposal...'!* How utterly, utterly charming... But this was not the letter Maud was now so intent on reading aloud.

"And you haven't changed your dress! Even the Carlton may be closed at this hour."

Maud's cheeks blazed. "Just listen! You must hear this! It must have been delivered when I was 'on'."

Waller set his top hat, scarf and cane on her rickety, crowded dressing table and undid his topcoat.

"We're not dawdling, Maud."

"No, no!" she said, "but I must simply read this or I'll explode!"

He smiled fondly. "Well we can't have that! Read away and then for gods sake come out to dinner! Like that if you must. No one will mind. I'm sure the Carlton has seen you in your nightclothes!"

"Sh! Listen!"

"I'm all ears, as they say."

Maud tossed back her head forgetting her head-dress, but the crown remained in place. She set her shoulders swinging the toga behind her so that her magnificent figure was outlined against the light. Waller tapped his foot impatiently.

"Well? I'm hungry, Maud."

"*'Dear Mrs. Tree,*" Maud read theatrically, "*The subject of your visit last Sunday has caused infinite pain, but I have since seen your husband, & had a long talk with my daughter. I am utterly convinced that the friendship which I have always known to have existed between them is only friendship'*- she's underlined 'friendship' – I must say I would too – and I quote, '*It is not that which you would have me believe. Yours sincerely, Henrietta L. Pinney.*'

"The 'L' is clearly important," he said dryly.

"Well either she's mad or I am!"

"What extraordinary women they must be – mother and daughter."

"I just wish they'd go away!"

He undid his necktie. "Did you visit May?"

Maud looked uncomfortable. "I was curious."

"Even now?"

She said nothing.

"I see." He picked up his cane.

"Where are you going?" she asked in alarm.

"To the Carlton. I'm hungry. I'm tired. Let's go."

"You're angry."

"No, I'm hungry, I think you may be too."

Maud made no effort to move. "Why are you doing this?"

Lewis made an exasperated gesture, then a great effort to control himself.

"I'm not doing anything. Let's go."

"I don't want to."

"Please yourself." He left his tie undone but draped his opera scarf carelessly round his neck. "I know it's impossible to love someone really and still treat them as you are treating me," he said carefully, sadly.

Maud was silent.

"Yes," he said. "It is, trust me. But I will not think of you every minute of the day and long for you and ache to be with you. I won't have it."

"I'm sorry."

"You told me you'd be alone – which you are at last but you've been gone hours – all day. This morning you said we could meet."

"And here we are."

"And here we are." He gave her a long look and for the first time she was afraid – afraid that she might have gone too far. As if reading her mind he said, "You abuse your power over me utterly and completely. I have to ask myself what my future will be if I am to go on for the rest of my life with such an utterly one-sided love!"

"It's not... one sided," Maud said above a whisper.

"No?" He spun round. "Then prove it!"

*   *   *

Maud entered His Majesty's theatre and came upon a scene of ravishing Pre-Raphaelite beauty. The set designs had been created by Sir Lawrence Alma Tadema and rainbow colours streaking a painted indigo blue sky seemed as real as any island sunset. Somewhere came the sound of cooing doves just as stagehands hauled a replica of a sixteenth century vessel up a ramp. Maud watched transfixed. The plushness of their theatre – it would always be theirs – never ceased to impress her but Tree had excelled himself with this latest production. And Tree, at least she thought it must be Tree, stepping out from the wings was almost unrecognizable. He seemed very tall, with an impressive lion's main sprouting from an exaggerated widow's peak. He wore a prosthetic nose and two huge canine teeth. The hairs from his bushy eyebrows were so long they all but covered his ebony black eyes, and hair appeared to be growing from his naked shoulders. Around his neck he wore a necklace made of animals' teeth. It was not such a stretch to imagine Tree as a wild beast, but never in all her wildest imagination had she ever expected to see their daughter Viola suspended above the stage by what seemed the thinnest of wires attached to her strait waistcoat.

"Fly! *Fly!*' Tree directed. Then "*Sing*! Sing!"

Maud, holding her breath, watched as Viola was raised higher above the very same proscenium arch that had collapsed so spectacularly during *Dream.*

"Das is goot!" Tree clapped his hands in glee. "Now. *Sing*!!

"But what shall I sing Papa?" Viola's voice could hardly be heard, at least by Maud, she was so high up.

"'Where the Bee Sucks' (only Tree pronounced it thucks) my beauty."

"Good Lord!" exclaimed Maud. "And who is she meant to be, pray?"

Tree looked stung. "Who?" He rounded on her. "Viola? Why Ariel of course!"

"And you are...?"

"Caliban," he pronounced the word very clearly as though she were a simpleton. "Isn't it obvious? I am surprised at you Maud, I would have thought you would (vud) know your *Tempest* better! But no matter, you see the ship though? In his silly review, Shaw calls it 'that confounded ship!' He says the waves are so realistic they made him seasick! Shall I show you?"

"No, thanks," said Maud hastily.

"I confess I am not displeased."

"Anything to annoy Shaw," said Maud under her breath.

"And it will sail away with the entire cast!"

"... Marvellous –"

"Caliban will be left, well that will be me, repining on a solitary shore."

"When you say the 'whole cast' – do you mean Prospero too?"

Tree swiped the air with a hairy claw. "Tch! He's not necessary. I have cut his Epilogue altogether."

"Gosh, well that should make for an original ending."

"Maud, Maud," said Tree patiently. "Of all Shakespeare's plays, *The Tempest* is a *fairy*-play. '*This isle is full of noises, sounds, and sweet airs that give delight and hurt not.*'"

"Precisely, and you have tampered with it."

"No, I have endeavoured to capture the *spirit* which animates the text–"

Maud felt suddenly weary. It was all too familiar, and they were as usual going round in circles. "You wanted to see me?"

Tree ran a hand through his elaborate hair and unused to its length found his claw-like nails entangled. Neither one of them heard the faint cries coming from the ceiling as Viola helplessly waved her legs in a cycling motion trying to attract their attention.

"Ah ... .yes. Come Maud, we'll go up to the dome."

"Er... no, not the dome if you don't mind."

"Then the office."

"What about Danes?"

"He won't be there. Probably looking for lunch. That boy is always hungry."

"A boy no longer, surely?" said Maud as they moved down the stage steps and out into the lobby. Maud held the corner of her new pink glacé silk skirt with its sweet white blouse embroidered with pink roses. The tight bodice had double revers of pink satin embroidered with silver and fastened with matching silver buttons. She thought pink particularly suited her.

"No, probably not. And that is just what I want to talk to you about." He glanced at her clothes. "You look as though you were headed for the Riviera." It came out 'Wiviewa.'

"You want to talk about the South of France?"

"No, no."

Tree pushed open the office door to find Tom sitting at this desk tucking his way into an enormous steak and kidney pie. Gravy squeezed from the pastry dribbling through his fingers. He froze.

"Sir? Mrs. Beerbohm. I mean Mrs. Tree." He stuttered, flustered. "I mean Mrs. Beerbohm Tree."

"How 'bout Mrs. B.T?"

Tom flushed. "Very good Madam, Mrs –"

"Oh mine Gott!" exploded Tree. "Just leave us!"

Tom wrapped the remains of his pie carefully into a napkin, grabbed the half opened bottle of ale and moved to the door.

"I'll be-"

"Yes, yes," said Tree impatiently. "Get along with you!"

"I – I want to propose anything," he continued when Tom had gone.

Maud twitched. "Something," she said.

"That's the one."

She waited. Tree paced the office, or rather padded in a loping motion. Maud now noticed he had prosethetic claw toes and enormous hairy feet. "It's ... very difficult to say."

"Try."

"Mr. Beerbohm, Sir." Tom's voice could be heard on the other side of the door, through the key hole.

"Gott! What is it now?"

"Just say it quickly," Maud too was becoming impatient.

"I think you should come!" said Tom, this time through the letter box.

"Is it important?"

"*You* wanted to speak to *me*!" said Maud.

"I do! It is." Tree bent down heavily, necklace swinging, so that his ear was level with the flap.

"Not really." Tom's voice was now muffled as he too bent down to speak through the gap.

"Then don't bother me. I'm busy!"

"And so am I." Maud put on her gloves, doing up the tiny buttons one by one.

"It's to do mit de bees!" burst Tree at last.

"Bees?" echoed Maud surprised. "I thought you'd settled on your music."

"Oh... you were never this difficult! I mean birds and ze bees. As in...?" He made a crude gesture.

Maud paused and looked at him steadily. "Herbert, are you seriously talking about the facts of life?"

Tree looked away abashed. "It is time to explain these things to Viola. I want you to. As you can see she's no longer a child."

"It was hard to see anything she was so far up!"

"Well will you?"

Maud shook her head imperceptibly. "And this is why you wanted to speak to me?"

"Yes. In part."

Danes was at the door again.

"I insist you come now sir," he said as firmly as he knew how.

Tree took a surprised step back. "Insist is it? Well why didn't you say!" And he swung open the door with such force that Danes, who'd been crouching, fell forwards.

"It's Viola," he said brushing down his clothes and leaping to his feet. "She wants to come down!"

"Gott, Gott! Is there never any peace!"

Maud followed her husband and Danes down the corridor.

"Papa!" the voice was more insistent as they drew near.

"I think you've rather left her hanging," said Maud as they entered the auditorium. "And I suspect she's going to be rather more waspish than buzzing bee. What was the other thing you wanted to talk to me about? You said 'in part.'"

"Mmm?" Tree's jaw with its two singular teeth now resembled an old man's toothless one. "Ah yes. So you'll speak to her? About you know?"

Maud wanted to suggest that Mrs. Reed speak to her 'about you know' but thought she might succeed rather too well. She sighed. "Yes, I'll speak to her."

Tree clapped his hands in Viola's direction. "Again! We start at the beginning."

Maud turned to leave.

"I'm doing *Winter's Tale* next," he said offhandedly. "Ellen Terry has agreed to play Hermione – fifty years after she appeared in it the first time - cause for celebration."

Maud smiled tightly, "Indeed."

"Viola will play Perdita and I want you– " Tree caught his wife's eye. "I would like," he amended, "I would *like* you to play Paulina."

"I see," said Maud her heart bounding in no small leap of triumph, although she'd rather have been cast as the beautiful, wronged wife rather than waspish servant. "And you?"

Tree sniffed. "Oh this time I direct only. No part for me."

There was a small silence. "So you're not in it at all?"

"No."

"Not even as 'Time' for example or a non-speaking shepherd?"

Tree shook his head. "Not even."

Maud pursed her lips. "All right," she said while wondering what *he* would think. "I'll do it."

"And the bees?"

"And the bees."

Thirteen

Oh I have suffer'd With those that I saw suffer

The Tempest

London October 1906

Maud halted her 1903 Ford tonneau (which could reach up to 28 mph) in front of His Majesty's as abruptly as a hunt mare refusing a fence. Open roofed and in pillar-box red, it was the height of modernity. It had two forward speeds and one reverse – Maud found she had little need of that one – and a side door. This extra had cost her a small fortune, as had the wheel caps and leather roof which had been an additional £50. For all its purported slickness, the car consistently overheated and the transmission bands had an arbitrary habit of slipping. She had expected to enjoy driving rather more than she did, or at least as much as she enjoyed fast strolling, but the pleasure in buying her very own motor car with the proceeds from her successful stint as director of Wyndham's, was rapidly being replaced by the sheer fear and frustration of driving itself. The car was handsome enough, and big enough given she'd opted for the four-seat tonneau – but she would never get used to the high steering wheel above which she perched. It made her feel like a clown on a unicycle. Added to this was of course the chaotic presence on the roads of carriages, horses and bicycles all designed, Maud felt, to further compound her dread. Today was no exception and she wished that the theatre were not overrun with what appeared to be school children attending Waller's matinée. She noted their K.O.W badges with a touch of envy. 'Keen on Maud' would probably not cut such a dash. Later she would rather wish she'd not let envy cloud her natural curiosity and taken time to chat to the gaggle of girls. But at the time they were nothing but an irritating wall emitting an equally irritating cacophony of sound.

Waller had starred and produced *The Three Musketeers,* the success of which had sparked Tree's professional rivalry to the extent that in a swift counter mood, graciously played out by all parties concerned (well almost all), Tree offered Waller the lead role in his own production, but this time at His Majesty's and for a longer matinée run. However, there was one proviso. Tree wanted Maud as 'Miladi' (a role in which she had triumphed) – replaced by the lovely American actress, Mrs. Brown Potter. And lovely she certainly was. While Maud's dresses were considered 'dainty little frocks' in an article *The Dress Play of the Season*, Mrs. Brown Potter's Paris gowns were given special treatment. An artist was commissioned to sketch her dresses, while feature after feature emphasized the difference between the American woman's dress sense and 'the simple but pretty English dresses of the other ladies.' A rival paper went as far as to state that 'if there was nothing else worth seeing, Mrs. Brown Potter's wonderful hat in Act III would alone repay a visit to His Majesty's.' Maud was furious with both Tree and Waller for their lack of support. Waller said she was 'a goose' for thinking it anything but business. Tree was more explicit.

"Do you really think I would have you in the same production as *him*?" he said calmly. "With your dressing-rooms side by side like some... do you want the whole theatre to look on you as nothing but a common harlot?"

Maud's eyes narrowed, she sucked in her breath but when she let it out again she responded sweetly. "Oh Herbie dear, what *is* a harlot?" But that was not the end of the matter and later he dashed off a furious note delivered by hand by Danes.

I am very sorry for the pain which you feel. I asked you to act in one way and you chose to disregard my desire. I did what I thought was right. There was no insult to you in my mind – you of course see things with different eyes – eyes, not always your ears!

Mrs. Brown Potter, as it transpired, did not last long in the role. She might be beautiful but her diction was distinctly unclear and the press made fun of her American accent. The author of the play himself thought her far too passionate in a role that he said 'required restraint.' The real reason however, as Tree knew only too well, was that Maud had refused to give up her principal dressing room for the Potter woman and indeed had changed the lock and would not give up the key. Maud might no longer be leading lady but she was still Tree's wife and absolutely no one but her would use the room.

"But we're so cramped!" protested Tree. "We are at our wits' end to know what to do for space! The green room has to be turned into a dressing room and the three other ladies are much upset at having to dress in one small room – indeed I think it out of the question!"

"Not my problem," retorted Maud fingering the key in her pocket with glee.

"Nor mine," said Mrs. Brown Potter, tearing up her contract and cramming the contents into the pocket of the most exquisite Worth gown, (of which Maud was completely envious) and Tree tearing out his hair swore in German.

Secretly Maud still smarted when she thought over the whole affair–especially as Tree might still have given her the role after Potter left – after all she knew Miladi's lines back to front. But it appeared neither one of them could let it go. '*For me to have given you the part after Miss Potter went might have seemed a slight,*' Tree wrote to her, '*you make the present situation appear a slight by staying away.*' And then added, '*I am very, very tired and unhappy.*' This last aside which finished with '*and cannot argue more – I repeat, do as you please*' did please Maud, inordinately. She was equally pleased at the thought of occupying her old dressing-room again. She would fill it with flowers every night and buy that darling dressing-table she'd spotted in Grantham with Duchess. She might even install a small sofa so that her friends might sit and chat to her while she changed after a performance, rather than have to perch uncomfortably on the window ledge as they had had to in the past. It would be like old times, she thought happily– well other times at any rate. She unpeeled her gloves and flexed her hands, stiff from clinging to the wheel. She wondered if she would ever get used to driving a motor vehicle. Still the opportunity for travelling clothes motoring afforded was a bonus she supposed. With Mrs. Brown Potter in mind, Maud wore a fetching new passe-partout, edged in chinchilla for warmth and a small violet satin toque also trimmed in fur. It was an outfit however that appeared instantly drab in comparison to that of Waller. As he strode towards her, his shapely legs gleamed in pale cream stockings and his green velvet britches flashed strips of pink satin as he moved. She thought with pleasure of the delicious limerick he had written and left for her in her dressing room. It was of course rumoured that Potter had left the production because having been to see her, the Prince of Wales had offered her an altogether more enticing proposition.

There was a young lady Brown Potter/Who quitted the land that begot her/In all winds and weathers she wore but three feathers/And adopted 'Ich dien' as her motter.

Waller now struck a languid pose against the car's bonnet, causing the K.O.W girls to squeal in delight. Waller, as if he were indeed royalty, turned to wave and throw a wide smile.

"Hello," she said smiling sweetly. "I adored the ditty by the way– " she thought this a good way to start – neutral with a bit of flattery. "A touch risqué don't you think?" she rushed on breathlessly. " I mean everyone knows Bertie-"

"New?" He patted the car's bonnet.

Maud flushed. "Yes but paid for myself! Of course you haven't seen it have you? It's the dernier cri! I hardly drive it in… town." She took a breath, noting his humour. "How is my favourite musketeer?"

"Not long from Eastbourne. Alone."

"Grumpy then," said Maud with a stab at humour.

"Maybe, but you didn't come, after telling me you would."

Maud hovered, resisting putting her hand into his to be helped down yet unable to alight without it. "I wanted to, really I did but Violet telegraphed from Belfield…" her voice trailed.

"And you had to go?"

Maud nodded, hoping to chat him out of his mood. "She had the Primer, Ettie Desborough, you know how I adore her – Sunny Marlborough (less sunny these days it has to be said), and Herman Merivale – he's become such a famous dramatist since *Fedora*." Maud mentioned Sardou's play arranged by Merivale, produced by Tree and starring no other than the great Mrs. Pat Campbell. This great lady had not taken kindly to being covered in zebra-like stripes as Tree sweated off his black face paint all over her white frock and Maud had replaced her with only an evening's notice. She'd even been compared to La Bernhardt for whom Sardou had originally written the play. 'You see darling,' Merviale had said to her after her first night. 'All you have to do is have a pet tiger in your garden or take to sleeping in a coffin and you'll be considered an actress of genius!' Maud felt the warmth of her car's dying engine under her hand. Ah... those really were the days thought Maud, momentarily wistful. At least she and Tree had understood each other... She considered Waller's furious face clouded with jealousy – she had her very own pet tiger right here in front of her and by the tail at that. She made a great effort to keep her voice light.

"Oh and you'll love this!" she continued foolishly, "he says that Mrs. Brown Potter – only he calls her 'that lady'– seems to spend her leisure time in trying to get hold of his plays! He says he's so glad that her 'terrible shadow and her accent' have been removed from His Majesty's!" Maud touched the arm that was sprawled casually over the rim of the car. "Oh, and the du Mauriers – he's rather charming. He liked my present – I sent him Louis Parker's *Disraeli*. The wife's a funny little mouse of a thing –"

"You never like the wives," Waller said bitterly.

Maud looked astonished. "Nonsense! I like yours!"

"The grand lot then." Waller ran a hand through his waved hair, his green eyes glinting, his beautiful voice low, melodious and weighty with repressed anger. "Too grand for me clearly."

"You know that's not true."

"Then why didn't you come?'

There was an uncomfortable silence while Maud wondered if she might get Danes to drive her home as the thought of negotiating the streets behind The Carlton in the tonneau terrified her. Waller was warming to his theme. She heard the words 'callous' and 'indifferent' and something about 'not standing for another year of this.'

"I think you're behaving *hatefully* and utterly abusing your power over me. Quite frankly, you make me miserable."

"I –"

"You *shall* value my love a little more! Maud?"

He was shouting. She was going to have to say something, if nothing else but to calm him.

"Of course I value your love," she said truthfully although she did take it for granted. She saw that now. "I don't know. It feels all wrong – at least not right."

"Not *right*! Good God woman, I'll tell you what's not right! Mrs. Pinney was seen driving with your husband again last week – and before you ask she's unmistakable because of her height. Even sitting down she appears huge! Did you know that?"

Maud blanched but when she spoke her tone was caustic. "What, that sitting down she is huge? Yes she's huge full stop. I knew that."

"No you ninney, that's not what I meant. And later they were seen at the theatre! He was very attentive I'm told. They were at the opening night of *Girasol*."

"Is that so?" She straightened. "Look, hand me down will you," she said but he made no move to help her. "I've been thinking it for a while," she added to pique him. "That it's wrong between us. I don't care about May or Herbert."

"I mean to marry you, Maud."

Maud's eyes widened. "But you just said I was abusing my power!"

"Well you are," he said calmer then grinned unexpectedly. It doesn't mean I don't love you dreadfully."

"Sh! Someone will hear you!" She put a finger to his lips.

"I sincerely hope they do!"

"You seem to forget we *are* married."

"Very funny." He had high colour in his face now and his eyes glinted fiercely. He suddenly stepped up onto the mud-guard and reaching up into the tonneau, pulled her forwards so that she fell into his arms. He swung her easily over the side. She gasped, clutching her new hat. The one she absolutely did not want falling into mud.

"You know it can never be!"

"It will be!" he said fiercely. "You know that there is only room for one love in my life. Only one." His eyes were dark with lust. "You know that I ache for you, and I for my part don't believe you don't want me."

Maud felt her heart pound in spite of herself. She could smell the linen of his shirt and the sight of a pulse at his throat made her stomach constrict. His fingers dug into her sides. He wanted her – he always had and she was used to his adoration if she could call it that, but did she love him? Desire yes. Sometimes yes. At Belfield in the beautiful white room with its pale pink velvet cushions with the light from the vale flooding the bed, unquestionably yes. A little niggling devilish voice however skewered itself in her head. But is it Belfield you love or Waller? It asked. And here in broad daylight? Outside His Majesty's? Did she?

His lips were close to hers – too close. She couldn't breathe.

"It's a dream," said Maud, fiercely turning her face away. "Nothing can happen, you know that."

"Why can't it? Your husband manages it successfully enough and his career hasn't suffered. Quite the opposite I imagine."

"Don't be ridiculous," said Maud. "He doesn't manage anything – don't think for a moment that without Danes and me… well let's put it this way – we work very hard to make sure there isn't any scandal. I've had to beg newspaper men not to run stories – I've had to give away boxes to perfectly detestable people in return for… I've had my own fair share of threatening letters. But we've dealt with them. And as for divorce! Well it would simply mean not only our ruin but Florence's and

Herbert's – the end of our careers, the end of our children's and anyone connected with us."

"Oh don't play the ingénue now my dear Maud. You knew the risks. We've acted in enough plays together to show you what happens!"

"Precisely!" exclaimed Maud passionately, thinking of *A Woman's Reason* in which she had indeed played the adulterous wife to Waller's lover, while more astonishingly his real life wife Florence, had played his onstage one! And in the end she (or the Hon. Nina Keith) was ostracized from society. She didn't end up quite as tragically as the heroine of the popular novel *East Lynne*, disfigured and abandoned, but almost.

"The woman always loses and the man wins out. Even a playwright like Barrie knows – the world forgives *him*."

For a moment Waller looked at her, almost regretfully and Maud for her part was disappointed when he dropped her arms suddenly so that she could still feel the imprint of his fingers.

"Things *are* changing," he said firmly. "There *are* women who want the vote, women who want all kinds of change. And whether you want to accept it or not, divorce *is* happening."

"But not for people like us,' Maud's voice was neither bitter nor sad, merely realistic. She knew with certainty she would never again be 'owned' by any man. "Besides, aren't you happy as we are?"

Waller punched his fist into his other hand. "Given that you didn't appear this weekend, I'm going to ignore you just said that."

"I see," she said leaning against her beast of a car, still warm against her back, the car that was all hers.

"No, I don't think you do."

"I see enough to understand that if we divorced our careers would suffer. Do you really think there would be no fall-out? What if we never worked again? Do you really want that? Am I worth that?"

Waller threw back his head so that his strong taut neck was level with her lips.

"You are, yes." His voice was gentle and he dropped her wrists. For a moment she fancied there were tears in his eyes. "But I don't for a moment believe the reverse is true."

*   *   *

With its replica of a shepherd's cottage, babbling brook and donkey – Danes had drawn the line at working with any more rabbits – Tree's *The Winter's Tale* was yet another indictment of dramatic realism. Maud, centre stage was as silent and still as the 'statue' itself. Viola as Perdita, knelt at the feet of her real life godmother, Ellen Terry, majestically draped in a roman style toga and paid homage to the great actress. Maud was moved to tears by the sight of her daughter's beauty as it acknowledged the professionalism of the older woman. The press was in equal raptures:

Miss Viola Tree need not fear that we shall accuse her of superstition when she kneels and implores Hermione's blessing, for we see Ellen Terry not only as a great actress and a great personality but as a great religion.

Bernard Shaw was not so sure, preferring Maud's 'perfect diction' to Terry's. He went further, stating that her acting 'passes on to the next length of arid sham-feminine twaddle in blank verse, which she pumps out in little rhythmic strokes in a desperate and all too obvious effort to make music of it.' Maud was secretly thrilled of course as was the press generally. Maud's performance was considered 'spirited' and 'noteworthy.' It was particularly praised for its ability to shift from strident tones to the gentle cooing of a dove. And 'shifts' there certainly were – Tree had cut the whole of Act V, Scene 2 (which amounted to a third of the play) reducing the whole to three acts. There were lines that Maud had never noticed before but which she applauded now. When Antigonus said "Hang all the husbands..." Maud sniggered inwardly. But it was the erasure of the word

165

'bastard' in the second scene where Paulina (Maud) forces Leontes to 'look on his child,' that ought to have made Maud suspicious. Looking back she would kick herself for being such a fool or not wondering that Tree was so unusually forceful in his insistence that the word 'brat' be inserted in its place.

Maud, passing Danes in the wings a few moments later, was comforted by the sight of the young man, his apron pockets bulging as usual with pies, as he rushed to wait for his master. His devotion to Tree (and to pies) at least did not change. What was surprising was that he appeared to have a young lady in tow. Maud wondered only vaguely if she were indeed *his* young lady. She was pretty enough but there was something unsettling about her. From under the brim of an absurdly frilly pink hat, she regarded Maud with blatant curiosity. Her blank stare, more than her fussy clothes made her appear like an oversize doll. Maud realized then that she knew very little about Danes's personal life. Did he even have one?

"Has she lost her mama?" Maud asked sweetly, enjoying seeing the girl scowl in reply.

"Yes, no," said Danes.

"Yes, no?" Maud shot him an amused look. So she *was* his girl. She looked rather young but then you never could tell these days. Maddeningly, neither one seemed inclined to move so that Maud found she had almost to push the girl out of her way to get onto the stage. The audience was going mad for Ellen Terry and for Viola, Maud noted with an unexpected twinge of envy. In their rapturous applause she had a sudden vision of the future and her place being superseded by her daughter.

"He's not here," whispered Maud as she strode once more on to the stage.

Dane shifted his weight and pulled out a toffee, considering it before popping it in his mouth.

"It's not-"

Maud shot him a look. "It's not what?"

She hurried on to the stage to curtsey but Danes and the girl were still waiting.

"Is there something you wanted?" she hissed, this time more impatiently, turning to the thunderous applause and to meet Viola half way along the stage to take her bow with Ellen Terry. The audience couldn't get enough of the great actress making much of the fact that it was fifty years since she had first appeared in this very play.

"Does she want my autograph?" Maud nodded in the girl's direction. There was something about the child Maud instinctively distrusted.

"No I certainly do not!" the girl said loudly turning on her heel.

"Ooo!" exclaimed Maud, riled in spite of herself. "We do have a manner!"

Danes looked at the huffing retreating flounces in panic and thrust an envelope into Maud's hand.

"This came earlier. Sorry! Got to go!" He rushed off after the girl. Maud watched them go in amusement before turning back to the audience.

"Darling," she said to Viola as they met and stood holding hands.

"Mother," replied her daughter calmly.

They sank to the floor in deep curtsies. When Maud looked to the wings, Danes was back.

"I said I'd wait for an answer," he mouthed.

Maud looked at him blankly, rose and letting go of her daughter's hand retreated behind the curtain. "You mean for the letter?" she said, gesturing to the as yet unopened envelope that she'd tucked into her skirt pocket.

"Oh very well!" she said fishing it out and tearing it open in front of him. She kept her head bent, her vision clouding.

"Everything all right?" Danes said concerned, nervous lest the girl return before he'd fulfilled his task.

"Perfectly," she replied tightly, drowning, gasping for breath. "No answer."

* * *

Maud steered her car up Putney Hill – at least steering was the easy part. Her hands gripped the wheel as if clinging to the reins of a frisky stallion and she knew she would not breathe properly until she had reached her destination. It was only sheer determination that had prompted her to take out the car unaccompanied. She had also dispensed with her driving hat, requiring all her senses about her and did not want to be hampered or distracted by a flowing veil. Maud cursed as the beast spluttered steam in short desperate spurts then stopped altogether. Somewhat relieved, Maud alighted realizing she could walk the rest of the way. She tucked a prettily wrapped gift under her arm and set off in the direction of the house, 'Daisyfield' which she knew to be only a little further round a corner and on the brow of the hill. Hot and perspiring, her formerly smooth hair frizzing by the second, Maud paused, afraid of what lay ahead, wondering what on earth had prompted her to make the trip in the first place. As she rounded the last incline, Maud could hardly keep her mouth from dropping open in astonishment. Prosperous, Victorian houses set amidst large well-tended gardens dotted this part of London but Daisyfield could not have been more different. Indeed she couldn't imagine why anyone of sound mind would want to live there. It was a vast, sprawling one-floored curiosity in the shape of an ecclesiastical crucifix. Seemingly without chimneys (she would soon discover it had no inner doors either) she could only imagine the cold in winter.

She took a deep breath before pushing open the gate. The garden at least appeared conventional enough with its neatly planted hedges and clambering wisteria. Maud rang the enormous Swiss bell that hung from the porch and waited uncomfortably. She regretted the present too. What was she trying to achieve? Why was she torturing herself in this way? What on earth was she doing here? At last, just as she was resolved to leave, a young boy answered the door. He was immaculately dressed in britches, a white blouse and floppy bow, for all the world like the child actor who almost stole the show in *A Woman's Reason.* In fact *The Sketch* had devoted rather too much copy to the chap, saying 'it is not very often that the interviewer can take the interviewed on his knee...' This boy was as mercurial – all life and motion and easy talk.

"I've come to see Mrs. P– your mother?" said Maud, her voice croaking.

The boy looked at her with those blue, clear eyes Maud never thought to see in another living person.

"Why?"

"Why?" Maud echoed, wondering why indeed and how she'd do anything not to have rung the bell and not to be standing on the doorstep as she was now.

"It's all right Robin," came the voice from within. "Bid her come in."

If the 'house' from the outside was bizarre, the inside was even more so. In the absence of any doors, arches separated one room from the other and strategically hung curtains ensured a kind of privacy. Maud shivered, although she wasn't sure whether out of genuine cold or a sense of foreboding. Without windows the series of long rooms that formed the vertical length of the 'cross' felt sinister. Out of the shadows the woman spoke before Maud had a chance to see her properly.

"Oh it's you."

Maud was silent, her eyes becoming accustomed to the dark and to a scene she had witnessed once before. The woman's bulky shape was huddled on a low nursing stool, a baby sucking at a fat exposed breast. In profile she seemed pretty enough but when she turned to the trickle of light, Maud could see that her face was even more disfigured than when they'd met in Paris. Her left eye drooped, giving her a comic air. Only her hair retained its burnished sheen. May Pinney pulled her nipple unceremoniously out of the baby's mouth and covered herself. She leaned back against the wall and Maud could see that it wasn't a post partum belly that made May's protrude so, but the fact that she was clearly with child again. Maud's heart constricted and she wished vanity hadn't got the better of her and she'd not had her stays tightened so dramatically. She felt dizzy.

"Yes, another on the way." May patted her belly. "Six months gone I am."

Maud felt blindly for any piece of furniture for support. Tree was fifty years old and their daughter Viola, twenty-two. For how much longer did he intend producing children?

"That'll make four in total!"

Maud cleared her throat. "And all boys?"

May cackled. "So far."

"Would you like a ... daughter?" What was she saying? Had she gone mad? Did she even care?

May's eyes narrowed. "Yes."

Maud remembered her present. "I've brought you this. For the baby."

May hesitated. "Here Robbie – bring the lady a chair." She took the gift, placing it carefully on the floor beside her. "Thank you. And tea? Would you like something?"

Maud shook her head. A bottle of wine? Maybe. Veronal certainly.

"We should talk," said Maud when the boy Robin had dragged Maud a chair and then gathered up his new sibling and taken her to another part of the house.
May held up a hand. "Not about 'erbie. You might as well accept nothing is going to change. He comes back to me – he will always comes back to me. The sooner you understand that the easier it'll be for you. You are his wife. I understand that too."

Maud had to steady her breathing. It was as though their roles were reversed. May was behaving like the wife, poised and in control while she was the young, taken-advantage-of fool.

"I came here to ask you to give him up." Maud's voice was so low she almost didn't hear it herself.

May frowned. "That's not going to happen. Besides, do you really think I want ... this?" she looked down at her swollen belly. "Or this?" she waved a hand in front of her face. "Time is not on my side, Mrs. Tree, I am aware of that. To be honest I never expected to live this long."

Neither had she! Maud felt an unwelcome twinge of sympathy. She could hear a faint baby's cry from another room. For a moment both women froze, accustomed to responding to their children's needs. May relaxed.

"And the prognosis...?"

May shrugged. "No one seems to know. Least of all the doctors."

Indeed a broken Reed at the foot of a mighty Tree. Maud heard her thumping heart fill the silence between them.

"Now that you're here, you are right after all. We may as well talk. I've been thinking of writing to you for a while."

May stretched out two swollen feet. Really Maud couldn't for the life of her see what the attraction was for Herbert. What charm the woman might have once had, it seemed to Maud, resided purely in her still abundant head of hair.

"You have?"

"I-we-" she corrected herself, "have another problem. One that affects you too."

Maud's thumping she was sure was now deafening. "Oh?" she said coolly.

"I'm being stalked."

Maud almost choked. "Stalked?" she croaked. Oh! That bloody Littlechild, thought Maud – I'll have his guts for garters! He assured her that he would never openly follow the woman, that a clerk in the Register Office would copy details that the Pinney woman would never know... She clenched a fist.

"I can explain!" Maud jumped to her feet, pacing the room.

"You can?"

"I was jealous, angry –" she shook her head. "I don't know – frustrated that he couldn't love me in the way I needed – and yes, as much as I hate to admit it, that he had found greater happiness with another. With you."

May smiled, the drooping eye almost meeting a corner of her mouth.

"That's very nice of you," she said smoothly. "But sit down. It's not you."

"It's not?" She sounded like a dolt.

"No. There's a young girl called Olivia Truman-"

"How young?"

"Young. By which I mean fifteen years old, but she was twelve when this started."

Maud was beginning to feel an uncanny sense of déjà vu. "You're not serious?"

May pursed her lips. "I wish I wasn't."

"Fifteen?" Maud's brow creased as she called to mind the image of a young girl in a silly pink hat. "But harmless, surely? A schoolgirl crush? We've all had those! " It was on the tip of her tongue to mention the ridiculous K.O.W. badges but she thought better of it. There was no need to confuse things. Something niggled at the back of Maud's mind but she couldn't pinpoint it.

May picked up Maud's present unwrapping it carefully. Folds of the softest cashmere spilled onto her lap and for a moment May held it to her one smooth cheek, closing her eyes. Under different circumstances, Maud thought in alarm, they might have been friends.

"It's beautiful, thank you."

"Swann and Edgar."

"I see, thank you again." May left the blanket on her lap, feeling it with her fingers. "Olivia is different. Purposeful. She has them both wrapped round…" She let the material fall through her hands.

"What do you mean both?"

"Max and Herbert," May replied quietly. "She writes incessantly to them both. Max while charmed, at least is no fool. He sees that she only writes to him to be close to Herbert but I can see she truly believes herself in love. And that her feelings are reciprocated."

"Good heavens! Are… they?"

May folded the shawl carefully.

"I don't know," she said quietly. "What I do know, is that she means us harm Mrs. Tree, that I do believe sincerely."

Maud's hands felt clammy and her heart began to beat irregularly.

"What makes you think so?"

May was very still. "I've seen some of her letters. And some from him to her."

"I see."

"She visits him at Her Majesty's."

"The *Dome*?"

May nodded. "And you remember the photo that appeared of Herbert and Max recently? The one submitted anonymously?"

It was Maud's turn to nod.

"Well that was Olivia's doing."

May reached behind her and it was then that Maud noticed a small table set out with a decanter of port and glasses. She poured one now and handed it to Maud, which Maud not only took but downed in one, holding it out for another.

"Steady goes, Mrs. Tree," said May not unkindly.

"What do you know about her?" said Maud in her grandest Mrs. Allenby voice. "I mean where do her people hale from?"

May shook her head. "As far as I can make out she lives in the New Forest with her widowed mother. *Her* mother, I believe had a barouche and an account at Marshall and Snelgroves. Quiet respectability. You know how it is."

"I can imagine it."

"There's more. She means to marry him." Maud choked on her drink. May nodded sympathetically. "She despises me for producing –" she waved a glass in front of her stomach, "but I am relatively safe, I'm not married. She sees me as a breeding cow. Besides which it's no secret that I won't be around for much longer, but you – you are his wife and thus in real danger. " She too downed her drink. "Do you remember that man who threatened Claudette Collier?" She referred to an incident in which one of the extras had been discovered with a carving knife down his pants, just waiting to leap on Tree's co-star. Maud nodded.

"Well I believe this woman is just as dangerous."

"Have you spoken to 'erb– Herbert– or Max"

"Of course."

"And?"

May filled their glasses. "Max is a vain creature. He loves to be amused and for some reason he finds this whole thing extremely amusing. I suspect Olivia spins him an entirely different story when she writes to him. Of course I've asked him to stop, but I simply don't have the authority… well the authority of a wife."

"I don't know what you want me to do," said Maud, beginning to feel like a very minor character in a very bad novel. "I may be Herbert's wife in name but you rule his heart!"

May sighed. "That might have been true once but I don't have to tell you what Herbert is like with regards to women."

"No, but she's a child!" said Maud fiercely.

"She's a woman now! Any flattery is better than none. It's what he lives for. Anything I say would only be counterproductive. I won't give up but I only thought it fair to warn you. I think the girl is ill." She put a hand to her head. "You know…"

Maud undid her jabot and fanned her face, suddenly hot from too much port drunk too quickly.

"Did you actually see them at the Dome?"

May paused. "I did." She looked away. "The girl was barefoot, wearing the most absurd hat. I must have interrupted something because he was flustered. 'I am doing anything!' he said."

"God, his grammar is appalling," said Maud bitterly.

"I couldn't agree more. Anyway, he could see I was shocked. The little minx smiled sweetly but 'erbie turned and said, 'You see I've found my Trilby.'"

Maud's stomach and heart jolted at the thought of the aging Svengali who bewitches an innocent young girl..

"He said that?"

May shrugged.

"The bastard." Impulsively Maud touched May's arm. "I'm sorry."

"Don't be. I think it myself."

"You must have been very hurt."

May looked at Maud levelly. "I was."

"And you really think this is so? It is as you say?"

May turned so that Maud had a full view of her ravaged face, puckered, scarred and swollen. Only one eye was still clear – it wouldn't be long before she was completely blind.

"We've both been blackmailed before – or at least there's been an attempt to do so."

Maud nodded thoughtfully. "Yes," she said. "Once when I was pregnant and Tree was in New York. I received letters alluding to an affair." Maud coloured, realizing now that May was the party in question.

"And he comforted you, assuring you there was nothing in it, that there were people out there who were just jealous?"

Maud nodded but her heart sank. Why had she ever believed herself to be so unique?

May nodded. "I know how it is. This is different. *She* is different. She can do a lot of damage and she's very young. She doesn't realize her power and what she could do to all of us. And I saw what 'erbert wrote in reply – " she clasped her hands together. "It must have been in response to a question of Olivia's – maybe even a journalist's – I know there are rumours circulating. There always are. But Herbert denied my existence. In his letter to that... that *girl*, he denied my children's existence and this house."

"How could anyone do that?" Maud murmured, thinking rather more of the extraordinary building.

May shrugged. A baby's cries drew closer and Robin returned with a red- faced screaming child.

"I think he's hungry Mama," said the boy.

"And your elder son?"

"Claude? He wants to be an actor."

"And Viola?"

Maud smiled when she really didn't know whether to weep or laugh hysterically.

"An actress. She is one already. By the way, whatever happened to the man in the Collier incident?"

"Dan Leno?"

"Was that his name?"

May nodded. "He was taken away."

"Ah yes…"

"Well I'm glad to have seen you Mrs. Tree." May held out her hand and for a moment in taking hers, Maud clasped it warmly. The woman still towered over her.

"And I you," she said.

"Ironic, isn't it?"

Maud raised an eyebrow.

"I came to see you once and now you've come to see me. I hated you once as surely you must hate me."

"I don't hate you," Maud said quietly. "Not sure about that Olivia creature though!"

May smiled. "Go carefully," she said.

"And you Mrs. Pinney, and you."

Fourteen

I do begin to have bloody thoughts

The Tempest

London September 1906

Danes had intended to have a quiet day, or at least as quiet a day as it was possible at His Majesty's. The play was in its eighth week and so far there had been no major domestic calamities. Maud's temporary exile in France seemed to have improved relations between the Trees and even Putney Hill had gone ominously quiet – no demands for out-of-season strawberries or fresh herrings from Bergen. Tom wasn't inordinately hungry, always his inward barometer that outside all was well, the donkey kept at the Hyde Park Stables had kept its teeth and the 'babbling brook' had not become a flood. Given the drama with *Nero* when the all-too realistic burning of Rome had set off the fire hoses and members of the audience fleeing in fear for their lives, this was no mean feat. Danes cleared a space on his desk, not for the contracts he'd brought with him from Sir George Lewis no less (Tree wasn't taking any chances) to be signed up by the actors engaged for Tree's next production but for the delectable ham and suet pudding he'd purchased from Fortnum's on his way here. In fact it looked so delectable he wasn't sure he'd be able to wait much longer. He glanced at it from time to time, his mouth virtually salivating as he imagined the first exquisite mouthful.

He glanced around the room assessing how much work there was to be done before lunch, and whether he could risk a tiny mouthful of pud first. Set designs for Tree's revival of *Antony and Cleopatra* were propped against chairs awaiting Mrs. Tree's approval and there was the usual social correspondence to wade through. He usually left the drafting of press releases and advertising business to Tree's theatrical agent Elisabeth Marbury, but he was capable of copying a text exactly. Tom was used to scouting for trouble, but as he could tell there was only one potential blip on the horizon. The Kaiser had invited his master, Viola and half the company to perform for him in Berlin. He had not invited Mrs. Tree and Tom had no desire to be in the office when she saw that invitation. Tom reluctantly settled in his chair away from the desk cluttered with newspaper clippings – Mrs. Tree still insisted on purchasing three or four dailies she later spent hours perusing. Eventually, but it really was only eventually, she cut out theatre reviews, pasting them into oversize, cloth scrapbooks which were left, he couldn't help thinking, for his master or himself to trip over. The rest of the room was no less chaotic. Programmes, account ledgers, prompt books and scripts were piled on the floor together with material swatches for costumes. Even the walls were plastered with black and white publicity photographs of the Trees. The one Tom liked best was of Maud in the plays *Madame de Pompadour* and *A Woman of No Importance*. There were a further two separate, somewhat surprising caricatures of Waller and Maud. The caption under Maud, who was dressed as a bride read, 'A gown typical of sunshine and happiness and right well does Mrs. Tree look in it.' Waller's read, 'First he proposes the renewal of their old relations.' Tom liked these less. The rest of the pictures were majestic, vivid portraits of Herbert as Svengali, Caliban and Richard II. Some were even by famous artists such as Charles Buchel who like Tree was German-born, and Sir Lawrence Alma Tadema. But the svelte lithe figure portrayed, Tom thought, was somewhat lacking in the original. Still, he found these rather comforting, especially at night when he was often the only person left in the theatre. He never thought he'd think it but alone was what he sincerely wished to be a few moments later.

"Hello Tom," said a voice Tom was beginning to dread, and today the apparition in white muslin was even less welcome than usual. Tom was well used to shooing the K.O.W. girls from the stage door but in comparison with Olivia Truman, they were no trouble, no trouble at all. Apart from the endless questions of, 'What is he really really like?' and 'Does he ever throw his shirts away?' They generally made little disturbance. They screamed and ooh and ahhed whenever Waller emerged from his dressing room, but often the sight of Mrs. Tree put an end to all that anyway. This girl was something else. Trouble was what. She wanted something but he wasn't sure what.

To begin with, Tom had assumed this Miss Truman was merely one of the K.O.W. groupies gathering for Waller's Muskateer performance. Her appearance at the first night of Tree's *Oliver Twist,* however, left Tom more than a little uneasy. For the life of him he couldn't remember who'd let her into the box – the royal box at that. After all it wasn't every night (or so the company kept telling him) you had the likes of Lilly Langtry, the Bancrofts, and Duchess's daughters all gathered together but there she was, a small pinched girl with the blackest hair he'd ever seen, hanging on the arm of Max Beerbohm himself and behaving for all the world as if she were family. At first Tom thought she was. They made an odd couple – the famous satirist and equally diminutive figure, with his own lacquered hair and pallor replicated in his tiny companion. After the fall of the curtain after the final act, there'd been such a stampede. Tom couldn't get to his master at all. He'd booked the Carlton as usual but not until 12.45 – and the actors were still packed onto the stage in their costumes, taking their bows and chatting through it all as if it were still a live performance. When he'd spied Mrs. Tree flushed and haughty, he had relaxed. She at least would make sure that Tree got to the restaurant on time.

"Here boy, would ya fix this?" Tom had looked up to see Mrs. Brown Potter flicking a fringed Indian stole in his face. "There's a tear see? And I need it double quick if you can. I'll be back to fetch it." Only she said 'fitch'. He objected to being called 'boy.'

At the sight of her rival, Mrs. Tree swooped down like a heron on a goldfish and in Tom's opinion looking not far off one herself. Both she and Duchess were similarly dressed in shiny, scaly gowns with so much material in all the wrong places and such low décolletage that Tom, as used as he was to seeing actresses in various stages of undress, was shocked. He had to avert his eyes as Maud's bosom threatened to spill over the elaborate corsage of once fresh (and now drooping) roses centered in the middle of her bon point. Duchess's violets were rather more successful, being smaller, more expensive and pinned to her waist as was her custom and not to a slipping neckline.

"And *who* is that infant?" said Maud in a loud stage whisper. "I don't know if you saw her Tom, but she was jumping on her *seat*! I'm sure Tree was distracted – who wouldn't have been by that commotion?"

"Oh darling," drawled Duchess, "never mind the child, I've spotted Lady Colin Campbell and Madge Kendal!"

"I see," said Maud dryly.

"And John Merrick. I know I shouldn't but really what a creature! Why bring him here tonight? Why bring him at all? You know they're calling him the Elephant Man! Ladies have fainted at the sight of him."

"Yes, I read that somewhere."

"And your husband!"

"What, also an elephant man?"

"No, clearly, ha, ha. Just look at Tree! What a glamorous trio – the actor manager between those two stars!"

Maud coughed so that her breasts wobbled and Tom felt his stomach constrict. He was never one for shape desserts.

"More like two ancient lights!"

Duchess threw back her head and guffawed. "Wicked, darling, wicked! No, don't go chasing the Potter woman!" A jewelled hand shot out to apprehend her friend. "'Laud the heat! I've never known a July like it, darling why don't you leave all this and come to Belfield? We miss you there."

Tom was grateful to Duchess. Another scene between the Potter woman and Mrs. Tree would have absolutely ensured he didn't eat the delicious suet pudding he'd been keeping for the party afterwards or more specifically for when the cast went to their party and he was left alone in the theatre to eat his midnight feast in peace. And there was that damn girl again at his elbow, cool in the terrible heat despite the number of silly ruffles on her dress.

"So which one is she?" said the girl breathlessly. Her cheeks were as pink as the elaborate bows sticking out like rabbit's ears on either side of her head. Despite the get up-she was pretty enough, but Tom found the single-minded pursuit of his master extremely off-putting. "She's got to be really *really* ugly."

Tom wanted to ask why but decided to ignore her. He pushed past her and went back stage pulling up a tall stool close to the piano. Planting his workbox on the closed hood he attempted to thread a needle, Mrs. Brown Potter's beautiful shawl draped over his knees.

"Go on Tom, tell me which one she is!" The girl had followed him and now jerked his arm to get his attention so that he dropped the thread.

"What? Who?" he said in exasperation, cutting another with his teeth.

"Why, Mrs. Tree of course! Which one is she? It's just that those two women look so alike."

Tom paused, the needle hovering over the silk velvet.

"You's joking ain't cha? Everyone knows Mrs. Tree!" But it amused him to know something she did not.

The girl's black eyes flashed. "I'm not everyone."

Tom sniffed. "Nah… you's just out of the schoolroom."

"I'm older than I look." Her eyes darted round the room following Tree and now that Tom observed her closely, they seemed to soften and grow misty. "You'll see, one day I'll surprise you – I won't always be this young."

"No you won't, I'll give ya that."

She pushed out a hip. "You think you know everything about him."

Tom knotted his thread.

"If you mean Mr. Tree-" But she wasn't listening. She twirled and flounced and just when he thought she had finally gone she was back, her eyes scanning the cloth on his lap as if committing every detail of its design to memory.

"I write to him, you know."

Tom stared blankly. She made no sense to him at all. He couldn't care less what she did in her time. All he wanted to do was finish his mending and think about his dinner.

"Why would'ya do that?"

She fiddled with a heavy gold bracelet and picked up the fringed end of the shawl. She was making him nervous. He was very afraid that one of the charms would catch on the silk. Why wasn't she wearing a modest strand of coral beads like other young girls her age?

"And he writes to me. He's told me to learn the lines to a song – very young and simple, he said."

Like you, he thought. Tom stuck his needle into the fabric.

"You've got me there."

"So which one is she?"

Tom scratched his head; he didn't trust the look in her eye. He would play for time.

"Look," she said and her eyes lost their softness, becoming hard and small. "Is... is that her?" She looked wildly round the room, her eyes alighting on the beautiful American actress Maxine Elliot.

But Tom wasn't having any of it. He was used to exacting leading ladies but not to hoity toity schoolgirls giving themselves airs and graces when they was not long out of nappies. He finished the mending and broke the thread with his teeth.

"Well?" she demanded. Tom folded the shawl with exaggerated care. His mind raced with excuses as to how to avoid her, even after the girl had pinched his arm and he had grunted in pain. He pushed himself off the stool just as Herbert's brother sidled up to them.

"Why helloo..." he said looking, thought Tom more and more like one of his own caricatures. In profile, his retroussé nose was really very pretty – too pretty thought Tom, and his lashes looked

184

artificially blackened. Tom glanced at a waistline that surely could only be achieved by a corset and stays. He looked away embarrassed. Was that carmine on his lips?

"I'm so glad you didn't drown the stalls with your tears, child," he said clearly delighted to have come across her.

The girl shrugged. "Then you obviously didn't know buckets could be obtained from the attendants."

Thrilled, Max clapped his hands. "Oh very good! Very good! So no buns and milk for the baby after all! What do you think eh, Tom?"

The girl flushed a most unbecoming colour, tossing back her hair – not that it moved much – hers like Max's appeared stuck together.

"No, baby is about right," he thought but merely shrugged.

The girl stamped her foot and then grimaced in pain. Max uttered a loud guffaw.

"I feel I have stumbled on a tremendous soul-stirring tragedy. I search the world's history in vain for any analogue to you."

"I don't know what you mean," she said haughtily.

"Oh I think you do." His eyes narrowed and then changing tack, sighed dramatically. "But no matter. I know you're only nice to me to get close to my brother," he whispered.

"Am I?" The girl tilted her head up. "Am I being nice?"

"Well I do think you could be nicer. Much."

"Would it have an effect?"

Max inhaled his tobacco.

"That would depend."

Tom cleared his throat. It was one thing to listen to his master make a fool of himself, but this particular scene felt more wrong than usual. The girl seemed to collect herself.

"Has he left?" her voice was panicked. "You've distracted me deliberately haven't you? I know you have? Have I missed him?"

Max laughed. "Dear oh dear," he said lightly but the girl turned on her heel in fury. "Yes you probably have! Try his dressing room!"

Tom scowled but Max only chuckled, and lifting the piano lid began idly playing with the keys.

"Pretty stuff," he said, gesturing to Mrs. Brown Potter's scarf.

"Worth."

"It wouldn't be anything else." He stubbed out his cheroot. He considered Tom as if on the point of saying something but changed his mind.

"Well tulaloo."

"Tu – goodnight, Sir."

But Max was slow to go. "Enchanting, don't you think?" he said, removing bits of cheroot from his lips. "Enchanting."

Not at all what I'd call it, thought Tom but then who was he to say?

Now a year later Tom felt a sense of foreboding as he raised his eyes to the smiling, smug face he was beginning to loathe.

"Oh Tommy, Tom," she said in her most childlike sing- song voice.

"What do you want?"

"Oh …nothing…" She twirled a parasol with the tips of kid-gloved fingers the colour of soft butter.

Tom began sorting out lighting scripts for the afternoon's performance. The girl had not moved but was watching him in a way that made him uncomfortable.

"Look, he's not here and I'm busy."

"Oh I know that," she replied smoothly. "He's with Putney, cooing and fussing no doubt with the imminent…"

"Imminent?"

"Soon, it means soon, Tom."

He bent his flushed face over the desk so that she couldn't see the fury in his eyes.

"Anyway I'm not worried. He's coming down to visit, to my mama's place at Lymington."

"Now why would he do that, Miss?"

His indignation made him look at her levelly, staring her down till she was the first to look away. When she regained her composure she tilted her head, taunting him. She ran a tongue over her lips. Tom watched in disgust. He'd seen this particular little play too many times. And all for what? A different dressing room? A chance to see his master alone? A reading?

"He's a very attractive man."

"I wouldn't know about that. I would say though that you're a bit young for that sort of thing ain't cha? And definitely with him. He's old enough to be your granddad!"

There was a silence.

"*Great* granddad even."

Olivia had been twirling her parasol and now she snapped it shut. Tom's heart began to beat frantically with the thrill of embarrassing her. It was short-lived.

"Don't be so sure, Tommy Tom," she said coldly. "He's a man, a sensual man and I am pretty – most importantly, I am fresh and young."

Tom stood his full height.

"Young yes. Not too sure about the rest." He began to shut the door but she laid a hand on his arm. For a moment they stared at each other. "You need to go now," he said. She wedged her foot in the door. "Now," said Tom.

"Oh Tommy Tom," she said ever so sweetly. "There *is* something. I *do* want something. I need your help." She batted heavily kohled eyes and once more Tom was repulsed. She dropped his arm. "I want you to tell me about... cars."

"Cars?" Tom could not have been more surprised had she slapped him. Or kissed him for that matter. Anything seemed possible. "Cars?" he repeated dully.

She smiled in a way that she must have thought would please him – her thin lips stretched over small fox-like teeth. He had to clench a fist to refrain from taking her white frilly frou frou parasol and snapping it on top of her ludicrous curls.

"Ah, there you are Tommy!" Smooth as silk, Waller appeared as if from nowhere, his head floating above the girl's so Tom was forced to open the door or appear rude. He flashed his white teeth smile and his voice seemed to drop an octave.

"Is she for you then? *Do*... introduce me!"

"Why I-" began the girl smiling and rocking on her soft-soled boots.

"She's just going-" said Tom.

"No I'm not," she pouted. "I want to know about cars... and no one will tell me."

"Is that so?" Waller's voice was like honey and sunshine and cream, Tom would give him that.

The girl made a moue with her mouth and shook her head til her curls danced.

"So."

"And why is that pet?" said Waller softly, pursing his own lips and sucking in his cheeks in a way Tom had seen him do in front of mirrors.

"Everyone's always so busy!"

Waller laughed. "It is a theatre, you do realize? And not any theatre – it's His Majesty's!"

The girl smiled winsomely. "Oh I know that!" she giggled and bowed her head bashfully. "I know exactly who manages this theatre! I've been writing…"

"Writing? Did you hear that Tom? My, what a clever girl!"

Tom gritted his teeth and nodded quickly. Waller ran a hand through immaculate locks, sucking in his diaphragm at the same time so that Tom thought it a wonder he could speak at all, and then beamed the girl the full impact of his dazzling eyes.

"I feel something… overpowering," the girl said.

Waller nodded, knowing. "As in a keen and strong feeling?"

She nodded, twirling her parasol and rocking on her feet till her hair and ribbons and flounces were all moving at once, and Tom wanted to slap her down or at least stop her turning as he would have done a spinning top.

"Then you can't be a child!" He waited for the impact of his words to fall, measuring them just as carefully as though he were reciting Shakespeare. The girl lapped them up. Tom could see her lips quiver with emotion. "No child has a crush," continued Waller, drawing out each syllable. "You must be a woman with a woman's heart!"

"Oh I am, I am!"

Tom frowned. This had gone on long enough.

"Then tell me..." It was Waller this time who was virtually licking his lips.

"Yes?"

"This feeling..."

"Yes?"

"Who's the lucky man? I mean, dare I hope that you too wear a K.O.W. badge?"

The girl shook her head vigorously.

"No," she said smiling, "'fraid not..."

Waller clutched at his heart, jerked a leg, stumbled and then fell dramatically.

"No!" he gasped, "Please don't tell me! I couldn't bear to hear that your love... was for ..."

The girl was giggling hysterically now and had thrown down her parasol to lean over him. With a sigh, Tom too went over to him.

"Oh do get up Sir," he said. "Mrs. Tree will be in any moment and she'll be very upset to see you on the floor. Better still... tell the girl what ever it is she wants about... motorcars!" And then maybe, with any luck, she'll go...

Waller continued to lie still but the girl had sprung up.

"Did you say Mrs. Tree is coming here?"

Tom nodded. He was tired of this now and of his office being used as a waiting room. He really would like that pint before curtain call. But the girl had sprinted to the other side of the room and was peering out of the window.

"Is that it?" she demanded. "Is that her car?"

"Charming," said Waller. "A man lies here wounded, heart sinew exposed and the little minx has moved on…"

"Are *you* going to move sir?' said Tom stepping over him.

"Well, you know Tommy I don't think I will now."

The girl was standing on tippy toe.

"What a magnificent thing!" she said "I bet it goes terrifically fast!" her eyes were burning. "I bet it needs incredible brakes to make it stop!"

Tom considered the man on the floor and the girl in her hat, neither of whom seemed to be in any hurry to leave. All he needed to make the moment complete was –

"Good morning, Tom," said Mrs. Tree in that tight, tinkling high voice that denoted trouble of a non-specific nature. For a moment he stared at her, wondering if she were dressed for a particular role. He had never seen anyone dressed head to toe in a block colour before and yet here she stood before them all in green. Had someone told her it was her lucky colour? To top it all her once blonde locks were now… red. When she swivelled her head though to look down at Waller, Tom saw in alarm that a parrot-like tail of yellow feathers hung down her back. She clutched matching yellow kid driving gloves – not the soft butter variety, thought Tom critically – these were more clotted cream. Her eyes darted from the girl to Tom to Waller.

"Tired my love?" she said sharply.

For a moment Waller hesitated, taking in her outfit. "Somewhat, my dove."

"Good."

The girl froze, blushed, and squeezing under the gap made by Mrs. Tree's arm against the door-stop suddenly vanished.

Mrs. Tree raised a carefully arched eyebrow. "And that was…?"

Tom closed the door firmly.

"That was Mr. Tree's stalker."

Waller struck his head. "I knew it!"

Maud started. "What do you mean?" she said, stepping over Waller.

Tom dug into his pocket for a sweet. "A figure of speech Mrs. Tree. Nothing to worry about." He went back to his desk hoping that they would both leave now. He rustled some papers noisily. But Mrs. Tree wasn't having a bar of it. She hovered by Tom's elbow, her green lace sleeves tickling his cheek.

"Why did you call her a stalker?"

"I didn't mean any harm by it," he said hastily. "I only meant that she writes an awful lot of letters and hangs around the stall doors. She sends me on errands."

"That's ridiculous!" Mrs. Tree began to pace in front of Tom's desk and poked Waller with her foot. "Your aren't her master." She drew in her nostrils, catching a glimpse of herself in the mirror. "What kind of letters?"

Tom sucked hard on his sweet. "Dunno... mostly to an aunt – she says they're to an aunt – sometimes to Max..." He felt uncomfortable now. "She asks to write them... here at my desk. It doesn't bother me... or at least it didn't... I thought you knew... she said..."

Waller got up slowly, realizing there was no more attention to be had from playing dead.

"Do you have any now?"

Tom felt in his copious pockets. There were two sealed letters and one as yet unfinished. He handed them to Waller. For a moment Maud and Waller exchanged a look. She shook her head over the sealed letters but shut her eyes as if in approval over the opened one. Waller's long fingers felt round the edges, hesitating before removing the mauve sheet.

'According to law,' read Waller, 'no preliminary canter counts – you may say morally it does –' Tom's stomach began to rumble. He didn't understand the first thing about what she'd written and he wondered that such a young girl could have those words in her head. Mrs. Tree had put a hand to her throat and a hand on Waller's arm. '... but I think not more than the original kiss.' They exchanged a look. Tom tried to inch his way forward but they were well and truly blocking the way. He wished for the hundredth time his office were not so visible from the vestibule. Maybe he should relocate to the dome?

'You need have no fear..." continued Waller, and Tom immediately did. "Remember," Waller's voice dropped, 'this is in italics' he whispered to Maud, 'his mistress cannot become his wife – come what may I must have that supreme advantage over Putney should Maud die –"

Tom stood still. Maud gasped. Waller had lost his cad's expression. "There's more I'm afraid darling."

It was the word 'darling' that motivated Tom.

"Right," he said gruffly, "some of us have work to do."

Neither appeared to have heard him.

"Besides," continued Waller, "it is so much easier to rule a man whose desire you have whetted and left unsatisfied, than if you have surrendered..."

"That's it Sir," said Tom in the voice he used when moving crowds in front of the ticket office. "If you'll just move along, I can get by."

This seemed to do the trick or maybe it was the appearance of a small boy Tom had never seen before bursting through the door.

"You've got to help Miss!" he said breathlessly.

"God! Who's this now?" exclaimed Waller, "Another stalker?"

"No sir," said the boy, "I'm Mrs. Reed's son."

"You can vouch for him?"

"I know who he is," said Maud quietly.

Tom, one foot out the door, withdrew it.

"What's the matter Robin?" asked Maud quietly. "And how on earth did you get here?"

"I walked," said the boy and now that they all looked at him they could see he was indeed exhausted.

"But that must have taken you hours!" exclaimed Maud in awe.

"It's my mother," he said. "There's something wrong."

And all at once Maud remembered a scene with blood on the sheets and on the floor and streaking her father's face. She stumbled against Waller.

"Darling," he said, "At last!"

"Oh for god sake," she said into his coat. "We'll have to go. We'll take the tonneau. Thank goodness I drove it here."

"Go?"

"Yes, to her. To Putney!"

Waller took a step back, a muscle ticking in his cheek.

"And you would do this?"

"Of course! Wouldn't you?" Her voice was hoarse, fierce. She opened her reticule and pulled out a shilling. "Tom, please take Robin and buy him a steak-and-ale pie – and one for yourself, and a pint."

Tom blinked and looked down at the boy. What was going on here? What did they think Tom Danes, front manager, really did?

"And Tom. Keep him with you. All day if needs must. Don't let him out of your sight."

"And Olivia? Miss Truman I mean? The girl –" he added in response to their blank stares. "Am I to keep her in my sights too?"

Maud looked at Waller.

"Absolutely not! Actually, yes. Find your master. As soon as you can."

"And this afternoon's matinee?"

"We'll be back by then, Tom. Come Waller, we must make haste."

She turned back to the boy. "I give you my word," she said, gently cupping his face in trembling hands. "I give you my word."

Fifteen

The moving accident is not my trade; To freeze the blood I have no ready arts:

Wordsworth

In her dream, Maud confused the blood staining her mother's hands – hands that had so briefly touched her dead child's – with the dark clotting pools of thick gunk spreading over May Pinney's and her own. There was the same sweet, sickly over-powering stench that was now so horribly recognizable to her. When she had first seen May lying there as she had seen her own mother, she thought she would faint. With May Pinney's every groan came the memory of her own mother's cries, the drenched counterpane once white and if not exactly fresh, then clean enough to her child's eyes and now testament to the terrible battle for life, by death. Above all, trapped in both rooms was the suffocating panic of knowing there was no escape. What would be was already determined in the too tight pelvis and the circumference of the child's head. Now as then, hushed voices were considerate of what was to come, of a fate that would determine an outcome unimaginable only a few hours before.

Maud had stood rooted to the spot, paralyzed before the all too familiar scene, her worst nightmare made real and her heart beat so that her breastbone ached just to think on it. She couldn't breathe, thoughts crashed against her skull begging for release. And while she longed to flee, the desperate cries from the bed propelled her forward and in the same instant she knew what she must do. She peeled off her gloves and removed her jacket, lace cuffs already crumpling with the perspiration soaking her wrists. Next she removed her hat with its trailing feathers smoothing them with one last caress as though in farewell, as if for luck and setting it on a narrow shelf and as far away from the mess around the bed as possible. Another boy hovered, his face white, shifting from one foot to the other. Maud hesitated before putting an arm around his shoulder and whispering that he should go to the well at the end of the garden, and to take his time about it and to pull at least 5 pails of water. Waller, who had appeared and now looked as green as Maud's costume, made a face of protest but Maud hissed something to the effect that getting the boy away from the room was her only concern, and drawing water would keep them both occupied for a time.

The cries from the bed had now become screams and Maud grimaced. She willed her physical body to go through the motions of aid, while in her mind she clung to the dialogue now playing there – anything to stop her re-living the scene from that other childbirth in which death stalked the room with its ravenous face. The extraordinary fact of her even being in this room at all did not bear thinking about. The windowless room with its hastily rigged curtain (thank God for the curtain) reminded Maud of the Ibsen play of which Wilde (and Herbert) had been so scathing. She revisited that image in her head now, scrutinizing it carefully. In fact it was almost exactly as he described it– words dripping in sarcasm and scorn for the bare room, the single chair, the green-brown drapes all anathema to the aestheticism Wilde personified. She had felt his complete confusion at seeing her in such a setting – that she who had played his Mrs. Allonby so admirably all those years before, could stoop to this.

*   *   *

And I don't give up happiness merely because it comes so late... Of all the lines she had ever learned, of all the lines she had ever spoken, these were the ones that stayed with her, that haunted her. Her breathing was ragged now as the morphine wore off, and consequently there was fresh pain unlike any she had ever known. This pain was greater than childbirth, greater than the knowledge that Herbert betrayed her. It was everywhere, ripping through her head and body. But *her* pain? Surely the pain was May Pinney's? In her dream it was the other woman's blood still pouring from her body, blood that try as she might, she could not stem... Maud strained to turn her head but found it pinned to the pillow. Pillow? She didn't understand. What had happened? Why was she in bed at all? It was not her own bed, that much was clear. Then whose? And again why? And what had happened to

May Pinney? Had she survived? Had the baby? Was that mass on the sheet...? Someone caught her hand, prevented her from feeling her face, to pick at the blood congealing beneath her fingers. She felt too the sting of glass embedded in her arms and face. *Never mind her head* she inwardly moaned – *it's the glass that is misery*... Hushed voices faded from the room, as did the distant traffic and a night-light that was too bright. She wished more than anything they could understand that it was the glass... *it was the glass that pierced the hollow of mine ear...* If only they knew this then they would hurry up, they would leave her head alone and clean her arm. Her lips couldn't move, the lower part of her face seemed to be wired shut; her face was tightly bound. She found that her hearing was impaired, that the only reality was inside her head, a reality to which at that moment, she must return.

*   *   *

Afterwards, when he thought he could get away with it, Tom Danes confessed that Maud's green outfit and hat (never mind dyed hair) had made her look like an exotic bird, and never more so than when her feathers were stuck to her face. Of course he hastily added that when he'd first seen her, he hadn't realized the red mixed in with the yellow and green was in fact blood. Nor did he confess to losing all appetite for a pie he had so tenderly placed in his back apron pocket earlier that morning – for there wasn't much difference between his smashed up pasty and the colours (and contours) of her face once he'd sat down heavily on it in shock. And shock certainly did not begin to convey the heart-paralyzing terror that gripped him when Herbert touched his arm to wake him. Luckily, on account of Putney's imminent accouchement, Tom had been sleeping outside his master's door, not on the floor but in relative luxury on a chaise longue pushed there from a spare dressing-room. Tree, more agitated than Tom had ever known him had muttered incomprehensible gibberish in a mixture of High German and low and together they had fled the theatre. It was with some surprise therefore, that Tom realized that it was not to May Pinney's bedside they hastened but to Maud's. Once there however, his master became a man with a mission, or at the very least one reminiscent of Jack Tanner in Shaw's *Man and Superman*. Mr. Waller, it soon became apparent had no such alter ego but did harbour a very real aversion to blood and nursing homes and had been all too happy for Herbert to take over. And take over he had. It was Herbert who had telegrammed Sir Arthur Fripps, the King's surgeon no less. Herbert, who had fetched Maud's things from her home and Herbert who secreted himself by the back door into the surgery to avoid the press that gathered there. Several times a day, Tom was sent for updates on Maud's progress. No, that had been the most surprising thing in this great drama – how his master had reacted to the news. So far he had not even been to Putney.

But Herbert's devotion to his sick wife was not the only transformation to take place. There was seismic change in Tom's appetite – or lack of, which was most troubling. Now that he could feed freely on the delicacies transported daily to the nursing home from the Carlton Hotel, meals Maud with her jaw wired shut could not eat, Tom found he had no desire to either. Tom fed her rather on snippets of gossip, but the pleasure was somewhat diluted as he realized now that it was Maud's witty ripostes that turned a bit of news into capricious enjoyment. She was a heroine to Herbert and his children for saving Mrs. Pinney, and bringing into the world the child that would almost certainly have died if it hadn't been for Maud – a girl to be named Juliet. Not that the world could know any of this, but he did and his master did and that would probably account for Tree's gentleness towards his wife in the aftermath of her motor accident. Maud pressed Tom repeatedly, or pressed his hand and he knew that she needed to hear again and again the details of what had happened because she could remember nothing of it herself. Not one for sentimentality, Tom did not take fright at the tears that pushed their way through the bandages at the corner of her eyes, nor questioned whether or not she could even hear him. She lay, completely still under the grand Dr. Fripp's orders, entombed like a mummy or at the very least a medieval effigy, her head and face immobile.

What of course he could not tell her was that there was all manner of really quite damaging gossip (Tom had no doubt that the greatest instigator of these rumours was that revolting girl, the odious Miss Truman) as to what Herbert Tree's wife was doing driving a Ford motor late at night and not alone at that. Some said it served her right for carrying on with a member of the company and right under Tree's nose, that smashing into a small cart in which the car's mudguards crumpled was only what she deserved. But of course that wasn't all that crumpled... Waller jumped clear unhurt, as did the driver of the cart who shouted, enraged that Maud hadn't sounded her horn – which she hadn't. Exhausted from delivering May's child, she had driven blindly, as though in a trance and for the first and last time she had not been afraid. Or so she told Tom much later. But then she had never expected to see another living soul emerge through the thick morning fog. And then suddenly, as from nowhere she heard Waller's voice in her ear telling her to stop. He didn't shout and she didn't panic but it was too late. She braked suddenly and they had spun and then there among the hedgerows of Putney Hill was a horse and cart and with nowhere else to go Maud had gone into them head on.

There was a deathly silence. Waller, not Maud heard the sound of breaking glass, the sound of metal crumpling and twisting, the sound of her bones snapping as brittle and as quickly as twigs in the undergrowth. But what Waller would always remember, he told Tom afterwards, was the horse's horrible shriek as its hooves landed on Maud's skull. Tom knew that Maud sustained three broken ribs and a broken jaw, the pain the nurses said would be intense – every breath she took an agony, a small death. The accompanying feeling of despair at not being able to talk or to swallow properly would be all-consuming. Tom told Maud, rather, though he could not know if she understood, how lucky she was not to have been killed. It was a miracle. It could have been so much worse. How lucky, how lucky and yet... and yet when Tom looked at his master's wife, small and shrivelled that formidable woman reduced to a still, sick person, all individuality neutered, he didn't think she looked lucky at all. There was nothing lucky about any of it and while it had brought about an unexpected show of compassion in his master, it had produced quite a reverse effect on the odious creature, as Tom had taken to calling her. The only time Tom had ever wanted to strike a woman was when he came upon Waller in the theatre foyer talking to that ... that girl. The thing he had witnessed but would never repeat was that Miss Truman had called Waller 'a Jew' to his face, adding 'why couldn't our troubles have been ended the other day – by something worse than a cut face?'

Meanwhile Maud lay oblivious of the goings on at His Majesty's or indeed any theatre, in her silent, secret world, a world that alternated between bouts of extreme pain and the all too vivid dreams brought on by morphia. Tom could almost touch those dreams as the shadows raced about her face. He could feel the tension seep from the rigid blue veins, when her eyes rolled into her head. And slowly even this became familiar – at least to Tom. They settled into a strange new routine and a peaceful one, his masters and he. Because it was secret it was also autonomous and Tom answered to no one, not even Mr. Waller. Especially Waller. Tom laughed inwardly. How much more did he know now! Waller delivered letters all right and sometimes twice daily, but it was Tom who read them to his mistress. He was after all the only one she trusted. And sometimes he imagined he saw a tiny flicker of hope, the faintest glint in her eye. *I love you & yearn for you & think of you! I found 2 more photos of you so now I have 4 in my study!* Tom knew he struggled to read these with anything like the expression demanded, the honey silk smoothness of a Waller. And over the next weeks, it didn't seem to matter. It seemed to Tom that Waller was more concerned with covering his own back, than any genuine concern for his mistress. Each letter seemed to be prefaced with *but we saw each other at such and such a time, didn't we sweet?* As if it could possibly matter now when all the world knew that they had been out driving together. *I first heard it from your maid that you have had a terrible night...*'. Tom quivered at that. *Yes but it wasn't him sitting up all night with her was it?* He hated the way Waller called Maud 'pet' and told her he had 'heaps of ready money' – why hadn't he said so before? *Do do do* – all this underlined three times – *do let me buy you things.* And in response to her silence he wrote again, *I wonder why, apart from the pain (& I fear it was bad today) & illness & weakness you were so depressed my love.* Why indeed? Thought Tom. The woman had lost her beauty; her face was a mess. Was the man such a fool? Why was it that his mistress had never before noticed his vanity? These people with the airs and graces considered themselves to be clever... Why Tom had never met a bigger bunch of fools in all his life! Waller offered to read to her in his 'low soft voice' assuring her that it would do her more good than anything Fripp and his nurses could offer. Tom thought not.

And then of course there was Maud's other great so-called admirer, although Tom was beginning to feel exhausted with all the fetching of water for vases and the demands that Duchess made upon him when she paid a visit. He was beginning to wonder which of the two was the more disruptive. Waller's letters at least could be ignored. Violet on the other hand made no secret of her displeasure, raging at Maud's unresponsive form. What was she (Maud) doing helping that trollop anyway? Violet was always under the impression that Maud despised her. When had that changed? How was it that the trollop's child had thought to even *find* Maud at His Majesty's? Could she imagine the gossip? (Tom could, never mind Maud.) And what in *heaven's* name was that trollop doing continuing to have children? Wasn't she supposed to be *dead* by now? He knew nothing about. No one suffered lead oxide poisoning for this long. Tom had sat up at that. He knew nothing about oxide poisoning either. It wasn't something his master ever talked about. Shakespeare (Tree) hunger (Tom) but never anything more serious. Maybe she wasn't ill after all, insisted Duchess. How could she be if she was still breeding? Really, how indelicate this all was and really Maud had been very neglectful to have allowed this state of affairs! Tom had almost laughed out loud at that. How was it Maud's fault? He was glad when at last Duchess was recalled to Belfield and even gladder that Maud could not respond.

But there were other less complicated well wishes, namely from Ellen Terry who had drawn smiling faces all over her writing paper – *'I'm so fond of you & admire you & most of all your courage'* and Duchess's husband who far from being the philistine illiterate his wife maintained, wrote a long moving letter wanting her to know how her 'wonderful pluck' had impressed them all. Only the great actor manager, Herbert Beerbohm Tree sat silently – the time for lengthy admissions of guilt or gratitude long passed – with tears coursing down his face, playing no one this time but himself.

*   *   *

"You know she's cut her hair?" said Violet, one day when Maud could move her head enough to look out of the window although still unable to speak. Duchess swept into the nursing home, a jangle of nerves creating disturbance and noise amid the calm quiet rooms. Knowing there could be no answer, she careered into her next topic – a frustrated tryst with Cust. "He was there do you know – all *night* and I couldn't get to him – not through my corridor or private passage – there was *no way!*" She wrung her hands! "Oh the *misery* dear of his being so near and not being able to … touch him!"

Maud closed her eyes, not only against the torment but the motion that was Violet and her romances. Her friend spun round in her new corselet skirt and matching crepe de chine blouse – both by far the most conventional get-ups Maud had ever seen her in. She made her eyes go large.

"Ah..." Violet touched her little coat, the short bolero edged with velvet and embroidered in gold and green. "This? Darling it's banana to you – well, the old biscuit colour re-christened."

Maud made a suitably admiring face. At least the top bit of her face still moved. It was actually exhausting not being able to speak – people still expected her to respond. Violet's hat was also banana or biscuit-coloured and trimmed with a band of velvet and pink and red roses.

"Oh no Maud dear, the toque as we know it, is quite dead." She made a violent gesture, no doubt thinking not at all of head attire but rather of her husband. "Although with this exception most millinery is tilted at an angle suggesting the grotesque and leads directly to the pathway of the aggressive which should always be avoided, and Maud dear, you'd do well to observe this, in modes as well as manners." Maud thought it would be rather a long time before she considered the merits of one hat over the other but Violet was warming to her theme, ducking beneath the tiny nursing home mirror to adjust its position.

"Small hats *de jour* are only ever acceptable when covered in one of the multitudinous varieties of anemones – ideally purple with black centres."

Maud blinked. Since when had Violet been remotely concerned with fashion? Why was it that visitors came to see her regaling her with intimate day-by-day accounts of their lives? And think to distract her with it? Maud touched her head once again and the bald patch at the front where her hair had been shaved. Violet had said that Danes was absolutely correct in saying she looked like a parrot, especially as her dyed hair was all patchy. Violet said she was more cockatoo. Maud shuddered at the thought of what she must look like. More Miss Havisham she imagined, than Lady in White.

"To cover the hair, yes." Violet nodded impatiently but Maud insisted until Violet, frowning and panting finally collapsed on the end of the bed and looked at her levelly.

"I don't know what you're talking about, Maud dear. You're simply going to have to write it down." She pushed the pad of paper that resided by her bedside towards her and a pencil badly in need of sharpening. Maud grasped the pencil with all her strength and it still wasn't enough. She touched her hair again and made a snipping gesture.

"Oh!" Violet clapped her hands. "You mean Viola?"

Maud blinked twice. Violet stared at her for a moment scanning the pathetic pale face under its patchwork of bandages and the shock of dyed hair that sprang through the gaps onto the pillow. Maud's fingers trembled as she pulled her friend's sleeve.

"Oh that…" Violet frowned. "Yes, well apparently, Viola cut her hair – you know the new bob – well maybe you don't – no, no, it looks lovely. The point is that she left her shorn hair on a tram! For all and sundry to examine and a fine mane it must have been too! That incredible red…" she glanced at Maud. "All right, not red but auburn in the sunlight." Violet patted her own lustrous locks. "Must say, she's got gumption your girl – more than us at any rate."

More than us *now,* Maud would have corrected. She sighed inwardly and her heart took up its steady and downwards trajectory from where it had so briefly been suspended. If Violet wanted her undivided attention she certainly had it.

"You know Maud dear, you're going to have to watch that one. I hear she's on her way to Venice now with the Cunards, Lord Vernon, Cust can you credit it –and the Premier who has, as you well know, quite a thing for her. Margot says she's the least hysterical of women and coming from Margot that's saying something. But she's also saying, which is quite *quite* wrong, that after herself obviously, she rather wished she'd married Squiffie. I mean really! The man is in his fifties! She says and I quote, that he loves Viola 'with the best kind of love.' Whatever that is."

Platonic love that's what, or that's what she hoped… Maud was grateful that she didn't have a voice. She didn't feel at all able to keep up with her friend and for once had neither the will nor inclination to defend her family. She was well aware of the odd, and yes passionate interest Herbert Asquith held for her daughter. Viola shared everything with Maud, including reading her mother extracts from his letters and although there were some that reassured her more than others, she was still persuaded that Asquith's friendship was one-sided. *'You cannot imagine how much rest and pleasure and joy you have given me...'* the Prime Minister had written. *'I know you feel strongly and deeply and I rely on you.'* Maud also knew Viola was very good at avoiding him when it suited and that her own theatre engagements often kept her out of reach. *His* reach. Worryingly he seemed to depend increasingly on Viola and Maud regretted that Margot his wife felt excluded. It could only end with the Prime Minister's interest going elsewhere, which it must surely do if the past was anything to go by.

And your daughter Diana, Maud wanted to remind her friend, *is also in Venice and enjoying a relationship that is certainly not platonic.* That certainly would have wiped the smugness from Violet's tone. Maud knew very well that other members of the Venice party included the Ettie Desborough's boys, the Grenfells, Horners and Ansons and that there would be lashings of wine, moonlit balconies and kisses.

"Mmmnn..." said Violet grumpily. "I suppose you really can't react much."

Yes and it has its advantages... Maud closed her eyes. The pain could still take her by surprise and it did now, shooting through her jaw and tearing behind her eye sockets. Tears pricked her eyes. Violet stopped mid-sentence.

"Oh darling, I'm sorry!" She moved up the bed. "I've been rattling on when..."

Maud gripped the pencil with all her strength. She pushed the paper towards Violet.

Violet glanced down and then her eyes too filled.

"Belfield, darling," she said gently. "Of course. I'm a fool for not having thought of it before. I'll take you to Belfield. I'll take you ... home."

Sixteen

Yet sit and see; Minding true things by what their mockeries be.

Henry V

Belfield Castle March 1907

Maud sat alone in what she considered to be the most romantic bedroom at Belfield. It was to be found at the end of Violet's corridor and was sometimes referred to as the Tapestry Room because of the large 16th century tapestries adorning the walls. The largest needlework – the one facing the bed – depicted hundreds of naked cherubs clambering up a vine to gorge on grape. Other round- faced, fat-limbed boys either carried or supported each other as they filled golden baskets with apples and other fruit. Some wore banners draped across their naked bodies in a futile stab at modesty. All sported that particular hue of Titian hair Maud described her daughter Viola's as, a colour Violet still persisted on calling simply red. And in the distance, against a silver sky, a fairy castle rose out of apple green hills. The picture was sensual yet at the same time innocent, delicious in its shades of indigo blue and pink. Unframed, it hung above a Charles II gilded table carved with putti and ancanthus foliage. Mirrors behind the bed and opposite the ceiling to floor windows, reflected this many times over. The rest of the furniture was also pink and the huge canopied gilt-painted bed was draped in the palest silk moiré. Maud ran her fingers over the embossed damask and wondered if she would ever again share a bed with anyone. Happiness may have come so late but it had also been snatched from her too soon.

She was dressed in one of Violet's cast-offs – a dress made up, Violet informed her, of two shades of helitrope – Maud would have called check but she bowed before her friend's superior artistic eye. She had breakfasted on a tray in her room – well breakfast was something of an exaggeration– she had only just graduated to lumpy liquids – but there seemed little point in going down just yet. Violet was in London with her daughters Diana and Marjorie, ostensibly to secure them parts in the new Shakespearean revival at His Majesty's. 'I'll do something, something!' Tree had sniffed at Maud's bedside and Violet, never one to turn down an opportunity had countered with an eager, 'Do you really mean *anything?*' With the result that Violet's daughters had walk-on parts in *Julius Sneezer* as Tree dubbed it, given the number of colds running among the cast. The youngest boy, John Manners, was at home ill being cared for in the nursery wing and the Duke was in his study not, Maud imagined, counting out his money.

The bed itself was strewn with half-read letters. Some had been written just after the accident and she re-read those as a source of comfort and encouragement in the dark, dead, cold hours of the early morning when the morphine had worn off. Correspondence from friends and her Tennyson had kept her marginally sane. Waller's had almost succeeded in doing the reverse. He was appearing as Robin Hood in a romantic version of the same name at the Lyric and wanted her bed moved so that she might sit up and wave to him before the evening performance. She had never noticed before how much Waller concentrated … well, on Waller. '*I 'spose*,' he'd written during that last week at the nursing home, '*even if a telephone in your room were possible, with your dear face bandaged up so tightly you couldn't speak into it?!*' No not speak, or eat or barely breathe or swallow...'*Darling, darling, please please stay another week at Netley House.' You stay another week darling!* Maud had wanted to scrawl back but hadn't the strength. And no matter how seemingly charming he was, Maud was unmoved. '*Surely we shall still see and love each other as much as before! Isn't it worth getting well to be in my arms?*', he had written after the performance. Maud had found it tiring not at all to reply with a single, *No!*

There had even been tentative hope in the form a note written by the eminent radiologist Edward Shenton.

'*Thank you for your kind letter and the cheque for two guineas,*' he wrote. '*I am much interested and hope very much to be the means of getting your chin eventually back in its right position.*'

Sir Alfred Fripps, her surgeon, apart from wanting to know if the swelling and discharge persisted (even after several months), expressed gladness that the pain at least was subsiding. *The physical pain that is*, thought Maud. He went on to say that he had been to see Shaw's latest play, *A Doctor's Dilemma* – the title of which was pure irony. She supposed he was trying to humour her by recalling that he had slept for 3 out of the 5 acts and that during the 4th, a man in the pit got so bored that he called out, "I say, you fellows, I *will* stay till the end if you will!" Well he had succeeded and she *was* amused and the smile that broke upon her face threated to break it again and was excruciating.

But it was the correspondence from The Lecture Agency (it cited Hillaire Belloc, Winston Churchill and Captain Scott among its list of contributors), which actually caused Maud's heartbeat to quicken. Although she had been on its books since 1903, Maud had been too busy with theatre engagements to be able to take up its employment. Now if she could recover in time, she would join the English drama critic A.B. Walkley and Oscar Wilde's former tutor the Rev. J.P. Mahaffy at the Hans Crescent Hotel to give a lecture on any subject of her choice. Maud's lecture would be the 'event of the season' according to Mrs. Baillie Reynolds, the popular novelist and writer on the supernatural because, as she wrote to her on behalf of the Agency, 'although not a suffragette, I think women should take more part in public effort than they do.'

Perhaps this really was her future then, thought Maud catching a glimpse of her lopsided face in the mirrors and not allowing herself, on this spring day any trace of sentimentality. Public speaking was something she had always had half a mind to pursuing. Now, more than ever, it might become her mainstay. 'To be eloquent is to be individual,' Tree had advised her once, ' to be strong is to be simple.' On that occasion she'd been told (not exactly asked) to open public baths in Paddington. ("The Baths are ready, you must open them.") In alarm, Maud had asked how that was to be done. "Very simply," was the reply, "you have to make a speech." Completely panicked and with only ten days to prepare, Maud veered from a desire to quote Homer, to Wordsworthian allusions to streams and Lucy. The great day came, the baths were tiny and the echo great. There were embarrassing and stifled tin giggles (verging on the hysterical) which reverberated from the roof and which, it gradually dawned on her, to her horror, were coming from her own mouth. She remembered making one heroic effort at self-control, fixing her eyes on a little far-away boy who clung to a diving board. *He is poor, unwashed, evidently an orphan!* Maud told herself, feeling unaccountably moved. Her speech might very well mean everything to him. She remembered looking around her at the sea of faces and drawing immediate inspiration from the touching sight. She rose majestically to her feet to proclaim the long-looked for message, "Ladies and Gentlemen, I declare these baths, open."

Maud sighed, almost shuddering at the recollection of the sound of the boy falling from the diving-board into the newly opened baths which momentarily drowned the applause (though thankfully not the boy) as she dropped exhausted from the platform. She would never know what temerity possessed her to turn to the bevy of eager reporters and say, "Gentlemen of the Press, I give you my maiden speech!"

Maud rose carefully from her chair. She still felt the thump of blood rush to her jaw with any sudden movement – and went to the window. It was so quiet here. She'd forgotten quite how quiet. Even Fripp's nursing home which prided itself on its peaceful environment (and discretion), so conducive to rapid recuperation, could not completely drown the general background rush of traffic – horns from the hansom cabs and horse drawn carriages. But the quiet at Belfield was of an altogether different category and releasing the window latch she let in a cacophony of bird-song – she identified spring thrush rising through the morning mist and woodpecker and wood pigeon – a welcome disturbance. She had been at Belfield three months and knew she could not stay much longer. Yes, speech-making might just be the very thing. She had written to Noel Coward, to Barrie and to Maugham, but to no avail. Coward had graciously replied, 'you may be quite sure, that whenever I have anything suitable, I will cast you for it as you have given me a good deal more pleasure on the stage than most people.' *Yes something suitable if she could wear a mask!* She was under no illusion that the roles she might be offered now would be limited.

Maud hit her left hand with her right fist. No, she would not give up, she would not give in and most of all she would not hide away like Mrs. Pinney! Ah... May... she too had written kind words. '*I am indebted to you... I owe you my life... and one day I will repay you...*' It was strange that initial dislike and jealousy had given birth to their unearthly friendship. She did nothing but sympathize with May. Moreover, she knew now what it was to lose one's beauty... But she must do more. She must do as much as possible to stay busy...

Maud slipped out of her room and down the long, seemingly endless spiral staircase that connected Violet's corridor to the library and rooms below. She felt along the walls with her fingertips, not because she couldn't see but imagining what it might be to feel cold stone beneath her skin as if for the very first time. She wanted more than anything to feel again with the intensity that she used to, to take pleasure once again in simple things. Increasingly, she felt disconnected, remote, enveloped in another worldliness. It was as if her illness had taken her somewhere else and in returning she was not the person she had been, though the memory of that self still lingered. Life had lost its shimmer and she struggled to imagine a time when she would once again feel desire – that heart-stopping tingling need for... well for anything really. Perhaps she never would. The thought no longer filled her with terror or sadness. In the past months she had sought oblivion from pain but even that was somehow preferable to this general numbness... She felt herself to be a spectre among spectres. Easily enough done here, she thought wryly to herself in a house so steeped in history. She knocked softly and on hearing the Duke's voice pushed open the door.

John Manners, the 8th Duke of Belfield was seated in his Wellington Chair at the huge George III partner's desk with its many drawers and hidden cachets. Above him, a Turner painting depicted Belfield as though floating over the Vale, its turrets awash with sunlight, with the suggestion of a rainbow in the distance. His 6 foot 2 inch frame was immaculately dressed in tweeds and riding boots ready for his morning ride. A starched thick white collar supported a head she felt certain would sink into its chest if left to its own devices. For the first time she noticed that the hair at his temples had turned white and there were dark shadows under his eyes. Even his pointy moustache seemed to droop. She started. There was always something so familiar about him while at the same time unsettling, and it had nothing to do with the fact that he was Duchess's husband.

"Ah, Maud dear." His voice was tired and Maud felt a sympathetic tug. An eyeglass hung on a long narrow gold chain around his neck and a spotless white handkerchief poked from his hunting jacket. He half rose to get up but she raised a hand in protest.

"No, no... please."

He paused, relieved she could see. And suddenly he seemed much older, more statesmanlike and far less stupid than Violet made out.

"You look…"

Maud smiled as much as the bandages would allow.

"You can say what you like but you know I won't believe you."

"Tiresome woman…" he said affectionately. He made a gesture to a low chair beside him, but fearing that once lowered into it she would have some difficulty getting up again, Maud perched instead on the window seat opposite his desk.

He looked at her, his moustache twitching. "No good turn goes unpunished. You must have thought that."

Maud shrugged. "I chose to go and it was an accident."

"The press…"

"… Can say what it likes." Maud held his gaze. "I did see where Lily Brayton's carriage careered into a milk float and her face was badly cut."

"Yes, Fripp has been in charge of her too. What a time for understudies!"

"And Ellen Terry…" Maud had been on the point of recounting a car accident they had both been involved in, but all at once there seemed little point in dwelling on more unpleasantness. Or perhaps it was simply that in his presence, Maud continued to be overwhelmed by this feeling of familiarity. Maud, facing Belfield with her back to the sun felt its warmth on her shoulders. Sunbeams danced off the beautiful objects on his desk. His rings lay on the papers he had been reading and twinkled in the shafts of light. Above them his face was illuminated, the lines suddenly smoothed away.

"You must always think of Belfield as your home."

Maud studied his kindly, troubled eyes.

"I know you mean that," she said.

He coughed and pushed away his papers – mostly letters she thought and a jumble of notices. He'd removed his rings while writing and now began replacing them carefully. His signet ring had a ruby seal, something she had never noticed before.

"She loves you know…" said Maud, her eyes still distracted by the colour in the ring.

"What?"

"Violet – she does love you."

Belfield pursed his lips, the moustache descending to the cleft in his chin.

"No she doesn't."

Maud took breath to speak but Belfield put a hand to her lips in an unexpectedly intimate gesture.

"Sh!," he said. "Please. Allow me this insight. I'm not such a fool."

Maud took his hand away gently and held it. "No, you're not."

For a moment he returned the pressure and then sat back in his chair, his arms hanging over the edges, the light playing with his eyeglass and rings. Again the ruby shone and she blinked, reminded by the memory of another such ring…

"What will you do now?" he asked at length, crossing one pristine boot over the other.

Maud leant against the window casement with a clear view of the parklands and woods. Silver trees along the horizon formed a natural boundary against the terraces and walkways of formal gardens. From here too, she could just make out one of Cibber's statues, 'Taste' – one of the senses. Which just about summed Belfield up, thought Maud. It really was, thanks to Violet's artistic influence that Belfield had evolved, despite its grandeur, into this elegant yet convivial family home.

"Public speaking, perhaps."

He guffawed. "You want to do that? Willingly? By God, I have to do enough of it as it is and hate every minute of it!"

"Yes but-"

"No – not in the blood-"

He stood up. Their morning interview, if you could call it that, was over. He stood up with the top part of his body in darkness and only the ruby red ring on his left hand aglow, just as a dying ember might appear in a sooty grate. A black grate... Maud felt a prickly sensation spread over her skin. *Not in the blood.* Because suddenly that's precisely what it was. Having stood up herself almost in unison with him, she sat down abruptly. All at once the image of another man came to her. In her mind's eye that other man wore evening dress certainly, but his neck protruded out of the same stiff white collar, giving him the appearance of an owl. He had on the same highly polished boots and his finger sported the same ruby signet ring. She had never clearly seen his face. Not then. But she remembered those hands – so pale against his dark clothes and the even darker shadows behind him. And no matter how dark *they* seemed – their clothes in the shadows – they only appeared dark from where she was standing. She and her father were dark in a different way – blackened by dirt and coal and poverty. And she was ashamed. She had slunk behind her father for the first time in her life, not because she wanted to be associated with him, not because she wanted to be seen to belong to him but because before that great man – the greatest she had ever seen – she was ashamed to be seen at all. Behind him had been the small boy.

Maud stared at Belfield. Although drenched in sunlight, he appeared faceless and only his hands and collar were illuminated. But it was his ring that fascinated her. She couldn't take her eyes off his pale hands.

"Maud?" he said gruffly.

"It was you," she said almost to herself. "It was always you. You are – you were the boy – weren't you?" Her voice tailed off so that it was hardly above a whisper, while her mind whirled to settle the rush of memories and to untangle and make sense of them. *You are the boy in my dreams!*

And then aloud she said, "I dream about you. I dream about you all the time."

"Oh my dear…" he said gallantly but clearly uncomfortable. "You know Maud – I – you know we couldn't– the Vanbrugh woman caused such upset." He mentioned Maud's actress and friend with whom Belfield had a love child – the cause of the Belfields' marital discord. Well some of it.

Maud stared at him. *Oh for heavens 'sake* she wanted to exclaim, but her thoughts were so confused, so jangled, she didn't want to waste a moment being diverted.

"All these years…" she said slowly. "All these years I've wondered…"

Belfield looked at her closely. "You love Herbert. Violet tells me so…"

And then in panic, he said forcibly, "Shall I call nanny?"

Maud shook her head. "I'm perfectly all right."

She was silent for a moment and then looked at his hands and the ring, and then back to Belfield. She could see it all very clearly now. She only wondered why it had taken this long. She could see the theatre that stormy night and her father's face stormier than any weather outdoors. She felt the fear and the strangeness as though it were yesterday.

"You were that small boy who came to the theatre with his father that night? Weren't you? It was you! We talked as children, that one night, the night –" Maud swallowed but this was too important to allow emotion to get the better of her. There might not be another opportunity to talk to Belfield in this way. There certainly had never been in the past. Maud drew on that same strength that had sustained her through her maiden speech that helped her to accept the loss of her looks, her voice. She enunciated very clearly. "We talked you and I once, almost as we are doing now, but it was the night our brother was born and my mother died."

Belfield turned on his heel, reaching by force for a decanter that stood on the small two-tier table that held drinks and glasses. He downed a whisky in one, squared his shoulders and turned to Maud, motioning to the bottle.

She shook her head then changed her mind. "All right. Yes."

She attempted a tiny sip but in the absence of a straw most of the liquid spilled down her chin.

"Here," he took the handkerchief from his front pocket and mopped her face gently. She caught his wrist.

"Your father was my mother's lover."

"Yes."

Her heart was pounding so loudly she wondered he couldn't hear it. She held his gaze. She'd never really noticed the colour of his eyes before or really very much about him at all for that matter. Over the years he had been the silent presence. Her friend's husband – a source of hilarity and mockery in turn. But she had to know.

"Are you my brother?"

"No."

"No?" Maud's tone was sharp. "No? You know so or no, you don't believe so?"

"No." Belfield's voice cracked. "I don't believe so."

"I see." This time Maud didn't care how much drink was spilled in trying to imbibe as much as possible in one go. "Your father paid for my education."

"Yes."

"Blood money?"

"If you like – no– Maud!"

"Does Violet know?"

He spluttered. "Of course not!"

Maud raised an eyebrow, or thought she might have. Bandages still covered much of her head. "Why of course not? Are you ashamed?"

Belfield poured himself another drink – right to the top this time, nursing the bottle against his chest, his eyeglass tinkling against the decanter's crystal. He met her fierce gaze with a candid look.

"A little." And then when she didn't respond he said, "Well aren't you?"

Maud looked away and suddenly all the fire in her evaporated and she strangled a sob. "Yes."

"Look, if it helps at all, for a long time I wasn't sure. When my father died and so young… there were affairs of his – I mean business affairs," he added quickly, "that I simply left to other people. It was only when Violet made friends with you when your sister–"

"Was her governess."

Belfield considered her. "Yes, but you know it wasn't like that."

Maud put down her glass on his desk and slumped back on the window seat. "I know. I'm sorry. You have always been so kind…"

"It was easy to be." He coloured. "You know how I love actresses!"

Maud said nothing. She might have added, *Like your father!* But didn't.

Belfield consumed the contents of his glass and then settled the decanter on his desk. He sat on the edge of his chair – the famous Wellington Chair that had held three generations of Dukes and Maud was momentarily distracted by the thought. He flexed a leg swinging that elegant leather-clad foot and Maud almost held her breath a second time waiting for the antique wood to give way. He shook his head as if to emphasize what he was saying.

"I don't know how they met – I don't know when they met. I *think* it

wasn' t long before –"

"You mean it was a quick affair."

"It was quick only because she died," said Belfield kindly, firmly now. "I mean to reassure you. That you and I are not related."

"You'd be happier wouldn't you if that were the case?"

"Well wouldn't you?"

Maud closed her eyes. "Yes."

"It would be easier." Belfield touched her arm. "I don't find this easy to say," he said, "but surely you must see that my father cared – that he wanted to do the right thing."

"The right thing!" Maud exploded. "And my father? You don't think he cared? That he didn't die of a broken heart!"

Belfield withdrew his hand.

"You're being melodramatic. He died of drink. And from what I observed then, he wasn't much of a father."

Maud couldn't stop the tears – tears that had not flown so freely in a long time, not even in the immediate aftermath of her accident.

"Maybe not, but he was mine."

Belfield let out a deep sigh. "You're right of course. I apologize."

For a moment Maud thought this was another dismissal, but to her relief Belfield sat back down properly in his chair.

"Look, we can't change what happened nor will we ever know the details of their affair. I'm not sure I want to, not really. There are times like now when I confess to being a little curious, but if only to … oh it doesn't matter." He poured himself another drink. His mouth moved under his moustache. He stroked both ends briefly as if working something out in his head. At length he pushed aside his glass and sat up straight, squaring his shoulders. "And please don't think that what I'm about to suggest has anything to do with that or this–" He motioned to her face which must look a sodden mess of discoloured bandages. "I can't give you cash." He looked to the magnificent view. "Asset rich perhaps but death duties have all but put an end to houses like this. It won't be long before I shall have to sell off land as it is, and the London house will certainly have to be sold. But," he rested his elbows on the arms of his chair. "I do have a personal allowance and I want to help you." He waved a hand to silence her as she attempted to speak. "It's not charity. Believe me it's in my interests to have you back in London. Keeping an eye on Vi is only part of it."

Maud blew her nose carefully, pulling off one of the wetter plasters.

"What would you do now that you've perhaps not had the time or opportunity to do before?" he continued.

Maud crumpled up his handkerchief. "Travel to Egypt."

"Good heavens!" spluttered Belfield.

"You thought something more modest?"

"Well yes, actually."

Maud smiled. "Well actually so had I until you asked me."

"No, you are right again. I did, so what will it be?"

"Egypt."

Belfield sighed.

"Alone?"

"No, I should like the N.K.G to accompany me."

"The who?"

"Oh I'm sorry – the Nice Kind Gentleman – W.S. Gilbert to you – it's how I address my letters to him. He calls me the Nice Kind Lady."

"As I'm sure you are." Belfield scratched his head. "Anything else?"

Maud hesitated.

"I'm beginning to regret this," said Belfield. "Last offer."

Maud took a deep breath. "I want to learn French. Or at least improve it."

Belfield picked up his eyeglass and shuffled his papers. "But you translated that little play didn't you – *On the Telephone*?"

Maud nodded. She wouldn't take umbrage at him calling it 'a little play.' "I did but I want to do more. There's no copyright on foreign plays – at least not at the moment, and the French ones are... well just so much better. And there are so many of them!"

"I see. Well don't let Mr. Shaw hear you."

"He knows how I feel."

There was a small silence. Belfield grunted. "Done. Now bugger 'orf."

Maud smiled. "And we won't-"

Belfield smiled back thoughtfully. "No. We won't."

Maud got to her feet just as there was a knock at the study door.

"That'll be nanny," he muttered. "There's no peace here when Vi's away. Well at least she can bandage you up again. Not sure what's happened to your face. He made a circular motion to indicate the unraveling of cloth.

Maud opened the door as the knocking became more insistent.

"Oh your Grace!"

Nanny, who had in fact looked after the Duke and was the oldest living creature Maud had ever seen, stood shaking on the threshold, tears streaming down her face, her small thin frame rendered vulnerable and pathetic with each sob. "Oh your Grace, it's Lord Haddon."

Seventeen

'Tis not the balm, the sceptre and the ball... the intertissued robe of gold and pearl... No, not all these, thrice-gorgeous ceremony...

Henry V

His Majesty's Theatre March 1911

It was a surprisingly warm spring – balmy and lovely with early lilacs blossoming through the gold-tipped gates of Waterloo Gardens and along the Mall, but despite the temperate weather Tom Danes was going through one of the most testing times of his career. Sun and hunger were the least of it. Tree's latest production, not at His Majesty's but at the Theatre Royal, Drury Lane, was a command performance to celebrate the coronation of George V, and the presence in England of Kaiser Wilhem II. The play was *Money* by Edward Bulwer-Lytton (*Baron Lytton to you*! Maud – now *Lady* Tree – endlessly reminded him). The other great actor manager, George Alexander was to play Evelyn, Irene Vanbrugh Clara, Tree Graves, Arthur Bourchier, Stout and Maud – *Lady* Tree (with a newly corrected chin that Tom did not consider an improvement) the grand part of Lady Franklin. Arthur Collins himself (director of the Theatre Royal) had personally written Maud a letter to the effect that he was sure that 'the inclusion' of her name in the cast would give 'great satisfaction in court circles.'

Excitement was at fever pitch. A command performance was still a command performance after all and a real live Emperor from a foreign country, even if he was the King's cousin was causing all round jitters. Emissaries from Buckingham Palace arrived on a daily basis with specific instructions– reams of the stuff – the audience was to rise, the audience was to sit, the King would receive... the Queen would decline... Sir Herbert would greet – although not in German – Maud said no one had ever understood his own peculiar form of the language – etc. etc. Five horse-drawn carriages (no motor cars to be present) complete with footmen would transport members of the royal household. Mr. Collins would accompany the Kaiser, his wife, King George and Queen Mary. Sir Squire Bancroft was in charge of the Prince of Wales and Princess Victoria. Thousands of onlookers were expected to line the streets around the Strand. Lewis Waller would make all the announcements – on account of that buttery voice and Lyn Harding, the actor who had starred in Maud's plays at the Wyndham, would pour sherry.

Tom's head fairly spun with the logistics of moving so many people, costumes and props from theatre to theatre, especially as his master had spent much of the previous month in America and when post or telegrams arrived, the information conveyed was invariably out of date. Maud's thoughts seemed utterly consumed by the beautiful new gown designed specifically for the event by Lady Duff-Gordon – *Lucille* to her customers. Lady Tree, Tom knew, had been involved with the designer's theatrically inspired 'catwalk' invitation-only tea time gatherings, where clients gathered to view the clothes and listen to the string band playing in the background. Madame Lucille called her collection 'emotional gowns' which Tom considered closest to the truth. Impractical dresses for hysterical women just about summed it up. None of them could take but the tiniest steps in the new 'hobble' skirts. The name said it all he supposed. At least the men-folk might be able to keep tabs on them for a while. Duchess told Maud she wasn't expected to do anything much in the dresses anyway apart from 'hover.' Maud said she would wear absolutely anything that drew the eye *away* from her chin. This Tom understood perfectly.

The dress itself, as Maud told Tom several times a day, (and took time to drop in and tell him) was in the palest mint green with a short train and chiffon draped stole and crisscrossed at the front. It was in the 'directoire' style (whatever that was) sporting, as everyone in London would instantly recognize, Lucille's trademark – handmade silk flowers in blended pastel colours. Despite the lovely weather, Maud was to wear Vi's own white fox stole and enormous fur muff. Atop her hair she would wear a vast feather and diamond comb. Her three ropes of pearls very nearly touched her knees. For the evening, Lucille had surpassed herself in creating a white silk skirt with an empire bodice in black velvet – the dress itself was to be exhibited later that year in the Paris collection for the autumn. That is, of course if the Empress herself hadn't snapped it up! Tom gave Maud a contemptuous look lost on Maud. The actresses were in a state, the actors were jittery and the stage crew clamoured for more pay. Tom was at a loss to see why. Never mind the hullabaloo surrounding the King's visit, the play itself was incredibly boring. It was full of justifications and come-uppances and moral retribution and everyone getting what they duly deserved and therefore very boring indeed. Tom had come to the conclusion that women liked a good cry – the harsher the story the better as far as he could make out. If the heroine was horribly disfigured, her life a misery from start to finish, then it was considered truly excellent. Extra handkerchiefs were provided, such was the reaction to this play and on more than one occasion a female member of the audience had suffered palpitations.

Tom sighed in exasperation. Gone were the days when his office and his time and his eating routine were his own. Gone was the time when a matinee meant just that – at least three hours clear when he could visit The Red Lion, enjoy a pint or two, and a good old-fashioned pie and saunter back with a bit of air in his lungs before pulling down the curtain on another Tree success. He even missed Tree's philandering. At least then, it had been Tom and his master with the womenfolk keeping if not exactly to their places, at least somewhere in the background. Now, Maud (in her new re-energized, re-sculpted form) had begun using his office as some sort of meeting-place for her friends and family. Well mostly family. Most days began with Viola's visit mid-morning – checking that her mother was occupied – then the PM (looking for Viola) and then Lady Tree herself looking for both the PM and her daughter, who by now were half way through their morning drive through the park.

"She's only comforting him," Violet hissed on one occasion when Tom returning to his office found the Duchess and her Ladyship at loggerheads – no infrequent occurrence since the loss of Lord Haddon – for a time the Duchess had been inconsolable after the death of her boy. Not only had Tom's office become a veritable studio but home to the hundreds of sketches of the child, and plaster-casts of his head the Duchess was preparing as a permanent exhibit of her son at the Tate. Macabre is what Tom thought them and he didn't need them cluttering up his space – may God have mercy on his soul. The small chap had been likeable enough from the little Tom saw of him, though not nearly as keen on the theatre as his sisters.

"Why does he need comforting? Surely he's got enough on his plate with that new bill of his! Doesn't parliament keep him busy? I hear the young Tories yesterday didn't let him speak and the sitting was suspended."

Duchess made a face. "Exactly! Even great men get lonely. You and I know that."

"He's married!"

"Precisely, and Viola is a sensible girl. Her head's not going to be turned by... by *Squiffie*!"

"Isn't it?"

Duchess made an exasperated gesture, throwing up her hands so that Tom saw diamonds glint in the strong morning sunlight. "Well your turning up here every morning isn't going to stop her, or him for that matter. After all he *is* the Prime Minister. If he wants a pretty young girl to go out with him on a drive – that's what he'll get."

Maud tossed her head, catching sight of herself in the mirror. At certain angles and from a certain distance, Tom supposed she didn't look too bad.

"I wouldn't care if he were the Kaiser himself – oh darling, and talking of which... what if I *don't* wear the fox but a picture hat instead but keeping the feather?"

And they were off. Tom marvelled at how quickly they could return to their subject of choice. But it was a subject soon replaced – too soon as in twenty-four hours later (and twenty-four hours before the great day) – by a furore the likes of which Tom hoped never to see again in his lifetime.

That same day, Maud received a letter – a type-written, two page affair which she declared to be just the beginning of the insults heaped upon her – and which she pounded on his desk as though he were somehow responsible. Pale, shaking with disappointment and fury and with all thoughts of the PM and her daughter well and truly obliterated, Maud paced Tom's office.

"The slut! The whore! I won't stand for it! *He* won't stand for it – I won't let him!"

Tom took a big bite out of the Bath bun he'd been keeping for elevenses, knowing full well that he'd not see it again that day and then pulled out the bottle of ale he kept for emergencies. Maud turned up her nose at that – not that she was able to do much facial expression these days, but Tom got the *impression* that that was what she intended. He glanced at the neatly typed letter with its crest of Drury Lane emblazoned in its centre and then to Maud's distraught face. She had been crying, and all at once the irritation he had initially felt seeped out of him along with the taste of the sugary bun. He licked the last traces of sweetness from his lips as if they were the last he'd ever have, quickly wiping his hands on his apron. He'd been about to polish the silver props that were to be transported later that day to the Theatre Royal. Maud stabbed the paper.

"See here!" she cried, "and here!"

"I-"

Maud whipped the letter from him. "How *dare* they!" she boomed in her Mistress Quickly voice. "Mr. Cyril Maude may be the *Manager* but Mr. Collins is the *Director*! And my husband– " she drew herself to her full height which was still considerably more than Tom's.

"Why, what's he done –*they* -" Tom corrected quickly, "what have *they* done?"

"*Done*?" boomed Lady Tree. "*Done*? My good man – why it's all here in black and white! Don't you *see*?"

Tom scratched his head. Maud swept passed him furiously, snatching back the letter.

"Done? Why he's only gone and offered his whore *my* part!" she screamed. "As if she could learn it in a day! That was *my* line! But I've not met another living actress who could do the same! Even that Bourchier woman wasn't able to learn her part for, and I quote 'I know not the Shakespeare!' Unquote. Bloody Colonial! Damned Australian upstart! She probably descends from convicts! Or natives... I bet she stole and was about to have her hands–"

"What, Irene Bourchier?" interrupted Tom now well confused.

"No, not *Irene,* Cyril Maude's wife – Miss *Emery.*" While Maud charged furiously back and forth, Tom managed to winkle the letter from her. She appeared not to notice until he began reading, at which point she stopped and stood absolutely motionless.

'*Dear Lady Tree*...' he read slowly ironing out the creases with one hand and turning to the light.

'*In reply to your letter of the 9*'-

"Mmm, " muttered Maud.

"*This most unfortunate difficulty,*' continued Tom, '*seems to have arisen in consequence of a conversation that Sir Herbert had with Mr. Cyril Maude yesterday. Sir Herbert then said you perfectly agreed to Miss Emery playing the part and were quite prepared to resign in her favour, but unfortunately Sir Herbert at this time had not heard of my letter to you or your reply –* "

There was a blood-curdling scream as Maud snatched the letter out of Tom's hand.

"*Agreed* to give up my part! As if! Of course 'Sir Herbert had not heard of my letter' as I never wrote one! The *snake*!" Maud began to breathe raggedly.

"Please sit, my lady," said Tom nervously, more used to fainting women in his office than he would ideally wish. "Please calm yourself. There must be a way to fix this."

"Well there isn't!" Maud collapsed into a chair and began to fan herself with the letter. Tom attempted to release it from her hand but she once again leapt to her feet.

"Just listen to this!"

"I will, but I beg you calm yourself!"

"You calm yourself! Oh – I'm sorry," she said quickly. "But just read! *Read!*" She stabbed once more at the paper that was by now grubby and wrinkled, torn at the corners.

Tom ducked under his desk and took a glug of ale – it was only 9.30 in the morning but he wasn't sure how much more he could take of this nor how long it would continue. He took a final glug and read silently. *You will understand I have had a great deal of anxiety over this matter, and perhaps I was a little rushed in writing to you owing to my desire to settle as soon as possible the cast to be submitted to the King… In the difficult circumstances that have arisen I think it would be a very charming and gracious act on your part if you would kindly offer the part to Miss Emery.*
"Oh."

"Oh? That's it?"

"I see the problem."

"So do I. Well I won't. Never. " Maud crunched up the letter and then punched her hand. "I'll never talk to him again. Not any of them. Oh! I expect Herbert is behind all this. He never has the guts to tell things to my face. Is he sweet on this one too? Don't tell me he's betrayed us both!" She put a dramatic hand to her forehead, closing her eyes.

"Both?"

Maud's eyes flew open. "Why May and me of course."

"Ah yes." Tom had forgotten how these two enemies were now bosom pals. His master, he knew rued the day they had ever met.

"Well?"

"No, no," said Tom firmly. "Of course not."

"Then why?" Maud's lip, still scarred and jarring, began to tremble.

"I hear she's only just returning to the stage after a bout of illness. Years even."

229

"A baby!" scoffed Maud. "Hardly illness and it doesn't take years."

"She almost died."

"Well so did I but I still was back in my corsets 6 weeks later! And Herbi- Herbert was in America."

There was a brief unhappy pause where Maud studied her velvet shoe, and Tom tried a different tack.

"Maybe," said Tom clearing his throat, "maybe her husband just wants to make it up to her?"

Maud's eyes narrowed. "So shou-does mine."

"Well then."

"Well then nothing. I am by far the better actress." She unfurled the now damp pages. "I am older," she sucked in her cheeks giving her face a comical twist where once it revealed rather fine cheekbones. "And grander, and I will not give way."

Tom's heart began to thud unevenly. She was indeed all those things and it did not look as though she might be leaving his room in a hurry. His stomach began to rumble as it did in times of distress and he wished he'd not scoffed the Bath Bun.

"Not even the Suffragettes..." he muttered under his breath.

"What did you say?" Maud frowned so that her chin appeared more protruding than usual.

Tom cleared his throat. "Nothing m'lady – just that there was that disturbance last week during *The Silver King*."

"Don't I know it! That wretched play has had more publicity thanks to those sulky lasses than all Miss Marbury's work put together..." Maud suddenly stopped frowning and the faintest of smiles broke over her face. Tom was now more alarmed than when she'd been shouting.

"Tell me…" said Maud thoughtfully. "Just how disruptive *were* the Suffragettes?"

Tom's brain spun but not quickly enough for Maud's moving double-quick time. He could see a trap being laid before him but could nothing to avoid it.

"Well… they stood up shouting for one thing."

Maud stood up too now, flicking the train of her skirt as though she were positioning herself centre stage for a soliloquy.

"How shouting? Was it loud? Where were they exactly? I mean the stalls? Balcony?" and when Tom inwardly groaning, remained silent she snapped "Think man! It's important!"

"It was in the papers…" he said stalling for time.

"Yes, yes we know that!"

Tom sank down in his chair and surreptitiously pulled out his second security measure – whisky – to be had only in moments of extreme need. If his master had only just stuck to Shakespeare… No one minded about him – and in retrospect, even the menagerie of animals didn't seem so bad…

"A bit of heckling. 'Votes for Women' is what I think they shouted. That kind of thing."

"Yes, I see." Maud also settled herself down in the chair opposite him, calmer now and Tom could almost see the whirring of her mind, certainly a pulse was beating uncommonly quickly. "And they were a nuisance?"

"I'll say! The women in the audience didn't like them at all! There was a lot of screaming – the curtain came down and the play was interrupted while bobbies were called off The Strand. My master wasn't best pleased."

Maud tilted her head. "No, I bet he wasn't." And then she smiled suddenly and rose to her feet. "Well, must be going," she said. "Can't be sitting here all day. I suppose *they–*"

"Haven't seen them today your ladyship," lied Tom for he'd had enough of the Trees for one day.

"No," Maud adjusted her hat. "I think he's losing interest."

Tom darted once more under his desk.

"What on earth are you doing?" said Maud as he came up, swirling the glorious hot, strong alcohol round his mouth and wishing more fervently than at any other time in his life that he were in the pub.

And then as if saved from the firing squad his office door burst open and Duchess swept in perspiring heavily in the warm weather, violets wilting all over her body.

"Do you know what he's done?" her usual languid voice staccato fast.

Tom took his time swallowing as Maud turned her attention to her friend.

"Who darling?" said Maud calmly, never for a moment anticipating what was to follow.

"Why, the Prime Minister!"

Tom sat back down very very quietly.

"Oh God!" Maud clutched at her throat.

"Margot is on her way."

"Just one more," Danes muttered under his breath, pouring himself a half measure.

"What!"

"It's never Viola?"

Duchess's voice was deep. She nodded. "*And* Felicity!"

"What the *two* of them?" Tom thought it had gone past the point for polite pleasantries and plonked his bottle on the table in full view. He fished out several more glasses – none of them particularly clean. Duchess took the bottle from him before he had a chance to pour, drinking from it directly.

"Don't be disgusting!"

"Bring another chair!"

"We can't put her here!"

"Well she can't be anywhere else!"

"She's the PM's wife for goodness sake."

"I don't care if she's the Kaiser's."

"Talking of which–" said Tom under his breath.

"Don't you *dare*!" snapped Maud under hers and hiding the letter behind her back.

"Look it's not so bad. Margot is offering to go with them."

Tom spluttered.

"This is too much," said Maud collapsing in a chair for the umpteenth time.

Duchess took another swig. "Excellent whisky ," she said, congratulating him as though he were somehow responsible for its distillery and hiccupped. "Actually I think it's rather decent of the old girl. You know how jealous she gets."

"Gad! I should think so! Well isn't she seething? I would be. I *am*."

Duchess paused, Tom's bottle half way to the mouth.

"No, no she's not. She's pretty good in a crisis – provided she's got the right wardrobe!"

"Darling!"

"I know."

"We must send for Herbert!" Maud swayed dramatically as though she might faint.

"Well only if you think so – I thought we might send Danes-"

Tom froze as both women turned to him.

"Danes?" echoed Maud.

"Send me where?" said Tom, not liking the sound of any of it. "Send me where?"

"Well, France to begin with. You'll have to go after Felicity and I don't think her Ladyship should travel. Tree can't leave the theatre on account of the Kaiser's visit tomorrow and–"

Maud reached for the whisky bottle and she too now took a swig directly.

"You said Felicity? What about Viola? Surely Scotland Yard?"

"Oh I don't think we want to be involving them, do we?"

"But surely Margot?"

"And the press?" interjected Tom then wished he hadn't.

"The Press! Oh!" said Maud letting out an Ophelia-type cry of anguish. "Oh my God, it will all come out now! That wretched stalker! May and her children! And he of the dulcet tones… Oh! Everything!"

"With all due respect," said Duchess calmly. "I'm not sure any of that is very newsworthy. I mean you could not compare it to the Duke and that … *actress*."

Both Tom and Maud looked at her dumbfounded.

"I mean is it?" They looked at each other, then at the same time lurched for the bottle but Tom was too fast and too determined.

"Mine," he said firmly.

"She's right of course," Maud said taking the bottle from Tom and passing it to Violet.

"I know it."

They passed the bottle conspiratorially, not bothering with glasses. Maud's cheeks were flushed. Duchess let out a belch. There was an astonished silence then a giggle (Tom's) which produced more giggles until Tom froze suddenly, the bottle mid air. Maud and Violet turned to follow his gaze. Waller stood within the doorframe, a quizzical expression on his face.

"Well... hello..." he said his voice even more fruity and honey-like than usual. "I say, have I missed a party?"

"What are you doing here?" Maud's tone was not exactly friendly.

Tom shot her a nervous look, feeling sparks ignite between them.

"Well that's a charming greeting," he said, eyes flashing.

"Have a drink," said Violet quickly passing him the whisky bottle. There wasn't much left and he looked at it and their flushed faces disparagingly.

"I'm not sure there's enough is there?"

"Why are you here?" Maud repeated, her tone no less steely.

Waller ran a hand through his long locks and leant nonchalantly against the wall closest to the door.

"Well I've just seen the PM," he said, weighing his words for maximum impact.

"What? Where?" Duchess said turning to the window.

"Well here," said Waller gleefully. "He's just arrived with … "

"Viola?" snapped Maud.

"Well no darling..." said Waller smoothly. "With Margot. They must be back together – I'm assuming. She was wearing the most exquisite Worth travelling coat, sort of blush colour with–"

"Not Lucille?" interrupted Duchess.

"Nope. Worth. Definitely Worth. You can always tell. I mean Lucille might have a French name–"

"Oh for goodness sake!" barked Maud, "it means they're back!"

Waller looked pleased at the sudden attention.

"Or that they haven't left."

Maud turned to Duchess who made a face.

"They've gone," she said quietly. "There's no doubt about that."

"No," said Waller, "I have just seen them. At the corner of the Carlton. They should be here any moment."

"Not *Squiffie* and Margo," said Maud irritably. "Viola and Felicity."

Waller looked perplexed. "Well..." he began patiently. "I spoke to them. Their motor had stopped. Margot was admiring the lilacs and I was on foot. As we were headed in the same direction, I said I would catch up with them here."

"So Margot is with them?"

"I thought I said, although quite frankly I'm beginning to doubt what I saw."

"Oh, she'll be so angry!"

Waller shook his head. "I don't understand. Why on earth my dear Maud, should she be angry?"

"You would be too," said Maud glumly.

"I'm really not keeping up with this."

Maud touched her head that had begun to throb.

"Squiffie has run off with Viola *and* Fit," she announced dramatically.

"What!" squeaked Duchess.

"Good Man!" said Waller reaching for the bottle.

"No! No!" said Duchess, "You've got it all wrong! That's not what I mean at all."

"Oh this is killing!" said Waller. "I don't know what it is about you two," he said looking meaningfully at Maud and Violet, "but whenever you come together something happens."

Maud gave him a withering look. Not even the sight of him leaning in what he knew was a most alluring pose could alter her humour. Tom swallowed nervously. None of it bode well. Violet had begun unclipping the violets from her waist in a decidedly Ophelia-like way and as if on cue was absentmindedly shredding them.

"That's not true," countered Maud shrilly, moving towards him. Instinctively, Waller took a step back and bumped into a low table. Hoping to right it before the vase of flowers that teetered there precariously fell to the floor, he reached blindly for support. There was a collective gasp and then a groan. Waller's hands hovered in the air before alighting on the newly sculptured shoulders of Lord Haddon. Tom could only watch in horror as the child's head dutifully and silently splintered as it had in life, into a thousand pieces .

"Oh!" screamed Duchess as Tom leapt forward and Margot Asquith, wife of the Prime Minister took it upon herself to arrive at that very moment, a vision of silks and jewels and glowing skin.

"*Hate* to be the bearer of bad news darlings," she said just as Maud, who sprang forward to help Duchess retrieve what was left of her child, fell headlong against Waller, her train catching in the shiny new buttons of his shoe spat. Margot assessed the chaotic scene dispassionately. "As I say... bad news, but don't shoot the messenger... Suffragettes have padlocked themselves to the seats in the royal box –chains and locks 'fraid this time. The PM is in rather a panic. And darling," she added almost as an afterthought, "I think you'll need some pliers, can't think how else you're going to separate the two."

Eighteen

*Here we will sit, and let the sounds of music Creep in our ears;
soft stillness and the night Becomes the touches of sweet harmony*

The Merchant of Venice

August 1914

Maud appraised herself in the little looking-glass that hung above the washbasin in her bedroom at Arche de la Tour. 'Appraise' was as close as she dared get to her face these days. The scars around her jawline had eventually healed although there had been times when Maud wondered if it ever would. For a year after the accident pus still oozed from the wound and she was still picking glass from her hands and arm even now. Her face was as good as it was ever going to be, at least as long as she didn't over exert it or speak in too animated a fashion. Then it became lopsided. Even she could see that. The change in her was more fundamental. She felt old, the skin on her neck every bit as scrawny as nanny's. Her hair, which in her thirties had begun to thin at an alarming rate, was past recovery and her once slight figure had thickened. Men no longer looked at her with that flicker of appreciation she had grown used to arousing. She realized with a shock just how much she missed that. She was no longer offered the parts of ravishing young women and was growing very tired indeed of playing Mistress Quickly or similar, virtually disguised in widow's weeds with her double chin embalmed in a wimple. Her very spirit was weary and her once famous wit deserted her more often than not. She mourned for the girl she once was, for that carefree person who loved her life. There was a time when she had looked to the future with joy, imagining it to be exactly like the present, just more of it.

In the years since the accident, Henry Manners had been as good as his word, and thanks to him Maud had embarked on a

French course which enabled her now to translate the plays that were the staple of British theatre. Between that and her new house, an exquisite folly in a sleepy little Normandy town, she saw herself moving towards an uneventful old age. Not the case with Herbert, Maud couldn't help thinking. She knew he had recently fathered yet another child and at the time of Viola's marriage – a ridiculously grand affair with over three thousand people lining the streets to catch a glimpse of the bride – May had been about to deliver another. Hey ho, thought Maud – that was the difference wasn't it between men and women and now she felt spent, dried up, no longer a figure of desire to set company aflame. The idea of Waller sprang somewhere at the back of her mind, but the wavering image dimmed almost as quickly. She was certain she no longer evoked the same sensation in him.

Maud caught a reflection of the bed in the glass. Bed these days was overwhelmingly inviting for all the wrong reasons. She thought of lying down on the cool sheets and pressing her face in the lavender-scented linen… In the closed house by the canal, the heat this August was unbearable. It was four o'clock, too late to begin anything useful and too early to make preparations to go out for the evening. Besides, go where? The house was in disarray as it was – full of house guests who came and went at all hours of the day and night. Felicity was one of them and together with Diana Manners, Duchess's daughter, they seemed intent on drawing as much attention to themselves as possible. Viola had heard from the Premier himself, who in turn informed Maud, that a recent sojourn in Venice had been less than conventional. It was enough to make Maud's thin hair stand on end. Felicity and Diana had accompanied the Asquiths and Lord Vernon, but as far as Maud could make out there had been precious little sight of Margot. How could there have been when the tabloids featured an extraordinary picture of the Premier dressed in a Doge's hat being pushed in a Bath chair round St. Mark's by no other than Felicity and Diana? Maud shuddered at the familiarity of the thing. And just where had Margot been? Or Lord Vernon? How was it that her daughter had been wandering the canals of Venice in the early hours of the morning, and in pyjamas without a chaperone? Besides which she had been given to understand that Asquith's fondness, if you wanted to call it that, was for *Viola.* Had he lost interest? Was he now after Felicity? Thankfully Duchess didn't appear to be anything like as au courant as she normally was, nor to have noticed that in one picture in particular, Diana was wearing the Belfield tiara – and nothing else. Maud should probably be grateful that at least Felicity was wearing pyjamas…

And thinking of pyjamas...Maud looked longingly at her bed. She really did feel so very tired...

Oblivion in any shape was tempting, while the peace she normally felt when she came back to this sleepy village after a frantic week in London with her charity work and new theatre engagement was shattered by the disarray in which she'd found her house. The 'new' or newish play of an even older one, *Diplomacy,* in which she was now appearing was hardly anything to get excited about. 18 years ago, Maud played the beautiful heroine taking over (in a highly publicized move) from the great Sarah Bernhardt herself. How she had sighed and pouted and been, she had to confess it, piqued to the core with that uncomfortable and unattractive jealousy that all but spoilt the pleasure of playing opposite Herbert, and learning the part in the first place. Dear Herman Merivale, sensing her malaise, had encouraged Maud by saying that if she were to lose a leg, sleep in a coffin and keep a tiger as a pet then she too would attain the fame and mystique that followed La Bernhardt even to the London stage. Tree of course had been antagonized by her success, but not even he could deny the reviews. The atmosphere in the theatre was said 'to fast approach the heat of a Turkish bath.' There had been a renewed flirtation with Waller, a new hat and a gown in the softest silk chiffon that even now Maud could feel caress her skin. If truth be told she preferred its touch to Waller's, who was beginning to irritate more than excite. The same could not, alas, be said of her present Lady Henry Fairfax – a role specially created for her but by comparison, even Mistress Quickly looked winsome. In the press release and accompanying photograph, she scarcely recognized the old woman who sat in a shapeless *voluminous* robe and granny's bonnet, beside the erect and distinguished Gerald du Maurier.

Ah... Gerald du Maurier... now there was something to creep under the sheets with! Maud startled her own reflection with wide eyes. There it was, thank goodness, the return of desire – faint, remote but unmistakable. Could she? (He had a wife.) Would she? Would *he*? She could always write to him, send him a slender obscure book of... well letters, poetry – she could always ask dear Bernard to recommend something. Better still she might request they meet – Gerald and herself that is – she was well aware just what Charlotte Shaw thought of *her* friendship with Shaw, and how on more than one occasion he'd been forced to write cryptic postcards in response to her rather longer and more prosaic correspondence. She could always request Gerald meet her when they were next in town, discuss how she might better improve her role. And then she sighed. Improve a role that was already, even she could see, stretched to the limit? The pretext of meeting was thin. Besides, she wasn't interested in making an old woman seem fascinating. She was tired of playacting. She wanted to be herself, to be fascinating, in her own right, all over again. She wanted to be, if not a girl again at least a desired woman. She wanted that more than anything, just one more time. Maud sank onto her dressing table stool and leant forward to push open the shuttered window, fanning her chest as she did so. Below, the street was quiet as villagers locked themselves indoors for their afternoon siestas. The smells at least were comfortingly familiar and happily helped by the fermenting cheese and milk she had found on her doorstep on her return. Indoors was hardly any tidier, with every bed slept in too. What lazy thoughts idled in her youngest daughter's brain, Maud could only speculate. But Maud wasn't sure she had the energy to either chase her or enhance her marriage prospects by improving her social skills. Felicity would do as she pleased. She always had.

A fly buzzed overhead as Maud sank into the cool sheets. She would only close her eyes for a few minutes. There was so much to do in the house but it was so very hot... Sweat trickled between her breasts and down the back of her neck. She mopped her neck with the sheet. Here at least she became weightless, ageless. In sleep at least, she could be the young woman of her mind. Where had the years gone? Everything had been so fast and furious when her girls were small, her life (and energy) revolving around the theatre and tracking Herbert's affairs. And their arguments? Maud marvelled at the devotion given to them. So many had had to do with other women – May mostly. Maud saw now that she too had been to blame. She hadn't known how to coax Tree, how to placate him, not at least in the way he needed to be, not as a mistress might. She had been so hell-bent on being an equal with her superior education, more specifically her superior *elocution*. She had been proud, too proud. She had only ever wanted to be Tree's leading lady. Tree had never wanted that from her. She had failed to understand that all he wanted was a stay-at-home wife. It had been the greatest shock when early on in their relationship she realized that Tree thought little of her talent – that is if he ever thought of anyone's but his own.

And Tree the man...? Maud pressed her face into the now wrinkled linen sheets, feeling the pang that was never quite absent from any recollection to do with him. He was complex and cruel, arrogant and dismissive but he also represented home to her. He was her youth, her history. He was the touch that made her flesh tingle, his was the weird intonation that insisted they do 'anything;' he was the Svengali to her Trilby, barefoot or otherwise, and Henry VIII to her doomed Nan Bullen. Perhaps he had simply been too worldly and she too Victorian in her prim desire to bring a veneer of respectability to the their profession. He was cavalier in his approach to everything. He genuinely did not care for what people thought of him, while she cared too much. And who was the happier? Yet no costume or grease-paint, no footlight or flat stage could disguise the torrent of passion that raged through them both. In the end however, it was a passion that was crippling and a passion that almost destroyed them. It was not that they saw through a glass darkly, but that they were seen darkly. Never far away lurked zealous critics and jealous opponents eager to see them fall... Maud stretched limbs that at this moment were too warm to be languid, bones too brittle to be seductive. She was glad to be alone in her bed. Glad... *Ah... but it was not always thus...* whispered a voice from the furthest corners of her mind... not always... and from the depths of half sleep, that silent secret sea, Maud remembered the ten days when she had had Tree all to herself. Ten days that stood as an isolated, lonely island in the global disaster of their marriage.

They had set sail together from Southampton, with Duchess there for the send-off (along with press and although she did not know it then, May no doubt hidden somewhere in the crowd). Duchess had lent Maud most of her jewels for the trip and she hovered nervously, anxiously eyeing the small portmanteau she had also lent Maud in which to carry them. Maud herself was swathed in a shocking amount of red velvet – yards and yards of the stuff and the whole thing edged in sable fur. Maud liked fur and she adored velvet, but together the costume was all too reminiscent of her Absent-Minded Beggar get-up. Not surprisingly, Duchess heartily approved.

"You want to stand out in the crowd ducky," she said. "There should be no mistake that you – are – his- wife." Even for Duchess, the words were more drawn out than usual. Maud dismissed as foolish the tiny hand of dread that crept over her.

"Stand out is all that's required. And you can do it very effectively." Duchess caressed the diamonds in Maud's hat and the enormous emerald broach pinning fresh flowers to her bosom. "In silent ways... in how you conduct yourself. *Tu comprends*? This trip is about *him*," Duchess swivelled her shoulders to face her, "not about scoring points, Maudie... there is no room on this trip for pride..."

Had Maud even heard her? She was elated as she all but pushed Duchess out of the First Class cabin – a sumptuous compartment smothered in flowers from almost every actor, agent, playwright and well-wisher they had ever met. She had no lady's maid but Max Beerbohm, Herbert's brother, had been hired as their press secretary for the duration of the American tour and he and she spent almost as much time trying on her (or rather Duchess's) jewels and hats as they did composing interesting columns for the American papers. Which was just as well, as there had been an uncomfortable hiatus when he was reported as telling the *Chicago Post* that he 'liked their American language – it was so crisp and different.' But that was later. For now there was a palpable and contagious excitement – the immense comfort in the knowledge that for eight days Maud and Herbert were together on this ship sailing towards their destiny, their hope.

At last the shouts and cries and sounds of the band died away as the steamer was hauled through the icy waters and reluctantly coaxed on its way. The ship lurched by the steep English cliffs before gathering momentum and disappearing along the horizon. Maud had stood before the small window, her profile reflected in the dying sun, which together with the firelight made her beautiful, made her glitter in her jewels, made her seductive in her red velvet and made her once again, someone else.

The door closed silently and Tree, also someone else, stepped into the cabin. There was no sparkle in him other than desire and she was stripped of the mocking wit that so often prematurely, deflated his mood. Wordlessly, he ripped open his shirt, tiny sapphire studs pinging soundlessly on to the rug. His own hair fell forward boyishly, rakishly. She caught her breath suddenly shy, uncertain, but as she half turned away from him, pinned by the extreme train of her skirt, he moved quickly. And this time she abandoned any pretence of coyness. Her arms dropped by her side, and with the velvet of her dress stretched taut against her body and back a soundless voice whispered she was more Lady Jane Grey than Cleopatra. His hands were on the outline of her jaw, in her hair, discarding Duchess's diamond clips as if they were mere tortoiseshell. His hands traced her throat, the pulse that spoke loudest, hovered at the buttons of her bodice.

"Tell me...anything..." he said hoarsely. She shook her head imperceptibly but he held her face in one hand, forcing her to look at him. "What do you see?"

She tried to look away, a retort at the ready, but the intensity of his touch made her respond unflinchingly. He raised her chin.

"What do you see?" he repeated.

Never mind about seeing, she thought wryly, it was a wonder he couldn't *hear* the pounding of her blood. What *did* she see? A German first, she would have joked, and yet a man desperately in love with all things English and more than desperate to be accepted by them. Above all she saw a creature, otherworldly and magnetic.

"I see... an actor... a great actor..."

Tree touched her lips, his eyes boring into hers.

"No," he said above a whisper. "You see a man – no more. Please..." he added so faintly that she had to strain to hear him. "Just love me as such ..."

And for the duration of that crossing to America every night had been the same and every day bedecked in what appeared to be Duchess's entire jewellery collection, Maud had indeed sparkled. She was abandoned, she was amusing and attentive, she devoted herself to Tree – after all there wasn't much else to do. They discussed plays to be produced, parts they would share, they made adjustments to the forthcoming tour. Tree would concentrate on the Shakespeare he had promised. Maud was to play Mrs. Murgatroyd and the Princess and Tree that cat-footed, loose-lipped (just how loose lipped she was soon to discover) Demetrius in the *Red Lamp*. She was young, she was beautiful and she was in love, and what was more she had Tree all to herself – no cast, no wardrobe or make-up acolytes, no one but the ship, the vast ocean cocooning them in tranquil expectancy, taking them onwards and with increasing speed, to a brave new world. And because there was no one else, Tree turned to her first thing in the morning and last thing at night and during the nigh,t reaching for her repeatedly – his muse, his lover. And Maud, feeling truly desired for the first time in her life responded and blossomed, her mind and body languid and smooth. And all the while of course there was Max, who flattered them both, amused them both and later, to their astonishment, became engaged to the actress Constance Collier.

But even as the ship docked, pulling exhausted into the New York harbour, the giddy, electrifying pace of this new world overtook them. Maud wrote to Duchess of the speed, the frantic energy where no one sat for very long. She wrote of the bustle and noise, the immense buildings, the women's shiny hair ironed so straight and dry it was a wonder they had any left at all. Duchess's jewels too seemed to pale into insignificance alongside the larger, brighter more spectacular hues of these American women's, and Maud's velvet, original gowns seemed somehow home-spun in comparison here. Only her feet seemed to attract attention from one fashion journal, being it reported 'small, straight and well-shaped.' And then, suddenly Tree was no longer there – always out, always interviewing, always auditioning. And back to his old ways. She had come back early one afternoon, having found the perfect blue for a silk handerkchief he was to wear in his pocket as the defeated husband in *A Bunch of Violet* ... And there he was... or more specifically there *they* were... he not defeated at all in his velvet smoking jacket, his tie undone and the woman – girl really... Duchess had had the temerity to quote Wilde to her when she telegrammed her – something along the lines of temptation and resistance. Not.

Maud punched the memory. Time and time again she swore she would never be surprised – taken by surprise – that she would not allow herself to be hurt, and yet time and time again Herbert so much as breathed in her direction and she crumpled. But in the end, she turned the trip to her advantage and her heartache was allowed its outlet. The Americans were gagging for interviews – interviews she had up until now refused, but now she (and they) couldn't get enough. A volley of telegrams (mostly from Duchess ensued), '*What* are you doing??? ' Had been the latest. There'd been scarcely any need to add 'stop,' thought Maud as she tossed these (and her newly ironed hair) into the grate and responded by synchronizing articles in London's *Tatler* – ('Mrs. Tree in Sloane Street' ran its title, and featured a winsome picture of Maud leaning against an artfully decorated mantelpiece) with the volumes appearing daily across America. 'Her personality is her charm!' screamed the *New York Rochester*. It would seem that every aspect of Maud's life was to be examined. She was quizzed on how to bring up children, on her clothes, her homes, her fast stroller – the fact that she sometimes wore a divided skirt, her acting (was it true she would rather act than eat?) and her scholarly background. Pages were devoted to this alone and the fact that before she took up acting, she was set on a Cambridge degree – 'Mrs. Beerbohm Tree is said to read ancient Greek as well as she reads English,' said the *Nashville American,* while the *Pioneer Press* called her a 'versatile mathematician, lady and scholar.'

And here Maud grimly went to town. If there was something that she knew irked Tree even more than her professional success, it was her formal education, her magnificent speaking voice and above all her Englishness. The *Louisville Post* had already said of Tree that he was 'tall and thin and talks with a lisp', while the *Chicago Tribune* said he was 'a peculiar actor who does not move the emotions...' Maud was elated. "Isn't it enough yah?" asked Max wearily feigning a German accent, but Maud was nowhere near finished. She gave solo recitals, reeling off huge chunks of Tennyson to a slightly bewildered American audience. (They were only marginally more enthusiastic about Longfellow). She had tea with Rudyard Kipling and was gracious about Mrs. Kendal who was also on tour in America. Despite her philanthropic attempts to publicize the plight of the so-called Elephant Man, Madge Kendal was even more competitive than Maud. But by now Maud had the ear of most of the male journalists, and the female ones tailed her doggedly.

"Apparently you Beerbohm Trees are the fashion in New York," said Max languidly to her one evening as they sat by a roaring fire in her suite, having already consumed one bottle of champagne and awaiting another to be sent up. Piles of newspapers lay discarded at their feet. Max was supposed to write a press release every evening but so far had failed to compose anything that met with his own punctilious satisfaction. "That is according to a certain Jennifer Hawter."

"Howler," corrected Maud. "Dear Jennirfer." Maud hiccupped gently. "I mean Jennifer." Max raised an eyebrow.

"Good heavens my dear..."

"Don't!" warned Maud.

Max lit a cheroot and crossed one elegant leg over the other. His head was thrown back against a cushion and he raised the paper in front of him, the cigarette hanging in the air precariously. "Altogether the BTs are very delightful English people and society has smiled affably on them. Mr. and Mrs. Kendal are for the moment eclipsed, and Mrs. Beerbohm Tree is very beautiful, which Mrs. Kendal is not!'

"Oooh!" purred Maud, "I like that!"

"Thought you would pet," replied Max pleasantly. "Now can we stop?"

Maud rose carefully, far from sure of her footing even on the plush carpet. She tilted her head in front of a small mirror.

"I don't know what you mean."

There was only the very smallest set-back that Maud adroitly managed again to turn to her advantage. While the American press skirted the subject of women's emancipation in coy and elegant captions, mostly thanks to Miss Howler ('Mrs. BT is up in Latin and Greek but it is not thought that she discusses the shortcomings of the members of her husband's company in either of these languages'), the English were more direct. The *Daily Sketch* went as far as to question her commitment to the Woman's Cause. Maud responded by holding a press conference directly and when pressed on being famously anti-suffrage, on having dismissed the new woman as a 'paper and ink individual', Maud merely smiled her most enchanting (and enigmatic) smile. Nodding, she agreed that she had indeed said she (the new woman that is) was a woman of 'no importance but that was long before Oscar Wilde...' Here Maud tempered the nervous titters in reminding the gathered journalists that she had long been an advocate of Ibsen in the 'Hedda is all of us' vein. Why, hadn't her own brother-in-law, Max Beerbohm, stated that the 'new woman sprang fully formed from Ibsen's brain?' (Why did you have to drag me into this? groaned Max later). It wasn't that Maud was against the franchise but that quite simply she herself had all the autonomy she could possibly hope for. Didn't she? Besides, she countered, the modern woman wasn't looking for contentment; it's the enlargement of her sphere she was after, wasn't she?

The press was in raptures. Maud BT was feminine, exquisitely learned and wise. As she said herself she could keep house, tend babies *and* earn her keep. She was in short the perfect woman. There followed a flurry of frantic articles. Miss Howler excelled herself with one entitled 'Garnered in Feminine Fields', devoting its weekend spread to the New Woman debate and citing Maud as its most credible candidate. Furious, Tree attempted to revert the attention back to his Shakespeare tour, from where he believed it should never have deviated. At an off-the-record meeting, he gave his side to a gathering of eminent playwrights and theatre practitioners. 'The public has set its face against sexuality,' he said in the manner of Falstaff, and in the manner of Hamlet he intoned, 'and it is revolting against stage realist treatment of modern life – the most inane of theatrical ventures.' Women's groups were not impressed, not least by his stab at humour. They weren't interested in the politics of the theatre. Tree tried again. 'Women,' he said, 'can have no more appropriate place in which to work than to engage in works of mercy.' Howls of protest to which he added limply, 'but women on the stage are very independent and their independence has not deprived them of any womanly charm. '

"We're even!" proclaimed Maud triumphantly as she and Max were out driving early one morning in Central Park. He balanced several magazines and newspapers on his lap and under their rug, on to which Maud kept diving like a hawk above its prey. He shot her an uneasy look as she emerged flushed, wondering what the occasional passer-by must think they were really up to.

"What?" she asked perturbed by silence.

He shook his head. "Nothing."

"It's never 'nothing' with you." For a moment she was distracted and Max seized this window to tell her how redundant he felt. "Besides, there are zillions of eager foot-soldiers – bright, brright– " he stammered. Like Herbert, Max was unable to pronounce his 'rs', or at least not very clearly – "*eager* young people who stay up all night writing copy before I've even set pen to paper."

It was a cold, sunny day but wrapped in fur, Maud felt elated. The horse shook its head so that the whole carriage vibrated. Max shivered in the icy conditions, none too fond of horses or rides in parks at the best of times.

"Well you could..." began Maud unsympathetically.

"I could what?"

Maud appraised him coolly. "Get up early."

"Oooh darling. That's mean. What do you think I'm doing now?"

The tip of Maud's soft kid glove hovered above his cheek, "I know, I know," she said soothingly as if he were a child.

"Walk on!" said their driver.

Max snorted, settling back into the carriage.

"I thought he was talking to me!" whispered Max.

Maud giggled and because she had stung him, Max tapped the paper on her lap.

"I wouldn't say 'even' exactly," he added peevishly. "You didn't read the end."

Maud grabbed the paper, her heart skipping a beat. "Actors and actresses hold a unique position," she read aloud turning to him. "And?"

Max made a face. "And..." he said, "Read on."

Maud made a moue, mimicking him and then was quiet. "Oh... I see."

Max leant over her shoulder to finish for her aloud. "Ours is probably the one profession in which there is equality between the sexes. The moral is obvious."

Maud snuggled into her fur cloak, tucking her hands into her enormous muff. "Eh bien," she said but her mind was racing. No, it was far from over.

Tree travelled to Harvard, choosing as his subject the philosophy of Shakespeare. Maud travelled to Vassar and talked about... infidelity. The women there wanted to know everything and Maud gave them everything they wanted. "Herbert's affairs start with a compliment and end with a confinement," she told one reporter. "But I didn't say that. Of course one doesn't believe everything one reads in the press," she added sweetly. Referring to his Washington production of *Hamlet* in which she had played Ophelia, insisting on fresh (and very costly) flowers at every performance she added tartly, "For some reason there seem to be a great many children in it."

A little underwhelmed by this marital banter and thoroughly bored by now, Max summoned up what creative energy remained in him to sum up their visit in a quip never intended for publication: "England might have its Beerbohm Trees but America has its Beer bums…" Tree attributed this leak to Maud, which she shrugged off with ill-disguised glea. Not that it mattered over much– by the time they arrived at the White House for a reception in their honour and in the presence of President Cleveland himself, they were hardly speaking. More importantly, it was only as they docked in Southampton that Maud realized her nausea had nothing to do with the sea journey.

* * *

Maud's brow was furrowed in sleep. Felicity. Joy. Oh joyful yet joyless one. How was it that she could have been so wanted, so conceived in love and yet born with such resentment of and for the world? How was it that everything said or done was misconstrued, misinterpreted? Taken badly and not in the intended spirit? How was it that with all the loving Maud felt for her daughter so little was reciprocated, and in its place and endless well of hurt and resentment of unintended damage? How was it that in the end she should come between them, irrevocably and always? And with the final mooring in New York it was as if the giddy world of light and colour, security, beauty and desire came suddenly to a stop. The world, Maud's world, collided with the hoards waiting to elbow her out of the way. As Maud looked for Tree in the crowd and saw him surrounded by laughing starlets, and recognized that familiar flush of excitement – he always said he could stand any amount of flattery so long as it was 'fulsome enough'– she watched with heart-stabbing sadness as he grew gradually smaller while her own shadow expanded on the gangplank and was consumed finally by the waiting crowds.

And it had never been the same again. Not ever. Not despite Duchess's best attempts at sending Parma violets, giant cyclamen plants and forests of lilies-of-the-valley to her luxurious Louis XVI cabin (which Maud was now occupying alone) in a last-ditch effort to create a romantic setting for their return. Despite the attention, the lavish parties, the fêting by Americans and Maud's tremendous reception, the tour was a financial fiasco. Perhaps she had been a tiny bit provocative, but the theatre criticism was for Herbert and his macabre intonation. Still it was not all bad news and there were two very positive outcomes from the tour. Maud had long wondered at Tom Danes's complete efficacy in the PR department, and she hired on their return the already notable Elisabeth Marbury to be Tree's agent. Tree, no less industrious, had purchased while in Philadelphia a little known play called *Trilby,* written by George du Maurier. The rest as they say, is history and no thanks to Max who Herbert had initially sent to report on the play. No longer making any attempt to combat boredom, Max only yawned and told Herbert *Trilby* could only fail in London. The success of that play (and another affair, another reconciliation and another child) enabled Tree to build his theatre, His Majesty's. The Trees become Sir Herbert and Lady Tree, friends to the aristocracy and politicians alike, counting the greatest personages of the age.

Maud woke with a start as sweat now soaked the sheets and the afternoon sun baked the little room. There was banging on the door and commotion in the streets which was rather more than the usual coming to of the little village after its daily nap. She could hear, if she wasn't much mistaken, a pistol shot.

"C'est la guerre!" There was a shrill cry somewhere between elation and terror. And the cry was taken up through the town. Doors and windows slammed, she could hear the neighbouring window creaked open, the jemmy scratching on the stone wall. Children cried and dogs barked and there was the clip clop of horses on the bridge. More banging and this time insistent, Maud woke, her head throbbed, her mouth was dry. She took a swig of the warm water by her bed and went to the window, dabbing at her neck with her handkerchief. The town doctor stood in shirtsleeves.

"*Rapidement!*" He called up to her, "Ah my dear Lady... you must leave."

"Leave?"

"It's war. It has finally happened."

"*War!*" breathed Maud. "You are leaving...? *Now*? But I can't – it's the afternoon. I can't go anywhere!" She gestured to the house. "The rooms need doing... besides I have..." her voice trailed as she realized how ridiculous she must sound.

"*C'est exacte*," said the doctor, reading her thoughts. "No more letters. You must send telegrams but these will take 6 or 8 hours. I myself will leave from Rouen directly and am happy to escort you."

Maud blinked, still dazed from her nap, her thoughts that had taken her so far into the past and from the import of the news. Herbert, she thought. A hand of fear clutched at her heart, coupled with the dizzy excitement she could feel palpably rising from the village. Tree had closed his production of *Pygmalion* prematurely – the very production for which Shaw had kicked off rehearsals by writing to its Eliza (Mrs. Patrick Campbell), "I am sending a letter to Tree which will pull him together if it does not kill him," – and set off in July with the faithful Tom on his annual pilgrimage to Marienbad. Nothing would deter him in spite of the fact that even a month ago, the whole population of France was agitated by the possibility of war with Germany. And so it had proved.

She nodded to the doctor.

"Do you know what has been happening in ... Germany? I mean what might happen to British people there?"

The doctor shook his head. "I think everyone is going home... while they can."

"But he drove– was driven!"

"Who drove, Madame?"

"My... husband."

"Ah chère Madame..." sighed the doctor. "Who can say? Is he alone?"

She shook her head. "He left with Tom."

"Son fils?"

"Son ..." Maud couldn't think of the French for manager. "Son ... *homme*," she finished helplessly. The doctor looked at her with sympathy, making an expansive gesture.

"Et voilà..."

For a moment they looked at each other, momentarily anchored by the small anxieties that made them human, that tethered them to the familiar routine of the mundane. But then the bustle and slamming of doors, the sound of horses clacking through the narrow cobble-stone streets and the sudden peeling of church bells reminded them there was nothing ordinary about this moment – that far from it these were extraordinary times, that nothing would ever be the same again – that in time they would remember every second, every minute and every hour on the day that war was declared.

"*Je descends*," she said, tucking her blouse into her skirt, "*Je descends immediatement!*"

Nineteen

The hawthorn hedge puts forth its buds
And my heart puts forth its pain

Rupert Brooke

She had been 'exalté' as she wrote to Duchess – she tried to use French words wherever possible so that Henry would be assured the money on her language course had been wisely spent – there was in this instance no other word for it. And it was strange to admit such a sentiment now after so much suffering, so many dead, but it was true. The whole world was gripped with an excitement not remotely comparable to the Boer fever she witnessed in 1899. No longer were her French neighbours able to joke that the English had Suffragettes and the Irish question in the shape of Home Rule, to keep them out of the war. This felt like the end of the world, and exactly as her youngest daughter Iris would later describe as days coming 'up as beggars in the street with empty hands, as summer without sun…' in a remarkable poem that would bring her fame at just 16 years of age. It was just as well that she had something to show for a war that was not spent in the charity work and nursing that claimed the imagination of most young women. They all despaired of the notoriously lazy Iris. Even Dora Carington wrote to her, "*You ought to be inspired by this war…Astound the world by a ballad. But then you are so lazy…*" Iris would astound the world all right, and her mother for that matter, by marrying a man she'd known less than two weeks. But that was still to come…

Propelled by the urgent need to get home, Maud left her little house on the Pont, following the doctor as far as Rouen as he suggested before travelling alone to Dover. At Victoria she had almost sobbed with relief to see Herbert, recognizable almost exclusively by the brilliance of his slightly (why had she never noticed before?) deranged blue eyes. He is an old man, she thought as he shuffled towards her, the long-suffering Tom a boy no longer– in tow. At last... But if she thought age might have slowed his libido, Maud was soon disabused of this hope. For out of the shadows, just as her heart stopped in her mouth with longing, with exaggerated patriotic emotion, stepped another.

Tree shrugged. "I'm going to telegram him of course," said Tree, ignoring Maud's wide-eyed shock (and Tom's uneasy jigging) and no doubt hoping to field this with a conundrum of his own.

"Telegram who?" said Maud stiffly setting down her bag to catch her breath that now came in ragged and unattractive gasps, more out of shock than exertion. Tom, after a brief tussle over Maud's bag managed to peel it from her. Tree took a step back, pushing a lock of white hair from his eyes as though reeling in disbelief that she could not know. Out of the corner of *her* eye Maud examined the creature who accompanied them. She had bright red hair – masses of the stuff, rather like the wig Maud herself had worn as the great villain Lydia Gwilt, and a very white face with overly inquisitive eyes.

Maud stole a second, more intense glance. Good God, maybe she really *was* Lydia Gwilt.

"Muriel, Ma'am," bobbed the girl. "Muriel Ridley."

Maud ignored her, walking on. There was only room for one May Pinney in her life. "Send whom a telegram?" she insisted.

"Why the Kaiser Maudie, the Kaiser, who else? I'll send him a telegram – I'll say that he gave me a third-rate order for acting in Berlin and I've left him a fourth-rate motor car for acting just as badly!"

Maud stopped for a moment, reflecting on that trip. "And jewels. The Kaiser gave Viola jewels."

Tree also stopped, as if searching for an inventory in the roof of Victoria Station.

"So he did."

"So you left your car?"

"Had to. In Cologne there was complete panic on the streets and children threw stones at us. We moved at a snail's pace and then we ran out of petrol, so there was anything to do. We caught the last train out of the city. Then at the Belgian frontier we had to walk several miles in terrible heat, as clearly German trains could not leave German territory."

"Good heavens!"

"Oh… it wasn't so bad. Quite liberating actually. All about us hoards of refugees were so terribly (tewibly) anxious about their belongs while Tom here and I couldn't wait to give them away!"

"I wouldn't quite put it that way," said Tom, shifting Maud's case to the other arm.

"Anyway, a train to Ostend in which we were crammed like sardines – I must have lost *pounds* in the process – a boat to Dover and here we are."

Maud looked at him. "And here we are," she repeated. And nothing, but nothing will ever change. Not even a war can stop the man from being unfaithful – but unfaithful to whom precisely? Presumably the Pinney woman didn't know about this latest dalliance? Maud felt strangely protective of May as she swept past the Ridley girl.

"Kindly ask Tom to drop me at Arlington Street. I must see Duchess."

"Oh…" said Tree clearly disappointed. "I thought we might have a light supper."

Maud raised an eyebrow. "What, the three of us?"

* * *

Some time later, Maud found Duchess in a high state of anxiety, her familiar, languid drawl replaced by an unfamiliar and rapid staccato that stabbed the air with irregular accents.

Servants hurtled through the Arlington Street house, which having been closed for the summer was now being 'opened' at speed. Dustsheets were flung from unidentifiable shapes to reveal the beautiful pieces of furniture beneath and trunks and valises were scattered throughout. Violet sat enthroned amidst the chaos wearing most of her jewels including, Maud was relieved to see, what was unmistakably the Belfield tiara.

"You do know Diana wants to nurse," said Duchess accusingly.

Maud didn't know. There was so much to take in – everything seemed to be happening at such a furious pace there was hardly time to catch her breath. She had barely got over the shock of the Ridley woman, although given there was a war on a husband's infidelity seemed relatively unimportant.

"She's adamant she wants to go to the front, wherever that is. No, a hospital isn't good enough for my lady. She wants to be in the thick of things." Violet toyed with the enormous pearls that hung like a bell-pull round her throat. "Your Felicity will be next, mark my words."

Maud wanted to say that Felicity going anywhere further than Cavendish Square was unlikely given her devotion to parties and Oxford men but surmised Duchess was in no mood to be contradicted. Duchess flipped her pearls so that they now hung down her back, almost garrotting her in the process.

"You just know they'll be ravished," Duchess added darkly.

"What? By wounded soldiers?" Maud could barely contain her astonishment.

"You know what men are like!" rounded Duchess fiercely. Maud did indeed know. But then she also knew what women were like.

"It's early days," said Maud calmly. "Herbie says apart from children throwing stones and a bit of hissing, there really wasn't any bad feeling in Germany."

Duchess's eyes were round as saucers. "Don't be ridiculous! They hate us! Anyway I've thought of something that might hold her ladyship back. I shall turn this house into a hospital – for a very few mind – very *select* – officers, – people I know, naturally."

"How... very ... generous..." said Maud at last exhausted, sinking onto a chair.

"Well I thought so. And of course there's no question of John fighting. I won't hear of it. He'll stay at Belfield. I've lost one son, I shan't lose another."

What man proposes... thought Maud closing her eyes thankful for the dim light and even the fatigue that made her limbs languid but her mind dart. And just as suddenly the yearning to be with her friend in a house she had loved dissipated and Maud wanted only to be on the familiar home turf of the theatre, her theatre, His Majesty's.

"I must go," she said with great effort.

"What!" exclaimed Duchess sharply "You've only just got here!"

"Yes and now I must go."

Maud gathered up her carpet bag and dirty coat and waving to Violet she all but ran from the room and down the stairs in a manner not attempted since she was a girl. And once in the street, in the great enveloping darkness exaggerated by the fear of expectancy that hung over the city, Maud took long full breaths. She thought of Herbert with Muriel Ridley and Tom, no longer the ingénue they had befriended all those years ago but a man now – a man who would be called up, perhaps never to return. And she thought of her daughters safe at home – Viola married to an asthmatic art critic – well he wouldn't be going anywhere, Felicity engaged to a major in the army and little Iris so indolent it was unlikely any Hunn would rouse *her*. And although Maud set off in the direction of her funny wedge house in All Souls Place (what an appropriate name given the slaughter that was to come) she found her footsteps dragging, gradually slowing till they came to a complete standstill. As tired as she was, she had suddenly no desire to return to an empty house either. Instead, she turned in the direction of Charing Cross. Apart from the headlines plastered on makeshift news stands – *Britain at War* – there was no other indication that such a momentous event had occurred. There was an eerie quiet that muffled Maud's careful steps. By the time she had turned into Trafalgar Square however, the scene was reminiscent of New Year's Eve and the place was packed with men throwing their hats into the air and yelping with excitement. Maud steeled herself as she pushed through the crowds in the direction of the Wyndham Theatre where for that briefest of time, she had directed three plays, appearing in two of them. The billboards continued to advertise *Diplomacy* although she had left it a month before for the summer's recess. What would happen now, she wondered, to theatres everywhere now that war had been declared?

Her own theatre was in darkness and in her desperation to reach it she hadn't thought how she might get in. The doors were securely bolted and the overhead street lamps were dimmed. Maud walked around the whole block, realizing that whatever vague plan she may have had to lounge in the foyer and think or loll on the stage steps had been quickly replaced with the practicality of gaining entry. In the end she threw her bag on the ground in front of the large poplar tree that stood almost directly in front of the entrance, and settled uncomfortably on its small grass mound. It was a warm, clear night, and she undid her coat.

"Of all the people..." said an unmistakable voice. Maud closed her eyes. No! she thought. No, of all the people in the world, absolutely no! She could not recall ever being more undignified, sitting with her legs akimbo as she was at this moment, travel-stained and unkempt – a torn stocking poking from dusty skirts and what little hair she had blown in every direction.

"Ditto..." she responded lamely.

A glow from the man's cigarette traced circles in the air, hovered above her as he muttered something along the lines of, "No, don't get up."

Maud muttered something inaudible. She had no intention of rising – to what? Sink down again?

"I shan't ask you what you're doing here," he said smoothly and she heard the sharp intake of tobacco. He made a vague apology for smoking but she waved aside his objection. "I expect it's the same as me."

"I've just returned from France, just a few hours ago," she said dully and suddenly the impact of the day's travel, the events, what was to come, hit her full on and she felt pathetic tears well in her eyes.

"Oh ... my dear..." Gerald du Maurier was compassion itself. He threw away his cigarette – she heard and saw him twist his heel on its stub then crouch on the pavement beside her. He brushed her shoulder. "You must be exhausted."

She nodded not trusting herself to speak, hoping he wouldn't come any closer.

"It's madness. The world has gone mad," he said quietly. "I brought Daphne earlier," he said referring to his seven-year old daughter. "I wanted her to see, to remember how it was... but when I dropped her with her mother... I couldn't stay." He paused and then added simply, "No other place would do..."

He gestured to the building that loomed above them with its graceful balconies and porthole windows and intricate carvings along the top. The billboards still carried both their names from the season's last run. "At least tonight..."

"I felt the same way." Maud's tone was unintentionally cool. He shot her a glance.

"And all this must change... So many have already been called up."

Maud started. "Of course. As I suppose they must. But so soon?"

"So soon."

Maud leaned against the rough bark of the tree, feeling leaves rustle behind her head.

"Herbert is going to re-open His Majesty's – he hopes the other theatres will follow suit. I don't know what to think. Herbert's argument is that by opening, those unable to enlist will continue to be employed and he intends the profits to go to the war charities."

"How... noble."

Maud failed to note the irony in his voice. "He says more than ever we need to keep the public's spirits up – rousing dramas – patriotic dramas... he proposes *Drake* then *Henry IV*..." Her voice dwindled. She could feel, if not see his look boring into her and her tone was thin, unsteady.

"Good old *Henry*."

"You *are* being sarcastic. I knew it."

"Not at all."

"You don't like him."

"Do *you*?"

"What, Henry?"

"You know who I mean."

There was an uneasy silence for which Gerald made no apology.

"He's my husband? What an odd question."

"Is it?"

Gerald too leant against the tree, bringing his head level with hers. He felt in his pockets for his cigarettes and then for matches, lighting one and holding it for as long as possible before waving it out. In the brief glow his long face was illuminated with its high cheekbones and dark blue eyes.

The face of a scholar thought Maud, or a priest.

"I've never asked you. It was always obvious to me – to everyone who's ever met you I should imagine. But I should have asked you. Even all those years ago when we first acted together... and given that there will no doubt be so very many more..."

"Ask me what?" Maud's voice was very thin, she thought it might crack at any moment.

Gerald drew long on his cigarette and then languidly blew out smoke.

"If you were happy."

Maud exhaled as if she were the one smoking. "Happy?" she echoed. What an extraordinary thing to ask now. She was about to comment, flippantly, but something in his eyes made her pause. "Happy enough." The words fell into the air – hollow once spoken. Her heart was beating too quickly. Suddenly, she was aware too of his long leg stretched beside hers and the width of shoulders she longed to lean against.

"No, it's not true," she whispered. "I'm not – happy. Not at all."

He threw away his cigarette. "Neither am I."

* * *

The months of that first year of war passed with dread and uncertainty. Every morning Maud heard soldiers of the Flying Corps as they passed her window. By the afternoon, ever increasing legions of men in Khaki swung through the streets, whistling as they sang their way to their deaths. Maud was busier than she had ever been in her entire working life. Following Tree's example of putting on additional matinée performances, other theatres soon did the same, with the result that Maud often rushed from an afternoon's play to an evening's poetry recital. She was now in her element, and as Lady Tree her name gave additional lustre and patronage to philanthropic benefits. And now too women's organizations, regardless of political affiliation, joined forces to raise funds for the war effort. She was inundated with requests for solo performances, which enjoyed renewed popularity in being inexpensive to perform and easily transported. Not only did Maud give her support to the Woman's Theatre appearing in one-character plays, but galvanized into action, she organized a Stage Skating Party, various garden parties and concerts. She was always on the look-out for new talent and ways of raising money, and spent days auditioning pianists to accompany her. Both Trees collaborated in a series of high profile benefit performances and events and their names as a result were plastered on bill-boards throughout the country.

"Surely you're not jealous?" she asked Gerald one evening in between performances, as she pushed a damp rag round her face in an attempt to remove the afternoon's grease-paint and replace it with the evening's.

Gerald appraised her reflection in her dressing-room mirror.

"Your hair is looking lovely," he said.

"Sweet of you to say it's mine," she breathed, and not for the first time before wrapping it up in her character's matronly bonnet.

Diplomacy continued to run because, due to a coincidental premonition of war, the adaptation of the play *Dora* had already transformed the two male lead characters from French officials to English diplomats working at the embassy in Paris. Having left the play in the summer, Maud now returned, not because of Gerald but because Shaw had written to her pleading with her not to abandon the Wyndham in its hour of need. In his last letter he had written to her complaining of an afternoon 'of lacerating anguish' partly contemplating Gladys Cooper's 'overpowering experiments in rhetoric' and 'partly in wishing I had never been born!'

"Why should I be jealous?" he persisted.

Maud paused, her hand poised at her face. There was a tone to his voice she had never heard before – a harshness entirely devoid of affection. Dressed for his part as Boris Ipanoff, he perched on the edge of her dressing-table and played with his cigarette case. His hands were immaculate, long elegant fingers toying with long elegant cigarettes. *Woodbines* for her soldiers – Maud made a mental note to pick some more up for them on her way to the hospital in the morning.

"The press records our every move – the social pages-"

"And you're happy to be associated with *him* after all the misery he has inflicted on you?" Gerald interrupted, lighting a cigarette and blowing smoke out of the side of his mouth.

Maud leant back in her chair throwing down her face-cloth.

"For the war effort, absolutely." Her eyes were fierce but she added more gently,

"He is after all, still my husband."

"You don't let me forget it."

There was a pause. "That was unfair," she said calmly.

"Yes it was. I'm sorry."

"I was only going to say," said Maud reasonably, "that so much of our activity is recorded in the press to… well to *encourager les autres*." Maud pursed her lips. She *did* like the phrase and Belfield was always so complimentary at the way she pronounced it. She dabbed at her cheeks. "An urgent pace has been falsely created, I agree, but it keeps everyone focused and busy. This continuous, frantic fund-raising can only ensure patriotism can't it? And it's so important when the numbers of casualties are so horrendous."

Gerald sighed, "Oh darling… I know you're right. There are rumblings even so… a number of articles questioning the opening at all of theatre in war-time – I mean the theatres in France and Belgium remain rigidly closed. There's more – actors are being called 'shirkers.'

"Well that's rich!" said Maud, annoyed. "To think what we go through! At least we're doing something – those of us who are too old to go to the front. Oh I didn't mean-"

"Quite," said Gerald tightly.

"How *dare* people make trouble!" protested Maud in her most commanding Lady Bracknell voice. "Entertainment is needed now, more than ever! Keep the spirits up – a rest from too much reality. Besides, it's what our boys want when they're on leave – they *need* distraction. It's what we *do*…"

Gerald put a finger on her lips, silencing her. "Yes," he said. "Distracting is exactly what we do."

Twenty

Dost thou know, my son, with how little wisdom the world is governed?

Count Oxtenstierna

His Majesty's Theatre, January 1915

Tom Danes, holed up in his make-shift office (his former room having been made over to the American Elisabeth Marbury) and amidst the mounds of scripts, coffee cups, gas lights and props, held a magnifying glass to his right eye to examine, in detail, the facsimile of Asquith's signature. The exquisite programme announcing the collaboration of theatres across the continent, also sported the signatures of the French, Russian, Japanese, Belgian and Serbian delegates in what Tree termed 'a Constantinople of the Stage.' Tom's job was to check for smudges, typing errors and the like when what he really wanted was a slap-up meal from The Pig – a nice little eatery down from the Carlton. But there was no rest to be had these days what with the war effort and the effort spent in keeping everyone busy and employed. If Lady Tree wasn't planning insanely short sketches to be taken around camps and hospitals she was knitting socks, somewhat unsuccessfully in Tom's opinion. The *Daily Mail* encouraged the knitting of garments to specifics printed every Monday morning and Maud was in a complete frenzy until he had secured several copies for herself, Violet and the girls. But now everything had escalated to a completely new level. The Trees had embarked on their most ambitious project to date– that of bringing together artists from all over Europe to fight with 'the banner of peace' as Herbert announced to the press, 'the Kaiser's hymn of hate.'

Danes wasn't sure he understood any of it– whenever Tree pontificated these days, there seemed to be an abundance of tears, not least from Tree himself but what was very clear to Danes, was that the war was bringing about changes he could scarcely cope with. Kitchener's bony finger seemed to reach out to Tom and Tom alone, seeking him out even through the tiny shafts of window light. His poster appeared everywhere from hoardings and trams to the base of Nelson's Column, which was completely covered with them. Tom was not displeased that just this once something else competed with advertisements for Tree's *Drake*. But the biggest change to affect Tom's life directly was the re-appearance of Lady Tree in any significant way as she firmly reinstated herself at the centre of His Majesty's. Things as a result were (uncomfortably) like old times. Except that a new restlessness gripped her and like a fever drew everyone with her in its wake. She was not at all satisfied with her role in the recent *The School for Scandal*, although tickets sold out in 2 ½ hours and over £2,000 was raised for the war effort. Tom had greatly enjoyed the excitement surrounding the event, which according to one evening paper had rarely been seen, even with Melba and Caruso. In coverage reminiscent of pre-war days, the press (for which Danes had been asked to retain every available copy) reported Lady Tree's 'flaming gown full of golden stripes.' But Maud continued to be stung, she confessed to Danes, by the criticism that actors might be 'shirkers.' She said 'she couldn't get it out of her mind.

"Look at this!" she said, hurling the *Sporting Life* at him, in which the titles 'Actors Fighting' and 'Theatrical Distress' barely caught his eye. "And this!" Danes glanced at a piece called 'Patriotism and the Playhouse' before Maud whisked it from him.

Maud was not to be calmed as she was propelled by a frenzy of activity the like of which Tom hoped never to see again. Quite frankly he didn't believe he'd *survive* such a schedule again, because whatever schemes the Trees were involved in, naturally involved Tom too. He was forever packing up for one or other – neither seemed to have reliable dressers or butlers – Tom therefore was forever taking Gladstone bags to the station and then collecting them when they were not required. Then there was the correspondence (delivery of) and the telegramming (mostly to Walmer). Lady Tree had begun to consider the Prime Minister's wartime retreat a second home. Why only the other night she had swanned in from such a stay with the Prime

Minister, all wistful and dramatic. "You see Tom," she had said, "it was at dinner that the naval battle came to him – such a heavenly moment." She had been referring to the battle of Jutland, so he'd taken an interest, but booking passages to France while they could still cross was more his line. Maud insisted on checking up on her 'little house on the bridge', as she called it. A total nonsense in Tom's opinion as he knew very well the only thing she was checking on was Mr. du Maurier...

And now this... this *Entente Matinee* as the press dubbed it – this Anglo-French theatrical extravaganza with the participation of no less than a stellar cast. If Maud was going to make a point she was going to make it royally, as she informed him several times a day. In collaboration with French and Belgian theatres, it would be the first time in forty-four years that the Comédie Française visited England, and the first theatrical performance the King and Queen would attend since the outbreak of war. Danes had never heard of the Comédie Francaise but he knew what a command performance looked like. He still twitched at the memory of the Suffragette padlocked to the stalls while another clambered on to the stage across the footlights and all this in the presence of the King! He felt positively dizzy when he thought of the ensuing rumpus for Tree's production of *The Silver King*. But now it would seem the Trees had the support of nearly everyone. The *Daily Telegraph* compared their benefit to the 'famous banquet held at the Crystal Palace some 44 years ago' while *The Era* said it 'recalled the famous company's' visit during the Franco-Prussian war of 1871 when 'la grande Sarah' was a 'very young woman.' Maud had sniffed at this. "Not so *very* young."

"You see, " said Maud triumphantly the evening before, "No mention of shirkers now! So many actors could never have left the French stage in *peace-time*. But now...!"

"But now...?" echoed Tom blankly.

"But now..." Maud's eyes searched the wall behind his head as if for some nameless audience. Her hands were clasped together at her breast and tears hung from suspiciously long lashes. She was definitely in her Mabel Vane mode and would have cried, 'Just call me sister!' if the situation had remotely merited it.

"We've scored a first!"

Not yet you haven't, thought Tom as he sorted the programmes into neat piles, carefully pressing tissue paper between them so as not to damage the delicate print. Max Beerbohm's one-act skit would appear last, coming directly after a Sarah Bernhardt monologue, but before Elgar who was playing music specially composed for the event. This grandest of all occasions was to be attended by no less than two Portuguese Queens – the dowager Amalia who had attended Duchess's dinner party at Belfield all those years ago and Victoria Augusta, consort of King Manuel, the Prime Minister Asquith, the Duc d'Orleans, the ambassadors of Japan, France, Russia and representatives of Serbia and Belgium. And of course King George V and Queen Mary. It would seem that Maud had cast her net far and wide (although not so far thought Tom, in the case of du Maurier) in soliciting the help of those old hands Mrs. Madge Kendal and Violet Vanbrugh. The effort of co-ordinating travel arrangements (on both sides of the channel) in order to bring these great stars together, however, was nothing in comparison to the headache of keeping some of them apart. Kitchener might want recruits, thought Tom but he should try dealing with this lot. Miss V, as she insisted on being called (one-time mistress to the Duke of Belfield and mother of his love-child) had to be kept well apart from his Duchess. For obvious reasons, Mrs. Keppel could not be invited on the same night as the Queen, while Maud was to be polite to Lady (Emerald) Cunard but not overly welcoming to her lover, Sir Thomas Beecham. Despite the fact that the latter leased His Majesty's for opera seasons and had done as much as he could to promote Viola Tree's singing career in Italy, (as they all knew this had come to a very sticky end in Genoa, but this was not his fault) he refused to offer his hand in marriage to the influential (and affluent) Emerald.

As if this were not enough, the troublesome Miss Truman took it upon herself to make a re-appearance. It had never occurred to him before to judge his master but the more Tom Danes saw of life, or more specifically life at His Majesty's, the more nagging little doubts began to worm their way through him. For example, was it quite right he wondered, that Tree should have spent the last Christmas of peacetime partly at Belfield Castle with Maud and those children and then the later part of the day in London with May and hers? And then complain incessantly to Tom that he was tired! While Tree kept parts of his life separate, Tom could happily pretend they didn't exist at all. During the long years of Maud's absence from His Majesty's altogether, Tom and his master had rubbed along very well. But only a few weeks before, Tom had been summoned to Sloane Street where Herbert was dining with chums. He had forgotten something or other – Tom couldn't for the life of him remember what excuse he gave to get him there, although he sure as hell remembered what came after. Whatever it was, was enough to warrant Tom's journey late at night from the other side of London to a little known restaurant. It was a clear, cold night – one of the coldest on record and from the street and under its dim light, Tom could see them clearly illuminated against the velvet curtains, framed in the window. But it wasn't his master that caught his attention – animated and bombastic as never before. No, it was the sight of that woman – that dreadful hair like an explosion at the front of her head, talking for all the world as if they *knew* each other, to May Pinney.

And by 'know', Tom realized then with a shock, it was as in *intimately*, which of course they did. It was only Tom who was out of the loop. They had never stopped knowing each other – that much was obvious. Somehow the evil one had wheedled her way into May's life too – though how she had managed it given how secretive Tree generally was about Putney, he could only guess. Not that secretive clearly. Tom had looked from one face to the other – not May's (he'd always felt sorry for the woman – for her *and* for Maud), but at Miss Truman's and Herbert's. His master's was flattered beyond anything he had ever witnessed, while hers was adoring and frankly insane. Tom stumbled on the icy pavement, unwilling to enter and deciding for the first time in his life on a course of action independent of Herbert's. But it was too late. Tree, on the lookout for his 'boy' spied him almost immediately, beckoning to the headwaiter, who clicked his fingers for the maître'd. Not even the offer of oysters, vast and waxy and unseasonal nestling amid ice and white linen, to which Tree encouraged Tom 'to help himself,' tempted him to stay. His stomach did a cod-flipping-on-the deck turn at the sight of the other woman seated with Tree. Lady Townsend was Tree's new 'reader', but Tom knew that she spent very little time actually reading. She might think she was in love with Tree, thought Tom, but it wouldn't last long. May looked subdued, but then well she might. Only earlier that day she had escorted her children to an afternoon performance, entering through one door while Maud swept through another. But now, the sly one with the flaming, coloured hair had also spotted him.

"Oh it's Tom, Tom," said Olivia Truman, lips pursed at the ready but her eyes were steely. She wore far too much jewellery –

the kind that didn't much sparkle and her bodice, covered in a fishing net of pearls, looked too much like chain-mail to be attractive.

Tom ignored her.

"Ah Tom..." Tree was somehow beside him, a heavy hand on Tom's shoulder. He'd never noticed before how heavy it could be. Tree's hair had fallen on to his forehead – it was white now and his flushed cheeks heavily veined. Tom realized with a further start that his master was no longer young. Tom was unused to seeing him as plain Tree, without the whiskers and carmine paints playing at someone greater than himself. Tom felt seduced by the warmth of the room, the plush velvet chairs, mirrors and cut glass. Apart from the sight of the odd man in uniform it was hard to believe there was a war on. Indeed there was every indication that the Christmas truce might hold – or so they were told and for once, even the initiatives of the Suffragists with their open Christmas letter to the Women of Austria and Germany, seemed to be achieving unimaginable results. There was a lustre to the room that had everything to do with hope, and a buzz of conversation that lulled him into a general feeling of apathy.

"I need you to do anything."

Tom no longer thought to correct him.

"Now?" Or induce him to reply humbly.

"Well yes, now." Tree's good humour was replaced by a moment's irritation.

Tom was silent. His eyes were drawn to the reflections of beautiful women – that is the ones not at Tree's table.

"I hope to travel to America," said Tree. He pushed his hair from his eyes beneath bushy eyebrows.

"Yes?"

"Yes, Tom. America. Soon – just as soon as I can get a passage – Iris is going to accompany me. You know how Maud frets that she is so terribly idle, especially given that even Felicity is a nurse 'auxiliare.'" He waved his hand with a flourish.

Iris? The Tree's youngest daughter? Duchess's daughter's pal? The one he was forever calling the press about? Not to give them stories but to beg them from printing them. The daughter who Tom knew did not live at home, but shared a flat with the aforesaid Duchess's daughter unbeknownst to either set of parents? Tom sat up, figuratively speaking that is, at the news. He wondered if Maud knew. Was he, Tom, to go too? Was he to stay? His thoughts whirled. Did that mean the odious Miss Marbury was to accompany him? Did that mean, most important of all, that he'd get his old room back?

"We're filming," said Tree. "I've been offered a contract in Hollywood to film *Macbeth*, with me..." Tree lowered his eyes modestly. "Well... with me as Macbeth. Constance Collier will play L-Lady Macbeth." Tree's voice dwindled and if he hoped to engage Tom's interest, he failed. Tom did not see the urgency of getting him out of his warm bed for ... well for this, the kind of news he would either read about or hear about in the morning. There was an uncomfortable silence.

"You are not happy?" Except that it came out 'heppy.'

"Not overly, no." Tom shoved his hands in his trouser pockets. "With all due respect Sir-" said Tom and was interrupted by Olivia's unpleasant cackle emitted through over-bitten lips. "With all due respect," he repeated, "what has this to do with me?"

Tree took a swift swig of champagne. Tom half turned towards the door, but reluctantly. If he wasn't careful, the warmth and delicious smells would draw him back into the room and into one of the over-stuffed seats from which he would find it impossible to leave. A hand on his arm stayed him.

"I need you to tell Iris about Claude," said Tree.

"Come again."

"I need," said Tree calmly, "I need you to tell Iris, nicely of course, that she has a brother. Claude." He jerked his head in May's direction. "Claude. You know. My – *our*" he corrected himself, "son Claude."

Tom had heard strange things in his time with Tree, had been privy to secrets he'd rather not have had the privilege of sharing, and witnessed things he thought best left on the stage. This was the most bizarre yet.

"Look," he said, pulling Tom out of earshot. "If a passage comes up we must be prepared to leave quickly. Everything's quiet at the moment but you know how that can all change. I've also been asked to be King's Messenger and I can do both, but I want Iris to know – don't want her hearing gossip on the ship, read anything in the papers. Claude is acting in New York... in fact he's planning on joining the company for my Shakespeare Season which we'll set up when– "

"*Planning,* or is going to as a matter of fact?"

Tree hesitated. "Going to." He mumbled.

"I'm sorry?" Tom's eyes bored into his master's until Tree looked away.

"He's going to!" bellowed Tree.

"All right, all right," said Tom. "Keep your wig on." He reached for Tree's drink, taking a swig of his now warm champagne. "So why me?" asked Tom calmly. "Why not *her*?" he spilled champagne in the direction of May's table. "Or her, for that matter." He shot Olivia a fierce look. "Or better still you and her ladyship. Together."

"Very funny."

"Well I'm not laughing," said Tom insolently, tossing back the glass's dregs. "But what I want to know guv, is why now? After all this time?"

"We –" Tree swept his arms as he had done so effectively as the spy Demitri in some play Tom couldn't recall – expansively, generously. Tom was unmoved. "We...concluded that you would be the best one."

"We?"

"May and I..."

"That's not what I meant, but never mind. Why then tonight? This very minute? When I was all tucked up nice and warm in me bed."

Tree smiled sweetly. "Oh I'm sorry for that, Tom. No time like the present? I s'pose…" he shrugged. "After so much champagne, "it seemed like the only time."

Tom blinked rapidly, incredulous at the man's selfishness and other attributes, of which the latter was the most redeemable. He pushed Tree's glass into his soft belly, against the crisp whiteness of his evening shirt with its tiny diamond studs. His eyes encompassed the room one last time, an unattainable haze of jewels and fur and thick brocades.

"And only Iris? I mean what about Viola and Felicity? Or do they already know?"

Tree frowned. "You have a point, yes."

"Well," said Tom, "Let me save you the trouble of that conundrum." He was quite proud that the word had popped into his head as if from nowhere. He'd wanted to use it for a long time. "The answer is…" his eyes narrowed so that he could see Tree lean almost imperceptibly closer and remain impassive himself. "Nein."

Tree reacted as if he'd been struck and it was his turn to blink furiously.

"*Nein*!" he echoed uncomprehending. "*Nein*?"

Tom paused, uncharacteristically lost in thought and went to the window where yet another of Kitchener's posters seemed to leap back at him, this time wrapped round the lamp-post opposite. There was more coverage of the forthcoming Entente with the *New Witness* stating that 'it was fine to think that we allies are joining hands in the field of art as well as in the field of battle.' He wasn't sure he could be bothered to keep any more cuttings or rush out to buy any more papers. The idea that he might actually stop working for either Tree was novel and exhilarating. It had never occurred to him before. He thought of the years of a life devoted to Herbert and his theatre and wondered what it had all been about. Had any of it really counted? If he left would he even be missed? The turning point was not the war – great decisions turned, he knew, on much smaller things. No, it was being called out in the middle of the night, in the cold – how little must they think of him – how little must he think of himself, if at a moment's notice he would leave his bed and cross London to run a fool's errand? What did that say about his life? It was true that there was a time when he was more than grateful for the meals in his belly no matter how long he'd had to wait for them. He'd been in ecstasy with half a pork pie to keep him going of a night, and happily sit in front of Tree's door all night if need be. But that was then and Tom Danes was no longer that biddable boy. Besides, they fed you well in the army didn't they? He looked up. Kitchener's eyes stared straight at him – 'Wants YOU'. There was no messing with that.

   And suddenly, as Tom looked round his tiny office, he knew what he must do, what he should have done some months before. He opened the window to breathe in the icy air and never had he felt so happy, so invigorated, so much his own man.

Twenty-one

How should I your true love know from another one?

Hamlet

Hollywood 1916

"Put your hands up!"

"No, no, I mean yes, yes of course! But don't shoot for god's sake!"

Instinctively Tree jumped from the director's chair in which he'd been slumped. This place at the uttermost end of the great world was all about sudden loud bangs and over-bright Kinetoscope and never-ever-ending chirping cicadas! Oh to sleep, perchance to dream! But it was evident not even he was to be spared. Everyone wanted a piece of him, his dollar of flesh. No chance of nodding off now that he was wide-awake and back in the land of make-believe. No allowance to be made, he thought grumpily, for the fact that he'd had to travel six days by ocean liner to New York (a treacherous journey in itself with the constant threat of U-boats), and then another five days by train to California via Chicago and then as if that were not enough, another westbound train to Los Angeles. City of Angels my… the place was full of Indians! He scratched the itch under his grisly toupee and hunkered back down in his chair.

It seemed equally fantastical that while he was wearing a ridiculous get- up of elastic-sided boots and false whiskers, the civilized world was at war. He was doing his bit to make Americans aware of what they in Europe suffered and what was at stake. He had made rousing speeches along the way, in Baltimore, Philadelphia and El Paso, addressing 'Feeling and Head-strong Americans'. He had spoken so that he himself was moved to tears of the colours he wore close to his heart; red for the blood his country was shedding, blue for hope and white for the peace that he hoped to come... But *here*...! The ground shook and pounded as a gang of cowhands drove what appeared to be at first guess, some two thousand goats and hogs. Tree shook his head, thinking this scene like every other he witnessed in the so-called art of photoplay was certainly extraordinary in its vitality. It was also disturbing, disquieting and extreme. Where was the stately, unhindered tempo of the stage reading? Where the flexibility and dramatic potency? And now that he was thinking in this vein, where was the historical accuracy of their costumes?

The sight of his own shiny britches, so unlike any he'd ever worn to ride in in England, provoked a shudder. He and Maud had both been passionate about attention to detail in the sumptuous, glorious creations commissioned for His Majesty's. Why, Tree had even devoted a chapter of his latest book to props and the importance, nay symbolism of getting the right ones. Shylock's gabardine and Orlando's blood-stained napkin were examples he had used, he congratulated himself to great effect. He thought now with acute nostalgia of Henslowe's Diary, that inventory that survived the burning of the Globe, in which not only he but any theatre director might read that Shakespeare intended Maid Marian to wear a green gown, and Henry V a white and gold doublet. Entries for French Pierrot suits, velvet coats, jerkins in yellow leather, red copes, taffeta dresses, calico petticoats, frieze coats, Turkish janissaries, Roman senators and costumes for Spanish and Danish soldiers, lances, painted shields and imperial and papal crowns had haunted him all his working life. God's nightclothes spare me! Tree pleaded silently as a bevy of cowboys dressed in full regalia and waving and firing pistols surrounded his desert-side tent. He shuddered. The whole experience was ghastly. Hollywood was ghastly, the studio five miles from Los Angeles might as well have been five hundred miles for all the amusement it provided... and the *people*! Truly a land of many babies and few children. Tree's head drooped. He really was too weary to move. He had only come at the behest of the lovely Constance who wrote glowingly of the wonderful weather – eternal summer, is what she'd said of the place. It was dazzling, she said, with its orange-groves, purple hills and beautiful waveless Pacific. But even she admitted to a mind-numbing boredom, and the filming of *Macbeth* was merely an excuse to get him away from May Pinney, never mind Maud, to be held in Tree's arms once again.

Ah yes... that had been a beautiful thing, their... re-acquaintance... It was a very good thing that she had never married his brother Max. History really would have repeated itself if she had... No, she had married another fellow actor who was, at this moment waiting for Constance in New York, with neither realizing the distances involved... He might as well have been back in England for the little she saw of him. And poor *katze*, poor little Constance, actually grown a little stout latterly but always his divine leading lady... how lonely she was away from Kensington ... Tree sneezed. This confounded weather! So much for bright blue skies! Ever since he and daughter Iris (Maud's brilliant idea) had arrived in California it had done nothing but pour with rain, water even came through the roof of the bungalow Constance had found for them. Encouraging them only to bring light summer clothes, he and Iris shivered and coughed and slowly froze.

"Perfect weather for the blasted heath!" Tree muttered under his breath.

The problem was that not even Constance as Lady Macbeth or United Artists with all its resources could make the film (going by the takes) a success, and Tree himself, so used to the challenge of linguistics, insisted on declaiming every single word despite the colossal cost in film footage. Unbeknown to Tree, a dummy camera was set up so that he could deliver the full text, while a concealed second took the few shots actually required. The plan to film a 'Tree in Shakespeare' sequence was consequently shelved and Tree, his pride stung to the core retreated, plaid cloak and dagger, not to Collier's bed but to that of a pretty young actress young enough to be his, well... young enough. And in order to save face, and more to the point to prevent further litigious action on behalf of Hollywood producers, he agreed not entirely reluctantly, to appear as a Senator in a film called *Old Folks at Home.* But Tree was tired, tired of starting for mountains at midnight, dressing by 7 in the frigid morning already bewigged, to stride forth on horseback (thank heavens he could actually ride!) in order to catch a trickle of sunlight as it seeped through gaps of cloud along the horizon.

"Sir Tree?"

Tree looked up into the beguiling, if ageing green eyes of Constance Collier. She was elaborately made up with thin arched eyebrows and the new- look platinum shingled hair so popular with the Hollywood 'stars.' Her face swooped low, but not to kiss him as he half expected but to sink into an adjoining chair. Her scent lingered in the air and shimmering, rustling fabric flashed before him. He half turned to appraise the evening dress – cut low at the front and back with its long train and diamond clips. A huge fluffy white fox stole, tantalizingly cosy, was draped over one shoulder. Tree had half a mind to drape it over his.

"Oh, it's you."

"Yes it's me," said Constance brightly stretching a still slender leg out in front of her. The silk fabric clung to her thighs, caressing her ankles and in spite of himself and his new lover, Tree felt the stirrings of desire.

"You aren't ready?"

"Ready for what?"

"Oh really Sir Tree," said Constance, jigging her ankle so that the velvet slipper skimmed the floor and then fell off completely, revealing exquisitely painted toe nails.

"Don't call me that," Tree said irritated, following the trajectory of her foot.

"I know, but it's too funny the way they get it wrong."

"Ha, ha."

"It's the first night you know…"

Tree sat up, suddenly alert.

"*Macbeth*? Surely I'd have remembered that!"

"Er… no." Constance fiddled with the clasp on her diamond bracelet. Her nails were highly polished scarlet lacquer and Tree watched, transfixed by the contrast they made amidst the long strands of pearl-white fur.

"Sorry, not your *Macbeth* but Barrie's spoof -"

"Barrie's *what*?" it came out as a roar.

"Not spoof exactly," Constance corrected quickly. Though her voice was calm a pulse throbbed at her neck and tiny blue veins shone under the skin of her considerable poitrine. 'That's not quite right, but you know that Barrie has made his own little film – a sort of advertising short for... well for yours. I think, though I may be wrong, there's a plan to release the films together. "

"*Barrie*? Barrie of *Peter Pan* and the Lost Boys? He has done this?" Tree was incredulous.

Constance nodded, afraid to speak.

A chariot galloped past at full tilt, kicking up dust in their faces.

"That's it," he said. "Let's get out here. This godforsaken place *is* the never never."

Constance made to take him by the hand but now he resisted, sliding back in his chair.

"Oh do come, your chauffeur is waiting. Chaplin's hosting a huge party for the screening on Sunset. In fact he specifically asked that you be there. You know how he's dying to see you again."

"I can't think why." Tree thought of the peculiar bowler-hatted tramp he had met for an excruciatingly dull cocktail-only evening before and winced. Constance was so homesick for English things and people that when she first met Charlie Chaplin she had latched on to the diminutive actor and found him easy enough company. When they had all met for dinner afterwards, however, Chaplin had been so awestruck by Tree, an actor he had idolized as a boy, that he barely managed to string a sentence together. Tree whipped through the cities and countries he had visited on tour, none of which meant anything to Chaplin.

"You really ought to travel more," Tree breathed at last, almost weeping with boredom.

Tree gestured to his costume.

"I'm not really dressed for a party," he said.

Constance raised an eyebrow.

"You know full well that here of all places you'll be perfectly at home. Chaplin never changes out of his get-up as you've seen, and filming has just been wrapped up on *The Birth of a Nation*. They're sure to start casting for *Intolerance,* which is going to be a kind of sequel and just as epic-"

"Ah so we're going because of you..."

"No! Yes ... well not entirely. You'll have fun, you will, and you know how they all have heard of you and want to meet you and how they love an English actor with a properly trained English voice!"

Still Tree was silent.

"And you do look so very ..."

"Yes?"

"Manly. I was going to say so manly in your breeches."

"Britches," corrected Tree but he glanced nonetheless at his own shapely leg. Women and the odd valet had always complimented his calves.

"*Birth of a Nation*, you say."

She nodded, wetting her already scarlet lips enticingly and twisting towards him so that her breasts appeared full and pert. She *knew* that Maud bemoaned her own sagging ones and she, Constance, who had never born children...

"They say this new film beggars all description," she purred, allowing her hand to travel up his arm. "It has taken two years to prepare and has already cost £200,000. Or the equivalent of –not sure what that is in dollars."

"That much..." murmured Tree, thinking that his own *Chu Chin* had cost a mere £5,000, the most lavish production ever mounted at His Majesty's.

Constance nodded. "D.W. Griffith doesn't care a hoot about money, " she said admiringly. "Watching his work is like... well like having gold flung in your face."

"Maybe he'll fling it in *my* face," said Tree dryly. "Yes, that would be a thing." He considered the vast re-created plains in front of him – the life-size elephants made from plaster of Paris that stood sentinel to eiormous pink pillars through which a marching troupe of Roman soldiers now appeared. Perhaps he was mistaken after all. He felt calm once again in the wake of such logic. Where would he be without it? There was no doubt that the moving picture industry was beginning to exert tremendous influence in America. After all steam, electricity and telegraphy were all scoffed at to begin with... He was proud of his analogy. And the actor's role within this burgeoning new industry? He considered Constance's strong profile. As blank as the plains beyond it – and like them a canvass upon which a Western, an Egypt, a Babylonia might yet be played...Yes, the photoplay will give the actor the enfranchisement of posterity... But this was at once a spur and warning to ambition...

"I suppose even Shakespeare lamented that he could not give an audience in the wooden 'o' of the theatre, the pride and pomp that filled his imagination..."

"Yes, yes," agreed Constance eagerly. "After all it is only what you have ever tried to do..."

"Indeed." But then he just as suddenly became homesick for His Majesty's and more particularly for the Dome, where he lived like a prince and where he might entertain after a gala night. The King and Queen would have attended with a retinue of courtiers dressed in full court dress and decorations, the women in gorgeous dresses and tiaras. And waiting for him always was Danes... he frowned. Constance, catching hold of his mood caressed his cheek.

"You cannot have forgotten Cleopatra," she said softly, seductively.

Tree looked up under bushy, artificial brows. No he had not forgotten. How they had enjoyed each other! Constance in her role of Cleopatra to his Antony... He had directed her, robed her sublime body in silver, crowned her, adorned and adored her so that not only the rest of the company took note but all London raved about their performance while Maud had simply raged.

"Ah yes..."

"That scene, Cleopatra, carrying a sceptre and the symbol of the sacred calf in her hand while processing through the streets of Alexandria towards the market place."

Tree frowned. "I remember *Antony* in his magnificent tunic and hand-made sandals, standing on carpet covered marble steps, head in profile turned to the glittering sea beyond...."

There was a small silence between them.

"Why yes, my dear, I have certainly tried. Theatre was the business of illusion. But as on the stage so it is in real life; we become what we imagine ourselves to be...'

Constance leant in closer, her hand caressing Tree's forearm.

"And what is that Sir Tree? What has become of the man you imagined?"

Tree blinked. "Why he's right here, little katze," he whispered softly. "The real man is to be found in his work. Surely you have been with me long enough to know that? I wanted to – to do justice to the great writers, and of course for me the greatest has always been, will always be..."

Constance's lips parted, showing small white teeth, pretty but pike-like too, Tree couldn't help thinking.

"Yes?" she breathed.

"Why, Shakespeare of course. My first and foremost love is and always will be, Shakespeare.

"Oh!" Constance let her arm drop.

"And *he* will be there?"

"What, Mr. Shakespeare?"

"No, no not *Shakespeare*! This... D.W. Griffith of course."

"He will."

"So let's go." Tree stood up and reached down to pull Constance to her feet.

"Why on earth didn't you say so at the start?"

*   *   *

They travelled in Constance's chauffeur-driven car through ostrich farms that had not yet been built over, down the one main street of Hollywood to the farm only recently purchased by the Warner brothers. Attached to the single-story building was a make-shift hotel where newcomers such as Charlie Chaplin and Mary Pickford were currently in residence. For that one night it had been transformed, so that it resembled an extension of one of the many film sets rather than the small bungalow-type dwelling it was in reality. In front of the curved amphitheatre that loomed over the existing buildings, some twenty or so identical Ford T model cars were lined up, their shiny red exteriors glistening in the sudden sunlight. Like a cast of extras their accompanying chauffeurs waited patiently outside, taking large yellow dusters out from time to time to wipe away imaginary flecks of dust and the odd unseasonal drop of rain.

As Tree helped Constance alight, a fire-engine pulled up and they watched transfixed as Charlie Chaplin's face appeared behind the wheel, still wearing his fireman's gear.

"That is so typical of him!" hissed Constance. "Anything these days for attention. Which is strange given his history. You know what they say–"

"No, what?" Tree was curious in spite of himself.

"He spent eighteen months in a workhouse in Lambeth with his mother and brother before doing a clog-dance routine round the music halls, then five years – I tell you five *years* as Billy in Frohman's *Sherlock*. Not so much tour de force as forced to tour."

"Ha."

"Funny all right. Except that he has just signed a contract worth $670,000 a year plus a signing bonus of $150,000 plus plus-"

"What!"

Constance nodded. "Not bad for a bowler-hatted tramp."

"Not bad at all..." agreed Tree in wonder.

"And..."

"And?" Tree had on his mad Beethoven expression look. How did this woman know so much when she'd only just arrived in this frontier country?

"They say there's to be film – Barrie has been invited to direct a screen version of *Peter Pan*. Who do you think is to be cast in the title role?"

Tree shrugged. "Mary Pickford?"

Constance motioned over her shoulder, and now the peculiar little man with the lopsided walk, twirling an invisible cane leapt gingerly from the fire-engine and threw himself on Tree.

"No!" said Tree more in response to Constance's revelation than to the fact that the boy wonder was attempting to cuddle him. "There, there," said Tree disengaging Chaplin's arms and finding that still attached to one was a slight, pretty fair-haired girl dressed in a tin soldier's tunic.

"Oh hello again," she said from somewhere near Herbert's arm-pit.

Constance also turned to Herbert. "Again?"

"It is anything," he said, suddenly flustered.

"Clearly," she said, lip curling while Chaplin once again in the presence of his demi-god could only stutter, his eyes enormous, his moustache quivering.

"I'm Muuuriel," said the girl taking Constance's limp hand.

"And English, thank God!" said Constance, the relief of being with a fellow countrywoman pushing away any twinges of jealousy she might be feeling.

"Yes I'm an English *giairl*," said Muriel in an attempt at gentrifying a Cockney accent. "And new to teown."

Tree blanched. "Spare me," he said under his breath "the slings and arrows of outrageous refainement!" Which was not, he conceded to himself something he had noticed the other evening. But then there hadn't been much conversation between them.

"Barrie for one has created a small corner of höme," chirped in Chaplin, gesturing to the vast atrium they now entered and though while open to the elements, was strung with antler heads and swords and shields in the style of a baronial castle. Black musicians in red jackets chiselled at their instruments while pretty young girls in tutu-length skirts and tartan sashes lined the walls ready to serve guests with cocktails and glasses of champagne. More Champagne teetered from ice-stuffed buckets while all manner of seafood sprawled from ice carvings and elaborate displays. Gigantic bowls of exotic fruits hung precariously from stand-alone columns and everywhere was the buzz of chatter, cigarette smoke and aspiration.

"Et tu Brutus?" muttered Tree.

"Ain't like any home I know," said Constance taking a glass of champagne from a woman dressed in ginormous ostrich feathers and little else.

"I feel I'm lost on the set of some film whose name I can't remember," whispered Tree.

"What was that?" said Muriel brightly.

Tree contemplated the smooth upturned face, line-free and clear. It was so fresh and seemingly pure his heart gave a lurch, not of desire but envy of her youth. Now she leaned in to him, her breasts skimming his arm.

"You know, I never thought of you actually existing off stage," she said.

"No?"

Muriel shook her head so that her carefully curled ringlets bobbed and her blue eyes shone.

"I saw you as Svengali and as Fagin."

"Really?" Tree's turned, his attention suddenly focused.

Muriel nodded, her ribbons singing vigorously.

"Yes, and as Antony."

Tree's eyes misted. "Ah my Antony... I'm glad you saw that..."

Constance tossed her fox over her shoulder so that its tail tickled Herbert's cheek.

"And my Cleopatra?"

Both Muriel and Tree ignored her.

"You were a legend!" breathed Muriel.

Tree took the little hand that lingered on his sleeve.

"Oh how touching, little katze, how touching."

Constance took his other. "It's show time," she said firmly.

* * *

Tree sat in stony silence, every muscle tense, tears pricking through his veins while all around him the audience erupted in hysterical laughter. Even Muriel shook beside him. He could feel her limbs twitching against his and he recoiled in horror. There was no mistaking the spirit in which this... *travesty* was intended. The lush, velvet curtains – so much grander and taller than those at His Majesty's, had swung back to reveal the huge screen. Nothing modest or discreet about this country! Oh no, everything to the greatest excess. The enormous white letters giving prominence to the title:

Macbeth: The Real Thing At Last

Was it revenge? Tree couldn't bring himself to even glance at Barrie, seated as he was on his throne, so small and delicate his feet didn't reach the ground! Was it revenge because Tree had declined to produce *Peter Pan* at His Majesty's? Was that it? Truth to tell it was a decision Tree often regretted – his usual Medusa touch failing on that occasion. He'd never cared for the wee little Barrie – more Maud's friend than his – but there was no more nefarious reason than that – it was an oversight, nothing more. He had simply failed to see how the story of a motherless boy who refused to grow up could possibly be of interest. He had been proved wrong. *Mea Culpa*. His nose bled for that decision on a daily basis. But it couldn't be helped and there was nothing personal in his decision. Tree had been so busy with his Shakespeare Festival, with Maud and May and all his own boys that he had not read the play as thoroughly as he might have. All right, Tree was completely honest, he hadn't loved the fact that Gerald du Maurier was Barrie's greatest ever Captain Hook (*or* such a friend of Maud's). But this! *This* because of *that*?

Tree looked up, a dizzying roar in his ears. Words were flitting past the screen faster than he could read them. The castlist included four murderers, two murdered, one willing to be murdered, one afterwards murdered, one nearly murdered, one not worth murdering and so forth. He clenched his fists.

A new byline read: 'The elegant home of the Macbeths is no longer a happy one.'

"I'll say," said Muriel in a stage whisper. "Isn't it a scream?" Tree withdrew his arm. "'If Burnham Wood moves, it's a cinch, has a poetic ring don't it?'"

"No," managed Tree, "it don't, *doesn't!*"

He untied his cravat, suddenly having difficulty in breathing. He shut his eyes, hoping that when he reopened them he would find he had been dreaming, a horrible, terrible dream but a dream all the same. Instead he stared at the image of an artificially aged letter skewered by an arrow that read, 'Dear Macbeth, the King has gotten old and silly, slay him. Yours sincerely, Lady M.'

"But look, it ends heppily," said Muriel happily, "it says so. The Macbeths repent and all ends heppily."

And completely and utterly undermines my own film. You fool – everyone can see that! Who will come to see any of my Shakespeare after this! Tree looked at her untroubled face with its rouged cheeks, the memory of that lithe body under his still fresh and prescient. He felt rather than saw Constance on his other side, remembering how he had wanted her, how strong and wide her hips had once been, how hungry he had been too to possess her at every instant but now her inane laughter as she too joined in repulsed him. As did the moving, vibrant faces, the energy, the exuberance, the emptiness. Hideous, distorted, *braying* donkeys is what they now resembled. He had done his bit more than any English actor for this new – new confounded medium! His own *King John* was the first ever Shakespeare to be filmed, followed shortly by that of his famous *Henry VIII.* He'd been canny with that one though. Only twenty prints were to be made, ten for London cinemas and ten for the provinces. Under no circumstances were they to be sold to cinema managers, but rather leased out for special exhibitions, then promptly destroyed so that they would not interfere with live theatre. There was still so much beauty in sound. How could Shakespeare be properly interpreted without it? Where was the golden timbre that left the spine tingling? Or the soft voice to melt the bosom? Where would La Duse be without her glorious incantation? What (he hated to conjure up that name) but what would Waller have been without his? No, Tree had not spent a lifetime giving voice or voices to his Hero only to be silenced now!

"Don't take it so seriously!" shushed Constance, noticing how the colour in his face came and went alarmingly. "It's only a bit of fun!"

"Fun!" scoffed Tree. "*Fun*? This is an abomination. An abomination of all that is true and sacred."

Tears now pricked his eyes. He shook his head. There's a war on! He wanted to yell, or holler as these Americans would say. You, of all people here, should know better! He wanted to make her stop watching this silly nonsense and remind her that Shakespeare was not to be mocked, not in this way. That Shakespeare was at the heart of all they were fighting for. Had she gone mad? Why, she had sailed from England only a few weeks after the sinking of the *Lusitania* – in fact that very manager Charles Frohman she had just mentioned in connection to Chaplin died on the ship – a hero by all accounts! Had that not moved her? What was heroic about any of this? Certainly Barrie's ridiculous spoof seemed to be producing far greater effect than the loss of life. Tree had given speeches in New York to drum up support for the war effort. He had written endless articles defending his actors, listing the men who had abandoned his stage for a more terrifying one. His very own nephew had died, as had Kipling's son and Asquith's – countless others, the greatest talent of their generation.

Tree pulled at his toupee and ripped off his moustaches. What on earth was he doing here amongst these odd renegades, these impecunious English? He looked scornfully at Charlie Chaplin. He might be making himself a rich man but he certainly wasn't fighting for his country. Tree got unsteadily to his feet, hampered by his ridiculous boots. And he felt ashamed of his weak nostalgia for this woman. Constance, who only moments before had aroused seductive memories now appeared overblown and faded compared to the other! But then the other was just a child! Both women, in their different ways, were distasteful to him. What was he thinking? What was she saying, this child? Heaven spare him, something about meeting in New York! That she could follow him and they could stay together? He could think of nothing he would like less. What did come to mind now were thoughts of his boyhood, his German schooling, of Marienbad and pine trees and a feeling of such longing almost overcame him. So much so that he swayed. And he thought of His Majesty's, dusty and magnificent and grand with the elegance and restraint of the true aristocrat. He thought of his children. At length he even thought of Maud. He had always loved her. Why had she never understood that other women didn't affect what he felt about her? That those tender feelings had never altered (well perhaps once or twice), but generally they were as intact as when they married. Perhaps she should be reminded of this? Why had he not done so in the past? Well he would tell her. At once. He would go home and he would tell her.

Home, he would go home.

Twenty-two

*What if my house be troubled with a rat,
And I be pleased to give ten thousand ducats
To have it baned?*

The Merchant of Venice

London 1916

Maud was early but so was May Pinney. Maud spied her rival and friend on the other side of the platform between the luggage trolley and wagon-lit. One could always see May, she was so tall, even taller than Maud's own statuesque daughter Viola. Maud's first reaction was to hide but then she began to giggle. What a couple of old trouts they were still chasing after Tree, still dancing round each other pretending the other didn't exist! And here they both were arriving breathless and excited because their Lord and Master was returning home! And just as had been the case for his departure in November 1915, the station teemed with children, grandchildren, wives – yes both of us, thought Maud– orchids – luggage and of course the Prime Minister. Hopefully now however,

spiteful rumours buzzing round Tree's Teutonic heritage would be quashed for good. Tree, in his capacity as King's Messenger, returned a hero. Tree had been hurt to the quick that his loyalty to England was questioned at all. Vicious articles had appeared stating that 'Sir B-T is a Jew' having had to 'change his German name.' Others said that there was a growing number of compatriots like him who had become 'naturalised for their own profit', but were nonetheless 'active and untiring agents of German propaganda.' His entry for 'Who's Who' was reproduced liberally.

"Second son of Julius Beerbohm... " read Tree aloud from *The Stage,* arriving unceremoniously one evening at All Souls House. "Educated Shnepfeuthall College, Germany... etc., amongst other honours 3rd class order of Prussian Crown!" Tree threw down the paper on the hall table while divesting himself of his coat in one svelte move, or rather he merely let it drop as he had so often for Tom Danes expecting him to catch it off him in mid-flight. The sable edged overcoat made for his role as Svengali, lay in a cashmere pool at his feet. He was white and trembling with a mixture of shock and anger. "As I told the Kaiser, it was a third-rate decoration," raged Tree. "But this! This because I want to play Shylock, *will* play Shylock!" Unfortunately (or fortunately as it was only to her) it came out as more 'vill' than 'will.'

Maud opened her mouth to speak but Tree interrupted her before she had a chance to reply.

"Do you realize they want to ban *The Merchant of Venice* completely? In America they are already campaigning to have it removed from lists of suggested reading in schools. As if Shakespeare were somehow responsible! My God! (Mein Gott!) To banish Shylock from the stage would be to banish one of the most important creatures of Shakespeare's genius!"

"Yes," said Maud, "Richard III was a wicked man – would we object to him? Henry VIII wasn't a particularly good man either but it doesn't stop playwrights from wanting to write about him."

Tree looked at her wild-eyed – more Svengali than Shylock. "I know why I married you!"

"Besides which wicked characters have always been more fascinating-"

Tree looked about to cry. "Why did you leave me Maudie?"

"To play... I was going to say wicked characters have always been more fun to play. Marriage is quite another affair."

Maud picked up Tree's coat off the floor. "You must write back – *figh*t back in the press. Say that Goethe was capable of writing about Mephistopheles but it doesn't mean he was in sympathy with him."

There was a small silence. "On reflection, perhaps stay with an English analogy and Shakespeare. Cite Iago."

Tree collapsed by the fire.

"Perhaps," said Maud gently coming to sit beside him on the fender, the coat resting on her lap. "Perhaps now is the time to stress once again that while the greatest drama in the world is being unfolded every day, it is only natural that the drama of our make-believe stage should seem insignificant. But we are all doing what we can. The theatre still has a place. It offers solace as never before."

Tree closed his eyes. "They also serve who keep high courage alive..." he said softly.

"What?"

"Elizabeth I–" Tree shook his lion's head, his hands running through his hair. "Her speech to her troops. Perhaps the greatest asset in keeping alive the heroic spirit of our troops will be in supporting their unconquerable humour. We need to play on that."

"Exactly."

Maud sighed at the memory. Tree had left with his entourage, his hopes, his mission to drum up American support, and Iris. He was retuning home alone. Little Iris, who seemed hardly out of the school-room, had met and married an American she had known for less that two months. The mayor of New York had married them on Christmas Eve and they were at this very moment honeymooning in the Bahamas. Maud was not at all appeased by the fact that Iris had become good friends with Charlie Chaplin while biding her time in Los Angeles, or that Chaplin had played Artful Dodger to Tree's Fagin in a charity production of *Oliver Twist*.

Maud sometimes felt as though the world, her world, was slipping away from her – sliding like grains of Norfolk sand through her fingertips. The boys she had entertained in Brancaster in her house on the edge of the purple marsh – Patrick Shaw-Stewart, Rupert Brooke, Ettie Desborough's glorious sons and little Jack Horner had all been called up. Every day came another tale of loss – the girl who was trying on her wedding dress at the very moment her fiancé was shot through the heart might have been her own Felicity, for her fiancé Lord Brabourne was killed in the early days of combat. The endless, damned lists. There was Herbert's nephew, Evelyn, a mere boy, Kipling's son, Squiffie's own boy too. And there was Lewis Waller, not killed in combat but dead on tour from pneumonia. After all those protestations of love what was left? Waller's last letter to her had begun, 'Dear Lady Tree... I am producing some time in the autumn, a play called Sir Walter Raleigh...' he had signed it 'yours sincerely.' Who could possibly tell from that, there had ever been anything between them, that at one time he had been willing to give up everything for her – had wanted her to do the same for him? Maud clenched her teeth. Honeymoons or Hollywood could not seem more fantastical.

And meanwhile, Duchess still insisted nursing her own particular terror that her daughter might be ravaged. Diana only added to Duchess's fear by saying that she rather longed to be ravaged too. Both however now accepted that the enemy really was the Hun rather than any of the wounded, who clearly were in no condition to do anything other than die nobly. Felicity in the meantime had of course defied them both and gone to Paris with a view to nursing in Serbia. She had lied about her age – no young nurses were being taken on ships to Serbia. With the outbreak of typhus the very young were considered too much of a health risk and Lipton (of the tea fame) was tired of mounting rescue operations, having put his magnificent yacht at the disposal of the Red Cross. Once was heroic – more than once was uneconomical.

Even so Maud hoped Felicity would be more successful at nursing than she had in the war office. Having spent a good deal of time putting war flags into a war map, very accurately, the General's cat sat on the German army and wiped it out. The Allies (and Felicity) departed for the summer in a blaze of taxi-cabs, and Maud was more alone than ever. Increasingly, her barometer was spinning out of control. She treasured Tree's letters as a lifeline back to her youth, to a simpler peacetime. *It seems a long time since you wrote and even longer since I wrote to you...* His were intimate, affectionate, as if they had never parted all those years and years ago. 'I haven't heard from you lately,' he wrote from Chicago, 'I am rather depressed just now and long to be home.' Yes, but whose home, she couldn't help thinking. And as much as he wrote to her, he must also write to May and Olivia and... It was inconceivable that he could care so much about them all, be so much devoted to each of them as if unaware of the other's existence. Perhaps she, Maud, unable to share, might have been happier if she had. Would things be any different? Dear Tom... she thought how it has taken your going for me to miss you – wish I had done things differently. She felt foolish tears prick her eyes and suddenly the fanfare for Tree's arrival seemed staged, like so many of his elaborate tableaux and just as hollow. She sniffed and turned away from the growing crowds. She spied Margot Asquith, as beautifully dressed as always, her tongue as sharp as ever now that she was no longer a Prime Minister's wife.

The station was a sea of men in khaki, some arriving, some departing and women of all ages and from all walks of life united in their attempt to wave them on their way, a forced smile hiding the pain of departure. Young girls in heavy black boots sporting whicker baskets strapped round their necks, sold magazines and Woodbines. A snow-covered train waited to take men back to the front, with steam settling beneath the station roof like a giant halo. Kiosks exchanged French money for officers and soldiers in uniform. Cues of men snaked round the station to the exit, with the wounded and exhausted lying on the platforms in between. The steam was heavier with the arrival of a train from France and crowds of waiting families surged forward so that Maud too was pushed unwillingly along. She lost sight of May in the crowd, in turn pushed up against the Mongolian fur of a soldier's uniform or shoved against the rough cloth of a coat or the pinching brass of a button. A child on his returning father's shoulders smiled down at her. Somewhere else lovers embraced.

She felt a hand on her arm. Still the steam enveloped them, swirling round her feet, whistling forwards. Everyone seemed taller than her and she could no longer make out the train's shape, gobbled up as it was by the throngs of men.

"My lady," said a familiar voice, an amused voice, as the band began to play and marching could be heard in the foreground. "All this ... for me?"

Maud blinked uncomprehendingly, momentarily confused. Please God, let this not be a dream. She closed her eyes. Please, please this once, let it be true.

"Maudie?" the voice registered more concern than wonder. "Such emotion... " Fingers wiped a tear, felt her cheek. "I must say I'm flattered. We've quarrelled so much of late I thought... It doesn't matter."

Slowly, carefully, she opened her eyes. The music was now deafening and the bobby's whistle came closer with the arrival of the PM. Everywhere there was chatter and noise.

"Oh," said Maud inaudibly. "Oh...Thank God... thank God... it's you."

"Well who else did you think it might be?" said Gerald du Maurier, shifting his bag to the other shoulder.

Maud swallowed. "I was early."

Gerald looked at her. "No, you're perfectly on time. Besides, how did you know? Did Sylvia..?" Gerald mentioned his wife. "No of course not."

Maud swayed slightly and Gerald took her arm.

"Come on – let's get out of here. You look done in – I'm taking you to Bentley's – it's a new place – just opened. They sell oysters and champagne and I'd say we deserve them both!"

Afterwards Maud was glad that she had not been there. The press reported the scrum as flowers were strewn in Herbert's path, and not only May but that dreadful Truman woman had clung to his arm. Viola, expecting a child, was not at the station and Iris of course was abroad. At least her children, thought Maud thankfully, were spared that sight. She had been curious of course. But when she'd written to ask Iris her impression of Claude Beerbohm, Iris replied, "Did you mean my cousin, Mama?" which lead Maud to believe Tree hadn't told Iris the whole story. Yes, Maud was very glad to be out of that circus.

They sat by her fire in Ayot Place. She had moved to yet another house, another life. What was she running from? What was she headed towards? She snuggled into her wrap – it was cold and for one evening only she would allow them the indulgence of a fire. She tried to keep coal and the luxury of hot water to a minimum, thinking of the hardship their soldiers were suffering. Gerald smiled with his eyes. A book lay open on his lap and his legs were crossed at the ankle. As ever his back was ramrod straight.

"And at home by the fire, whenever you look up there I shall be… "

Maud held his gaze. "Hardy."

"Hardy," affirmed Gerald. He put aside his book." Maud my dear, I want us to be together. For always."

Maud's heart sank. She'd heard this kind of thing before, from a married man before. And as before, she was still a married woman. The difference between then and now was that now she was no longer young, and what illusions of love she'd had were long gone.

She touched his lips with her finger. "I know," she said.

He moved his mouth against her hand. "I don't like your tone. It makes me uneasy."

"It's merely realistic. You know how things are."

"I know how *you* are. I know that you are still waiting for some – some kind of affirmation that a loveless marriage is worth fighting for."

Maud let her hands fall from his face. "You know it's more complicated than that."

"I know what I see," said Gerald angrily. "And what I see is a man who takes what he wants whenever he wants it with absolutely no thought of the consequences and I see what that has done, continues to do, to you. I also see how much life is wasted and I'm not talking about the war."

"I've been through this before'-"

Gerald got abruptly to his feet. "But not with me. Things are different now. The war will change, *is* changing, how people think. You were so worried about the theatre – your careers – how society would view your affair – all that will change."

"Nothing changes that much for women though. Not really. The world will forgive *him*," said Maud quoting from Mary Archerson in *The Likeness of the Night.* "It always does."

"This isn't a penny novel, let alone a bad play."

"Oh," said Maud piqued. "Mary was one of my better roles – and contrary to tradition I was the mistress in that, not the wife. Critics said I played with wonderful empathy."

"Well they would."

"You can be so ... charming."

Gerald made a mock bow. "But really, Tree's career hasn't fared so badly."

Maud's eyes widened in disbelief. "Because he's a man! Just look at dear Ellen Terry. She played in *The Winter's Tale,* a mere *fifty* years after she appeared in it the first time, but she hasn't been recognized for her contribution to theatre. At least not yet. I suppose there's still hope that she'll be created a Dame or suchlike before she's too doddery to know what's happening. When she had her children all those years ago she was almost banished from the stage completely."

"While Tree seems to go from strength to strength…"

"Yes, but that's also thanks to me. I've been like a *banshi* – vigilant at all times – denying everything all the time no matter how much I hurt, no matter how much I wanted to reveal my heart…" Maud swallowed. "And I nagged Belfield and Margot to put in a good word to the PM."

"You've been ... Caesar's Wife... beyond reproach."

"You're laughing at me."

"I've never been more serious."

Maud sniffed. "I'll have you know that recently we've been ... close actually."

Gerald shot her a look. "Well I hope that's not true."

"You know what I mean. But do you really think people just left Herbert alone? Of course not! There has always been the risk of blackmail. Ever since – well ever since his second trip to America when I couldn't go." Maud fought back tears as she remembered the shock of that nasty little letter mentioning Tree's Daisyfield set-up with May Pinney. She remembered feeling the child in her belly leap as if mimicking her mother's distress. And it was ever thus with Tree.

"I took my own measures."

Gerald shook his head. "What measures?" It was less a question than a command."

"Love is a possible strength in an actual weakness..." Maud murmured. "Also Hardy."

"What measures?" repeated Gerald, ignoring her.

"I have an ongoing... relationship with a Mr. Littlechild – an appropriate name given what I'm going to tell you."

Gerald lit a cheroot and slowly let the smoke escape his mouth.

"I think I can guess."

"Littlechild is a private investigator. He gives me a copy of Tree's children's birth certificates – May and Tree's children that is. I've known all along about those and certainly about the later additions – the ones my *husband* has never thought to mention."

"And you're happy with this?"

Maud made an impatient gesture. "Of course I'm not happy! Every..." she closed her eyes. "Every time I learned of yet another... son... it was an agony. I died a little bit more."

"Then live your life," said Gerald forcibly. "Surely it's time? Live it with someone who isn't – wasn't," Gerald corrected himself, "a dandy. More interested in himself than you."

"He just got bored of waiting," said Maud, knowing that Gerald meant Waller and not wanting to talk about him now that he was dead. Gerald raised an eyebrow.

"Let that be a lesson then," he said lightly. "I'm no Waller."

"Clearly."

"I'm not prepared to wait or be side-stepped. I'm not in awe of Tree or his theatre. I have my own." He threw his cigarette into the fire. "We will do great things, I know we will. We have already. You've worked with Barrie and I like his plays – I want to do *Peter Ibbotson* next and a revival of *What Every Woman Knows*."

Maud inwardly groaned at the mention of the latter play – Maud knew the script so well she not only inhabited the main role but often wondered if she had just continued to play her throughout her life.

"I plan," she heard Gerald say, "to go on directing plays till I'm a very old man. And I want you with me." He pulled Maud to her feet so she was pressed against the length of his body, taking care to keep her from treading on his highly polished shoes. "And now I just want you."

Twenty-three

It is because I think so much of warm and sensitive hearts that I would spare them from being wounded.

Oliver Twist

Maud looked down at Tree as he lay ramrod straight on the narrow bed, his limbs stretched abnormally taught, toes pointing up towards the ceiling, his hands clasped she imagined, under the sheet. Tree never slept like that, but rather in a curled foetal position with his back to her, to the bedroom door. The skin on his face was smooth, gravity pulling at the lines and crevices and someone had parted his hair on the wrong side. Whatever essence of the soul, whatever spirit concoction that made up a man, was completely absent now, in death. She touched his forehead with her lips and almost recoiled at its coldness. She suppressed a sob and her hands shook as she smoothed his shirt. She removed the bedclothes with a sudden inexplicable desire to see his hands once again, hands that were more familiar to her almost than her own. They would always be the most beautiful hands she had ever seen on any person male or female. But while the shape was familiar, there were unfamiliar red blotches and bruises where the blood had clotted and spilled – blood that had clotted too soon, too permanently.

Maud made the sign of the cross and moved away.

"We are ready my lady," said the undertaker and she nodded. She pressed her body against the wall of the small chapel where Herbert had lain the previous night. The brick was cold against her back, damp against the velvet of her coat. Despite the warm summer's day she shivered. It was untimely, Herbert's death. But then there was so much death during the war that was untimely. She had not said goodbye and the last time she had seen Herbert they had not exactly argued but there had been no peace, no resolution. They had not come to accept one another. Everything felt jagged and incomplete. No sooner had she given the word than strangers seemed to appear from nowhere and Maud sank further into her corner. She had wanted a few final moments alone with Herbert before the spectacle began, before he was fought over and shared with so many others, each and every one jostling for position, each and every one alleging greater and greater ownership. Already, May Pinney claimed to be the last person alive to have spoken to him, while the odious Miss Truman had reared her ugly head one final time, stating she had been his mistress these past sixteen years, which given she was hardly more than a child now... Even Viola...

Maud could not bear to think of Viola... just yet. Instead she turned the events of the past week over and over in her mind re-playing the moment when she knew. The moment when her world stopped and her heart opened itself to unimaginable pain. It had been said before so many times, but then only because it was true. Death was so final.

"He was just sitting up in bed," the nurse had wailed as Maud, already breathless from the climb up to his first floor room, her arms weighed down with clean linen and flowers, thought she would stop breathing altogether. "Sir Herbert asked me to open the window, it was that warm. It was such a lovely warm, balmy evening. He was paring a peach – (the peaches Maud knew Ettie Desborough had sent from Taplow) and when I turned to him he was..." and here the nurse had cried so much that despite her own shock and grief, Maud was impatient.

"*Was*?" Maud snapped.

"Dead!" sniffed the nurse. "I turned to Sir Herbert and he was dead!"

And so it proved to be. A minor knee injury inflicted when Herbert fell headlong down Constance Collier's cottage steps (Maud had thought *that* affair long over) had not only resulted in an equally minor op but in Herbert's death from a blood clot. The irony was that Herbert had *wanted* to get up from his sick-bed, had been desperate to get up and visit his theatre. Desperate to begin rehearsals for *The Great Lover*, the play Tom and Maud were so against him producing, and which if they had their way would never be. Only Sir Alfred Fripp had prevented him from moving, keeping him immobile long after it was safe. Maud grimaced at the futility of it and the enormity of the loss she was shocked to feel now. The next morning, Maud left her home early. She had an unbearable yearning to see Herbert again and would have given anything, anything to hear his voice just one last time. She would have given anything too, to feel his cheek on hers. She hadn't slept; she had hardly spoken to Felicity or even Viola, and Iris would only learn the news by telegram. She knew it was her duty to comfort *them*, they had after all lost their father but all she could feel was her own grief, and beyond that she could not go. She rounded the corner of Fripp's nursing home and all but recoiled in horror. The steps were crowded with reporters. She stopped short, unaware that a man had been hurrying after her.

"M-Maud," stammered Max Beerbohm, wincing as she trod on his foot.

"Oh Max," said Maud bursting into tears.

Max took her by the elbow and together they made their way to the back of the house and the tradesmen's entrance. Max hurried Maud through basement kitchens, guiding her through tortuous corridors and rooms housing the tools of the surgeon's trade. But if Maud had hoped to be alone with Herbert she was disappointed. Already he was half buried in flowers like a male Ophelia, his face seeming as waxy as the wilting petals.

"Always a baronet in the sight of God."

"For those who treat God as minor royalty," quipped Maud, although it had been one of Tree's favourite epigrams.

"I'm sure he was smiling," whispered Max, "when he died. I'm sure he was radiant."

* * *

The theatre world was out in force. Ellen Terry drew her own following as she processed majestically amongst the mourners, her presence testament not only to a great friendship but also to a great institution. Politicians rubbed shoulders with artists, aristocracy with flower-girls, religious men and women with other creators of make-believe. And George Alexander, who had only recently made his last stage appearance because 'Herbert was coming' and dying himself, had outlived his great friend after all. Maud walked slowly behind the coffin, draped in its flowing velvet cloth and smothered in huge lilies that made her sneeze. She was grateful for the Spanish veil she had chosen to wear, more to hide from prying eyes than as a fashion statement. The press would later report her dramatic attire, the thousands of celebrities, the pomp of the occasion. It would also report the tremendous and typically theatrical commotion, caused not by Chopin's funeral march or Clara Butt belting out her number, but by the crack of anti-aircraft guns and the flashes of blinding lightning as a day time air raid sent huge oaks crashing on the heath. Maud's usual composure in public left her, and not because she was in fear for her life. She felt neither spiritual nor close to Herbert, but rather consumed by an irrational anger. She shook her fist at the sky. The callous, random disposal of life on such a colossal scale left her shaking with fury, as did Herbert's ludicrous carelessness.

Maud lifted her head. There were so many friends amongst the mourners. Duchess, Maud feared, was losing her reason. She had hardly stopped nibbling on the crumbly Bath biscuits she now took with her wherever she went. The front of her very ancient costume was littered with yesterday's tea and around her neck and despite the clammy weather, she wore a once fashionable fox, whose head seemed to arch in the direction of its mistress's mouth as if it at any moment might leap forward to snatch the food into its own. Her famous eyes, once beautifully deep-set appeared shrunken. Harry Cust's death in March, despite her protestations to the contrary, had hit her hard. Little Jim Barrie tripped ahead between the headstones, coming to an abrupt halt when he realized that Tree was to lie not only beside George du Maurier, author of *Trilby* the success of which when produced by Tree had led to the building her His Majesty's, but also alongside George's daughter Sylvia Llewelyn Davies and her husband Arthur. It was their boys Barrie adopted when they died tragically young. And it need not be repeated that all his life Tree had berated himself for ignoring the opportunity of producing *Peter Pan*. There was, Maud thought, a beautiful irony in that. Barrie thought otherwise and appeared to be almost hopping mad as he sprang up from behind the du Maurier monument.

"Did you k-know this?" he hissed.

Maud sucked in her breath. "Of course not!" Maud's veil caught on her lips as she spoke. "Don't you think *he* minds rather more?" Maud nodded to the coffin. She had no wish to lift up her veil, but speaking was becoming problematic. The sultry air and her own breath made the organza stick to her tongue.

"*She* would not have wanted this. *They* would not have!"

"Well maybe you should consider –" Maud had meant to say 'lying beside them too,' but the word came out as 'dying' instead.

Barrie glared.

Maud gave an exasperated sigh.

"My nerves are quite s-shot," he said, a twitch beginning under his eye. "What with the a-air r-raid and now this… I'm not sure I can withstand another sh-sh-hock."

There was a momentary lull in the bombing and Clara Butt took the opportunity to embark on another hymn – she and La Melba. One diva really should have been enough. Maud stared at the sky ahead, streaked with the traces of anti-aircraft fire. What did any of this mean? Maud wondered too at the intense secrecy of Herbert's life, of hers for that matter. All the effort in keeping one family so apart from the other, all the pain caused by children seeking a parent, a wife yearning for her husband. Or two 'wives' seeking just the one, Maud thought wryly. But then she'd played that part hadn't she? Maud lifted her head abruptly. One of Shaw's so-called 'Pleasant Plays', that was it. Maud had played the 'progressive' Mrs. Clarendon in *You Never Can Tell*. She remembered now. Only progressive wasn't quite the word Maud would use to describe Mrs. C, or 'pleasant.' The play had been about a mother returning with the three children who had never known their father. It would seem there was an embarrassment of children in the Tree saga. Only a few days before, when Maud didn't believe things could get any worse, she had received that disturbing letter. And from Lady Lyttleton, president of the Victoria League no less. A 'certain' Private in the Canadian Army, claiming to be Herbert Tree's 'nephew', wished to head up an Entertainments Committee for the League. Lady Lyttleton had been asked to find out whether this was true and whether he was a person to be trusted, *'I am so sorry to bother you about such a matter,'* continued Lady Lyttleton, *'but you know how people claim relationship with anyone so prominent as Sir Herbert was and no one on the committee but myself knew you well enough to ask this question.'*

Maud didn't dare look around to see how many of Herbert's 'nephews' were in attendance now. She suppressed a sob. Not even Duchess could comfort her now. Maud wanted only her daughters. She still had them. Well she had Viola. Felicity was always distant and Iris was lost to America. It had always been Viola there at her right hand to comfort her. Just where *was* her eldest daughter? Maud frowned, peering through the bright haze left by the gunfire in the sky.

She also had Gerald. Her heart swelled. Maybe she had not felt it properly before until now. Maybe there simply hadn't been the space. Maud thought of his long thoughtful face, his absolute belief in her. He kept telling her she was the only one for him, that she was what he wanted. Maud blinked. Why had she been so blind? He was her home now. He was what she must focus on. She would go to him now and tell him. Let the dead bury their dead, thought Maud, seeing all the elderly great and good tottering over Herbert's grave. She wasn't part of this. She never really had been. Maud spun on her heel. Ripping her hat and veil from her head she all but ran from the cemetery. Let May and Olivia jostle for position as to who should throw the first clump of earth. Maud would have no part of it. This bit of her life was over. She would begin again and it would be wonderful. She would have a new theatre, a new manager and a new play. That is what she needed now.

*   *   *

By the time Maud made her way back to Eaton Square it was twilight, the city still warm from the buzz of the afternoon's air raid. It had taken much longer than she anticipated by the time she had procured a hansom and walked the final hundred yards. Her skirts were dusty and her hat and veil were crumpled from where she had been holding them under her arm. She almost wept with relief at the sight of Gerald's flat. She paused to savour the moment – a moment she knew would herald a turning point and a new phase of her life. It was not to be embarked on lightly. Maud closed her eyes. It was time. For so long she had lived under Herbert's shadow, his larger than life persona, a presence that had done its best to obliterate hers. It was time. Maud tilted her head, peering above her. The curtains were drawn in Gerald's first floor drawing-room and she could see him crossing the floor from time to time. He appeared animated and carried a decanter in one hand, a cigar in the other. He was probably listening to his new gramophone and dancing in his new spats, she thought indulgently. He really was a bit of a dandy in spite of his protests to the contrary. Maud's spirits lifted and her heart began to thump. How surprised he'd be to see her, how thrilled by her decision! She had never been more certain about anything in her life! Maud took a step forward, breathing in the intoxicating scent of lily of the valley. The air was young and fresh.

I an old turtle, will wing me to some wither'd bough...quoted Maud softly to herself, only my mate is not lost... She pushed open the little iron gate at the front garden. *And is found.*

Her heart began to pound. At last... hand poised to ring the bell Maud thought better of it; if the door was open she would go in and surprise him. Removing her glove she felt the smooth brass surface of the knocker. Everything seemed exaggerated in memory, everything from that moment forward, of significance. She dropped her unbecoming hat and veil on the marble-topped table and shook her skirts free of any stubborn dust. Smoothing her wild hair and pinching her pale cheeks for colour she set her chin. Who was she now? No shrewish Paulina, no Mabel Vane or aged Countess, not even a grieving widow. No, she was, Maud choked back the tears, simply a woman in love. An *old* woman in love corrected a sulky voice at the back of her head but still in love. Maud took the steps two at a time. Well at least I can still do this, she thought. She paused on the landing. Not a sound came from within the room, or not the ones Maud expected. So Gerald was not, after all, listening to music. Maud hesitated. Could he have slipped out of the room? But no, she'd been standing outside beneath his window all the time. They would have had to pass on the stairs if he had gone anywhere else in the house. And then she heard murmurings. Murmurings? Maud frowned. There was another voice now too, a low unmistakable voice. Maud pushed open the door.

"Mother!"

Maud blinked as Gerald unceremoniously pushed Viola off his knee, not a graceful gesture given that Viola was over six feet tall and Gerald as ever was conscious of his polished shoes. She landed in a heap of disarrayed clothes on the carpet.

"M-Maudie – we- were-" Gerald swept a hand through his hair.

Maud grappled for a moment with the array of roles open to her, but this was not one she had ever played before in public.

Maud ignored Gerald but her eyes bored into Viola's.

"What is this?" she asked coldly. Viola made no attempt either to get up off the floor or arrange her décolleté.

"This," she said holding her mother's gaze, "is hereditary."

Twenty-four

Move him into the sun... If anything might rouse him now The kind old sun will know.

Wilfred Owen

31 July 1917

Tom Danes had never heard of Ypres and even less of a little village called Passchendale – his experience of anything remotely 'French' was based on the stories Lady Tree had told him of her mad capers in Paris, and her funny 'insane' house as Herbert called it in Pont de l'Arche. Thus he was only mildly surprised to learn that Ypres, which he soon learned to call 'Wypers', was in fact in Belgium but he nonetheless conjured up visions of delicious if different food, of steaming plates of stew laced with bracing foreign brandy and though probably too rich, Tom looked forward to holding his sides in the pain of indigestion. He imagined a light camaraderie with other like-minded East End men as they jostled beside each other in the trains carrying them towards Dover. But he was not placed with other working-class men – the truth was that many of them were declared too unfit for physical exertion of any kind. In fact over one million men this year alone were considered unfit for combat. It was the upper classes that proved the fittest in the end – or rather the beginning. He knew this, for his Captain Horner with whom he was placed as batman on account of his remarkable 'dressing skills', had told him. If you were nobly born, Horner told him, if you joined up green and keen in the early months, the more certain you were of death. He should know. Of his most inner circle, that coterie made up of children of the Souls, there was only himself and Patrick Shaw Stewart left...There were many things Tom would rather not have known. 51 months of hell,

Horner told him, scratching off the months on the rotten beam that held up their trench hell-hole, 51 months of hell.

And it was worse than hell, thought Tom wiping the rain from his face, worse than anything Tom could ever have imagined. As was the incessant rain that coursed through their boots in rivers of clay and mud. The pock-marked landscape turned into a never-ending quagmire, churning up its wounded and its dead at every turn. Danes fought his way through a foot of knee-high quicksand, feeling himself sinking with every attempt. On his back he carried a rucksack weighing 60 pounds of a soldier's equipment– rifle, bayonet, entrenching tool, bombs, wire-cutters sandbags, French wire, 170 rounds of ammunition and one roman candle. But the difficulty with which Tom struggled to move was nothing to what the bearers faced as they battled to carry stretchers to the casualty clearing stations only yards away. On normal terrain a stretcher would have required but two bearers; here sixteen men in relays of four men each were needed to transport the half drowned men from their shell holes. The smells emanating from rotten flesh made Tom want to vomit, as did the sight of wounds inflicted by the Germans' recent delight, shells filled with mustard gas that damaged the eyes and stripped the skin to the bone.

This was not the noble (if somewhat prolonged) death-scene Danes had heard Tree pronounce so many times on a well lit stage. There was no room here for King John or Henry or even Bill Sykes. This was not the death described by the poets. There was nothing as far as Danes could see that was remotely honourable or enviable. Danes had survived – God only knew how – what was nothing short of a massacre, a massacre in which the French moved 600 yards. Following that debâcle thousands of French soldiers deserted, fifty-five men were shot for desertion and all-told there were a quarter of a million casualties – 150,000 of them British. There was more to come. Herbert may have been elated that his youngest grandchild was to be named Virginia, but now that one and a half-fresh American troops had entered the war, there was a stronger impetus to sacrifice even more young men, if that were possible, in the interests of securing a longer-lasting peace.

Danes no longer cared about peace, not even about food; his existence, measured in minutes, was governed simply by clay and mud. Mud was everywhere, in the guns, in the shells, mud and slime mixed with the gore and guts and limbs of the maimed. His feet were sodden with squelching, insect-ridden mud, his body shook with fever and his recent stomach wound seeped with puss. The horror of it was so out of context, such a world away from His Majesty's Theatre and the simplicity of that life, as it now seemed, that Danes trapped in his line, wondered if he were already dead. They all moved as if in slow motion, every movement took all their energy, every effort repeated again and again as they struggled against the suction and weight of the mud. The men were half dead too, their eyes had seen too much horror to enable them ever to go home now. For who would believe them? Who would understand all they had seen and done? Danes couldn't believe it himself. He stole a look at his Captain. Horner no longer slept. He sat with his eyes open, clutching the little book in which the names of his friends, his closest friends, who had been killed, were written. There were 25 men so far, all boys with whom he'd grown up, including all three of Ettie Desborough's sons. That was the hardest, he said. They had all been in love with Ettie Desborough, but her sons had been demi-gods. She would lose her reason, he felt certain of that.

It was still dark when battle began at ten to four in the morning. It was supposed to be dawn, but there was so much cloud above that it was pitch black when the alarm came through. Ypres, rising 20 metres above sea level with a coastal strip of sand, seemed to be melting into the very gravel silts of marl from which it was formed. 21 mines had been dug under the Messines ridge and German position, and soon what little was left of the branchless trees and stumps would be decimated. For several hours, Danes sat with Horner in their rat-infested, sodden burrow beneath a barrage of sandbags, waiting for enough light to advance. Yellow-coloured water seeped through their clothes and down the sides of the slippery steamy earth. Through cracks in their roofless dug-out, Danes could see the coils of barbed wire and flares of artillery. Horner told Danes that he had been to His Majesty's on several occasions. His 'set' comprised Viola and Felicity Tree and Duchess's daughters. Horner didn't say if he was in love with anyone but he mentioned Duchess's eldest daughter Diana just too many times, thought Tom, for a man to pretend to be that disinterested. He also seemed inordinately excited by the fact that Lady Tree was Diana's godmother. Tom looked at his Captain with renewed admiration. Duchess was an acquired taste – he knew – he'd spent far too long in her and Lady Tree's company not to know these women inside out. As for her children...Tom recalled Tree's intense irritation at finding Diana behind the scenes, plastering her chin with Henry VIII's hair while the baby covered his arms with Caesar's blood. Their nanny was more direct. "*Quelle famille de serpents!*" she muttered, dragging Diana from hee- hawing through Bottom's head. Conjuring up those names – so far removed from this place – was as fantastical as though indeed a magician had appeared before them.

Now that he had begun, it would seem, Horner had no inclination to stop. His family, he told Danes, had not been like the others. He also seemed entirely serious when he said his family was poor. His mother was a true artist and collector of someone called Burne-Jones and that's why she and Duchess had got on so well. Tom thought Duchess many things but true artist wasn't exactly one of them. Horner's expression was rapt however, and Tom could see he was far away. His happiest memories, he said were of staying at a house at Brancaster on the north Norfolk coast next door to the Trees with his friends Patrick Shaw Stewart, Charles Lister and Rupert Brooke. Of course Diana was just a little girl then, no more than fourteen years old but already a beauty. They had all been in love with her, especially Patrick, and Charles Lister had written that he loved her as 'Tristan loved Isolde'. Whatever that meant, thought Tom. It didn't sound good though, by the bleak look on Horner's face when he said it. Edward Marsh had taught her the Greek alphabet and told her she looked like the moon. Tom would have said more unappetizing blancmange himself.

Ready to charge with their pennants flying, they waited in squalor and talked of life before. It dawned on Tom that he was once more a servant. He had left Tree's side to be his own man, and now at Horner's the only difference was that he could add the word 'soldier' before the word 'servant.' He wondered too what impulse had prompted him to volunteer. He did not feel the pride in killing that Horner described of some of his friends. Men who, brought up on a diet of bludgeoning wild-life for sport now went out at night to single out as many Germans as they could and shoot them dead with sniper fire. Not all are like them, Horner said ominously.

"No Sir." Tom was beginning to feel afraid. The glow from their talk was wearing off.

"I mean," said Horner. "Rather they had that kind of courage than none at all."

"Yes Sir," said Tom. But he added, "I'm not sure I understand you Sir," because he didn't.

Horner put his head above the parapet. "Diana's brother John has been kept out of it. From the front. Duchess wouldn't countenance losing another son."

Tom blinked. "But so many families have. Lost more than one."

Horner ducked down. "One rule my lad for us and one for you."

"Poor bugger," said Tom. Horner looked surprised.

"Not lucky?"

"No," said Tom. "How will he face us when we get home?"

Horner looked at him thoughtfully. "How indeed."

By the evening Horner had been shot through the ear.

"I've ordered you a gold tie-pin," he told Tom as he was being hauled from the dug-out. The wail of shells and rattle of musketry was deafening. Tom was shocked at how light Horner felt in his arms, like a child. "The pity of it is that it… well it will arrive after –"

"There's no after, Sir," said Danes gruffly, attempting to staunch the blood that now seeped from Horner's nose.

And Tom was right. By the end of the third day Horner too was dead and with him four hundred years of a continuous line died too. Male succession meant little to Tom but he did know the nursery rhyme. Horner had pulled a rum plum out this time. In the silence, in the lull that followed when mud and silt had clogged up the German guns and buried so many unexploded shells, Tom laid out Horner's possessions – a picture of his mother and a copy of *Henry V*. It was only then, when touching the leather-bound volume of the play, that he began to cry.

Twenty-five

The gods are just, and of our pleasant vices make instruments to plague us... The wheel is come full circle.

King Lear

London February 1917

Maud's shoes were beginning to feel uncomfortably wet, the fat sticky snowflakes gathering on her wool stockings like crows along a telephone wire had quickly melted. The evening light was fading fast. Under the provocative picture captured at Herbert's funeral, of Maud clenching a raised fist, headlines in the evening papers announced the sale of His Majesty's. *'I'll get my revenge says Lady Tree!'* screamed the tabloid. There were more flattering pictures of Maud scowling under that ridiculous hat. She was at a loss as to why she thought a veil of such thickness could ever be flattering, while the long black and yellow plumage looked as if the entire crow population of Hampstead had come to nest there. At least there were no pictures of May or Olivia Truman, for which she would be eternally grateful. But *revenge*?

There was, of course none to be had. How could there be? May Pinney was to have £1,000 'for her own use absolutely' and for her immediate needs. Maud's share was in trust. But she supposed May was only marginally better off than she was having so many younger dependents – if not older ones. There was over twenty years' difference between the ages of May's older boys and her younger ones. It was a long time since Maud cared about that. Not even news that there was yet *another* child really surprised her. After Gerald's betrayal nothing could come close. And now? What now? Herbert had always said it was 'difficult to be thoroughly popular' until one was quite dead. His popularity was only beginning, but it didn't pay the rent. There was no one she could really talk to either. Since liberating herself of Arlington Street Duchess seemed to be on a permanent sea voyage. She spent very little time at Belfield, very little time eating and even less on clothes. She had truly reverted to the free spirit Maud had known as a young girl. Unencumbered as she now was of her London abode, and preparing to hand over the reins of her former stately home, she had very little sympathy with those who still concerned themselves with dwellings and their upkeep. It would seem that Duchess had no intention of ever disembarking, and if so not for long.

If only Tom Danes were alive, thought Maud, I'd have talked to him. Maud was surprised at how much she missed the man and how much she had come to rely on his smooth management of the theatre and their lives. It had been a surprise too, she had to admit, when rather late in the day, he had left them to join up. A boy for so long, it was even more of a surprise to learn he was almost too old to fight. It was his luck or not, as it turned out, that an officer in the Greys had been in need of a batman. The officer wasn't specific on age or background – there wasn't a great deal of choice by 1917. She had somehow known too that he would never come home. Tom had been mentioned in dispatches, his bravery commendable, and had he a mother to mourn him she would have been proud. In the absence of any next-of-kin, however, his pathetic box of personal effects had been returned to the theatre. Maud had turned over the few items – a framed publicity photograph of Tree as Svengali, a half-eaten tin of boiled sweets, an odd sock wondering at a life half-lived. Maud closed her eyes. She was thoroughly wet and for the first time in her entire life had neither a part to prepare for nor an engagement in the theatre. Any theatre.

"Maud? Lady Tree I should say?" The voice registered unguarded pleasure but no curiosity as to how the grande dame of the stage came to be sitting on a cement step in the snow.

Maud's eyes snapped open. She peered above her. A woman, a very handsome woman, no longer so young, with deep-set eyes rather the way Duchess's had once been, looked down at her, expressing nothing but concern.

"Yes?"

"You don't recognize me do you?" The voice was familiar, the original American tonality neutralized by many years in England. "It's Elizabeth," said the woman hoisting up her skirt to join her on the step. "Elizabeth Robins." She grimaced as her bottom sank into the wet but made no attempt to get up again.

"Ah... Elizabeth..." Maud smiled. "Of course. How are you?"

"How are *you?* More to the point. I heard about Sir Herbert – I'm sorry. We had our... differences as you know, but it must be a great loss."

Maud frowned. *Loss?* She thought. The word did not begin to cover what she felt. "Yes it is," she replied. "It's stranger than that. It leaves... death leaves... one feeling very... disconnected and angry too. But you know how it is. The war... We've all..."

Elizabeth grasped Maud's hand.

"I do understand and I'm sorry," she repeated. "But you must know you were always so much more... than he was."

"Oh I don't know if that's true!" said Maud embarrassed. "He was certainly my sparring partner. And there was His Majesty's – no doubt you know all about that too. I don't know what I shall do now... now that..." her voice trailed.

Elizabeth shifted her skirt, rearranging the folds to make a cushion. "That's better," she said smiling. "Where are you living?"

Maud motioned to an unspecific point behind her. "Um...round the corner from here – All Souls Place, thought not many souls left in mine."

"You mean that funny wedged-shaped house?"

Maud smiled. "That's what Herbert called it."

"It looks like a slice of cheese."

"And with just as many holes."

Elizabeth shook her head. "You haven't changed."

Maud could feel the damp entering her bones. She would have given anything to be in a hot bath at that moment with a bottle of veronal on the side. "I wish that were true." She gave

Elizabeth a sideways glance. "*You* certainly haven't. Your hair is still as thick as ever. I'm very envious."

Elizabeth patted her bun. "Don't be. It's not real." Somehow the knowledge cheered Maud.

"Well it's lovely all the same."

"Too kind. Are you acting at the moment?"

Maud made a moue. "Not at the moment, no. But I see your *Votes for Women!* is a success – a film even – at The Coronet."

Elizabeth nodded. "Not such a success though. Of course I would like nothing more for it to be loved by all. You may remember how nervous I've always been about the critics, but this time the Examiner of Plays has called it a penny dreadful – a bad penny dreadful.'

"He hasn't!" said Maud genuinely surprised.

"He has," said Elizabeth soberly. "There are moments when I find it terribly amusing. I laugh even. But mostly I am stung."

"Of course you are," agreed Maud warmly.

"And that old turncoat Squire Bancroft did me no favours either. I'm beginning to think your Herbert wasn't so bad after all."

Maud was beginning to think the same. She thought too of the run- ins Herbert had had with Elizabeth or with any aspiring director for that matter who threatened his position, his *mission* as he saw it, to produce Shakespeare.

"He could never abide a clever woman, that was the problem. You see what happened to me!" said Maud wryly. "It really is good to see you Elizabeth," she added, carried away with the friendliness of the other woman and not realizing until that moment just how lonely she had been. "But what did he do, Squire I mean?" She said eager to keep her by her side.

"Well if you really do want to know I'm very happy to bore you! I really am peeved about the whole matter. The thing is that although the Examiner said the play was obviously 'well intentioned,' Squire persuaded his good friend that he couldn't pass my play when he'd banned Shaw's *Mrs. Warren's Profession.* They both deal as you know Maud dear, with similar themes. You know what I mean."

Maud knew only too well. She'd had her own challenges in getting her trilogy that included *Caesar's Wife* to the stage – especially when the word adultery couldn't be mentioned or at least not in so many words.

"Men!"

"Yes men," agreed Elizabeth. "If only they could accept that we women are here to stay and the sooner the trade unionists acknowledge this the better. Do you realize that the Woolwich Arsenal now has 25,000 women munitions workers, whereas it had only 125 at the start of the war?"

"Yes I did. I've given interviews on the subject and Gerald –" Maud swallowed. "Gerald and I wrote a sort of playlet about the subject and it was performed at the Theatre Royal."

Elizabeth looked at Maud with her strong clear face, the high cheek bones and sculpted jaw, without a trace of pity.

"I see where Gerald and Viola are acting together again," she said. "And they've penned a play under their combined names – Herbert Parsons."

"I think that's not all they combine," said Maud grimly, thinking of the recent photos spread over two pages in *The Sketch,* in which Viola was wrapped round Gerald's torso. The accompanying caption stated simply, 'The Dancers.' On another occasion *Tatler* reported Viola 'stripping off,' at some party onboard his yacht in the Cap Ferrat. 'Swimming by Moonlight' accompanied that one. The pain was still acute.

"Ah this war..." sighed Elizabeth. "As far as I can see women are either helping to provide the means to break men to pieces or helping put broken men together again. I mean that in the *broadest* sense."

"I like the way you put it."

"Oh Maud, if you don't mind me saying this but you have to learn not to mind so much. You have a life ahead of you. You must learn to live it and live it differently."

Maud couldn't help smiling at her friend's enthusiasm.

"I'm old, Elizabeth. I may just be done with the living bit."

Elizabeth made a swiping gesture as though she were swotting mosquitoes and not the swirling snowflakes. Like a child she held out her tongue to catch them.

"Sorry! I can't resist snow. It reminds me so of Boston."

She took one of Maud's hands in both of hers. "What tosh," she said kindly. "We're the same age – or close enough. Besides there's much to be done. I blame this war entirely on man's will-to- war. It's us woman's- will- to *peace* that must be heard more loudly. It's the only way. And the only way we can achieve this is by women learning to serve the interests of other women. You said you weren't acting at the moment."

Maud's coat was now too wet to squirm properly but she shrank further into her aged fox. It sounded like an accusation but beginning to know Elizabeth as she did, sensed it merely a statement of fact.

"Well do you *want* to?" Elizabeth's tone was firm, in much the way Maud's had been once with aspiring young actresses.

Maud studied her friend – well not so much friend as one time colleague. Why had she ever felt threatened by this well-meaning woman? Why had she been so quick to mistake kindness for rivalry?

"I suppose so… I hadn't thought much about the future." *Liar! screamed a voice. You've thought of nothing else because it terrifies you so.*

"Mnm…" said Elizabeth letting go of Maud's hand. "William –"

"William?" interjected Maud gently.

Elizabeth blushed. "William Archer... you must know that he and I... we are friends. I mean we are now... Once I would have had things differently but –"

It was Maud's turn to touch Elizabeth's hand.

"You don't have to explain, I just wasn't sure if it was the same William..."

"No it's all right. I am resigned to this... partnership. And I'm writing about it. At least Archer has done that – given me plenty of material to write about!"

Maud looked at Elizabeth in wonder. "Do you always do that? Turn every experience into something... so...so... positive?"

Elizabeth shrugged. "Not always, no, but I'm still an American remember. We're pioneers if nothing else – at heart anyway. I hope that I am ... positive as you put it. Besides, what other choice is there? My last novel was about a woman who does not choose to remarry after her husband dies." She looked at Maud pointedly. "My agent said I would sell more copies if I changed the ending but I refused. The book I'm working on now is somewhat different. *Time is Whispering* is what it's called."

"Well that's true enough. It sounds... carpe diem- ish ..." said Maud gloomily.

Elizabeth smiled. "Depends on your perspective, I guess. I find it very... uplifting actually. It's about two very different people and explores the feelings among those no longer young. But it's more than that," she added hastily. "While these two eventually marry they do so because they have *chosen* marriage and make it fit with their demands. They have companionship and harmony and together they achieve something wonderful." Elizabeth moved closer, to Maud as much for warmth as to prove a point. Her eyes were bright. "Our hero and heroine set up a home for women, a sort of training place if they want that, or rest if they need that too. In short a haven."

"Oh?" Maud too was interested now and despite the cold. Elizabeth was a warmth radiating comfort.

Elizabeth nodded. "Yes, and it's what William and I have done in reality at Beckett's Farm."

"Oh?" said Maud expressing surprise. "You mean companionship?"

"Well, that," said Elizabeth, "but I mean a haven – a place for women."

"Only women?" Maud repeated foolishly, her pulse quickening all the same.

"Only women. And William, of course." Elizabeth smiled. "He's not there very much actually. But we intend a woman's theatre – not like *Smallhythe*," she added quickly, "it's not a *Barn* Theatre like Eddy Craig's." Elizabeth mentioned the place in Kent where Ellen Terry lived with her daughter and her daughter's lover.

Maud was no longer listening, recognizing the familiar surge of energy that coursed through her body when there was a new project in the offing. She straightened, no longer feeling the wet snow melting on her even wetter gloves, no longer seeing the sandbags propped against the pillars or the posters or the blackout. *A women's haven.* The thought was unbearable – appalling but oh so so *appealing!* The thought was dangerous, delicious and made her spirits soar in a way they hadn't since... well for a very long time. She tried to imagine what it would be like not to have to worry about children or grandchildren and scraping to make ends meet. To live unencumbered... to return to a time devoted only to theatre. To concern herself with– well with only her own welfare... She could live on very little – she *had* been living on very little. What heaven it might be to escape the city gossip-mongers, Herbert's former lovers – Herbert's other *children!*

She stared ahead at the Haymarket Theatre opposite – the first theatre Tree had managed on his own, and realized with a start that her whole concept of theatre, as far as she could remember, had always been linked to some romantic ideal – some *male* ideal. Why, her very first experience – the reason she had wanted to act in the first place had not been because she'd seen Tree but because she'd seen Irving. Her older sister Bertha, who was employed at the Lyceum had taken her to see Irving in *The Bells.* Thereafter she was smitten, seeing the play some twenty times and taking to haunting the street where she believed he lived. It was only years later when finding herself seated beside the great though by now aged actor, she confessed this to him, only for him to say, 'Alas, they were not my windows! That was not my street.' Maud smiled at the memory.

And then she had seen Tree and her passion switched to him, and then to his theatre. The play for power between them had been ferocious and the ebb and flow of their love had been extinguished in the process. And why was that she wondered? Even now she could hardly remember the cause of their rows other than she had wanted to be his leading lady and he had tried to prevent it. She had envisaged a life together – together in all things, and he had not. His ego was too fragile to be satisfied by her devotion alone and yet in the end she had been closer to him, she knew than at any other time in their lives. He may have sewn his last oat but that coupling had held no meaning. He had wanted to come home. And she had waited – how she had waited! There had been other loves of course, but only to assuage the terrible loneliness that gripped her once the curtain had fallen on yet another provincial play. Waller had certainly loved her and for a time she had needed his blind loyalty. She had enjoyed being lavished with gifts and sweet love letters. But his fantastical belief that they could be together, marry even had become an obligation neither one could fulfil. In the end they were strangers to each other and he had died alone in some northern city, forgotten by most of their generation. She had, for a considerable time, loved du Maurier, astonished that love could surprise her at her age, that she could once again feel the fluttering in her stomach, the beat of her pulse against his, the jubilation of seeing him waiting at the stage entrance after a performance. She could, *they* could have enjoyed a future had it not been for... well the thought of his and Viola's betrayal made her want to wretch even now.

It had taken her a long time to recover, a long time to sleep without waking, drenched in perspiration, from a nightmare. She no longer dreamed about her mother's death or her car crash. Now in her nightmares she saw herself running to a table where du Maurier was seated, only for him to turn and be faceless. It had taken her months if not years to kill a desire not to wake up at all. And behind all these dreams, nightmare or otherwise was always Tree. There had been more reasons to hate him than to love him and yet he was always there, always in her mind. And in her mind's eye he would always be centre-stage, always splendid with a voice guttural and comical in turn, that despite the numerous guises, was always, as he would say, 'anything.' And without him? Without, more importantly, the *idea* of him, where would she be? She had spent her professional life fighting for autonomy *away* from his theatre, knowing full well that her success often was brought about because of it. She was no fool and she understood that being aligned to His Majesty's gave her kudos. Now there was no Tree, there was no His Majesty's. She was on her own.

"So will you?" said Elizabeth. Maud was jolted from her thoughts.

"Will I what?"

"Will you come and help us? Run the theatre? You'll be paid –" she added quickly. "That goes without saying. You'll have your own cottage and garden. Meals are taken communally if – " Elizabeth's voice faded but her mouth still moved.

Maud no longer heard her at all. Absentmindedly she felt her damp cheek. Who was she? Who was she without him? His death had made her lose all sense of self, of who she was, even of whom she had been. It was a very long time since she'd thought about herself completely independent of a husband. And as if called up by a genie, an image came to her from a long time ago, of a woman in her prime – no longer young but with an air of mystery shaped by experience and sorrow. She did not see beauty in that face but it was all the more memorable for being sometimes fantastical, sometimes whimsical and always exaggerated in its placid imperfection. If there was movement it came from the hands, restless, expressive but never captive. It was an image that she just one more time in her life, Maud would like to recapture.

"Yes," she interrupted, calm at last. "Yes I'll come."

Elizabeth got to her feet, shaking out her skirts in relief.

"Good. Very Good," she said stretching out her hand to help Maud up. "Then in that case, I've come to take you home."

Gratitude and affection to my editor Frank Hayes

Printed in Great Britain
by Amazon